BLACK WIND BLOWING

Peter Essex, the son of a British engineer, was born in Hong Kong. He has lived in Hong Kong, South Africa, England and Australia. *Black Wind Blowing* is his fourth novel.

D1089708

By the same author

THE EXILE
WE THE ENEMY
CANDLE IN THE WIND

Peter Essex

BLACK WIND BLOWING

Fontana
An Imprint of HarperCollinsPublishers

First published in 1990 by Collins

This continental edition first issued in 1991 by Fontana,
an imprint of HarperCollins Publishers,
77–85 Fulham Palace Road,
Hammersmith, London W6 8JB

9   8   7   6   5   4   3   2   1

Printed and bound in Great Britain by
HarperCollins Book Manufacturing, Glasgow

To Eve with love

Contents

1

MONKEY TRICKS

The dawn breeze blew warm and damp and the rain-mist shrouding the mountain tops swirled lazily in its current. The rain awoke the streams. Feeble trickles strengthened and rose up, quarrelling through the gulleys, bending the meek ferns, shooting cleanly down the slopes over thudding cascades to the sombre forested valleys far below.

Near such a waterfall, and in such a green valley, a little village clustered. There were eight small houses built of mountain stone and cement, and roofed with unglazed tiles that were mossy and chipped with age, and one great ancestral hall where the souls of twelve generations of the family Tang lay at rest, memorialized in dozens of dusty, small spirit tablets in a dark chapel. Above and below the village, terraces had been cut from the mountainside; basins of black earth planted with rows of lettuce and chives, and crisp sow cabbage. As for the rest of the village: it comprised six concrete pigsties where three pigs lived well, some broken-down chicken coops and a communal, open latrine pit; a sort of shallow pond into which the villagers contributed towards the propagation of the good, green veg. Which produce was then plucked and carried off to market in the nearby town of Sai Kung.

Not many people knew where the village was; it was not recorded on any but the most thoroughly surveyed government charts. Yet there it lay in the lap of the mountains, dawdling towards extinction, unaspiring and meek. The inhabitants called it Stone-wall Village.

A crooked pathway ran through the village from the coast up to the inland heights, and when the weather was fine small children played there, and dogs emerged to scratch and mate and bark at the sweating, swearing coolies who came occasionally along the path bent low beneath their heavy carrying poles. Wrinkled women, too old to work, sat there talking of youth and thinking of death.

This was the village where Tang Tsun awoke that misty, rainy morning; yawned; stretched, then suddenly remembering what day it was, unclenched himself from sleep with the instant vigour of youth. He was sixteen, yes, sixteen years old that day – a *man*. He'd vaulted the gateway of youth at last, and landed upon the sweet territory of maturity. The prospects were enthralling. He could, if the mood took him, change his given name. Likewise, he could marry. He might (this was not altogether a foregone conclusion) be expected to voice an opinion, now and then, before his elders. So, all in all, it was a memorable awakening.

He dressed in a hurry: a knee-length pair of cotton trousers, and the same vest that he'd slept in, clothed him; a pair of cheap rubber thongs shod his feet. He scooped from a cold pot on the stove a handful of stodgy congee, chewing as he made for the door. He breathed the soft damp mist.

It seemed that, no matter how early Tang Tsun arose, his father, Tang Ten-thousand Blessings, would always be ahead. A natural law. And thus it was on that damp dawn. There was the elder Tang, resplendently dressed in black ankle-length silk, gathered up for hygiene's sake, perched like a shiny blackbird on the rim of the latrine pit; in no position to return Tsun's first respectful bow as a full-blown adult. And it was this man's fine robe that reminded Tsun of the greater importance of that day. For Tsun's birthday could be counted as a non-event when compared to the *other*; the birthday of Great Sage Equal to Heaven (parochially called, Monkey). Yes, it was Monkey's birthday that would be vigorously celebrated by all who could walk the distance to His temple that morning. Tang Ten-thousand Blessings was dressed as befitted a man of his position – a ritualist of that hilltop temple. And Tsun would go there too.

10

And so it was that father and son voided as one, then took the well-woven stone pathway on to the verdant wet slopes of Horse Saddle Mountain; a long walk made shorter by tales and proverbs and good fatherly advice – man to man stuff, on subjects that but yesterday had been considered too succulent to chew. Over trickling streams; through bamboo forest; past scented pines and over grassy crests, the stone-paved pathway wandered on. The rain-mist slunk away; the mountains swelled powerfully and the track wound upwards, ever upwards.

There were fellow travellers, slowly ascending, like Father and he, bent to their task, murmuring in conversation, with now and then a jerk of laughter from tired lungs.

They walked through a feng shui forest and where it ended, in the cusp of a valley, lay Monkey's splendid home. There were gardens with scented hedgerows, and a green pond with a quaint bridge, purling with frogs. Wide steps fronted the temple, and its walls were of red brick. Red pillars buttressed a gem-green upswept roof. Long flags of red and saffron hung limply and a fine trail of grey smoke chalked the still air.

Tsun felt a jet of excitement. Hundreds of people had come. They stood on the steps and in groups within the balustrades, quietly waiting for the miracles of Master Kaan.

'Unforgettable things,' Father whispered, 'that's what you'll see today. Memories so commanding that they'll master you, mind and soul, heart and sinew, and lead you through life . . . For those called to greatness the consequences could alter the destiny of a nation . . . It's true. It's written.'

In Father's house a clay image of Monkey sat on a god-shelf, and was honoured by the elder Tangs. And he'd heard their whispers in the night about the Great Sage and the invincible power that came with devotion. But whenever he asked what was truth and what was fable, his parents would share hooded glances and invariably answer: 'You'll see – one day when you're a man!' . . . Well, now he was a man. And there was the temple with all its secrets – and he was ready for the truth.

Tsun's eyes were drawn then by a bright red-painted ladder

11

that dominated the centre of the courtyard. The ladder stood straight up in the air like a mast, with guide wires to hold it firm, all decorated with flags. Tsun counted the rungs; there were forty-nine, and to each rung was lashed a gleaming sharp silver sword. As he came closer he could see the marks of recent sharpening on the cutting edges, and each sword-edge was set slightly higher than its adjacent rung. Thick shoes to climb that ladder or your toes would not be part of you at the end of the journey, thought Tsun.

Yet he could see a man kneeling at the foot of the ladder who wore no shirt and no shoes, and who seemed prepared to climb it. He heard his father: 'The Ladder of Truth. Master Kaan will climb it . . . You've always looked for the truth, ha, boy? Well, there it is. You can feel the swords if you want to, but not just yet. Firstly, let's honour the Great Sage. Come, we'll buy incense.'

Many others were upon the same mission, all crushed and jostling at the incense vendor's stall. But Father was taller than most and more impatient, besides which he had sharp elbows, so they were soon served. They lit their joss stick bundles at a cluster of burning candles and planted them in a big brass censer . . . And then they went deeper into the temple to the splendid, carved altar of the Great Sage. There he sat, draped in sequined red silk, half man, half monkey. His face was golden, his red mouth curved in a thin and prankish grin like an archer's bow. Wide, bulging, mischievous eyes stared down at his humbly bent worshippers. Monkey the fearless. Monkey the loyal. Monkey the heavenly trickster, whom no one but the Lord Buddha could subdue . . . And here was Tang Tsun (sixteen years old today), who wanted no more than the truth. So if the Great Sage could see his way clear to provide some substance to all those legends, that would be a great kindness. And, in the light of the fact that they actually shared the same birthday, he would like to wish Monkey a thousand years' good luck.

Tsun's petition was cut short at that point. Some monks dressed in grey tunics arrived at the altar and lifted the Great Sage from his luxurious niche. They set Him upon a sedan chair and marched off with Him, chanting, waddling in step to the bitter, brass crash of gong and cymbal. So Tsun followed them through the temple interior and the smell and smoke of incense, back to the sun.

The crowd was thick but they parted to give the musicians and the sedan chair passage, and Tsun followed in their wake. He halted when he had reached the front rank of a wide circle that had formed around the Ladder of Truth and, kneeling, Master Kaan. From that spot he peered around for his father but failed to see him.

The bearers set down the sedan so that Monkey faced the middle of the circle, then they stood back. The musicians, some flute players and cymbalists and the two men who worked the big gong, kept on playing.

Now look at Master Kaan! As though wrestling in the grip of some remorseless, invisible power, the muscles of Kaan's back and arms knotted and bulged. His head dragged back, trembling with strain. He rose from the ground as though lifting a mighty weight, and as he came up he pivoted and Tsun observed his face. Kaan's jaws were clamped, his teeth bared and foam leaked from his mouth . . . Then as if his invisible antagonist had suddenly released him, his whole body slumped, his face smoothed and his eyes opened. His gaze fell unwaveringly on Tsun – bright and startling, and the boy stared back as one who has been caught out in some monstrous misdeed; unable to think or act or do anything but stare. He tried to look away but Kaan's dark gaze had entered him and stolen his resolve.

Tsun blinked, and that moment of darkness was enough to break the bond. Master Kaan turned away and walked towards the red ladder, and the big gong boomed and the cymbals hissed, which quite surpassed the small sound of Tsun's trembling sigh.

'The spirit has entered Kaan Wing – the spirit of Monkey.' That was the whisper of those who stood near Tsun. And it must have been true, for what other explanation was there for the events that subsequently took place?

Kaan came to the ladder and grasped it with his hands and

13

looked up. He lifted one foot and rested it lightly on the lowest sword. The music quailed. The blade took his weight – *crash* went the brass. *'Wah!'* gasped Tsun's and a hundred other throats. And so it was with the next step, and the next. Heads slowly raised and eyes turned skywards, as Master Kaan climbed higher with his bare soles on the sword edges – *and did not shed a single drop of blood.*

Tang Tsun swelled with excitement. His feet tingled with every step, as though it were his and not Kaan's bare soles that trod the sharp swords of Truth . . . Truth! Here was water for the thirst of the Seeker. The power of God come to earth. Man who could be tested by the razor's edge and not be cut. Look at Kaan as he climbed invincibly and weighted his flesh upon the sharp steel so firmly that the ladder shook. Aie*yaa*!

At a rung near the top Kaan stopped. He leaned his body against the highest sword and raised his hands, palms pressed together as though poised to dive upwards into the distant, blue heavens. He held that position, while those below looked on, all grateful in the knowledge that blessings, thus earned, were sprinkling liberally down upon them at the very moment. Tsun thought: if only I could do such incredible deeds. How wonderful to defy the law of injury; to be part of this world and yet able to visit a place beyond pain. There would be nothing that I would not dare to do if the Great Sage would grant *me* such power . . . Some clouds drifted by and the high red ladder seemed dizzily moved by their passage. A loud *ba-room* of the gong startled Tsun; the musicians had been resting, now they started up again and as they bashed out their tune, Kaan came down.

When Master Kaan's feet finally touched ground, he leaned his face forward so that his mouth rested on a sword, he laid his tongue upon the edge, and Tsun knew what was going to happen then: Kaan was going to lick the blade and nick his tongue. The blood of the wound would fall upon the charms that hung from the lower rungs. Tsun had seen such magically stained yellow papers on the god-shelf in his father's house. Now he knew where they had come from, and he wanted one.

It happened as Tsun had predicted. Kaan ran his tongue along the sword edge, blood spurted and he trailed the red stream over the spells. With an excited roar the crowd surged forward . . . Tsun was not prepared for it. He was left behind. He thought there would be nothing left when he came to the ladder, but the very last yellow paper was his. He took it and read it and was thrilled by the message:

> Obedience to the Ways of Heaven.
> A mountain of swords will not cut you.
> A lake of fire will not burn you.

The paper was blotched wetly in two places with Kaan's blood. Tsun held it in both hands and knew he had arrived at the gateway to great power. This was his day, his birthday shared with the God of Gods. He felt wonderful – earthborne yet with a spirit that soared amongst the clouds. He looked up to the high ladder and he thought: I can climb you. I'm not afraid. He truly was not afraid.

The crowd drew back and re-formed into a circle. Tsun found a new place from which to observe, nearer to the sedan throne of Monkey, which was an even better position than before. Master Kaan came to kneel close by, facing a wide brass cauldron set upon a brick hearth that leapt with flame. The cauldron held boiling oil. No doubt about the contents, Tsun could see the bubbling fluid; he could smell the aroma of hot oil. He could not help the gasp that escaped him when Master Kaan stood and thrust both hands into the oil. Kaan did not make a sound; he did not flinch. He did not hurry to withdraw his hands from the scalding oil; nor was he burned. He lifted up his unscarred arms for all to see.

'Honour the Great Sage,' exalted the monks. 'Invincible trust,' shouted the people. 'Ten-thousand years!'

'I can do that,' said Tang Tsun. 'A lake of fire will not burn me. I am not afraid.'

He stepped forward and came up to the cauldron. Master Kaan

glared at him, just as before, but Tsun's will stayed undiminished, all doubts were gone. High on the rapture of great courage, he said:

'Let me do it, Master Kaan. I'm not afraid.'

He plunged his right fist into the seething oil, and screamed, and screamed, snatched into a white heat of agony.

Only one small area of Tang Tsun's right hand was undamaged by the boiling oil. On his palm where his fisted fingers had pressed there remained a patch of good flesh – and this was very odd, for the design thus left was in the definite shape of the Sun-Moon character, Ming. Ming, as in Ming dynasty. (At least, that was the whispered opinion of the monks of that monastery.) The remainder of the hand, from fingertip to wrist was burned and horribly blistered. Fortunately for the boy he was in a place where help was immediately available. A monk of the temple of the Great Sage knew how to treat burn wounds with root balms and poultices and herbal concoctions. So the monks agreed with Tang Ten-thousand Blessings that his Eldest Son should stay at the temple until the worst of it was over.

The boy thought that it would never end. The pain raged on without stop, and it had monstrous power. It could drag his entire being into its furnace and hold him there all day. And at night, in short spells of shallow sleep he dreamed that hideous demons were gnawing at his arm, and often he awoke to the shock of his own screams. A coma-like fever set in after a few days and in its transport he visited frightful places: sunless valleys strewn with knuckled rocks, where cave openings scowling like the eyes of human skulls led down to great seas of groaning, swirling mist. He sank into this awful dreamscape as though never to return. But he did return.

He was cleansed of this nightmare by the deep, swelling chant of the monks at morning devotions. He lifted his burned hand and looked at the livid, raw flesh, all the more grotesque for the bright yellow balm smeared on it.

16

'It's mending in a wonderful way.'

He turned his head to see who had said those words, and found Master Kaan. The disciple of Monkey was seated, adjacent to Tsun's sleeping mat with his legs crossed and his back rested amiably against the wall. He leaned slowly forward and contemplated Tsun; who thought: How changed Kaan is without the spirit of Monkey driving him. After a while Kaan spoke again.

'Do you feel stronger, boy?'

'I thought I wouldn't burn.'

'Your thoughts are your enemy . . . Can you stand?'

Tsun kneeled, then stood. The wound throbbed for a while, then eased. 'I wasn't afraid.'

'You don't understand. Fearlessness is a false friend . . . Never mind, you'll learn.'

'I want that. I want to learn.'

'Perhaps you'll have no choice. It seems that you're marked with the Ming . . . Now let me see you walk.'

'What Ming?' Tsun asked. 'What does it mean?'

Kaan gave a wry, amused look. 'You want too much, too quickly. Are you always so impatient? . . . It means, boy, that Heaven is one inch above your head . . . Make of that what you will. Come. Come. Walk . . . That's right.'

Tsun took a few steps. 'It hurts.' He contrived a pained face.

'It hurts!' Kaan waved him towards the door. 'What do you expect, ha! You're as strong as a plough-ox. You can go home now. I'll walk with you to the edge of the garden and no further. Go on now,' he gestured impatiently.

'Can I be your pupil, Master Kaan?'

Kaan gave no answer. Tsun thought he'd been too zealous. He made amends for his cheek: 'I'd be respectful. I'd kow tow to you.'

If Kaan had heard this earnest request, he showed no sign of it. He walked in silence over the bridge that spanned the noisy green pond, then onwards along the stone pathways bound by fragrant hedges. And Tsun followed on, dawdling; hoping for a favourable answer.

At the feng shui woods at the edge of the monastery Kaan stopped. He stroked his chin and peered at Tsun. 'Your mother has been taught how to treat your hand,' he said. 'We'll watch how it heals.'

Tsun looked into his palm.

'The Ming,' Kaan said. 'If it doesn't fade in the healing then I'll teach you all I know.'

'It won't fade,' Tsun said.

'Yes. I believe that. Go now.'

Tsun turned his back on the temple of Monkey and strode towards the mountain. By midday he was back at Stone-wall Village.

In the defeating heat of the midday sun a steamy quietness settles on Stone-wall Village. The farmers set down their big watering cans and come home for rice and tea. The village dogs, with lolling tongues, flop down in the shade to blink the flies from their eyes. Some chickens cluck reprovingly from their roosts, and the three pigs grunt a quiet welcome to Dull Boy Chan when he comes to whisk cooling water on their fat, pink backs. The liveliest sound is the splash of the small waterfall in the nearby bend of the mountain.

That day the customary lethargy of noon was pierced by shrill female shrieks that came from the area of the communal latrine-pit. And that was the sound that surprised Tsun on his way into the village. He needed to take but a short detour to discover what was wrong. Little Tik-kat, youngest son of Fourth Uncle, had somehow found his way to the bottom of the pit and was resisting extrication. There he stood, knee-deep in night fragrance, with his thumb plugged deeply in his mouth, staring up at his would-be rescuers. Second Aunt and some other women were on their knees, outstretched at the pit edge, with beckoning arms, but Tik-kat was either too bemused by the ruckus, or having too good a time down there to respond. The distraught women saw Tsun and invited him to join them but Tsun walked on. Tik-kat was a

18

favourite of his; he wouldn't dream of spoiling his little cousin's fun.

Tsun went to his house and found his mother there preparing dinner, swirling watery rice in a basin to make dumplings. 'You're back.' Her eyes smiled. She stopped her work and dried the water from her fingers on the pants of her faded blue tunic-suit.

'Pain, son?' She inspected the scorched hand on both sides, her own hands hovering – not quite touching.

'Pain, Ma ma . . . but not so much as there was.'

'Aieya-tss!' She took on his agony.

'Aieya.' That single frowned statement was pressed upon Tsun as many times as he was stopped by the villagers in the days that followed.

'Does it hurt? Aieya!'

'Is it mending? Aieya!'

'Aieya!'

Some spoke with concern; some wonderment. Others, especially the muddy vegetable growers (who always did things as a group), thought Tsun's actions to have been inspired by a hungry ghost, and shunned him completely, muttering, giving him black looks when he approached. Their awe of him intensified when news of the weird stigma got out. Tsun made a point of casually airing the Ming as he passed them on the terraces. 'What one can not change, be proud of,' Father advised. And so he became proud of the Ming.

Tsun went about his daily tasks as best he could, but there were many things that he could no longer do. He could not work on the chopping-block cutting greens to mix with the pig food. He was unable to eat properly holding his chop-sticks in his left hand. His nightly calligraphy lessons at clever Third Uncle's house had to be forfeited, as he could no longer manage the delicate brushstrokes, and that seemed like a terrible punishment. But the worst thing about the injury was that it prevented him from earning his keep: his crippled hand lacked the power to wield a hammer.

19

Sai Kung Bay, just one hour's walk from Stone-wall Village, was a market town of blue Canton brick and tiled-roof houses that stood so close that the bamboo poles used to dry washing spanned the street. The Tang family ran a money factory there; a print shop that turned out big denomination 'bank notes' payable on demand at the Bank of Hell: currency of the dead, to be used by departed spirits to bribe their way past those most venal watchmen of the underworld. Of course it was the responsibility of living relatives to see that their ancestors did not run short of cash on their forty-nine-day journey through these dark caverns. And therein lay good profit for the manufacturers.

Tsun had wielded Boss Hammer in the pounding-shop; a place where thick ingots of Singapore tin were hammered and beaten until paper-thin, a task that wore calluses and crushed fingers, for the pounding-hammers were heavy and painfully unforgiving. He could no longer grasp a hammer, so he was set the task of cutting the tinfoil into little squares, then pasting it to the notes, and he failed in that too. He was further 'promoted' to the position of overseer of the tittering, chattering women in the ink-shop. He hated that, and told his father so. Thus he received his final promotion. His eventual employment (which, thankfully he could cope with) was to hang up the sheafs of printed, pasted notes over bamboo rods in the small yard of the factory, there to dry. Here he also doubled as a sort of weather-watchman. While the sun shone, the paper should enjoy it, but beware the sudden rain squall that would run the ink and spoil a day's production. That's all there was to it; a child of six had been holding down this job before Tsun had made her redundant.

So Tsun scanned the sky and listened to the rustle of the breeze-stirred paper. He had time to observe lazily the crumbling blue-brick world beyond the factory yard, and found there much to interest him.

There was Fung Sham the police sergeant who pedalled down the lane every Friday on his squeaky black bicycle, stopping at every factory, stall and shop along the route for a brief visit – smiling Sergeant Fung whose black leather belt was polished to a

20

gleam, who always straightened his cap before the factory gate, and sometimes spoke to Tsun.

'Let me see the hand . . . *Tcha*! Tsun, such a small wound. I shouldn't worry. I've seen so much worse, and it's healing well.'

It *was* healing well; the new skin shone lividly but for the unburned patch – the Ming character on his palm – and if he attempted to make a fist the skin wrinkled oddly, and it was numb. But the pain only came slightly now, at night. Fung was intrigued by the Ming, he swore it must mean something startlingly profound; he didn't know what. Tsun liked the cheerful policeman. It did not take him long to discover why Fung was so optimistic about life. Fung Sham was very rich. He wore a white-gold Rolex wrist-watch, and owned a gold-topped fountain pen, and it was rumoured that he kept three concubines in fine style. He played mah-jong at the 'top' table where 500 dollars could be lost or won in a single night . . . And how had Fung Sham on his black police bicycle become such a big-balls on the miserable pay of the Hong Kong government? The answer to that question was that Sergeant Fung was a 'caterer' (as less than honest station sergeants were known). His nickname was The Fixer, which seemed an apt description of his role. Fung took bribes from every store, tenement and factory owner in the market town of Sai Kung (in order that no legal problems should impede their trade). Tsun spied on his father, and had seen him seal fifty dollars in an envelope and give it to The Fixer. 'A little tea money, hah?' Both men had laughed, but Fung's smile was the more enduring.

Why pay The Fixer at all? Well, the story of Lai the incense-maker could be regarded as the perfect lesson for those who might harbour such doubts. Lai had lightened Fung's purse, and had consequently found himself in court in Hong Kong, where he'd been ordered to explain to a foreign devil, a gwailo magistrate, how twenty-nine adults and twenty-four children could work in one tiny room with no window, no chimney and no running water. Of course Lai was out of business now.

There were other interesting and equally regular visitors to the factory. Two men, always the same two, came on Sunday evenings just before closing. These were sharp fellows. They wore jackets over their vests, long trousers and leather sandals, and they owned good watches too. They walked with a swagger and never spoke to Tsun, even when greeted by him. One of the men had a harelip.

Tsun questioned his father about them one night after they had eaten.

'They look like bad guys, Ah Pa.'

'What would you know about that, ha? Bad guys, where did you hear such chat?'

'They sway their shoulders when they walk . . . like this. I should think they were gangsters, just from seeing them.'

'You better do your work, boy. Pay more attention to what you're paid for. Forget the rest.'

Youngest Brother San-kiu came into the room then, bare but for a short grubby singlet. Ten-thousand Blessings puffed his cheeks and pursed his lips then blew a rude noise that delighted the kid, who toddled, giggling, towards his father. Always messy, now there were rice grains stuck to San-kiu's fat cheeks.

'You walked like that once, Eldest Son.' Tang laughed. He dipped into his pocket and brought out a matchbox with a buzzing insect in it that San-kiu made a grab for.

'Not two years yet,' Tang raised his arms proudly, 'and look how he goes.'

Youngest Brother let fly a jet of golden urine that caused a little stream to trail across the concrete floor. His father shifted his feet to avoid the spill and it ran on until staunched by the body of a sleeping dog called Lucky Boy. Tsun thought it was amazing that someone so small could void such vast quantities of water.

'Look, I'll tell you about those fellows,' Tang said. 'You're a man, even old enough to marry, so you should know . . . They can make a lot of trouble for us, those men. If we don't want trouble, then we've got to come-up. Everyone pays. It's always been like that. It's not so bad.'

22

Tsun thought about that. Tang Ten-thousand Blessings took from his shirt a packet of Tarzan brand cigarettes, set one between his lips and lit it. Tsun's mother came in and threw a rag on the urine puddle and mopped it with her foot. She wore her usual faded blue floral tunic-suit with the trousers rolled up to the knees. She smiled at her husband; a loving smile, Tsun thought.

'Clever boy,' said the mother to her baby.

'Some bladder,' said Tsun.

Everyone laughed.

'What sort of trouble would those guys make?' Tsun said. 'Only two of them, all counted . . . How much trouble can two men make for our great family?'

Tsun thought that his father was not going to answer the question. Tang smoked the Tarzan down to the stub before he spoke again.

'Three United Society, that's who they are; triads, ha. Two people? Do you think that's all there are? Two hundred, more like it . . . two thousand, I don't know how many there are. They're big. I show respect. I pay . . . No more to be said.'

There ended the conversation. Tsun sat with his father for a while longer and mulled over the lesson: They're big. I show respect. I pay. So the little shrimp were food for the big fish, and that was all there was to it. How easy for the big fish, he thought; no sweat at the hammer and dye vats and print-press for them. They simply held out the hand and said: 'Pay up, brother' . . . So Father smoked Tarzans while the big-balls smoked Lucky Strike, and wore fancy Rolexes, and bragged about their losses at the mah-jong table . . . Respect? Tsun knew the difference between respect and fear.

He didn't like the idea of his father in fear of anyone, no matter how strong they might be. He had always thought of this man as being heroic; tall enough to scrape the blue from the sky . . . Yet here was a less than invincible man. He did not like this smaller man.

The paraffin lamp spluttered so Tang leaned over and turned up the wick. But Tsun did not stay to enjoy the light. He went and

23

lay down on the board-and-trestle bed that he shared with Youngest Brother, but could not sleep. Later, when the lamp was blown out, he heard the muted throat-sounds of his parents as they struggled to do the 'secret thing' on the hard concrete floor. Imagine it; he had come to life in just such a pathetic encounter.

No soft life for the shrimps, thought Tsun.

At Sai Kung there is a cinema-house called Ten and Ten, where one hundred people can sit down at a session on wooden seats to watch movies. Posters in the town tell of the forthcoming attractions, and Tsun read them, and sometimes he went after work to watch a movie that he judged to have prospects. Cantonese movies he shunned, for they were so repetitive. He disapproved of the traditional make-up that the actors wore and found their carping, falsetto voices to be a strain; and Chinese fight scenes were predictable and boring. Japanese films were better, but American films were the best. He never missed an American gangster movie. When such entertainment was advertised, Tsun bought a ticket in the stalls – thirty cents, but it was worth it.

Two other people who had a liking for such movies were Rabbit-lip Poon and Crooked-boy Luk. Moreover, for them it was a matter of education. They too sat in the stalls, but the Ten and Ten made no profit from their attendance.

It required therefore but a minute nudge from the elbow of destiny to cause the paths of the three men to cross one night in the foyer of the Ten and Ten. Tsun was standing contentedly at the roasted-peanut vendor's stall, munching hot peanuts, when it happened:

'Wai! It's the son of the "buy-a-passage" money-maker.' Tsun turned to see who had addressed him thus, and found it to be one of the men who collected squeeze from his father on Sunday evenings. And there next to him stood his braggart, harelipped partner. Both of them had women linked to their arms, one of

24

whom was quite beautiful. This lady inspected Tsun in a most profound way, then, unseen by her boy-friend, she poked towards Tsun a wriggling, wet, pink tongue-tip. Tsun's eyes widened.

'Ha!' said Crooked-boy Luk, on whose arm she hung. 'So what's to stare at?'

'Beg your pardon,' Tsun said. 'Some mistake.'

'Penis brain.' Luk thumped Tsun's chest.

'Son of a turtle.' Poon imitated his colleague.

There wasn't much aggression in the blows but they had the intended effect – a hearty thud that everyone heard – a total loss of face for Tsun. The girls tittered and Tsun blushed hotly. He felt he had been lured into this, but there was nothing to be done. He *had* been staring and this was the price of discourtesy. The wisest course now was to apologize and leave as quickly as possible.

'Confess my error,' he said. 'No harm was meant. I will pardon your stinking language, too.'

Luk frowned but said no more. Tsun turned away, then gasped as sudden pain rammed up through his spine. He turned in time to see Luk's next kick, but not to avoid it. Luk's leather sandal crashed into his ribs. Then Poon kicked out, and missed and kicked again. Tsun caught Poon's foot and held on to it, and both men lost their balance as they staggered into the roasted-peanut stall. Luk jumped forward punching as he came; stone-hard fists that burst with brilliant pain in the shell of Tsun's skull. Tsun felt the bones of his nose crush. The world went away – a great lazy emptiness yawned open. Still holding Poon's foot Tsun toppled, and as he came down he heard a sound like the snapping of a branch. But it wasn't a branch, it was Poon's ankle fracturing. Tsun's swooning zone of nothingness quickly dissolved, and hurt filled him up. He heard Poon's shout: 'Oh fuck! The bastard's done my ankle. Look at it.'

Tsun looked at it. It *did* look done. It extended from Poon's trouser-leg at an unanatomical angle and Poon was screaming bloody vengeance. Tsun thought: why such savagery? why? But

25

his mind lay in rubble; too shattered to reason. Only the barest instinct still stood and that warned him: be ready to fight. It's not over yet. So Tsun stood and wiped his knuckles over the raw wounds of his face, then brought up his fists like a boxer. But the battle of the Ten and Ten was over.

Luk jumped forward but it was all show. He gestured – a rigid pointed finger punctured the air near Tsun's face. Then the man turned away, and helped his broken comrade to stand. 'Bastard,' shouted the harelipped man as, with his arm drooped over Luk's shoulder, he hopped away. And the girls went with them, with angry backwards glances at the son of the 'buy-a-passage' money-maker who had caused so much trouble.

Tsun noticed then for the first time the other people clustered there, all of them watching him. He wanted to tell them: I didn't strike first, but his jaw was too sore to move. They stood well back from him as he limped through the foyer of the Ten and Ten and into the dark street.

Tsun walked towards the bay, drawn by the thought that the water might shrink his pain. His ribs were so badly hurt that each breath ended in a jagged gasp, so he pressed his hands to the bruises, hugging his chest, and in that way he could go on. He would take off his clothes, he thought, when he reached the water, and let his body float freely, and that would be good.

A warm night-breeze was blowing off the sea, and the bay water lay black-skinned and quiet. Here and there where the bright-light fishermen were at work floated circles of white, and further out the lights of the deep-sea junks rode slowly by. Naked, Tsun waded out, and when the water lapped at his thighs he knelt down and gathered it to wash his wounds. The sea was warm and flimsy waves flopped against him with the barest splash. He was better for it. The question returned: why such a savage attack? Because I possess courtesy, and they mistook courtesy for weakness; and strength for numbers . . . But the score was even – a broken ankle for a broken set of ribs. He'd gained back all his lost face in that fight; and not a moment of fear!

Those and other brave thoughts were Tsun's good friends for a while. But there were doubts too and they surfaced then, and gave the dark sea a menace it did not deserve. Could the allegation that a hungry ghost *was* on his trail be true? And if it was, what misfortune would it bring next?

The answer to that question arrived seven days later. And who does not know that seven is the triad number of death?

When Tang Ten-thousand Blessings failed to arrive home one stormy evening there was immediate consternation. No one of sane mind would walk in the mountains after dark, the track was beset by vampires and man-eating demons and wall-building ghosts that could entrap a man for ever. There was an old hanging tree growing quite close to the path and even in daylight it was best to hurry past that spot.

Concerned wife of Tang and Tsun went about the village knocking on doors, calling the menfolk from their meals to join in a search of the path to Sai Kung. Tsun wasn't surprised when no one would come out. Look at the sky, they said; listen to the wind and thunder. Impossible to keep a lamp lit on such a night.

'Look at your hearts,' Tsun told them, 'listen to your consciences. Don't you know that Tang Ten-thousand Blessings would do the same for any one of you?'

They were unmoved by his plea. But their prediction was correct – it was impossible to keep the lantern alive in that gusting wind.

Mother and son went back to their small house. 'It will be all right,' she kept saying. 'He's as strong as a tree. He'll come home with the dawn . . . ' But Tsun knew that his father was just a weak man, an ordinary man, and Tsun was filled with dread. They sat up all night, hiding their fear, waiting for the storm to die. They burned incense at the god-box of the Great Sage, and they comforted each other.

At cock-crow it was still pouring with rain but every man was up and waiting, glistening with water as though they'd stood that vigil all night long. No one said a word or looked Tsun in the eye.

They simply fell in behind him as he led off towards Sai Kung. They did not find Tang on the path.

Tang Ten-thousand Blessings was dead. Tsun knew that even before he pushed open the unlocked door of the factory. 'You wait here,' he told his mother. 'You men wait with her.' They obeyed; hunched against the rain.

It was dark inside the shop. The front windows were grey and opaquely washed, and the wind-song whistled and sighed as it always did on such days. How it could blow right through those old blue-brick walls he could never fathom, but there it was: the wind, and the drip, plop, drip of a hundred leaking roof tiles on the pine-plank floor, and the squeak and rustle of rats, and Tsun's frightened voice:

'Ah Pa? . . . Are you there . . . Ah Pa?'

He switched on the light in the print-shop and a single brave bulb came alive, drifting slightly in the draught, giving the shadows movement. There were the hand-carved printing-blocks, and brushes and pails of purple and yellow ink. Stacks of paper lay ready to be printed; nothing else. The cutting-room held the big, sharp scythe and bundles of rough-edged paper and the litter of off-cuts, and not much more than that.

Tsun's father lay face-down on the floor of the pounding-shop. Tang Ten-thousand Blessings was broken and dead. The back of his head was a pulp of bone and blood, and a bloody pounding-hammer lay near by. It was Tsun's hammer.

They heard Tsun's howl of anguish from the street, and came running.

Desolate wife of Tang knelt at her husband's body, rocking and keening, her face screwed tight with misery. The police came: first Sergeant Fung and a PC, and soon thereafter a tall, well-knit white man who wore silver stars on his shoulders and to whom Fung gave much face. The big gwailo inspector gave orders in Cantonese which Fung quickly obeyed. Then Sergeant Fung gently prised loose Ma ma's fingers from the body. With her hands clawed and trembling and her face rigid with grief, she allowed Fung to lead her from the room.

Tsun's head ached for the want of tears. His eyes would not cry, nor would he allow egress to the sob and whimper of his throat. He was borne down with anguish, he was crippled by it. He could not bear to look at the frozen horror that had so recently been warm-smiling, fine-featured Tang Ten-thousand Blessings. So he stared at the grey, worn pine planks at his feet and the pounding-anvils; shiny like mirrors where the hammers struck, and the heaps of Singapore tin. He looked at the mottled, wrecked fist that held the Ming, and remembered many things: 'Memories so commanding that they'll master you, mind and soul, heart and sinew, and lead you through life . . .'

'You can go if you want to,' the white police officer said in a kind way. 'Go home. Be with your mother, she needs you.'

Tsun looked at the provider of this advice and was conscious of unwavering blue eyes – trustworthy, Tsun judged. Then he turned away. And Father had said: 'For those called to greatness the consequences could alter the destiny of a nation . . .'

'I have many things to do.' Tsun stood. 'So much to learn . . . I will never forgive. Never.'

'I understand. My deepest regrets.'

'It's time to start.'

'Yes, it's best to go home; be with your family. You are the first son.'

In the darkest hour the seeds of dawn are sown: that was Tsun's faith as he walked away from the deathroom. Yes, he would go home, but not for long, and not to fill the shoes of Tang Ten-thousand Blessings, or to be a shrimp in the waters where the big fish swam . . . Father was dead. First Son would never forget him, nor would he imitate him. If there was a man worthy of imitation, then his name was Kaan. Master Kaan had provided a vision, and now it was time to follow it. He wanted the secrets of invincibility, he wanted the god-spirit of Monkey, and he sensed he had something precious to offer in return. *For he bore the Ming.*

He reached the gate of the factory and walked into the rain. He did not acknowledge anyone. He did not say a word, and he did not look back.

Even then he could hear the thrumming chant of the monks of Chai Tin Dai Sing calling him in.

2

STEAL THE SKY
– SWAP THE SUN

Nine floors above ground level is a world apart from the heat and constraint of the streets of Hong Kong. From that tranquil height one looks down upon crawl and march of machine and citizen with genial detachment. It is a pleasant distance to be from the sweat and scrimmage of springtime Hong Kong. Reven Forrester, at least, thought it to be so.

He turned away from the window that provided that lofty view to face a wide, well-polished desk, and the dashing little fellow whose rank entitled him to that fine furniture.

Assistant Commissioner Lo Ping-kin wore his shirt-sleeves puffed with springy arm-bands, and sleek waistcoats which gave him the waspish look of a seventeenth-century fencing master. A dapper moustache (an excellent growth by Chinese standards) completed the image. The AC held an open file before him. He looked up from it to say:

'Do you remember the case, Reven?'

There were several reasons as to why Reven Forrester should remember that case. It was a murder docket; the first of many, true. But there had been other circumstances that made that case unique.

'It was my first assistant sub-divisional command as a two-pip inspector . . . Sai Kung was just a sleepy little market port in those days – a bit of petty smuggling, fish dynamiting, some opium. No overtime, you follow. That case was my introduction to triad-style violence. Sure I remember.'

'Tang Tsun; what was he like?'

'He was sixteen, seventeen, it's written down there; very mature, intense . . . slightly built. I liked him. He came from a bottom-soil family from the nearby hills, but there was nothing of the peasant clod about him. He kept his grief to himself, and his anger too. God, he was angry. I could see it in him but he masked it, as only the Chinese can. There wasn't a line of emotion on his face . . . One of his hands was badly scarred, I remember . . .'

The telephone on Lo's desk rang then and while the AC addressed his caller (the Regional Commander, Marine) Forrester paced about a bit. A headache was swirling vaguely at the base of his skull; he needed, occasionally, to be pounded with stiff sport to keep that pain in check.

'For God's sake sit.' Lo gestured to one of his good leather visitors' chairs. 'I've never known anyone pace about so. Where were we . . . You were saying how well controlled you thought he was.'

'Amazing, considering his upbringing. He wasn't the son of a mandarin; just a peasant boy . . . I spoke to him; said the usual pathetic things I suppose. I don't think he heard a word of it. I remember what he said, though: "I've got so much to do . . . " Very quiet. And: "It's time to start."'

'So much to do?' Lo stroked the edges of his moustache. 'So much to do, ha? Well that was no lie. Look where he is today. Not every peasant boy grows up to be a triad boss, thank God for that. Go on, Reven.'

'I sent him home. I'm not sure how long he stayed there. But he never did go back to the hell-money factory after the murder, nor did any of the other workers. I heard that the landlord had the building exorcized, but even so no one wanted to rent the place after that, and in the end he had to board it up.'

'Understandable,' Lo said. 'Bad joss.'

'Tang Tsun went up to the monastery of the Monkey God on Horse Saddle Mountain. That's where I saw him next. It was a few months after the killing, and we'd made an arrest: a triad enforcer from Sun Yee On.'

'And one shot dead resisting.' Lo delved into the murder docket again . . . 'Crooked-boy Luk. There's a copy here of the coroner's report.'

Forrester touched his fingertips to the jagged little scar enlivening his left eyebrow and thought back to the day of its painful arrival. He said:

'One learns as one goes.'

'A fighting chain,' Lo closed the file with an air of finality, 'nasty weapon . . . don't see them about much these days. When I was a probationary inspector a friend of mind was maimed by a triad wielding one of those flails.' He closed the file and passed it over the desk. 'Do you know that this is practically all the material that we have on Tang Tsun.'

'Why should there be more?'

'There should be more because according to good sources, Tang Tsun is not the quiet and observant monk he pretends to be . . .'

'I don't believe he's a triad boss, PK. If anyone in this world has reason to hate the triads, it's Tang. It was Sun Yee On enforcers who beat his beloved father to death with his own hammer, remember. You ask me what I observed that day, twenty years ago. I saw a youth who would never forgive the killers of his father – I saw simple courage. Why should such a man aspire to be a triad boss?'

'Not just a triad boss, Reven; a Celestial Dragon-head. That's my information . . . Ambition, ambition. It drives us Chinese crazy. It makes the devil turn the grindstone. The triads haven't been controlled by a Dragon-head for a hundred years, or more. It's a grave situation, if it's true.'

'Grave for the Communists.'

Lo's expression barely changed, but his voice carried an edge now: 'Some of us have no option but to remain and work with the Communists, Reven. Some of us don't possess British passports, you see. And some of us even look forward, with pride, to the day when Hong Kong will be reunited with China . . . But why should we quarrel . . . Yes, grave for the Communists. With the triad societies divided they'd be able to control them at least as well as this administration has. Triad unity they see as a nightmare. And so do I. And so, Chief Superintendent, should you . . . For God's sake will you sit.'

'No one has tried to do more damage to the triads than I have in the past, PK. But I know their culture. They will unite in a small way, occasionally, in order to combine talents for a one-off job; a drug shipment perhaps. But the major gangs all hate each other; they're territorial and they war from street-level up. And the dragon-heads are fat cats. "Would we get any richer under a Celestial Dragon-head?" That's the only question that would occur to them. "How many more illicit casinos would such subordination facilitate? How much more heroin could be injected into Hong Kong's veins? How many more prostitutes could the Celestial Dragon-head guarantee? . . ." And the answer would come, "Not a dollar, a catty or a single girl more. So to hell with unity. To hell with a Celestial Dragon-head."'

'Maybe . . . maybe,' Lo conceded. 'But there's no waves without wind. Tang Tsun has made enemies . . .'

'The Chinese Intelligence Service?'

'What about the Ch.I.S.?'

'The Ch.I.S. are paranoid about the triads. If the Communists are behind this, PK, I would be sure to find out. I would not be manipulated by the Ch.I.S.'

'What a crassly naive suggestion, Reven. The Chinese Intelligence Service do not as yet initiate investigations by the Royal Hong Kong Police, and I hope they never will. From midnight on the thirtieth of June the Chinese will govern Hong Kong. Until that exact second I take my orders from the Commissioner . . . And until then, at least, you will be my Chief Staff Officer, Crime. So you, Reven, as our foremost triad expert, and because of your special understanding of Tang . . .'

'It's ridiculous, I only spoke to him for a few minutes, twenty years ago. Give the job to a Regional CID.'

34

'We feel you're the man to follow this thing through. You arrested Tang's father's killers. The fact that one of them died in the process is even more to your advantage. You've got face with Tang and that might be put to good use.'

'The thought of the triads uniting under a Celestial Dragonhead appals me, PK. It would be a bad thing for Hong Kong. But I think you're wrong, and if Tang isn't a triad officer I shall prove it.'

'I would expect nothing less from you, Reven. But if he is, I want him. I've stood by you, Reven, have I not?'

'More times than was good for your career.'

'In a few months, when His Excellency has waved his last salute, and is gone, and the Commissioner too, and a red flag flies from Government House, I'll still be here, with my family. If the Chinese feel that I've seriously failed them, then my head will be on the block. I confess the thought of it frightens me, my friend . . . My God, the fire's so close it singes the eyebrows.'

Forrester at last conceded to sit. He flopped into the good leather visitors' chair so that he was almost at eye level with his host; improving his view of the coldly determined eyes of Lo Ping-kin. He saw neither deceit nor sincerity, but bloodless detachment, selfish detachment, and pride. Lo would have his way, Forrester knew. He said, 'No matter how much face I've got with Tang, he's not going to invite me in for a fireside chat. Assuming that he is guilty, it's going to be very hard to prove . . . I'd prefer to take an unorthodox approach. I don't want to throw the full weight of the Group into this; I'll leave Intelligence Bureau out of the investigation and just use a few hand-picked men.'

'I don't see the point in doing that.'

'How many Dragon-heads have we convicted over the past decade? . . . The answer is, one. That's not a good record in terms of orthodox crime detection. We make deals with the triads, PK, and they make deals with us, and they betray each other for the sake of peace, or profit. I have five hundred men infiltrated into the various gangs, and they probably have triple that number of policemen on their payroll. And all these factors influence crime and its detection in Hong Kong. But PK, you can't expect me to catch you a Celestial Dragon-head in such a flawed net. That is the point.'

'Make whatever arrangements suit you, Reven . . . We live in pitiless times.'

Chief Staff Officer, Organized and Serious Crime Group: Reven Forrester thought the title to be abstruse and far too ponderous, nevertheless it was his – published in Orders, and screwed to his office door, so that was that. He had nothing against the job. It was a fine job. His was the task of the chessmaster contending a hundred hard-fought battles all at once. At his command were two bureaux – a Bureau of Criminal Intelligence and a Bureau of Organized and Serious Crime – and each bureau had four teams of men, and those were his pieces on the board . . . In opposition stood murderers and robbers and rapists and blackmailers and arsonists and kidnappers – all with one thing in common: they had been cunning enough in the execution of their various crimes to escape detection by the regional crime units. So Forrester and his men campaigned against these most vicious, shrewd people, and frequently beat them. There were charts and graphs on his office wall that proved that, and photographs of policemen who looked pleased with themselves, and villains who did not. And a glass-topped show-case beneath the window held all sorts of implements of failed crime.

Charlie Lam was in one of those photographs; grinning broadly over a wall of packaged heroin. Charlie had cut his teeth in the Triad Society Division. Now he was a superintendent in the Intelligence Bureau, leading a specialized team; he also disagreed with PK Lo's supposition:

'Can't see it, Reven. Tang Tsun as a Celestial Dragon-head? Doesn't fit, does it? For a start his father was killed by triad enforcers. Does the AC know that?'

'That docket was on his desk. He thinks that ambition could have driven him to do it . . . But I can't see that. One can't just *do* that sort of thing; One can't buy one's way into office in a triad society by being a major shareholder. It would have taken years for Tang to fight his way through the ranks. He'd have to have done some pretty serious things to prove his competence along the way . . . There's no question, we would have found some thread of evidence over the years to connect him to the triads.'

'I'd have thought so, Reven. But here's something interesting. Tang has a twenty-two-year-old brother: name, Tang San-kiu, calls himself Sandy. Sandy Tang has been investigated by Special Investigation Unit and they've got a fat file on him.'

'Good grief! SIU. The Bum Squad?'

'Yes, Sandy was with the Tung Wong Opera Company at the time. I've asked SIU for the file. Should arrive any minute . . . the gist of it is that Sandy was being buggered by a VIP barrister' – Charlie smirked the name – 'David Bruton-Jones. SIU pushed for conviction but Jones was never sent down. He threatened to name names – some VIP names; many of whom were too close to the Governor for His Excellency's comfort . . . You won't find that on the file, but that's what SIU believes.'

Forrester sat at a desk, smaller and more strewn than his superior's. The chairs were less luxuriant too, and definitely did not exude an odour of good leather. He said, 'Yes, I remember the case. I didn't know it was Tang Tsun's brother . . . It must have cost Tang plenty in black-money to keep the Chinese press quiet.'

'They'll print what they're paid to print – and not print what they're paid not to print. No problem. Besides, homosexuality is "Foreigners'" disease. It doesn't exist amongst the Chinese – we're too pure; and if we're not we're too sensible to admit it.'

'Sandy must have given the family considerable face problems . . . Naughty boy!'

'He's back in Hong Kong. He was banished to England for a year, but now he's back.' Charlie gave that statement the sort of wry shrug one reserves for the prodigally stupid in our midst.

'Now he's a star singer with Tung Wong; a perfect voice. Believe me, I've heard him – magnificent in military roles. You should hear him.'

'I'm not a Cantonese Opera fan, Charlie. I can't make head or tail of it.'

'Too subtle for hairy foreign barbarians.'

'Too jarring for hairy foreign barbarians.'

'I'll take you and explain the ritual . . . make you a fan.'

'No thank you, Charlie Lam; better that I should remain hairy and barbaric. Anyway, my crystal ball foretells that you won't have much time for opera in the near future, and neither will I.'

'Tang Tsun . . . a tricky one, ha?'

'Yes, very. I do not have a good feeling about this, Charlie. It is possible that Ch.I.S. are in the background here, somewhere, manipulating things. You will handle the case personally. Do not involve more than two members of your team; and they must be utterly trustworthy. It's seldom that a case makes its way on to my desk by this route, and in this manner. And when it happens, I tend to regard it as one might a large and dangerous snake in a wet paper bag. Be very cautious, Charlie . . . I will be working closely on this case too, and I will advise you of my moves.'

'I'm going to Sai Kung today. There's someone there I want to speak to in connection with this case. Did you ever meet a station sergeant, Fung Sham, known as The Fixer? . . . No? He retired quite recently. The greatest "caterer" in the business, but the Anti-Corruption Squad could never nail him. I had him more or less where I wanted him when I was his SDC . . . My first sub-divisional command, my God, those were good days. Life was an old tin can to be kicked up the street; and no more to it than that.'

'The pulse of youth; it never returns. I'll have to be leaving soon, Reven. Rehearsal at the church, you know – five o'clock . . . hell, I'm nervous.'

'It's high time you were married off, Charlie, that eel of yours has been roving free for too many years. Is there a woman in Hong Kong whose black-rose hasn't been nibbled by it? . . . Give Lulu a big hug for me and tell her don't worry. I'll be there

38

on the day to see that you don't make a last-minute break for freedom.'

'That's what Lulu says, too.' Charlie gave a squeaky impersonation of his school-teacher fiancée: 'High time that man Reven was married off . . . No girl safe in Hong Kong until then.'

'I know what Lulu thinks . . .' Lulu Wong was a close friend of Caroline O'Shea, and Lulu used every ounce of influence she possessed, on every possible occasion, to marry him to the flame-haired Caroline . . . 'Maybe some day, Charlie. Who knows?'

'A marriage made in Heaven, Reven.'

'More of Lulu's poetry, I think.'

'Caroline will be at the wedding. Did she tell you?'

'Lulu told me.'

Charlie grinned nervously. 'Guests of honour. Great face for me to have you both there – honest truth.'

'Your Lulu, Charlie Lam, is one hell of a manipulator. And you are her willing right hand. Of course I'll be there. Not even wild horses, Charlie . . .'

Sai Kung Hoi means Inner Port Shelter, and it is that. The harbour is boot-shaped, about two hundred metres long and five hundred metres wide, and so positioned that the bay is barely stirred no matter what the season. That summer sunset clung heavily to the air; hot and moist and vexed with mosquitoes. The fishing craft of Sai Kung floated lifelessly in the torpid lisping water.

The wooden-hulled motorized lighter of Fung Sham lay at anchor in the throat of the bay. A stocky, blunt-prowed vessel, its deck was wide and made of thick teak planks that were scarred from the years of hard-bottomed cargo. From its foredeck a stubby mast arose with a jib-boom hinged at its step to form a crane. Stretched from the lighter's box-like superstructure was a green oilcloth canopy, and Reven Forrester sat there. He wore a loose shirt and shorts and a pair of rubber sandals, and so did

Fung Sham, The Fixer. A single small neon strip gave light, and a large fan hummed upon a stand, trailing tiredly, to and fro, as though in forced observance of the play of conversation:

'Good times, Ging Si, ha? . . . Do you remember the sea-food eating-house of Fat-boy Shum? Best fried squid and celery in all of Hong Kong. And *you* could eat then; *what* an appetite . . . and what a thirst, aieya. But forgive me for being such a miserable host; dreaming of the past and forgetting the present. Let's drink another beer.'

From a galvanized bath of crushed ice came more beer. Fung lifted the bottle tops to his mouth and bit the caps off with his strong white teeth.

'*Yum Sing!* Ging Si,' Fung filled his glass. 'Drink to victory . . . Well, I can call you Ging Si with pride, because I knew you when you were just a "help man" inspector. So now you're top of the heap – a Ging Si, Superintendent. But I knew you when you were mustard-green of the tenth moon . . . Do you know what the PCs called you then? I'll tell you, they called you Monkey Without a Chain – Lat Sing Mah Lau. A good name for you; no one ever knew where the hell you were. No one but me . . . I knew.' Fung roared with laughter, bulged his eyes and wagged a finger at such saucy memories.

Forrester looked at Fung and thought: you haven't changed a bit; still the great josh-artist. Then he laughed too, and nodded towards the lighter. 'You've done well too, Ah Fung. But I knew you would prosper; Sai Kung was good to you.'

'And I was good to Sai Kung. It was policed as well as any town in the colony.'

'I've no argument there.'

'You're a gwailo with a Chinese heart, Ging Si; you understand that that which cannot be changed should not be seriously opposed. Can you stop the north-west wind with a shout? So I have prospered, but was Sai Kung a blacker place because of it . . . hah?'

'There's nothing that we do that doesn't leave a mark . . .

you judged what crime was acceptable and what was not. I'll grant you, some sort of order was established in that way.'

'When a hard crime was committed I stood against it, and so did every PC in the station.'

'Yes you did, and it's just that that I've come to talk to you about: Tang Ten-thousand Blessings.'

'Aah.'

An old woman emerged from the deck house then, carrying mosquito-coils. She set them down on the deck and lit them, and a haze of pyrethrum rose. They chewed on trivia until she had gone. Then Fung said:

'So long ago, Ging Si. But of course I remember it well; bad business. But you were there too; you know as much as anyone about that case.'

'Once I thought I did; now . . . I'm not sure. I want to know more about Tang himself, and his family, especially his father.'

'Tang Tsun, well there's a man who can touch pewter and make gold. He became a monk, didn't he? Well, he'll never need to carry a begging-bowl. His cousin Tang Tik-kat sold off the bottom-soil rights of their land and made some shrewd investments with the money in Hong Kong. I hear Tik-kat owns more buildings now than he could visit in a day . . . racehorses, and whatever else money can buy. You know what we Chinese are like; we like to show our wealth; to boast about our luck . . . Tang Tsun was born lucky.'

'He was born lucky?'

'Of course; he was born on the sixteenth of the eighth . . . triple wealth, and not only that, it's the birth date of Monkey . . . ' Fung belched in a vastly satisfying way. He finished his beer and tossed the bottle overboard, then bit the tops off two more bottles. 'He went to the temple of the Great Sage after his father's murder, don't you remember? The monks took him in like a long-lost son.'

'It's not so lucky to cause your father's death, Ah Fung; even so indirectly.'

'Tsun caused the Sun Yee On enforcers to lose face. So they

41

punished him by destroying his dearest possession – his father. He should have expected it after the fight that night in the Ten and Ten.'

'Did you ever have any doubts about that? Could Tang have been killed for any other reason?'

'I don't think so.' Fung dwelled on the question for a moment. 'What other reason?'

'Triad warfare?'

'Tang wasn't a triad member. He paid squeeze to Sun Yee On like every other businessman in Sai Kung, but he wasn't a member. He hated Sun Yee On, Ging Si, they all did. The only group he might have joined was his temple society.'

'Chai Tin Dai Sing Temple Society. Yes of course. How badly our minds sometimes serve us. Tell me what you know about this society.'

'I can tell you in a breath: I know nothing about them, excepting that they do exist . . . Oh they're very old . . . It might be called White Lotus Society.'

'White Lotus?'

'A whisper in the wind.' Fung drained his beer. 'I've no facts.' With a flick of his wrist he turfed the empty bottle over his shoulder. It was accepted by the sea with a subdued plop.

'White Lotus was a Ching Dynasty secret society. They mounted an uprising against the Manchus and were totally eliminated,' Forrester said uncertainly. 'Eighteen thirteen, I think.'

'You're the historian, Ging Si, not me.'

'Do White Lotus still hold initiation rites?'

'As I said, I know nothing . . . but there are rumours. I'll try and find out more if that's what you want, Ging Si.'

'No. Not at this stage.'

'As you say . . . Well then: let's finish this miserable beer, then go and eat.'

They drank the remaining bottles from the bottom of the tub, and thus protected from the heat rode a slow sampan to shore, then walked the dark streets to the seafood restaurant of Fat-boy

Shum. An uproar of a place, all clamour, shrieks and laughter and the blare of TV; the noise of Fat-boy's restaurant reached out into the night and drew them on . . . There were the bright windows with their aquariums of sluggish gape-jawed fish, staring in shock at those who had come to eat them, there was Fat-boy himself grinning like a buddha, trawling with a scoop-net for a slippery garoupa. He saw Forrester and Fung and yelled:

'Look who the God of Travellers has brought to me – the Monkey Without a Chain. I thought you must have lost him, Ah Fung . . . Well, there's your table, and there's your guests . . . Come on, come on, you're late for the party.'

Four men sat at a white-clothed round table, three Chinese ex-police officers, and Mike Hempstead, who, had he been dressed in uniform, would have borne three pips upon his shoulders. He greeted Forrester:

'Just like old times, Reven.'

'Yes.' An obligatory lie. Everything but the venue was different. He had served with all of these men at one time or another, and had drunk with them at Fat-boy Shum's restaurant to the point of obliteration. But with the exception of Mike Hempstead they had all soberly advanced in their careers, then gone into business.

Mike had marked time on the square of chief inspectorship for so long that he was rut-worn into it; no one really noticed, or expected good work from him any longer, so no one nudged him on.

Forrester greeted the Chinese. There was Yin-nam, an ex-detective sergeant; Liang, who had retired as an inspector; and Kwan, who wore a gold Rolex as proof that business had never been better: 'Import, export, Ging Si – make a million.'

Mike Hempstead put his arm on Forrester's shoulder and said: 'The only two cops left,' and everyone laughed except Forrester who saw his old friend closely now, and was aghast at the booze-blown face. Cops were expected to drink – cheap alcohol and long hot summers drew the men into the messes with desert thirsts. But this man was sick and rotten with the stuff. He escaped from Hempstead's embrace with the question:

'How's Tessa, Mike?'

43

Lovely Theresa Hempstead – was she rotting with her husband as some expatriate wives did?

'Sends her love to you . . . of course.' Hempstead almost emptied his glass at a swig. He didn't seem to have to swallow, but simply open his mouth and pour it in like a bucket to a drain. The Chinese cheered this feat. Hempstead licked his moustache and refilled his glass, flattered by the acclaim; a drinker of repute.

Food came; dishes of crisp tender squid and lotus roots, crab and mushrooms in wine sauce and green vegetables. Forrester set his chop-sticks to work – he knew how good the food would be. As they ate they spoke about the Sai Kung of old, and they chaffed and made up outrageous fiction about each other that brought mock-serious denials and great bellows of laughter. A listener would have sworn that these men had never known a moment of tedium, or seriousness, or rage. Quart bottles of beer were quickly emptied and food plates replaced in an instant – crunchy water chestnuts, oysters and wild rice-shoots. Shrimps, garoupa; the supply seemed endless.

Forrester drank when a toast was called for, and only then. That was the secret of staying sober in such company. The Chinese drank less moderately, and Mike Hempstead quaffed down his liquor with prodigious style. When Forrester asked Yin-nam why he had resigned from the force Hempstead answered on behalf of the ex-detective.

'I'll tell you why Yin-nam resigned, Reven. You want to know I'll tell you . . . He left because the Ch.I.S. have got long memories . . . Right, Yin-nam?'

'I got a better job . . . more money.'

'That's bullshit, OK. He left because in sixty-seven, when the Commies were rioting and screaming their fucking heads off about what they had in store for us British pigs, he stood his ground and got spat on, and called a yellow running-dog . . . Right, Yin-nam? And when the order came through to crack heads, he cracked heads . . . 'scuse me.' Hempstead scraped back his chair and stood . . . 'Fucking Commies have got long memories.' He wandered off unsteadily towards the toilets.

No one at their table spoke for a while, then Yin-nam said: 'It's true, I was there. I was there on the day when Peter Godber commanded us. Wah, Ging Si! There was a man: "Stand *firm!*" he ordered, and so we stood. I think we would have broken ranks, and run if it wasn't for Godber. He had *such* face!'

'Those PCs thought something of the Brits then.' Hempstead was back. 'Godber was a hero to those cops. When the Commies came on chanting their crappy Mao-thought, and waving their idiot little red books, our boys faced them down. *Bloody* brave! We told them that the Brits would never desert them, and those stupid cops believed it . . . until Maggie-bloody-Thatcher came on the scene and sold Hong Kong to the Reds . . . So now the good cops like Yin-nam and Liang here and a few thousand others have had to get out before the Ch.I.S. get in . . . God help Hong Kong.'

'To victory,' said Yin-nam.

'To victory.'

'It's time for brandy.' Hempstead belched irascibly. 'I've had all the beer I can fucking drink.'

So they ordered brandy – best French cognac. And that put Hempstead in roaring form for a while, and then he slumped into his chair and turned his dull, drunk eyes on Forrester and said: 'Jesus, Reven, I'm tired of this *fuck*ing life, honest I am. I'm forty-four and what the hell have I achieved?'

'I'll take you home, Mike.'

'A *fuck*ing chief inspector. I haven't got tuppence to my name . . . no pension, and a moaning wife who's never forgiven me for marrying her.'

'We're going, Ah Sham, many thanks. Great honour.'

Fung Sham clasped his hands to his chest and gave the smallest of bows: 'I'm ashamed to stand here having offered this pitiful meal.'

'Yin-nam; Liang, Kwan. You've all given me such face.'

Hempstead swayed towards the entrance like a counted-out boxer. At the glass doors he halted and turned to Forrester. 'No need . . . ' he frowned, 'for a fucking nursemaid, Reven. I'll drive myself.'

There was no question of that. He took Hempstead's arm in a harsh grip. He wanted his displeasure to get through to this man's piss-addled mind; but said no more than: 'I'm taking you home, Mike, so don't give me a fucking hard time, OK. Now, where's your car?'

'Up this street.' Hempstead gestured vaguely in the direction they should take.

The car was as beaten and dejected as its owner. The doors banged hollowly against worn locks and the driver's seat rocked beneath Forrester's buttocks as he drove. At the outskirts of Sai Kung they met with heavy rain which the wipers slapped at ineffectually.

'Pak Sha Wan,' Hempstead said dully. 'You know where the house is, ol' buddy.'

'Sure.'

'Not far, you know. I could have driven myself. Done it in worse shape than this . . . No fucking problem.'

Bloody fool. 'Why do you do this to yourself, Mike? Why don't you get out of Hong Kong . . . Make a new life somewhere else for Tess and yourself.'

'No lectures please, Ging Si . . . I know I've got no future here . . . known that for a long, long time'; all this slopped out unmediated by movement of lip or tongue. 'I love the place, you see . . . Don't wanna go anywhere else.'

He felt defeated by Hempstead's sheer dumb-drunkenness. Conversation was too much of a chore. He drove the miserable, leaking car at the beating rain and thought of some of the drunks he had known: good, intelligent men like this. And you could not shame them from the bottle, or argue them from it, or slap it from their hands. And all of them loved Hong Kong because Hong Kong was submerged in liquor, and they soaked and softened in it like prunes in a bowl. He drove up to Mike Hempstead's gate and on to the driveway. Pretty, lilac begonias clambered over a picket fence and low-swept flamboyant boughs kindled flame-red in the headlights. Tessa loved her garden. The house was of double-storeyed pre-war

46

colonial style, typical of the immoderate, government-owned houses of that era. Hempstead extricated himself from his seat-belt.

'C'mon, Reven.'

'I'm going to drive back now to Sai Kung, Mike. I'll organize a driver to bring your car back here in the morning.'

'Tessa won't like that.'

'It's midnight, Mike. Go get to bed.'

'She'll want to see you . . . old times' sake.'

'Get going. Get out of the rain.'

Mike Hempstead said, 'Right.' He took a few paces, turned around to wave and disappeared with a crash. A dog barked, an outside light came on and Theresa Hempstead's peeved voice floated down.

'Is that you, Mike?'

Hempstead had fallen face forward into the hibiscus shrubbery, where he lay, hooting with laughter as the rain soaked him through. Forrester got out of the car.

'Get up.' He prodded him unkindly with the toe of his shoe.

Mike did not get up, he just went on giggling. Forrester waded into the shrubbery, gripped the soggy material of Hempstead's shirt and hauled at it. It rended into two parts.

'Oh God!' Tessa Hempstead's words. She stood beneath a dripping umbrella holding a torch; its beam directed at her husband's face, then at his torn shirt, then towards the destroyed hibiscus foliage.

'Oh God,' she said with utter desperation.

Forrester gained the better of Hempstead. The man was still giggling, but he had risen, at least, to one knee. He pulled at this unmanageable bulk, and Hempstead gained his feet. By instalments, in constant danger of collapse, they progressed to the front porch.

'Hello, darling.' Hempstead blearily noticed his wife. 'I brought a visitor.'

Tessa Hempstead gave a sharp little gasp. 'Reven.'

'I 'vited him home, darling.' Hempstead began to giggle again.

Then he hiccuped loudly and vomited hotly down Forrester's arm.

Tessa Hempstead shouted, 'Filthy; rotten . . . ' Then fled. Forrester dragged Hempstead into the hall, and from the hall to the lounge, to a leatherette sofa. There he lay down his troublesome, eructative burden.

Tessa came back carrying a towel and a basin. The basin came in handy immediately as Mike then threw up the remainder of Fat-boy Shum's seafood cuisine – a bilious, stinking aggregate of crustacea that he was well rid off. Tessa Hempstead had things completely in hand now. A petite, energetic woman who taught aerobic classes, and was thus used to command, she directed Forrester to the stairs.

'Shower,' she ordered. 'Through the bedroom and to the left. I'll bring fresh towels.'

'I'm sorry about this, Tess, really. What a mess.'

'I'm not sorry,' she smiled with her small good teeth. 'What's left to be sorry about? Now go on, and don't scald, the water runs hot.'

He went into a petal-soft bedroom with a big frilly bed piled up with plump cushions, dented where her petite form had recently lain. One wall was filled with photographs, mostly of groups, always with her pretty face somewhere to be found. There was a wedding picture of a much younger Mike Hempstead on the steps of St Andrew's, Kowloon, sternly handsome and fervent with promise, with lacy-veiled Theresa at his side. And there stood Reven Forrester, one pace behind, one step above – three silver pips and a glinting sword, forever in escort . . . Just another golden dream. He stripped off his befouled vest and stepped from his shorts. The hot water in the shower, as promised, came bursting through and he took soap and lathered off the sour stink of Hempstead's stomach.

Tessa came into the bathroom while he stood in the shower cubicle. She'd brought fresh clothes, she said. He'd find them on the chair . . . She'd left on the steamy air the trace of her perfume too – an intimate deep woman smell, and he liked it. He drew at the scent and delightful memories swirled from forgotten mossy ditches of his mind: warm, moist, soft, sensual Tessa. Tessa, so brightly nice, and as fickle as a dandelion clock. Tessa, who, as petite as she was, could hurtle black anger like a spear at those who displeased . . . He had displeased, and gallant Mike Hempstead had gathered her with fine vows. And so it was.

When he was clean and dressed in a white T-shirt and faded blue rugby shorts (that he suspected had once belonged to him anyway), he came into the bedroom. Tessa arrived then too, bearing a tray with cups and a tall coffee-pot. Coffee, she said, was the least she could offer him by way of compensation.

'He's sleeping it off,' she gestured contemptuously to the lounge below, 'just a normal, boring ending to a normal, boring day for him. For me, thank God, it's quite different; you're here, and that is wonderful.'

She had coloured her mouth with pale lipstick and brushed out her thick blonde hair. She cleared some magazines off the seat of a chair for him, then sat on the bed folding her fine legs beneath her.

'No one can tell you what it's like being married to a drunk. Booze, it just melts your conscience, dissolves it like an ice-cube. Mike used to have such high ideals. He was a wonderful guy . . . but now. There's nothing left. No will, no thought that isn't mixed fifty-fifty with a jigger of brandy.'

'I don't know what to say, Tess. Mike's a good cop; a friend of mine.'

'Is he? So why do you avoid him? . . . He's a bloody embarrassment, that's why. Because he can't drink without getting legless . . . I know the gwailo cops aren't angels, but what the rest do or don't do doesn't concern me. Most of them know when to stop; Mike doesn't. He's hardly come home sober once these last few years. Oh, he was thrilled when Fung Sham invited him to Fat-boy's to a reunion dinner in your honour. I knew how it would end though.'

She poured coffee from the tall bone-china pot and when she reached out with the cup the lapel of her gown fell forward and he saw the swell of her breast – milk-white on her smooth golden

49

body. She saw where his eyes had strayed and unhurried fingers closed the gap. She said:

'And yet I wished that he would get drunk tonight, and you would bring him home. There, I've said it. I wanted to see you, Reven; I've missed you. This is the first time that we've sat together, just the two of us, for years. Do you know how you've changed most? It's your eyes. They're just as blue and startling, but once they darted like a squirrel in a tree, full of tricks and lightness. Now that's all gone. It's because of Shen Woo, isn't it, Reven? You loved her so much.'

'A paper-chase, Tess, that was blown away on a high wind. I'll never find it again; nor do I want to. It's gone. Best leave it alone.' He drank from the virtuously slim white cup, and watched her pink lips purse at her cup rim, sipping quickly, like a bird.

She spoke in a tautly soft way: 'I had a place in your life once. I can recall glorious carefree hours; such joy as I've never known since. Those memories haven't been lost in time have they . . . we were close; or is my mind a liar?'

'We were close.' Yet the mind was a liar; perfidiously so.

'I'm jealous of Shen . . .'

'She's dead.'

'And yet I envy what she had. It must have been a great love that you shared.'

'She would have been better off without it. Then she would have been alive today . . . Here's the hard truth: I hated her brother. I hunted him down. And she was caught up in the violence of it, and didn't survive it.'

'Neither did you, in a way. No, let me speak. Look at yourself. You're hollowed out with bitterness and guilt, Reven. You've enshrined your grief; you've made it a cruel and self-punishing creed.'

'That, Tess, is absolute fabrication.'

'Oh, it's true.' She put down her cup; he watched her fingers, tenuous, small fingers; now earnestly mitred. 'I'm a cop's wife, so I hear about other ex-pat policemen and the things they do. Most of it's gossip, nonsense, I'll agree. But the truth has a ring to it that sets it above all the daft babble – it clamours like a school bell in a playground . . . The word is that you've become hard, embittered, and cynical . . . Oh shit! And now I've made you angry, and I didn't want to do that.'

'Angry? Me? I'm just amazed at you. This is Hong Kong, you know, Tess, rumours grow in this climate like bamboo-shoots after rain.'

'I know. I'm sorry. It's none of my business, anyway . . . But I wanted you to know that I care for you.'

'For God's sake why?'

'The man asks why?' She mused, widening her eyes. 'OK; because I'm crazy. Because I hurt for you . . . On that rainy day, three years ago, was it, when Shen Woo was buried, I was there. I cried for you. You looked so weak and stooped. I wanted to go to you and hold you tightly and stroke away your grief. I wanted to feel your tears on my skin . . . You see, I knew that day that I still loved you, and nothing has changed since then.'

The rough-shod gentleness of such pretty-talk. What defence was there against these velvet words that would not stamp him as a brute? 'I don't want that. No . . . I don't want you to love me.'

'Well that's immaterial, Ging Si. I do. No fault of yours, and nothing to be done.'

'I can't love you.'

'I think you could. I see the way you look at me; the magic's still there, Ging Si.'

'Of course I've thought about it, Tess. It would be fantastic. And then what? A furtive, panicky affair that would be sure to get out. It's a bad idea, Tess . . . you'd hate me for it after a while. I won't let this happen.' Re-examined, this defence was sophistry, and unlikely to succeed. He watched; he watched all of her.

'I'm going to leave him, Reven. So it wouldn't be as you describe it. I love you . . . I wouldn't allow you to be tarnished in such a way . . . Do you hear me, I love you.'

'I know something about love. It's a power for destruction, Tess. Don't touch it, I warn you. You think it's Nirvana, but it's a hoax, a treason of the mind upon itself. A madness.' Yes it was. Well said!

51

So serious and taut; her neck had two sinews that made deep, fervent valleys in this light. She argued softly: 'I want that Nirvana, I want that madness. God, how I want it. I don't care if it's just a trick; it's a magnificent trick . . . A secret, dear Reven: my husband hasn't touched me for more than a year.'

Then your husband is crazy. That was Reven Forrester's conviction; unspoken, but stated just the same.

'Touch me.' She held out her hand and the love-drug scent of her wooed him again. So he touched her hand until the bond could not be broken. Then they drew each other in. Even as the wrongness of it shouted at his conscience, the wild need to fuck this woman drove him on. They binged on each other's juices, lick-kissing at the sweat of neck and cheek – then deeper.

Perhaps there was love in it; he did not think of love. His mind was sodden with sex, and God knows what she thought. His eyes were closed and so were hers as they thrust and gasped for orgasm . . . While downstairs the cuckold husband snored louder than the drumming rain.

There is an Old Man of the Moon, Yueh Lao Yeh, with a great white moustache and a river of beard, whose task it is to keep the Book of Marriages. So when a boy is born his name is registered, and next to it the name of his wife-to-be. Yueh's choice is irrevocable, but in order that there should be no confusion on earth, he ties to each babe's ankle a long and unbreakable red cord to join those he has coupled . . . In adulthood they will be drawn together by this cord. That is fate.

So Charlie Lam of the year of the Dragon and pretty Lulu Wong of the year of the Rat were destined to marry. The only possible point of discussion was that of the date for the event. So the omens were considered and after due consideration with the feng shui professors, and the Almanac of Respected Master T'ung, a date was set. It was day eight of the second moon. And that day had now arrived.

Lulu Wong's eyelids sprang wide open at the instant of dawn.

She rushed to her window and saw that it was to be a fine day. She drew a full bath and scrubbed and soaped until she was clean all over. Yin-san her maid of honour came into the bathroom while Lulu was at a delicate task. Yin-san had a vile wit:

'Close up your little purse, my dear, don't wash away your luck. The Buddha of pleasure has no sense of smell.'

'Awful!' shrieked Lulu. 'Aieya!'

They giggled over that joke, and others, all the way to the hairdresser, where Lulu's long black hair was washed and brushed and styled till it shone brighter than a raven's wing. Then they went back to Lulu's parent's house where all her fine wedding garments were laid out. Lulu drew on her new underclothes:

'As sheer spun as the spider's web.' That was how Yin-san saw it – 'To trap the spider and *gobble* him up.'

The dress was of white taffeta, cut tightly into Lulu's small waist, then flaring off her hips with masses of pleats that spilled widely to the ground – beautiful. Mrs Wong came into the room then, as did several curious aunts, all agasp and with one voice: 'Beauty enough to shame the moon.'

'Tolerably nice,' joshed Yin-san. 'If Lulu weren't so fat and ugly, ha?'

'Yin-san!'

'Well, she'd better get used to being teased. All of Charlie's relatives will do it . . . You really do look a fine sight though, Lulu – like a film-star.'

That compliment mollified the aunts.

A beautician came and cherried Lulu's lips and smeared and rouged and plucked and painted, and hid her pretty face so completely behind a mask of make-up that the aunts threw up their hands with delight:

'Empress for a day!'

Yin-san sighed and hoped she would look this grand on her wedding day. She doubted it though, her parents weren't as wealthy as the Wongs.

'That sex-wolf Charlie had better know his luck,' Yin-san said. They could all agree with that.

Lulu put on her best jewellery then – a gold link bracelet and a gold necklace with a jade charm that would save her from all adversity. Mrs Wong brought out a beautiful ruby ring: 'To bring luck, Lulu. It was your grandmother's. She was very lucky.' The ring unfortunately was too loose, even for Lulu's biggest finger.

'Never mind,' said Mrs Wong. 'Wear your glove over it. That will hold it in place.' And it did. 'Tonight you give it back.'

Also to ensure luck Mrs Wong had set out a table of rice cakes and sweets, stamped with red characters – food for the gods. And though she was devoutly Roman Catholic and wore a crucifix, no one thought it in the least strange that a god-box with Kuan Yin set serenely within it should decorate one corner of the living-room with offerings of oranges and smoking joss sticks before it.

Lulu was dressed in her beautiful white gown, a veil of lace fell to her chin. Yin-san wore a blue dress with seed-pearls at the neck. Mrs Wong stood out in wine-red brocade and the aunts had long since gone off, dressed in an assortment of auspicious shades . . . The time had come for the bride to leave her parent's home and to go to her husband-to-be's side at the Church of St Francis of Assisi in Sham Shui Po.

That was where nervous Charlie Lam waited for the woman he loved. There was no tangible reason for his unease. He was delighted that at last he and Lulu were to be wed. It was a splendid day – no dashing around with umbrellas to save precious hair-styles. The church was bright with flowers and profuse with friends and relatives, and there was his guest of honour. He gave Reven Forrester a furtive little wave – a mere tremor of the fingertips. But Reven saw it and winked the way gwai los do to cunningly acknowledge a deep secret.

The Perfect Golden Phoenix restaurant was to be the venue for the wedding-feast, and Charlie had visited that establishment that very morning to discuss a last-minute change in the menu – beggar's kitchen in place of chicken and melon in fragrant sauce . . . The bitter melons required for the latter dish were too immature and tart. But no one would find cause to complain, the Perfect Golden Phoenix was renowned for its beggar's kitchen.

And that was just one of the dozen sumptuous dishes laid on for his guests. Let it be known that this feast had cost him a fortune.

So all preparations were complete, and all was as it should be. So how come his bowels were in such a grovel of apprehension?

Then came a buzz of excitement. Charlie turned and caught his breath . . . The most beautiful woman he had ever seen had ascended to the porch of the church – *and this was his bride*.

Lonnie Huang and Noona Cham were waiters at the Perfect Golden Phoenix. Both had been born in Fukien province, which gave them an ability to turn on a dialect that was barely understood by their Hong Kong born colleagues, and so by origin they were natural friends.

They had also both dropped out of school at an early age, and they were both part-time homosexual prostitutes – full-moon boys. They worked in the Phoenix until closing time – one o'clock in the morning. Then, if the weather was fine, they would go to the Star Ferry terminal at Tsim Sha Tsui and there trawl for a tourist with a wallet full of love. The reward: a hotel bed in an air-conditioned room. And the alternative to that was a rat-hole tenement eight filthy flights of stairs above the street in the old sector of Kwun Tong.

It was natural, therefore, that Lonnie and Noona should share secrets, and money, and occasionally a client who wanted a double run, and could afford the luxury. For money brought new clothes, and Mandrax tablets, and laughter. While poverty was a triad loan-shark, and a knife at the neck. They tried very hard to have money, but mostly they were hard-up.

They were particularly broke on the afternoon of the wedding-feast of Charlie Lam, so as they lined the walls with the other waiters and watched the guests file to the tables, they bobbed and smiled respectfully, but their quick little gestures were sharp with want. They poured out tea and brought brandy and beer or soft drinks, and answered questions as to the menu (the shark-fin soup, oh yes sir, that will come later) but their hard-eyed vigil did not cease for an instant.

'Be careful, the room is full of *wind*,' Lonnie hissed to Noona. Lonnie liked to impress with triad jargon. *Wind; black-foot* – these were sly terms used to refer to the police. 'That one over there . . . the gwailo, isn't he just the most typical *black-foot* you've ever seen.'

'And look at the gwaipor hag sitting next to him, my dear. Her knickers are likely to catch fire with that torch in her crutch.'

'That hair!'

So much for Reven Forrester and Caroline O'Shea. Such conversations were snatched in passing. It was rush here, and rush there, pouring and carrying and dodging little children who were bent on tripping waiters at every opportunity.

Chopped pork with cabbage and water chestnuts with side plates of mixed vegetables: that was the first dish to come forth from the Phoenix's hectic kitchen. Three hundred guests were seated now and they took up their chop-sticks and went for the food like wolves at the kill . . . More food; duck pieces with diced pork on a bed of ginger-root, mushrooms, fish stomach, lotus seeds and onion. All bolted down in a minute.

'More soya sauce, waiter!'

'More brandy, ha. You gone to sleep, or what.'

A drum roll for the bride and groom, but Lonnie was all plates and bottles and yes sir, no sir, and had time to offer but the briefest glance. Her dress was beautiful he noticed, then he dashed for the kitchen to produce more food, more drink.

The bride made her way to the change-room, a quiet room near the ladies' lavatory which was reserved for her, whence (having shed the white gown) she would reappear in more gorgeous attire. Lonnie had seen the new outfit that awaited her there, which was, to his mind, quite tasteless – a traditional Chinese wedding costume – an elaborately embroidered, long, red silk skirt and jacket.

So Lonnie and Noona sweated from kitchen to table, and the guests ate and drank (mostly drank, for they had cleaned out all eight courses by then), and gambled. The music boomed, and the bride sat before a bright red screen beneath the characters 'Double Joy', all lit up like a Barbie doll in a toy-shop window. The children shrieked, the mah-jong players clashed, and the night wore on.

Then came the moment that Lonnie had awaited: a lull in appetite and thirst, an opportunity to steal into the bride's change-room and have a sniff around. Brides were amazingly negligent in their hurried change of clothes. Once he had picked up a Dunhill lighter there, on another occasion a bottle of Guy Laroche perfume had been his reward . . . This woman's lovely dress rested on a hanger; Lonnie tweaked the fine taffeta and pursed his lips in approval. He looked on the shelf where her white gloves lay; he searched beneath the seat where the Dunhill had been discovered . . . not even a hair-pin to be found. 'Bitch!'

He turned to go and trod upon something hard and small – a ring, a gold ring with a huge square, red stone mounted into it. Lonnie's mouth dried and his stomach kicked. He whispered: 'Ruby . . . no, can't be so.' For if it was, then it was the biggest, brightest ruby he had ever seen.

Lonnie dropped the ring into his trouser pocket. He hid his jolting heart within a blithe furrow – the eager, mandatory smile of the waiter at work, then slipped out of the room and back into the tumult of the wedding-feast.

Mrs Wong was the first to notice that Grandmother's ruby ring no longer decorated the hand of her newly wedded daughter. She came to Lulu and whispered:

'Better let me keep it if it's too loose . . . ' She tapped Lulu's hand. 'The ring.'

Lulu looked down, and thought she was going to faint; and the swirl of her mind said, *It's gone, it's gone*. But as though she did not believe that she clutched and twisted at the barren finger.

'Where is the ring, Daughter?'

'It was . . . I . . . don't know.'

'But Lulu, you had it when you came here, didn't you? When you took off your gloves it was there.'

'I don't remember.'

'Well, it must have been, ha? That's common sense, Daughter.'

Lulu rushed off towards her change-room. She did remember now; she had seen it on her finger when she'd taken off her gloves . . . Then what? . . . Then she had changed into the red silk outfit, and she had seen it then too, and so had Yin-san. Her mind's ear heard Yin-san say: 'Red on red – it glows like fire against the silk . . . ' And then she had combed her hair where the coronet and veil had disturbed it.

Lulu reached the change-room and cast around quickly; begging the ring to make itself visible. She looked on the shelf and on the floor. Hope dwindled. She ruffled the folds of the white taffeta gown, and with mounting failure felt sicker and more panicked and swooningly drained of blood. The ring was not there.

Mrs Wong came into the change-room and Yin-san also, and all of them began to search anew. But Grandmother's ruby ring was elsewhere. Yin-san was the first to acknowledge that dreadful truth.

'It's not here; not anywhere in this room.'

'You saw it on my hand while I was changing,' Lulu's aghast voice pleaded. 'Tell Mother that, Yin-san.'

'Oh yes, I saw it . . . maybe it fell on the floor of the restaurant. Perhaps someone has found it and given it to the owner.' Yin-san offered that sprig of hope. 'Surely that's what's happened.'

But it was not on the restaurant floor in the places where Lulu had trod, or where she had sat, nor had it been handed in to the manager. An announcement was loudly broadcast: a reward for the person who found Grandma's ruby ring. There was much hopeful scraping and bending done then by guests and waiters. No luck. The children were set to the task but not even their magpie eyes were able to discover it, and the brats soon lost interest . . . The immense loss threw a pall of suspicion upon all those present, so it came as no shock when the guests quickly left. And who was to blame for the entire unmitigated disaster? No one but thoughtless and uncaring Lulu, who now sat languidly buttressed against her husband's shoulder, her skin aglisten with perspiration, as translucent as pearl.

Mrs Wong left everyone present in no doubt where lay the burden of guilt: 'Aieya! That a mother should ever imagine that a child can be trusted . . . A bamboo duck for a daughter, no care, no care. Aieyaa! And now look; parents shamed, all guests gone . . . '

That wasn't quite true. Reven Forrester was still there and so was Caroline O'Shea . . . But who would argue with Mrs Wong that such contagious bad luck as Lulu had brought there had scattered the guests like rice-chaff in a storm.

Caroline hugged her unfortunate friend, but this was a family affair, all of them knew that. And so she and Reven Forrester soon went away, too.

Charlie Lam took charge then. He told Mrs Wong that she should shame her daughter no further: 'If there's blame then it's in the size of her fingers, not in the magnitude of respectfulness for things given. Now then, was the ring too big, or the finger too small?'

'The fit was wrong,' admitted Mrs Wong. 'But such an expensive ring, how could she lose such an *expensive* ring?'

'The answer,' said Charlie, 'is that it was not lost, but stolen. There are thieves who would steal the sky and swap the sun, and there's no protection against such crooks, don't you see? I'll do what I can do.'

'Your wedding ruined, Son-in-law.'

'I paid for it, and I have what I wanted from it.' Charlie Lam gathered in his bride and stroked her hair. 'You dry your tears, girl. You don't worry now. Something will happen, something good.'

But Charlie was wrong.

*

Lonnie Huang knew he was as close to big money as he would ever be, and that thought was wildly exhilarating – a kind of tingling, sexy feeling that danced and chuckled in his body – to drop away occasionally in surging apprehension that left his mouth dry and his palms damp with sweat. My God! there was danger. Look at the number of policemen in the restaurant. He could sense the weight of the ring in his pocket, and if he smoothed the cloth of his trousers he could feel its outline at his thigh . . . God! What if he were searched? He'd be done for then . . . He joined in the mêlée, shifting tables, down on hands and knees, sweeping and patting with outstretched fingers in corners and crevices with commendable zeal. It was while in this servile position that he bumped heads with Noona, who was similarly engaged, and who said straight out:

'You've got it haven't you.'

'So fucking loud . . . why don't you shout so the wind can hear?'

Noona whispered, 'Shit, no one here who can understand us. You've got it. What have you done with it?'

Lonnie thought that he might refute Noona's accusation. Why should this avaricious bitch share in the proceeds of his enterprise? Because Noona might otherwise betray him, that was one excellent reason that instantly occurred to Lonnie. It was better to share than have nothing at all. Lonnie whispered:

'It's in my pocket.'

'My God!' Noona giggled nervously. 'What are you going to do?'

'I'm going to get out of here with it, of course.'

'Let me see it.'

'You're crazy, Noona.'

'Just quickly . . . Right here under the table; who's to see us? Come on. Come on!'

Lonnie dipped into his pocket and wriggled the ring on to his finger. Then he drew it out.

'Wah!' Noona gasped. 'Hot rat!' He squeezed the ring from

his friend's finger and held it to his eyes. 'Money, money, money! . . . So what now?'

'I'm going to smuggle it out.'

'How?'

'I don't know yet. I'll think of something.'

'Swallow it, Lonnie. No one can see inside you.'

'Wah, good idea . . . give it back to me.'

But Noona had no chance to comply. He felt the toe of a shoe painfully prod his rump; and accompanying this discourtesy came the voice of Pock-face Lai the restaurant owner:

'You two Chiu Chau queers going to spend all day fondling each other down there? Get your full-moon arses the fuck out of there.'

'Just searching like you ordered, Ah Lai.'

Noona emerged, and then Lonnie. Lonnie was slowed with shock – the encounter with Lai had almost paralysed him, and he had no idea what Noona had done with the ring during those frantic moments.

'Bodysearch,' said Pock-face Lai. 'Line up with the others.' He gestured towards his office where a queue of waiters and kitchen staff had formed. Pock-face scowled at his staff. He had a warning for them:

'Let this sink into your shit-bucket brains. Because one of you, and I'm sure it *was* one of you, stole Wong Grandmother's ruby ring, we have all been cast as criminals . . . I have lost face, and that makes me very angry. And all of you who are innocent must be just as angry. And so when I discover which leprous little toad is guilty . . .'

The threats then laid on them seemed quite believable, and wholly appalling. The more so as treacherous Noona who stood squarely next to Lonnie, punctuated the entire tirade with the prod of his elbow.

'Cut his penis off and feed it to him . . .'

Noona nudged.

'Hammer chop-sticks into his eyeballs . . .'

Noona again. The idiot thought this was fun. Did he think Lai was joking, or what?

'Brand "Thief" on to his forehead, then give him over to the mad-dog gwailo cops.'

So the search began: one suspect at a time in the secrecy of Lai's office. And as Lonnie advanced he grew bolder. He did not have the ring on him, after all; Noona had it, and when it was discovered on him, as it certainly would be, he would not find Lonnie as his friend . . . If it came to that, he'd do the surgery on Noona's private parts himself, and with relish.

And now the door opened to accept Noona and Lonnie stood back, waiting stiffly for Ah Lai's triumphant roar . . . But no, the door re-opened and Noona emerged without a wrinkle of worry on his pretty face.

And so the search ended in frustration for Ah Lai. Lonnie and Noona walked home, the fingertips of their hands trailing, touching one another, in a new and tactile sense of togetherness that both of them greatly enjoyed, and which would last certainly for as long as it took for Grandma's ruby ring to work through Noona's digestive tubes.

'So clever, Noona . . . As quick as a sparrow.'

'And all the time you were so worried, Lonnie. I tried to let you know.' Noona sighed, 'Think of all the things that we'll be able to buy.'

'Clothes, that wine leather jacket at Wing On department store . . . and a massive Sony portable . . . A Nikon autofocus.'

'Much more than that. But who will we sell the ring to? Where will we get the best price?'

'I've worked up a brilliant plan, Noona!'

'Tell.'

'Same person who owned it before will buy it back, of course. She stinks of money.'

'Did you see how she blubbed, Lonnie, when her mother laid a heap on her?'

'That's what I mean. The bitch will shit fourteen-carat gold if we ask her to. And it will be easy to find her phone number.'

'You know, Lonnie, you turn me on.'

'I'm hot for you too, Noona.'

They laughed; they kissed. It would have taken a pack of Mandrax to make them feel this high on any other day.

The voice on the telephone enquired: 'Lulu Wong?'

'Yes.'

'The same Lulu Wong who one week ago was married at Perfect Golden Phoenix restaurant?'

'Yes.'

Lulu listened to the nervous, warbling male voice and wondered if someone was engaging her in a practical joke. Whoever it was was speaking from a public telephone, there was a rumbling of street traffic and the murmur of many people. The jagged-edged bray of a police klaxon came and went, and did her no good.

'Is it her? Is it her?' A different voice emerged – wriggling with pique it came again: 'Tell her, tell the bitch . . . ' Then the sounds went mute as though her caller had blocked the mouthpiece with his hand.

'Hello?' Lulu said. 'Who is this?'

'Never mind.' The first speaker came on the line again, with more confidence than before. 'We've got your lovely ruby ring. Do you want it back, rich Lulu Wong?'

Stay calm, she told herself. To the asker of that question she said, 'Yes . . . yes. There is a reward, a big reward.'

'A big reward.' He aped her as though to amuse his partner . . . 'Shit on your reward. That ring is worth a hundred . . . no, a thousand times more than what your stingy Ma ma offered.'

'You were there, then, at the restaurant. Who are you?'

The line became muffled again. Then: 'No more questions. I can get a good price for this stone anywhere in Hong Kong. Do you want it or don't you? Yes, or no?'

'Yes, I want it.'

'Listen carefully then, and do exactly as I say . . . '

Lulu listened carefully. She would have done exactly as

instructed had she been able to. Her difficulty was that she did not have sufficient funds to meet their demand:

'One hundred thousand Hong Kong. Bring it with you.'

'One hundred thousand . . . I don't have so much.'

'Then, no ring.'

'*Please* . . . '

'No!' The voice shrilled. 'Fuck you. You're rich.'

She winced at the piercing anger of this ugly, invisible person. 'I'll bring all I can. I beg you, let me have my ring back. I'll give you money, a lot of money, all I've got . . . '

The line went dourly dead.

Lulu rushed to her bedroom and changed from her housecoat into a slax-suit. She took her bank-book and checked the balance – 64,000 Hong Kong dollars and a few cents, which amount fell abysmally short of the demand. She rummaged through her handbags and found a few hundred dollars more. 'Hopeless.' She locked the flat and rode the lift to the ground, then walked to the underground Mass Transit Railway at Kowloon Tong, which swallowed her whole, and sped with her like a snake in its burrow to bustling Yau Ma Tei. Elevators and tunnels and quick-walking people thrust her back to the sunlight. Portland Street was her destination, and that street was just around the corner.

She had arrived nearly an hour ahead of schedule, and that was simply because she had not visited her bank to make the withdrawal as instructed. A far more expedient arrangement had occurred to her whilst in the bowels of the MTR. She would show these thieves her bank-book. They would then see for themselves that their demand was impossible to meet. She would plead with them, face to face, to be reasonable. She felt sure this approach would win them over. Sixty-four thousand Hong Kong, she would tell them, was a huge amount of cash. It was her life's savings. And they could have it all. Lulu knew that at a greater or lesser depth there existed compassion in even the blackest of hearts and she would tap the source of it within these men.

Some parts of Portland Street have a sinister reputation, and should not be visited by those of feeble bladder. For here there are several Taoist chapels – *chai tong* where the burial rites of the newly dead are attended to and so bad luck is in the air. From noon until late at night there is a clash and boom of cymbals and gongs and the wail of bamboo flutes. White ash falls like snow from the incinerators where paper hell-money and offerings are stuffed in by the armful.

Lulu stood at the appointed spot on the pavement outside one such chai tong and blew at the white dust on her sleeves, and waited. A feather-touch thrill of fear brushed her spine. Silly girl, a Christian shouldn't be troubled in such a place. Yet there it was again: an inner voice that warned that something awful might happen . . . Best go, she thought, there are bad things here. But she did not go. She stood with rigid Christian obstinacy in the spell of the dust and the music of the dead, and waited.

Her watch gave five minutes to the appointed hour – five minutes to one. Charlie might be going to the mess for his lunch hour – though his hours were never fixed. She wondered for the first time how Husband might react to her initiative. Perhaps she would have to fabricate a little: 'Some anonymous kind-hearted caller, Husband,' she would say. 'I have Grandmother's ring, I want you to have it back.' Yes, that might do. 'Of course I want no payment; unthinkable' . . . That lie would add a nice touch.

Now it was time. She bit on her lower lip and peered around. No one who looked remotely like the owner of that snake-cold voice came in sight. A minute past the hour . . . five minutes past. A tug upon the hem of her jacket made her start. It was just a small boy – a street kid in dirty vest and shorts and he pointed to the chai tong. 'There, Auntie.'

'I must go there?'

He nodded – a big head on a scrap of a body; mischief-bright eyes followed her as she walked to the chapel doors. And there she halted, and looked back, unsure. The urchin nodded – go on. So she did. She passed from the afternoon glare into a place of gloom and candle flame and old priests in red silk robes, all bowing and swaying in slow, stiff-jointed dance like giant string puppets, while flutes piped and wavered and cymbals crashed with startling stridor.

Some wrinkled women in black tunic-suits sat there, fettered by the boredom of great age, oblivious to all but this ritual of death that they knew by heart . . . And suddenly the street kid was with Lulu again, pulling.

'This way, Auntie.'

Through the yard past the glowing warm mouths of the brick incinerators into a lane, that was where they went. He skipped ahead with his quick little feet, turning impishly at the corner to stop and beckon her onwards, leading her deeper, deeper into the maze of old Yau Ma Tei, its godowns and tenements and neon promises of love. At the end of a dog-leg lane the kid vanished.

'This way, Auntie.'

She heard his voice but could not see him in the dull brick hallway, from where he called again.

'Over here . . . *here*. Come on.'

The building reeked like an unclean urinal. The walls were darkling-damp and the floor was strewn with foul refuse that squelched sickly as she trod upon it. Lulu's courage began to retreat. She stopped. She might have turned and fled in the direction of good sense had the kid's voice not come hollowly, invisibly, beckoning:

'*Wai!* Can't you see me? This way, Auntie!'

She saw a broken hinged door, and in the gloom beyond it a shadow that moved and firmed up indistinctly into the shape of a man – a perfumed man, who announced:

'It's the rich bitch . . . Welcome to Hell. So what are you waiting for, a gilt-edged invitation card? Come on in. Have you brought the cash?'

This sounded like the voice she had heard earlier; puniness swollen by conceit, quiveringly excitable. She came closer; past the broken door and into the room. Her shin struck a plank and she stumbled but did not fall.

'Forgive the lack of light,' shrilled the man. 'They had a fire here and so all the wiring is burned out. I thought it would be a good place for us to get acquainted though . . . and for you to make me rich.'

'I don't have one hundred thousand . . . '

Ahead of her explanation the man began ranting: 'Fuck . . . I warned you. I warned you.' A hand flew at her and slapped her hard across the cheek. Then she fell.

'Bitch!' he spat sourly.

All the convincing words that Lulu had stored up were knocked from her mind. She had never been hit so hard. 'Bitch!' Another swipe from the gloom raked her, with less force. Lulu opened her throat to a tearing scream.

'Don't scream,' said the perfumed man in a most palliative way. 'I'm sorry that I slapped you . . . You made me angry, you see. The ring is worth a hundred thousand, easily. So you should have brought it.'

Lulu retrieved some of her scattered good logic: 'Sixty-four thousand is what I've brought. It's as much as I can get.'

'Sixty-four thousand? Well, if it's all you've got . . . '

'I can prove it.' Lulu straightened the quail of terror in her voice. Such lightning-quick violence she had never experienced before. Would he hit her again, she wondered, if she stood? 'Can I get up?'

'I'm a reasonable fellow. Though the ring's worth much more . . . Still, sixty-four thousand . . . '

'Make you rich.'

'A modest sum. Much less than the going rate.'

Like old business associates striking a deal; that was the tone of it. Lulu drew herself warily up, her eyes were keener now in the dark, still she could not make out this man's features. He was slight, though; not much bigger than herself – but stronger, very much stronger, and seething with wicked energy.

'Well I suppose that will be all right then,' the man said. 'Let's have it.'

Lulu took her bank-book from her bag and held it out.

'What's this shit?'

'It's the proof; my bank-book. I brought it so that you could see for yourself.'

The book was snatched out of her hand. 'You stay right there,' he ordered. Then he walked past Lulu to the landing. His trailed perfume tinted the charred, black air.

'I'll draw it all out,' Lulu called after him. 'The banks are still open. We could go now, if you like.'

Lonnie Huang, slowed by deep thought, walked down the steps and into the lane. He set his dark-glasses on his nose, then peered around. The kid, called Fish-boy, who had escorted Lulu was there, and so was Noona. He beckoned to his friend. Noona came, breathless with excitement.

'Did you get the cash?'

'She's smarter than we thought.'

Fish-boy came to listen. Lonnie waited until the kid had drawn close, then swung his toe-cap into his skinny rectum with such force that Fish-boy shrieked like a squeaky-toy, then bolted.

'She's brought her bank-book.'

'No cash?'

'Just the bank-book . . . Look: sixty-four thousand dollars.'

Noona looked. 'Hot rat! Not bad for one day's work . . . Could be a trap, do you think?'

Lonnie squinted at that thought for a moment, then happily discounted it. 'It's not a trap. If it was then there would have been wind at the chapel. That was the place to set up the trap. There weren't any cops there, and there aren't any cops here; so no trap. She came all on her own.'

'What now, Lonnie?'

Inventive Lonnie, of course, was never too distant from a clever plan. He reasoned: 'Well it would be stupid to let her go now, wouldn't it? Maybe then she'd change her mind; you know what bitches women can be . . . then there would be big trouble. We'll just tie her up. You go to the Po Shai Bank and get some withdrawal slips while I tie her up. Then we'll get her to sign the forms . . . We can take our time after that. We can go ourselves to the bank and pick up the cash – no problem.'

Noona's eyes glowed in admiration for the mercurial mind of Lonnie Huang.

Death? There is neither decency to it, nor tact. It seldom chooses the right time, or place to come. And often it draws in, in a tawdry way . . . Like this:

Lulu was bound by a strong thin cord that lashed her thumbs together tightly behind her, with her elbows drawn up fully and the ligature completed with a slip-noose that circled her thin neck. This was the preferred Chinese way of seeing to the immobility of a prisoner. The slightest slump of the spine or downward pressure of the arms would irreversibly tighten the noose. In desperation, a person thus secured might easily strangle themselves. Lonnie had apologetically warned of such an eventuality when he first tied and gagged her: 'It's awful, I know, but what else can I do? You just keep still and you'll be fine. I'll be back soon.'

She had kept still, and he had come back soon, with bank withdrawal slips for her to sign:

'You see, Lulu, I kept my word – now you keep yours.' He had untied her, not in a rough way, and given her time to massage her wrists and shoulders.

'So now you sign . . . that's right . . . three times. You see we brought three forms, just in case . . . Ten thousand pardons for having to tie you again. I'm sure you see the reason. Quite obviously I can't part with the ring until I have the cash . . .'

The scented man had gone, and had not come back.

The hours passed in rigid brutal torture that built and built until the roar and rage of it was greater than hope and prayer, and was testing the will to survive. She thought, surely if I move just a little it will ease the pain . . . *Yes, just a little*, screamed her body, *just the merest twitch will help*.

So she unstiffened her spine, just a little, and immediately the noose grew tighter. She jolted with alarm, and it tightened more. And there was no way to ease the strangle-hold. The thin cruel cord bit into the muscle of her neck, choking off her air. Her nose began to gush with blood. Her vision sputtered with light and her head swelled to bursting, yet she managed to think a small prayer. *Holy Mother of Jesus, help me.*

Help came in the form of new resolve which kept her rigid, and taught her how to feed on sips of air. Lulu kept up the courage with thoughts of her fine husband – she must live for him. There were children to be borne, life had only just begun. In this manner she outfought the awful night.

With the grey of dawn came hope . . . footsteps? A heavier sound than the scudding of the rats; yes there was someone there.

It was the street urchin. He came into the room quietly and squatted down a few paces from her, resting his elbows on his knees. She could see him well; big brown inquisitive eyes, head cocked like a contemplative monkey. He watched, quite relaxed and totally absorbed; he did not take his eyes from her. Lulu knew that he would help her and she thanked God for sending him. Let him hurry though. With her precious air she made small whimpering noises in her throat . . . Ah! now he heard her and his face wrinkled in sympathy . . . But still he did not move to help. He took a cigarette stub from the pocket of his vest, lit it, then tossed the glowing match to one side, a trickle of smoke rose from his nostrils. Then he stood up, stretched his bony frame and walked away.

The time arrived when Lulu could take no more. Her body slumped forward – the slip-cord ran tight, and soundlessly choked away her life.

3

SWEET GREETINGS OF THE DAWN

She gasped and prised and clawed at the tightening noose, but the pressure was monstrous and relentless, and her life began to slip away. Then Caroline burst loose from the grip, and awoke with a gasp, still caught up in the rage of the killer nightmare, still defending herself from death. Even when she realized that it was no more than complete fiction – an aberration perpetrated on herself, by herself, the horror lingered . . . then a sudden new panic rose up to appal her and she bounded from her bed and dashed to her daughter's bedroom.

The dawn had arrived, a spare breeze tugged at the curtain edge, licking quick chinks of sunlight into the nursery. Shannon lay with her bed-mate rag doll, Sweet-Sue, pulled in to the crook of one arm, her other arm rested high on the pillow, her small breaths, barely sufficient to stir the bedclothes, filled the room with peace. Caroline drew a white, wooden rocking chair close to the bed and sat there contemplating in wonderment this perfect creature she had made. God at his most generous . . . She looked on quietly, there was no need to hurry the girl's awakening. It was Sunday, and Hong Kong, worn out by a week of frantic energy, lay in a giant slumber in the first hours of that day.

'Shannon,' she whispered the name and bent her cheek so close to her child's that she could feel the soft puffs of breath from her cherub mouth and hear the minute sounds of her breathing. She sniffed the milky-clean aroma of her daughter, then, though she knew it might wake the child, she kissed her. Shannon stirred and rubbed her pudgy knuckles over her face, then yawned. She opened her eyes – God what depths of ocean-blue! She stretched her arms upwards towards her mother demanding to be lifted, which of course Caroline did at once. For this first dawn pledge of love was Caroline's enchantment; it was a miraculous, perfect and impenetrable cocoon of protection that she threw around this little girl. She enfolded the warm, sleep-limp bundle and stroked her sorrel-brown hair. Her mother's flame-red and Reven Forrester's storm-black, mixed like paint on a palette, had gifted her child with this gorgeous rich mane. 'Lucky girl.'

'Momma?'

'Oh I was just thinking . . . just remembering.'

''Membering.'

'Yes, remembering.'

'What do you 'membering?'

'Long ago, before you were a real person.'

'Who was I then?'

'Part father and part mother . . . '

'Which part is?'

'Which part is what?'

'Father?'

Good Lord, the questions that bounded from this child – and not yet three years old. Which part is father? Well that depended on the turn of the breeze. One moment, iron-willed and tight with defiance that pressed her little lips into an ugly pout – then, without a hint of remorse, a melting of all opposition with podgy wet kisses and love abundant and real. She was quick to sense her mother's sadness, when it came; to stroke it quietly away. Which part father? Why, all and none. Caroline took the easy way:

'You have eyes just like your father.'

'Yess . . . ' drawn out. She knew there was more to it than that.

'You have his stubborn chin.' She poked her finger at Shannon's chin.

'What's stubum, Momma?'

'It's when you do . . . no it's when you *don't* do what is right for you. You just hold out for no good reason.'

Shannon thought deeply about that, fingering her chin like a wise old sage. Then she wriggled off her mother's lap and ran off. Caroline heard the toilet flush and the patter of footsteps receding further down the passage. A chair scraped. The fridge door slammed.

'There's orange juice on the shelf,' Caroline called to Carlotta the Filipino amah. 'Lotta, pour her some juice, will you.'

Shannon came back without the recommended orange juice, but with a glass of milk to her lips. There, that was her father – rankling against instruction.

'Don't drink and walk at the same time.'

Shannon picked up a doll called Judith, and laid her on the vacated cot next to Sweet-Sue, then hopped into the bed and addressed her family:

'Today we are all going on Momma's boat to the islands . . . so I want you to be good, and don't fall over the side like you did before.'

Caroline quaked with silent mirth and walked away. It was true; they were going to take *Dolphin* out. And Reven had promised he would come with them . . . Stubborn, Reven Forrester whom she loved, and who loved her too but feared to give in to it – feared to love, and feared to let it slip away.

'Is Uncle Charlie coming too, Momma?'

'Yes, and Auntie Lulu.'

'So you see,' Shannon reported to her dolls, 'there will be presents and sweets.'

Lulu doted on Shannon, and showered upon her an incessant supply of good things to suck, or wear, or play with. 'Godmother's duty' was the rationale offered for this untameable largesse. Of course, Shannon and her dolls adored Lulu.

Mother and daughter and dolls dressed for the day at sea. Caroline wore white slacks and a cotton blouse with a square nautical neck and sailor's cape. Shannon chose her polka-dot dress; Judith and Sweet-Sue sat stiffly in their Sunday best, and thus attired they arrived at the Yacht Club.

Dolphin was the ugly duckling of the Aberdeen Marina. She had been born a jung-dang fishing junk and had seen long and rough service too, as a *kai-to* island ferry. Caroline's affair with this vessel had begun one drizzly day when she had observed the old junk wedged up in a Cheung Chau boat-yard – holed, with engine blown and prop-shaft bent. Not even Caroline could explain the sudden need that had come upon her then to redeem this knackered beast. But there it was. She had known at first sight that this was the vessel she must own, and so, of course, had the shrewd boat-yard owner. So it was smiles and handshakes all round, and a new life for the battered jung-dang, with hydraulics, electronics and radar, a stateroom with toilet that flushed, two new Lugger engines, tens of gallons of varnish and a fine new name – *Dolphin*.

Dolphin rode bright and ugly amongst the haughty sleek aristocrats of the marina, awaiting the arrival of those she would carry to sea that peaceful day.

Reven Forrester came along the floating walkway soon after Caroline had arrived – ever punctual, slightly hurrying after a quick glance at his wrist-watch. She watched him approach, and so did Shannon who climbed to the deck-house roof and yelled:

'Daddy! Daddy!'

Reven, in faded jeans and T-shirt, grinned and waved and Caroline wished for one jealous moment that she was the sole recipient of this beaming joy.

'Get down, Shannon . . . hello, Reven.'

He came aboard and gathered up his daughter and hugged her. He glanced around and stated the obvious:

'Charlie's not here yet.'

Still holding Shannon, he kissed Caroline on the nose and then retreated. She said: 'They'll be along. They're never late.'

'I've got a new handbag,' said Shannon. 'It's got money in it.'

'Has it then?' He hoisted his daughter and shook loose squeals of delight.

Ah Tsai the master of *Dolphin* came on deck then carrying a big cold-box in his sinewy strong arms: 'Beer.' Reven declined the offer of a beer. He claimed he had things of importance to discuss with Charlie. Caroline wondered irritably whether that was the main reason for his presence there that day.

'Well you've got until we reach open sea to get your business behind you, and then you are to relax, both of you.' Caroline went to the companionway steps; half-way down she stopped. She warned implacably: 'Do you hear!'

'What's relax?' enquired Shannon of the upper half of her mother.

Carline pointed. 'Something *he* does not have a clue how to do.' She disappeared.

Reven Forrester said to his watch. 'I'll give him half an hour.'

One half-hour later he walked back along the walkway to shore; to the clubhouse, to check the message board. Nothing was pinned there for *Dolphin*. He dialled Charlie's home telephone number and there was no answer. He then put through a call to 'A' Department, Headquarters and was told by the duty officer that Superintendent Lam had signed in at 07.00, for a brief visit: 'No, sir – no idea where he went after that.'

Forrester dawdled back to the marina, sure that such a protracted pace would bring the latecomers in before him. But Charlie and his new bride did not precede him, nor could he see them from the high poop-deck of the *Dolphin*. He then took a beer, muttering something about the heat, and drank it and by that time Charlie and Lulu were almost an hour late.

'They've forgotten.' Caroline had reappeared. 'Shit!' She swore flimsily; like a cat sneezing.

'Unlikely.' Forrester scrunched the empty can and slung it into the waste bin. 'He never forgets, and he's never late.'

'Well he is now. Shall we wait a while longer?'

'Something's wrong. I'm going to HQ to see what's happened.'

'What would that achieve? If he's out you'll never find him. He'll 'phone you sooner or later. Look, you've got your bleeper on your belt . . . There's a radio-'phone on the bridge, so . . . '

'I'd better go.'

Shannon, who had sensed for some time that her party was about to break up before it had begun, had taken vehement hold of her father's leg, fettering it as best she could with her weight.

Caroline said: 'I'm just as concerned as you are. This is what I suggest: let's put out for a while, and sail to Repulse Bay – no further. If Charlie doesn't come through by lunch time to explain things, we'll sail directly back.'

Forrester lifted Shannon who stared at him with her bewitching blue eyes. 'All right,' said the enchanted man. And before he could change his mind Caroline gave Ah Tsai orders to cast off.

Repulse Bay was a short run from Aberdeen, even for their unswift craft, and there was calm water in the bay and good swimming. Far beyond the crowded shore they dropped anchor and lowered the dinghy. Shannon clad in naught but a blow-up ring was first into the water. She pinched her nose and with flaying arms threw herself into the green – no fear in her for the inky depths. Forrester followed his child, more gracefully, and the two of them splashed and romped and he dived around her like a porpoise, surfacing, roaring, with hair plastered flat and teeth bared, scaring her into delighted piercing shrieks. Standing precariously in the bobbing dinghy Caroline trained her video camera on these two humans whom she loved so dearly, and breathed in the goodness of it all in deep and happy sighs. She wanted all that moment had to offer. The video was no more than a silly attempt to hold on to the imprint of time, tick by tick; to spin out beyond its stretch this precious filament of pleasure. Well why not? She was possessive of every laugh and blink and splash. At that moment she was glad that Lulu and Charlie were not there to be part of this. This was her family at play, and it was good times like this that would gather in Reven.

When the bleeper that lay nestled on a towel sounded off she was not surprised; was pleased in a way. A small interruption of her joy . . . It was Charlie, no doubt, to apologize for his and Lulu's absence – some perfectly ordinary reason, she was sure. After that they could get back to the serious business of play; then they would dry down and Ah Tsai would lay out warm food. She had packed an excellent lunch.

It was Charlie. Reven spoke to him on the radio telephone and his features became grave. Caroline went on to the bridge so that she could hear. Reven whispered to her: 'Lulu's disappeared,' then spoke into the mouthpiece: 'When, Charlie?'

'Don't know, Reven. I was on Lantau Island yesterday . . . until late . . . at Shek Pik. You know, we discussed that.'

'Yes, the prisoner.'

'It was hard going. I didn't get back until zero four hundred . . . She wasn't at home. I've been checking hospitals since then; no luck. My God, I'm worried, Reven.'

'Her mother?' Sometimes the obvious was forgotten.

'She wasn't there. I've checked the report books of the regional stations; not a thing . . . I forgot all about our arrangement with Caroline and yourself, I'm sorry.'

'All right . . . of course. I'm coming in at once. Meet me at the office.'

'Sorry, Reven,' he said again, then the line went dead.

'If those bastards have harmed her . . . ' The threat hung nervously unfinished. A twitch of anger plucked at his jaw muscle.

'What's a bastard?' said Shannon, muffled beneath the fabric of a thick pink towel.

Caroline had returned to the choking horror of her nightmare; the jerk of the garotte and the ghastly struggle that had torn her from sleep that morning. She raised her hands to her throat and pressed, and said very quietly,

'Reven, I have the most awful feeling about this.'

Hong Kong's streets brim with humans like gutters filled with rain. People burble along, shoulder to shoulder, blank-faced, blind-eyed, eddying at a corner, compressing at the traffic lights, slow-moving because there are so many of them in so confined a space. It is no great event when one person amongst so many

77

simply swirls away – gone, as water into the porous earth, never to be found. Dozens of such mysteries occur every day – some reported, some not. Those who go missing are mostly women, and not everyone cares what happens to a mere woman. It's also reasonably argued that many of these girls vanish of their own accord, to become 'family girls' in the brothels of Kowloon, or to follow triad boys for the glamour of it.

Lulu Wong's case was different of course, she was the wife of a senior police officer, and so the efforts made to find her were great. But the case was just as hopeless as any other such case, really. The streets had taken her, as they took so many others. Why? Where? It was a massive riddle.

Her photograph was pinned to the bulletin-board of every police station throughout the territory, and appeared in every newspaper – Chinese and English. The TV stations broadcast her likeness. And of course Mrs Wong offered a reward. But the publicity failed and the bounty stood unclaimed – days passed until they numbered weeks. Current excitements and new mysteries overbore Lulu's case until they in turn were borne under in the rough contest for public attention. There were dedicated, tireless men like Chief Inspector MacNaughton, whose mandate it was to see this case through personally; there were Reven Forrester and Charlie Lam, of course, and others who never gave up. But generally speaking the public lost interest, and the hard-pressed police force was compelled towards greater priorities.

As Assistant Commissioner Lo Ping-kin said over coffee in his office: 'If you don't find them within seventy-two hours your chances are reduced by fifty per cent. After two weeks make that ninety per cent . . . How long has this docket been open, Reven?'

'Four weeks, PK . . . and a few days.' God! Was it that long ago?

'Thirty-four days to be precise,' Lo supplied. 'And no sign of her – no reward claimants?'

'No.'

'No ransom note; no suicide note. No trail or message whatsoever?'

'Not a thing.'

'Did she have any money with her when she left? Sometimes that's an indication of intent.'

'Charlie doesn't know whether she had cash or not. He knows little about her financial state. She's a "modern girl", independent, you follow. She didn't talk about it, and he didn't press her. Her mother reckons that Lulu is a hoarder, but she doesn't think that she has much, a few thousand dollars at the most.'

'She should know.' Lo poured coffee and ladled four spoons of sugar into his cup, stirring vigorously . . . 'What resources have you assigned to the case?'

'I've got two teams on it, and some specialists.'

'Trim it back, Reven. Put it on a back-burner. We can't afford the luxury . . . I'm sorry for Lam, but there it is. You're his friend, explain our position to him.'

'Of course. He's an experienced cop, PK. He knows we can't sustain the effort endlessly.'

'He looks really bad, Reven. I saw him in the lift this morning. I was shocked.' PK Lo slurped coffee, musing; then modified his position; 'Well not really shocked. I suppose if such a thing happened to me . . .'

'He's not going under, if that's what you're worried about.'

'It does concern me when I see one of my men in such a state. It affects the morale of the whole directorate. Can't let that happen.' Lo nodded in righteous agreement with himself.

'Lam's doing his job, PK. I've no cause for complaint. It's the uncertainty that's gnawing at him, the possibility that she's dead.'

'Watch him closely, Reven. I mean that. He's a good man, but good men break too . . . More coffee?' Lo sighed and wiped the fine foliage of his moustache. 'I don't want a messy ending to this. If this turns out badly . . . as it surely will . . .'

'I'll keep him under my wing.'

'Keep him busy and keep him well away from the case from now on . . . In fact, I think he should be transferred right out of the Intelligence Bureau. Place him elsewhere . . . on one of the crime teams.'

'He's working on the Tang Tsun investigation.'

'Then make sure he has no time for anything else. How is that case progressing?'

'Slow progress. Charlie Lam in fact interviewed a long-term prisoner at Shek Pik who was sent down as an accomplice in the murder of Tang's father. If you still have the case docket . . . '

Lo still had it. He paged through it.

'Rabbit-lip Poon,' Forrester said. 'You'll find his name there.'

'Here it is: Poon.' Lo trailed a pencil around that paragraph, lassoing it in a filament of grey. 'One of your arrests, Reven.'

'He got twenty years and no time off, so he's due for release. Poon's not a great talker, but he did say that Tang Tsun's father was not a member of Sun Yee On. He just paid squeeze, like the other businessmen. It seems there's no triad connection there . . . From another source I learned that Tang was a member of a temple society called White Lotus; a Buddhist society devoted to the Monkey God. Quite an interesting history they've got; it goes back all the way to the Ching dynasty – the Eight Trigrams uprising of Eighteen Thirteen . . . I'm working on it.'

'It's urgent, as you know.'

'One other thing. Tang Tsun's younger brother, San-kiu, better known as Sandy, is a full-blooded homosexual, SIU had a file on him. Interesting development, isn't it?'

'Is it?' Lo said prissily. 'Amazing how randomly the rotten seed falls. Awful for his family.'

'Tang sent the boy away for a while, but he's back now; a star singer with Tung Wong Opera Company; a perfect voice I'm told.'

'I don't follow opera.' Lo glanced pensively at his watch. 'I have a meeting with the Commissioner in ten minutes, Reven. I wish there was more to report on Tang Tsun . . . Still you've come quite far.'

Lo gave his watch further attention. Frowning, he stood hurriedly. He gathered up his jacket and drew it on, then departed his office without another word.

Reven Forrester went back to his office. A 'phone on his desk chirped irritably. Theresa Hempstead was the caller and she spoke in the muted, secretive way of a lover. She had left her husband.

Forrester winced. He covered the mouthpiece and said, 'Oh shit.' To her he said, 'I don't think that was a good move.'

'I told you I was going to do it.'

As if this collusion made it *their* decision. He wanted no part in this, yet he was involved. By his own free will, and with horrible enjoyment, he had buried himself to the hilt in her, and by that mad caprice was still firmly coupled. The mucilage of sex was an irremovable adhesive. Never again! He said: 'Are you OK?' and immediately regretted this line of enquiry.

'I'd be better if I could see you.'

Tell her no. Tell her this has gone far enough. He said: 'Hell-a-va day. Can't get away for hours. Absolute mayhem . . .'

'I'm at Trixie Welldon's flat. Midlevels; you know it. You came to a New Year's do here.'

He recalled Trixie's prissy style; antimacassars and porcelain knick-knacks. 'Can't come, Tess.'

'I want you, Reven . . .'

Oh shit.

'I've just had a bath and I'm stretched out, naked as sin . . . I'm touching myself as I speak to you . . . I'm soaked – oo-ooh.'

Momentarily he wondered if she was having him on; then dismissed that thought. This was vintage Tess Hempstead, or rather, Tess Lindsay, as she had then been known. Hot memories writhed. His penis thrust suddenly and urgently against the fabric of his trousers. He whispered infirmly:

'Forget it, Tess.'

Before his courage defected completely he set down the handpiece, and within seconds the 'phone began to ring again. This time it was Hempstead, and his words flopped drunkenly into Forrester's ear:

'Tess's left me, Rev.'

'Sorry, Mike . . . really . . . Hell, that's bad luck.'

'You don't sound very surprised.'

'No, I'm surprised . . . Look, Mike, she 'phoned me, just a minute ago and told me about it.'

'Thought she might. Soft spot, ye know – you. Well there's fuck-all left for me, fuck-absolutely-all left for me.'

'Hell, no, Mike. You two will get together again, for sure. All marriages go through rocky patches like this. Give it another go.' He thought, *please*.

'Naa . . . no chance. I've blown it, Reven. No more chances; the end of the road. You know what I mean?'

'No I don't.' There was a long silence, then Forrester said, 'Are you there, Mike?'

'Yea . . . I'm still here.' Hempstead began to sob, then pulled himself up. 'Well I 'phoned to tell you that.'

'You'll be OK, Mike.' He felt numbly ashamed of that platitude.

'It's the best way out, Rev.'

'I don't want to hear that kind of talk . . .'

The line went dead.

Forrester set the handpiece down staring abashedly at the instrument, then rushed through the 'phone directory for the number of Trixie Welldon; found it, and dialled.

'Tess . . .'

'Reven, I'm waiting for you.'

'Tess, listen to me. Mike was on the line, he sounds bad . . .'

'Had he been drinking?'

'Yes. That's not the point. I'm worried, Tess. He might do something stupid. Do you know what I mean?'

'He's always doing something stupid.'

'Has he ever threatened to do himself in?'

Tessa Hempstead laughed shrilly. 'Not *that* again.'

'Do you know where he is at the moment?'

'What time is it . . . he'll be at home now. Do you really think . . .?'

'I'm going to the house. I think you should go there too.'

Tessa Hempstead did not go to her husband's house. Forrester arrived there within the hour. He found an empty brandy bottle by the telephone in the hall, and a further empty bottle lay on its side on the lounge carpet with Hempstead's forearm and hand and fingers stretched unmoving towards it. The bulk of Mike Hempstead sprawled behind the couch. He was still dressed in his khaki twill uniform. He wasn't dead, but mortally drunk; spread-eagled, and quaking with fitful gagging, twanging snores. The room stank sourly of vomit. Forrester would have left him then and walked away if Hempstead hadn't quietly slurred:

'Aah . . . Chesus.'

'Stupid bastard; this shit is getting boring, Mike.'

Forrester gripped Hempstead by his leather Sam Browne and hauled him to the couch. Hempstead moaned limply, providing liberal percentages of drool along the route. That was when he noticed the revolver. It had been hidden by Hempstead's body – a police issue .38 Smith and Wesson. Forrester broke open the chamber and saw that one round had been fired. There was a smell of nitro.

'You tried to do it, you idiot . . .'

Hempstead groaned some more and his arms flopped lumpishly around, as though searching. Rendered incapable of any well-arranged movement, like some amoebic absurdity, he slid back into the couch.

'Too drunk to get it right. You missed by a mile.'

Hempstead's eyes blinked open, he squinted towards the source of this taunt and muttered something unintelligible, then, 'It's the bloody Ging Si . . . gimme the gun, Reven . . . fucking get it right this time.'

The impulse to oblige this stupid man passed. Forrester slipped the revolver into his waistband.

'Some fuck-up, you are, Mike.'

Hempstead held out his hand. 'Gimme.'

'You want to shoot yourself . . . here. Here's your thirty-eight. I'll even advise you in its employment this time. Stick it in your mouth, you can't miss that way.'

Hempstead took the revolver. He frowned into the barrel, his lips moved slackly, mumbling something that could have been – 'Fuck Reven Forrester.' Then he thumbed the hammer back. It cocked with a positive metallic click. Forrester said quickly:

'I don't get you, I wouldn't have thought that this was your style. Look at the cops who shot themselves in the past, a bunch of wankers. If you want to add your name to that list, I've no real objection. But I always considered you had more in you than that . . . You don't fit in with that lot.' This could be disputed.

Hempstead pointed the revolver unsteadily towards his forehead. He was drooling; wetly whimpering.

'You can squeeze that trigger, Mike. A few pounds of pressure and your brains will splat all over the wall. An ugly grey mush, but it will be all over – no more problems. And then we'll add your name to that list of losers – Evans, Mayburry, Machochlan, and the others. Is that how you want to be remembered . . .?'

Hempstead closed his eyes, frowning. The revolver muzzle jigged and trembled on the bone of his temple.

'On the other hand you could put that gun away, and start out afresh. No one will ever hear about this incident . . . I need your help, Mike. I need a chief inspector with your background in OSCB. Davidson is getting a leg up. I'll need a new man to head up OSCB Three. You're ex-Kowloon Crime. You'd do me fine.'

'You're lying, Rev. Don't lie to me.'

'I'm not lying, Mike . . . I was talking to Lo Ping-kin this very morning about it. We're hard pressed. We need a seasoned cop; an expert who can speak Cantonese well. I put your name forward.'

'Bullshit.'

Hempstead opened his eyelids and focused with clown-like effort on the man before him. 'Bullshit,' he said again. 'Isn't it?'

'A new job. Maybe a new rank soon. It's up to you.'

'You swear. You fucking swear.'

'So help me.'

In stages, Mike Hempstead lowered the revolver and gingerly eased forward the hammer-spring. There was no need for such extreme caution, though. Forrester had set the chamber to present the dead cartridge to the firing-pin.

Chief Inspector Gilchrist MacNaughton was florid-faced and stocky. He could trace his ancestry back to the MacNaughton chiefs of Inis Fraoch (which name is today taken to mean Heather Isle), who had thought nothing of entering combat with fierce dragons or warrior Picts, on whatever terms. He was as stubborn as granite, which great fortitude suited things admirably, for his task was to solve crimes that verged on the unsolvable. He applied himself to his cases with an inexorable will, and with no expectation of good fortune. So when luck did come his way he regarded it with the suspicion that his ancestors might have held for the sprite of Loch Awe. Still, he was quick to follow up a lead. And so when bank clerk Susan Li thought she had something to offer in connection with the missing person, Lulu Wong, MacNaughton went directly to see her.

Susan Li had a bad skin, protruding speckled teeth, and she wore spectacles. She stood deferentially, and somewhat nervously, one pace to the rear of her manager, Mr Wu, who knew just how to handle thick-headed gwai lo policemen who trashed the Cantonese language, such as this one: 'See here,' (sternness was the thing or they would walk all over you), 'no regulations broken in this bank, ha. When someone comes in with a signed withdrawal slip that matches the bank-book specimen, and funds are available, we pay up.'

'Good,' said MacNaughton. 'And that I presume was the case here.'

'Exactly the case.'

'I commend you on your policy.' MacNaughton wished this bumptious little squirt would step aside and let him get on with the interview. But Wu wished to hear more of his own voice.

'Hundreds of clients come in every day to make withdrawals or deposits . . . This is a very busy branch of the Po Shai Bank, as you must have already observed. I cannot possibly check everything myself. I have to rely on subordinates; tellers and clerks.' Here he gestured towards Miss Li; who perceived that her moment of interrogation was imminent, and wrung her hands. 'As I said: no regulations broken.'

'I've no argument with your system, Mr Wu. Most efficient, I'm sure. I can see how very busy you are. I don't wish to detain you for a moment longer.'

Wu's smile came and went in a second. Still unsure that he had satisfactorily made his point, yet having no more to say for the moment, he turned to his subordinate and shooed her forward: 'Come, come, Miss Li.' Miss Li came. 'Tell the inspector your story.'

In a rather dejected way she did that:

'Twenty thousand dollars . . . that was how much I paid out . . . that was the first time . . . and then another thirty thousand dollars . . . The signatures were perfect. I'm very careful.'

Wu hopped forward again, holding a clear plastic file. 'See, Inspector . . . Originals. No doubt in my mind that these are Lulu Wong's signatures. Look for yourself.'

MacNaughton took the file. It held two yellow withdrawal slips, a ledger print-out and a perforated card upon which some specimen signatures appeared. The signatures seemed to be all from the same hand.

'See,' Wu said again. 'Are they the same, or what?'

'I'll have them checked to be sure . . . The dates interest me. The first transaction took place weeks ago. This one took place only yesterday.'

'Yes . . . ' Miss Li was on the point of tears and could manage no more than, 'I didn't realize my mistake.'

'*M seng!*' Wu roared. 'Can't say that "mistake" is the right word. No, "mistake" is the wrong word; "mistake" is *definitely* the wrong word. As you can see, the first transaction took place before Lulu Wong's disappearance was advertised. The second, regrettably, a while afterwards. Can't argue. But how could this be helped?'

MacNaughton agreed at once. 'There will be no blame attached to your bank, Mr Wu; to yourself or any of your employees. You have my word on that . . . There might even be a commendation in it for both of you. The *only* matter of concern to the police is the finding of Mrs Lulu Wong.'

'It wasn't her,' Miss Li's eyelashes were dewy with tears now. 'It wasn't Lulu Wong who came in. It was a man. I didn't realize my mistake until this morning . . . '

Wu threw up his hands at the repetition of that most dreadful word: 'Ah, Inspector . . . '

'Go on, Miss Li.' MacNaughton shouldered him out.

'I couldn't sleep last night. There was something bothering me . . . Then I remembered . . . '

MacNaughton ended her seemingly interminable pause: 'What did you remember?'

'I remembered the name Lulu Wong, and the face . . . I'd seen it on the TV. I remembered that she was a missing person . . . '

'That's right, Inspector,' Wu was unstoppable. 'Then Miss Li came straight to me. You see, we didn't know Lulu Wong personally. Look at her ledger sheet and you'll see that she seldom came in to make a deposit – once, twice a year . . . Look at the ledger sheet.'

MacNaughton did as bidden. Lulu Wong had made her last deposit three months previously, a date close to her birthday. But of more interest than that was the very last entry on the sheet: Lulu Wong's current credit balance.

'There's fourteen thousand dollars still in this account.'

'Fourteen thousand . . . and thirty-three cents,' Wu corrected. 'Plus mid-term interest.'

'Mr Wu, Miss Li,' MacNaughton drew in his chin and faced the odd couple squarely, mayorally, as if about to bescroll and bemedal them: 'you have acted in a most responsible and public-spirited way. Yes, indeed. And I'm sure I can count on further co-operation . . . yes?'

Wu nodded and smiled, and so, tenuously, did Miss Li.

'In which case,' MacNaughton concluded, 'we have every chance of finding this poor girl.'

Lonnie Huang bought the wine-coloured Italian leather jacket that he had coveted for so long, a brutally loud Sony twinspeaker portable, and a Nikon autofocus camera. Noona Cham bought with his share of the cash some genuine Gucci shoes with a handbag to match, a gold neckchain with a jade charm, and some exquisite filmy silk underwear from Lane Crawford's, that made of Lonnie a slobbering sex-wolf. Of course they were careful not to show off their new wealth, or even to speak about it in public. The police came back to the restaurant and everyone was questioned again, but nothing came of it. Clearly, the police knew nothing about Lulu Wong's burgled bank account.

So Lonnie and Noona lived secretly, very well. And besides all the other luxuries, now they could afford Mandrax in sufficient quantity to stun a plough-ox. But a mere twenty-thousand dollars could not support this high-flying life-style indefinitely, and before long they were broke again. Something had to be done, and quickly.

Noona made the second withdrawal. Thirty thousand dollars this time; which was ten thousand more than the first withdrawal. 'No problem' – Lonnie had forecast – 'you simply smack down the withdrawal slip and bank-book on the counter; the signatures are checked and the money's handed over.' And so it was.

Now they started to search in earnest for somewhere decent to stay. Upmarket Yue Wan Estate was their mark. They had the money to pay squeeze to the officials who controlled the housing priority lists. They acquired more clothing – only imported labels of course, and they began to window-shop for good furniture. Mandrax: they could not do without that magic bullet, and Noona started on marijuana too, which wondrous haze bedimmed all anxiety; especially the haunting disquiet as to the fate of Lulu Wong. Lonnie wouldn't tell Noona what had happened to the girl, although he asked him often. In fact his enquiries caused Lonnie occasionally to become quite angry:

'What the fuck you worried about? Do you think I'd do some harm to her or what?'

'No . . . It's just that . . . '

'You think I'm keeping her on the quiet; fucking her behind your back?'

Vicious words; hurtful Lonnie. 'No,' Noona said. 'I don't think that. How can you say that?'

'What then, ha?'

'Well the papers reported that she'd disappeared.'

'So what?'

'Well, I wondered . . . '

'Wondered what?'

'Why should they say that?'

'Shit, Noona, how the hell do I know. Maybe they're lying . . . of course they're lying. It's a trick to frighten us. The police would try to do that – to draw us in.'

'Do you think so?'

'No doubt about it. Look, I've told you. I set her free. Where she went after that, I don't know. She could have gone missing for a few days and then gone home. The papers wouldn't report that she'd gone back home, would they? That's not news, is it? And now I don't want to hear one more fucking word about Lulu Wong, you hear?'

'You didn't hurt her did you?' Noona flinched as Lonnie drew back his hand, but he was too slow to avoid the stinging slap to his face. Lonnie, however, was as quick to forgiveness as he was to anger. He drew crying Noona in and kissed him and made love to him for a long time, and with marvellous passion. When he was finished he said:

'We need more money, Noona. Will you go into the bank again?'

It was a nice way to phrase that demand. 'Of course, Lonnie. When shall I do it?'

'Tomorrow would be fine.'

Noona did not ask why Lonnie was in need of more cash, so soon. And here was another question that he did not voice: what had become of the ring that Lonnie had said was their insurance against betrayal by Lulu Wong? Lonnie had kept it on him at all times, and his pleasure was to take it out and admire it. But lately he had not done that. Noona had searched through Lonnie's possessions and not found it, and he suspected that his lover had sold the ruby ring; which made the topic of Lonnie's need for money all the more intriguing. All Noona said was: 'I'll go in tomorrow . . . that will be the third bank-slip; the last slip.'

'Fourteen thousand dollars,' Lonnie chuckled, 'will last us for ever.'

Silently, Noona suffered his doubts. He thought about his impending visit to the Po Shai Bank. He would act exactly as he had done before. He would go to the same counter, and hopefully he would be attended to by the same pimply woman teller.

'No problem,' breathed Lonnie sleepily. 'You'll just walk in and walk out.'

Noona believed that, too. Still, a knot of apprehension squeezed his stomach. In the morning it grew tighter. Lonnie walked with him to the bank, and together they waited on the opposite pavement until business looked to be in full swing. The Po Shai Bank had glass windows and big glass doors so they could observe the banking hall from where they stood. And when Lonnie judged the time to be right, he nudged Noona into action. Noona felt as though every eye was upon him, every step was an ordeal. He followed the actions he had rehearsed, and hoped that no one noticed his trembling trouser cloth.

A small queue had formed at the counter of his choice. The pimply woman was dealing with the clients slowly. How horrendously ugly she was. He turned around to discover if he could see Lonnie. The opposite pavement was crowded, but he spotted him. The wine leather jacket stood out amongst the drab human swirl.

'May I help you, sir.'

The pimply teller's voice. He turned to face her, the withdrawal slip outheld. She took it and read it. She looked up and her eyes grew wider, wider, until the lenses of her spectacles were filled with her staring pupils. Her mouth popped and worked up and down, and out came, 'You, you, *you!*'

Noona gasped and pushed away from the counter. His mind shouted 'run' but his body went hollow and lame with shock. Men pelted towards him with shouts and pumping arms. In a panic he dodged them. Then a fist as hard as steel rammed into his throat. Choking he fell back. Another fist exploded in his face and big black doors closed with a slam on all and everything.

They photographed Noona, then drew a jute sack over his head and tightened the drawstrings at his neck. They searched him and took his identity card and wallet. Then his wrists were pinioned with handcuffs at his back. To Noona Cham those minutes were totally and irretrievably lost. When next life and light returned it jolted with a skull full of pain and the bray of a klaxon. His body rocked – he was in a speeding car. There were men around him; he could smell the tang of cigarette smoke, but he could see no further than the tip of his nose, a wreath of white fabric smothered out all else, he could hardly draw breath. He had been caught by the police, and he was more scared than ever he had been in his life.

When the car at last stopped he was grabbed by the shirt front and propelled forward so violently that his legs could hardly match the required pace. He stumbled along, lift doors opened, and closed, then came a smooth ride upwards, which ended with his violent expulsion into a passage. A further quick walk brought the slam of a steel door, then absolute darkness. Noona flared angrily at his treatment, he stood up straight, ready to deny, to defend; to spit back their questions at them. But no questions came. Nothing came other than darkness, a sombre, dimensionless darkness that sucked him ever deeper into its bleak, purple void as it went on and on. It was hot and airless, too, and sweat dribbled off his face, soaking the jute bag and making it even harder to breathe. He sat; the floor felt cool so he lay on it;

on his side, then on his belly. Self-pity welled up and quite smothered the small flame of anger; pity for his abysmal state. He would never betray Lonnie though. Here was his story: some man whom he vaguely knew (but had never been formally introduced to) had asked him (seeing that he couldn't find parking for his car) to go into the bank, on his behalf, and to make that withdrawal. Which good deed he had agreed to do, but had been prevented from so doing because he had been viciously assaulted while waiting to be served . . . That was his version of events, which he would stick to no matter what torture was applied. But no one came to ask him for this unshakeable alibi. It was as if no one cared. They had judged him guilty and dumped him there and would leave him there . . . for how long? Until he died? A horrifying possibility – and they could do it; the police could do anything. Noona writhed to his knees and sobbed; but the never-ending purply blackness offered no respite.

Noona became thirsty – sweat trickled down his cheeks, past his lips and he caught the droplets with his tongue-tip and sucked them into his mouth. The thirst mounted until his need for a drink was as constant as the suffocative darkness; two vicious monsters that united to force out every other thought from his mind – except for self-pity. That remained fervently strong; at times whiningly phrased: 'Oh no. Oh why? God why?'

If the gods did not hear a word of this lament, CSO Reven Forrester heard it all. It was relayed to him by the remote microphone tied to Noona's neck. He could see the prisoner dimly too, through a one-way mirror, and he judged the time to be right to take the interrogation one stage further. He said to Detective Sergeant Dun:

'Do it.'

The lights came on in the interrogation room. Noona's bagged head snapped up and he attempted to sit. Sergeant Dun came into the interrogation room. He said: '*Tcha!* They still got you tied up, ha. Well, they'll do anything those guys.'

He undid the handcuffs, took off the bag. 'I'm glad I came, they'd have left you here for a week.'

Noona said: 'Water . . . *please*.'

'Look, I'll go and get some in a minute. Hell, you're in big trouble, Noona Cham. *Big* trouble. Still they shouldn't treat you like this. That's not right. Even a kidnapper – even a murderer, shouldn't be treated like this; like a dog.'

Noona's mouth dropped. He looked stunned. Dun produced more sympathy.

'You know what, Noona, the Ging Si, my boss, he's quite mad. You know what I mean – crazy, howl at the moon, dog-mad. All gwailo cops are crazy, but this one's berserk, ha. He doesn't fucking care about anything . . . Sit down here, Noona. Sit on this chair. It's not right that they just throw you on the floor. Shit, it's not right.'

Noona whispered dryly, 'What's this about, murder? No murder.'

'Well I don't know. I heard those guys talking. I heard the Ging Si and some other guys saying stuff like that. They've got Lonnie Huang you know . . . '

'*Wa!*'

'Hell, I thought you knew . . . I'll tell you something – that Lonnie is as clever as a sewer rat. He's told them that the whole thing was your idea.'

'No . . . Want a lawyer.'

'You've got a right to one, but the Ging Si won't let you talk to one yet. He can do it you know. Talk about power . . . Now look, I'm going to get you some water, would you like a bowl of noodles, a cigarette?'

'Cigarette,' said Noona.

'Here . . . You know, Noona, what I would do if I were you – I'd ask for immunity. You could get it. All you'd have to do is give us the goods on Lonnie. Hell, the boss knows that Lonnie's the bad one. Lonnie Huang has got black hands. He's been inside before; aggravated burglary, and assault on police, and some other stuff. You're clean. They'd take your word before his, any day . . . Think about it; I'll be back soon.'

'Soon,' pleaded Noona.

93

Dun walked out. Noona drew heavily on his cigarette and looked around the room that confined him. What he saw were grey acoustic-tiled walls, a wall-mounted telephone and a VCR camera pointing straight at him. Two microphones hung from pulleys. There was a blue cabinet holding some VCR tape players and a monitor screen. What drew Noona's interest more than all that, though, was the large, one-way mirror behind which sat hidden Forrester and MacNaughton, and his erstwhile adviser, Detective Dun. Obviously it was his own reflection that he enjoyed. He passed his fingers through his long hair a few times to repair his looks. His face was restless, moving in a lively series of deep frowns.

'What do you think?' Forrester said to Dun. Both men studied the prisoner for a while.

'He's confused,' Dun said. 'You should go in now, Ging Si, with Mr MacNaughton, very hard.'

'Do you think he believes your story about Lonnie Huang?'

'I think so, sir. He nearly laid down a heap when I said that. Shake him some more.'

'Ah know it works nine times out of ten,' MacNaughton complained as they walked the interleading corridor, 'but Ah find the role of the crazy gwailo a strain. Aye.'

'Just be yourself,' Forrester said. They went into the interrogation room. MacNaughton slumped grimly on his chair, then leaned across the table towards the prisoner.

Noona cringed away from MacNaughton as though hell-fire might flame from his mouth. What emerged was the detective inspector's incredible brand of Scots-Cantonese. All Noona probably made of it was that he was as close to savage death as ever a man was; he squeaked.

'I want a lawyer.'

'No lawyer.' Forrester sat down too.

Dun came into the room then with Noona's promised glass of water. Noona followed him with pleading eyes. Dun kept his gaze averted; set down the glass, then scuttled away. MacNaughton took a swig from the glass, then snarled:

'Lonnie's told us what you did. *Fucking little rat*, you killed my friend's wife.'

'No, on my mother's life.'

'You deny it?'

'Yes.'

'Better tell us your side, then.'

Noona's tongue probed the stickiness of his mouth. His eyes fixed on the glass as it rose to MacNaughton's mouth again.

'Was it Lonnie Huang who did it?'

Noona whispered, 'I don't know.'

Out spewed MacNaughton's execrable Cantonese; a searing, barbarous invective that popped Noona's eyes and rocked him backwards on his chair.

'What this man is telling you,' Forrester translated reasonably, 'is that you are in desperate trouble. It's your word against Lonnie Huang's. I can help you. I'm the only person on God's earth who can help you now. But if you want to sit there and talk shit, you've had it. Here are the facts. Lulu Wong is dead. You were in possession of her cheques. Your accomplice has named you as the murderer. Open and shut case. Life sentence for you in Shek Pik. They'll love you there.'

MacNaughton leered, 'They'll ride your arse raw, ten times a day.'

Noona's eyes rolled back as though about to faint. But he didn't faint. Bleakly he enquired:

'If I talk will I get immunity?'

'Can't guarantee it. Depends on how good it is. I'll do my best for you.'

'Lonnie is lying. I didn't kill her. If anyone killed her it's him . . .'

'Hold on,' said Forrester. He worked the buttons on the VCR deck. A small, red eye glowed in the camera.

MacNaughton said calmly and diligently, 'Noona Cham, it is my duty to warn you that everything you say is being recorded and may be used in evidence against you.' He gave the case number, the place, the date and time. Then said, 'This is the voluntary confession of Noona Cham, obtained without duress or coercion . . . Carry on Mr Cham.'

Noona said, 'Sorry to worry you for water.'

'Of course; that's for you. It's hot in here . . . A cigarette? We'd like you to feel comfortable, Mr Cham.'

Thirty cigarettes later Noona realized that he had been duped. Lonnie was not their prisoner. Nor did they know for certain if Lulu Wong was dead. Noona had by then confessed truthfully as to his part in the crime, and it was too late for retractions or denials. It was all on tape.

'It's probable that Lonnie's killed her.' The tall gwailo, the one called Ging Si, reached out and switched off the VCR, then shrugged a smile towards Noona that said, So we lied to you – so what. He put the VCR cassette into his briefcase.

'She's disappeared,' said the other cop. 'And so has Lonnie. Unfortunately for us, and in a way for you too, Noona, the home address you registered with your employer was a false one. We've been there – no Lonnie. Where's Lonnie, Noona?'

'That,' said the Ging Si, 'is the immunity factor. You help us find him, and I'll save you from Shek Pik. It's a good deal . . . You'd be a hit in Shek Pik, mind you. Perhaps you'd enjoy it there.'

'She's not dead,' Noona said. 'I'm sure.'

'How do you know that?'

'Lonnie wouldn't do that.' Noona's faith in Lonnie was slightly restored. 'He had the cash; fifty thousand dollars, and the ring for insurance, so why would he kill her? He set her free after she had signed the withdrawal slips.'

'You saw her go free?'

'He told me he'd done that.'

'You're a stupid cunt, Noona. His best chance was to kill her. Do you think he wouldn't take his best chance?'

The Ging Si stood. 'So now, Noona, you're going to show us where that building is in Yau Ma Tei where you say you saw her alive. Thereafter we'll go looking for Lonnie Huang. And if we don't find him, Noona, you're in it alone. Don't forget that for an instant.'

'I'll take you there.' Noona rose wearily. 'I'm sure she's not dead.'

They drove there in unmarked cars. Dun drove the lead car, with Forrester and MacNaughton and Noona Cham as passengers. Two other vehicles carrying detectives followed on. Portland Street was packed with evening traffic. At a shop where shiny lacquered coffins were stacked, like huge logs, Noona pointed: 'There, over there, that's where she stood. The chai tong is at the back of the coffin shop.'

'Should we walk from here, Noona, or ride?'

'Walk.' Noona had declined into a sulk.

'Cuff him,' Forrester said to Dun. 'Lock him to your wrist.'

A service was in progress in the chai tong chapel – an ear-drubbing crash of brass and twittering flutes. Some of the detectives bent the knee in polite but quick *ta him* as they passed through. Even Noona hurried to be distanced from the stridor and the slow-falling dust – yellow in the fading sun. But once beyond that place, in Yau Ma Tei's miasma of grey alleyways, Noona slowed and dragged and shrank further into sullenness. His eyes, bleak and hateful, roved this way and that, seeing little beyond the mantle of his own misery. He jerked harshly at the steel cuffs that connected him to Dun, and led them on.

When he stopped next, it was in a dismal smoky street hung with illuminated yellow and green signs: 'Jet-fire girl', 'Thai Princess – big headlights', 'Red-hot Phoenix – knows what you want'. Noona lied in miserable fashion.

'I'm lost.'

'Take your time. No hurry, boy.'

While walking they had provoked scant interest; now as they loitered, the hostile eyes of the community caught them up. A flower pot crashed upon the pavement near MacNaughton and the voice of its ex-owner followed on: 'Cops, go fuck your mothers.'

'Shit aim,' said Dun. 'Nearly wiped out Noona.'

'Hard for them to see who is the prisoner amongst all these cops; they'll probably kill us all.'

'I think I remember,' said Noona Cham. 'This way.' He led them towards a burned-out guest-house.

He pointed. 'Maybe this is it.'

A peeling, painted sign read: Nine Dragon House.

'Can't you be sure?'

'Sure . . . *sure*. This is it.'

'What floor?'

'Fuck, how should I know. I never went in. I told you that.'

Swift darkness closed on Yau Ma Tei. MacNaughton said: 'We could have driven here, damn it. That would have saved half an hour.' He produced a beat-radio. 'I'll call the cars in, Ging Si; we've got hunting lights stashed in the boots.'

'Get on to SO, Support,' Forrester instructed. 'I want a forensic team on stand-by . . . and call in Kowloon Region HQ, and OSCB Three and Four.' Forrester remembered that Mike Hempstead had arrived to head up OSCB Three that morning. Clear-eyed and clean-breathed; he'd looked more like the Hempstead of old, but for his hands, they had worked in that sparrow-quick, nervous way that betrays the alcoholic. Perhaps Hempstead would take his chance, more likely, not. This would be his debut with OSCB.

The unmarked cars they had left in Portland Street arrived then. Forrester looked on as MacNaughton with clipped, Scots efficiency, issued torches – 'One for you too, sir' – and broke his men into teams: 'No civies in, no civies out; right. You know the drill . . . We start at the top and work down . . . Check lanterns.' White circles of light splotched the darkening walls. 'Any questions?'

There were no questions. MacNaughton looked to Forrester for final approval.

It was given.

'Right, in we go.'

A mish-mash of bad smells – decay – charred paint – excreta, stung their nostrils and soured their throats. The entrance was a bog of squelching litter that gave off more foulness as they trod it. A man fell wetly, and swore, and a gallery of torches swung to light him in his plight, men snickered softly. There were the stairs they would have to take, every step clogged with more muck. While platoons of rats squeaked and scampered to the defence of their kingdom, MacNaughton's men climbed, cutting at the evil air with the sword-bright torches. And if there was one common thought amongst them it was this: if this is the prison of Lulu Wong, how could she have survived? Six floors from the ground they began their search.

Dead or alive, she was not upon that floor, nor was she found on the fifth. Upon the fourth floor was discovered a maggoty, dead cat; on the third, a row of empty wine bottles, a half-burned candle and a flopped-out, used condom.

'No sign of her on this floor, sir. We're moving on.'

Down to the second floor, the third floor by Chinese reckoning. The fire damage was not total at this level. Charred door frames still swung upon hinges and the skeletons of chairs and tables and mattress springs littered the rooms. Lulu Wong was not there.

On the first floor the teams fanned out again. MacNaughton's bellow brought them running.

'There.' He jiggled his light. 'There.'

It was a woman's high-heeled shoe.

'Get Noona here,' Forrester said. He knelt and examined the small shoe. He did not doubt that it belonged to Lulu Wong. And at that instant he was sure that she was dead.

A camera clicked, a flash-bulb burst blue light into the desolation.

'Here he is, sir.'

Forrester's torch-beam probed the blinking frightened face of Noona Cham. Then he shone his light down on the shoe.

'Recognize it, Noona?'

Noona's breath shuddered: 'I don't know.'

'Look again. You're part woman, Noona. Your type wouldn't forget a thing like that.'

'Don't know,' insisted Noona Cham.

MacNaughton whispered, 'Liar.' They found cigarette butts on the floor; a short length of nylon washing-cord and a ballpoint pen. Each item was photographed from many angles.

Forrester walked to the landing where he stood alone while the search moved on to further, deeper rooms. He knew that Lulu's body would be found soon; there was a smell about that floor of rich decay. He didn't want to be the one to find it. He switched off his torch and stood quietly, waiting for the shout that would call him in. A man came up the stairs, his torch-beam caught Forrester.

'The teams have arrived,' the man reported. 'They're waiting to be briefed, sir.'

'Send up the Forensic Chemist.'

'Forensics only?'

'Yes.'

When the man had gone Forrester lit his torch. The beam fell on to the abutment of the staircase. He lowered it further and found there a storage cupboard, the kind of dwarf-doored locker that's wedged beneath stairs, that stays uncleaned for years. The door was charred on the surface but seemed to be otherwise intact. He kicked it, and it shifted. He kicked again, hard. The door fell in and a rash of angered ruby-red eyes reflected from the depths. A stench-wave, thickly rotten, swelled from that hole. Forrester was beaten backwards, the whole length of his gut convulsing.

Lulu Wong's remains lay puffed and gnawed. The torso was rolled in a tatty square of carpet through which putrid juices leaked. And everywhere moist grey rats, long-tailed and fat-bellied, swarmed at the feast, squeaking, scampering, glaring at the intruder. Rottenly swollen, they scuttled past his feet.

Noona was brought there. He heaved and vomited. He jerked away but Forrester scragged his neck and forced him to kneel. Detective Dun, linked to the prisoner, was obliged to bend too, gagging horribly.

'Lonnie's work, Noona. Or was it you who did this?'

Noona choked: 'No, no, not me.'

'So where do we go to look for Lonnie Huang?'

Shuddering, gagging, squirming from the adhesive stench, Noona gave no answer.

'Where is Lonnie Huang?'

'Let me go.'

Noona the little full-moon boy who had seemed as weak as chalk, shivered like a spring under tension, but he did not break. He whimpered and sobbed but he would not betray his murderous lover. Forrester relaxed his grip. He said to MacNaughton:

'Gilly, would you mind uncuffing our boy from Detective Dun. What Noona needs is a close-up perspective of things. It shouldn't take more than a minute.'

Detective Sergeant Dun readily released his prisoner. MacNaughton distanced himself and his men from the effluvial stench of the dead human being in the store cupboard, then lit a cigarette and drew in hard on it, careful not to let his fingers touch his lips. He knew what Forrester planned to do in order to break the little queer. Noona would never feel clean again.

Inside the half-gutted building there was absolute quiet for a while, then a desolate scream of torment tore loose. It rose up harsh and guttural and darted through every room. And MacNaughton who was as superstitious at heart as his ancestors of Inis Fraoch, shuddered deeply. When the shrill suddenly ended he was greatly relieved. Then he began to laugh and laugh. Hell, he couldn't hold it back.

Mike Hempstead slumped languidly on the bar counter of the Foreign Correspondents Club, allowing the arctic blow of their excellent air-conditioning to cool the sweat of his back. The heat that day had wilted him to the root, but a pint mug of draught might restore some vigour. He lifted the glass handle of the mug, thought: Cheers! then stuck the lot down in three gulps – good news. He tongued the foam from his moustache and crooked his finger towards the barman. The long looping counter was beginning to fill now as the midday thirst drove the herds down to drink, so he had to wait for a while for service. He didn't mind. There were those who believed that Mike Hempstead had no control over his liquor consumption. Well, they were quite wrong. What people like Reven Forrester and dear Tessa did not realize was that, though he enjoyed alcohol, perhaps more than most people, and sometimes did take a spot more than was good for the old liver, he had absolute mastery over the stuff . . . As demonstrated now, as he patiently observed the arrival of his next beer – rock-steady hands, mark you, then gazed into the fluted froth-capped glass to ponder at the physics of the tiny bubble trails within. Did he need to hurry it down? No he did not. For God's sake he was no lush, and that he had proved to himself on countless occasions. And if anyone cared to observe him here and now, could they dispute it? With eyebrows arched he surveyed his fellow drinkers. There were no overt challengers. The only person watching him, in fact, was a very attractive Chinese woman, who also seemed to be on her own. She quickly looked away. He took a short pull from his mug, and then another, and the third slug quite emptied it out. Once more he looked up; once more he caught the gaze of the pretty Chinese girl. That time did he detect a flicker of a smile before she turned aside? He thought: Yes.

He did not take his eyes from the woman after that. He ordered a beer and drank it and watched her as she sat with her eyes downcast, demurely sucking through a straw at some pukey cocktail topped with slushed ice and multi-coloured vegetable flotsam. She was, indeed, stunningly good-looking, dressed in red, which the Chinese women wear so well. He willed her to look at him again. He was poised, he flicked his hair and readied a smile for instant dispensation . . . And she did it. She raised her eyes lazily to his and at that moment he realized that he knew this woman. He was sure he had met her before . . . But where; and when? No wonder she had smiled at him. He mouthed:

'Hello.'

She grinned: 'Hello.'

Very friendly . . . Mike thought: in for a penny. He took his drink, squared his shoulders, and sauntered along the periphery of the bar counter until he stood puissantly at her side.

'Well,' he said richly, 'fancy seeing you here.'

She looked up. 'Yes, fancy that.'

Even the voice was familiar: educated, fashionably Americanized. Where the hell had they met? 'When was it last?'

'When was what last?'

'Oh God,' he slapped his forehead, 'I'm so bloody embarrassed.' Now he knew exactly where and when he had last seen this woman; in his very own lounge, last night – reading the news on ATV.

'You're Connie Tam. I *thought* I knew you.'

'Don't feel bad. It happens to me all the time.'

He regarded his glass, the contents of which had mysteriously vanished. 'Can I buy you a drink?'

'If you'd like to, why not.'

Why not indeed. He called for a repeat of her concoction and a refill for himself. Then he drew up a vacant chair.

'Cheers.'

She set the straw in her mouth and sucked, dimpling her cheeks. He said:

'So . . . what's it like to be a TV star?'

'It's hard work and the pay is lousy. It's not half as glamorous as you might think.'

'It's amazing, you know. I saw you and I thought: "Hell, I know that girl." And I suppose in a way, I do.'

'Friendship by proxy.'

'That's right . . . yes, absolutely.'

'Well you know my name, and I don't . . . '

'God, how rude of me. I'm Mike Hempstead.'

'And what do you do?'

'Work for the government.'

'Are you a cop?'

'Is it that obvious?'

She pulled a wry face. 'Don't you like your job either?'

103

She was marvellous. The sweetest, most natural girl he had ever met. They chatted, discovered that they had common interests. They were both jazz fans. They both read 'Crime Club' thrillers in bed, and had authored short stories (rejected for publication). He pretended an enthusiasm for a couple of other things – Indonesian curries, and horse-racing.

'Oh I love a gamble; spice of life.'

'Bet on Power Drive, this Saturday, Mike. Third race at Happy Valley. Put on ten thousand.'

'On a cop's pay? You've got to be joking.'

'Bet on it anyway. It's a sure thing.'

'I will.'

And he did. That afternoon, at the Arsenal Street HQ he gave a tote runner 300 dollars to place on Power Drive – for a win. That was the measure of debonair optimism that his encounter with Connie Tam had inspired. He couldn't get the incredible creature out of his mind; the way her fingers had dallied in his, the thrill of eye contact as they had said goodbye. Then, they had exchanged cards. He lifted hers from his wallet:

Connie Tam.
ATV News Desk.

Wow! And they had arranged to meet again at an Indonesian restaurant for a late dinner. Mike, me boy, the old charm has not deserted you; you're OK . . . Connie Tam; my God! The woman was a household name; a celebrity. And *she* had made it quite clear that she was interested. He felt great. It was as though he had emerged from the mire of disparagement that marriage and previous employment had caused to bind to him, to stand in a new light – a place of warm and deserving approbation. Yes, the future wore a smile.

That afternoon he led OSCB Three into Yau Ma Tei in a search for a street kid known only as Fish-boy (presumably because he was so quick and slippery). A ghostly Noona Cham had assisted in the compilation of an identikit, and with this supposed likeness of Fish-boy, and a verbal description too, they had proceeded to question the inhabitants of the area surrounding the murder site – dingy tenements infested with resentful people; jobless men in singlets and shorts, some stunned with opium, all bent to their mah-jong as though the assemblage of those tiles explained the absolute masonry of life. They shook their heads; they knew nothing of Fish-boy. Kids ran underfoot; squealing, crying, staring saucer-eyed at the advancing Wind. Women quarrelled and quacked like herded geese in the steamy communal kitchens. More children milled at the stoves, and more yet were strapped to the backs of those sharp-tongued women. No, they didn't know of Fish-boy. They knew to make congee in the day, and to open their legs wide at night – was there more to life than that?

Chief Inspector Hempstead returned from Yau Ma Tei in the pelting rain and thunder of a late evening storm. He was soaked; he was tired, and empty-handed. And he was exultant.

In an hour and a bit he was scheduled to escort one of Hong Kong's most celebrated personalities to dinner. And after that, if he played his cards right . . . Well, Mike, my boy, there's just no knowing how such an evening might end.

Mike Hempstead played his cards right . . . With Brut-shaven jowl and spearminted tongue he wafted scented, yet manly, conversation towards Connie Tam. And she bent to this source of suavity like willow-wood to water. He told her brave, modestly played-down tales of heroism (of proven influence on the female psyche). He put across the philosophy of a tough, but caring cop. He bought her lots of spicy food and bottles of wine. And on that regime Connie Tam was won.

And there began Mike Hempstead's nightmare. They rode in a taxi towards fashionable Quarry Bay, and her flat. And as they drove the memory of a recent, most distressing sexual encounter arrived to swamp him with apprehension – the woman had been Filipino, dusky and voluptuous, and madly carnal. She had lain next to him, naked, and as wide as a gate. And he had been unable to raise an erection. He went cold at the thought. My God, what if his bloody penis refused to perform again . . . It's all in the mind, he soothed. Just relax, and all good things will happen. So he relaxed. Connie's hand squeezed his. He turned towards her and the musky, warm smell of her steamed from her bosom, and her lips parted in anticipation of his kiss. He kissed her marvellous mouth and they clung then in glutinous unity in the sway of the taxi . . . but where there should by now have arisen a thunderhead, there lay a recalcitrant, shrivelled and totally unemployable polyp of a thing.

By the end of that journey Mike Hempstead was in an absolute funk. Connie's flat was spacious and filled with good furniture, deep carpets, long soft leather couches and whisper-soft music. It occurred to him that she managed well on her 'lousy' salary. Her balcony gave a wide view of the bay and the twinkling lights of Kwun Tong, and was furnished with cane chairs that creaked expensively as they took his weight. A drink?

'Yes please . . . a large brandy.'

She brought him that, then came to sit close to him. Mike Hempstead gave an inner groan of anguish. He tilted the brandy to his lips – good cognac – its velvet heat rushed through him. They kissed again: she squirmed her youthful-limbed body against him, and her full wet mouth came over his . . . There was no stirring at his loins. That time his groan was audible.

Worldly, Connie Tam knew at once what was troubling him.

'Just relax, Mike. It doesn't matter.'

Of course it bloody mattered. It mattered more than tomorrow's sunrise. He begged:

'Can I have another one of these?' He jiggled the ice-cubes.

'Of course, but I've got a better idea.'

The better idea was a joint of marijuana. Its pungent aroma preceded her return. She had changed too, into a black-skinned cheong sam, split from hem to waist. She knelt before him, drew in hard on the joint until her cheeks were puffed wide, then pressed her lips over his and kissed into him a full chest of smoke.

'Is that better, Mike?'

He hadn't smoked dope since college days. He'd forgotten its rapture – its sorcery of riches. His head swelled wonderfully, his skin tingled warmly. A plummy, slow voice rose from within him:

'Much better.'

'I thought you'd like it . . . More?'

'Mmm.'

She drew hard and the joint burned crookedly up the side. Soft lips came to provide the magic breath. Soon all bad thoughts, all fear and furore had vanished. They sucked into each other's mouths and a roar of manhood filled his groin; invincible hardness built. Let her feel it. My God; solid steel!

'Make love to me, Mike.'

Lithe thighs stemmed from black-petalled silk – such raw beauty that it stopped him in awe. Then his hand plundered in, eager for her secrets; dewy, warm, darkly entrapped secrets. Her eyes glowed, black jade in the ferment of wild love, and he rode her, whooping, yelling like a Vandal prince on a wild horse called ecstasy.

The early sun didn't wake Mike Hempstead. He slept on, sprawled face-down into the pillows of Connie Tam's wide bed. She awoke with the dawn, and eased herself carefully, secretively, away. She went straight to the bathroom and cleansed herself of the slough of sex. When she was clean she put on a silk gown. She took a white scarf from its pocket and folded it into a band, then tied it to her forehead. It was embroidered with the outline of a lotus bloom and beneath that the characters: 'Entrusted by Heaven to Prepare the Way.'

Connie went to her veranda and bowed in greeting to the rising sun. She sat cross-legged, then brought her fingers towards her face and brushed her eyelids closed. She took a slow, deep breath and began inwardly, silently, to chant.

> 'My faith is on high.
> Three Buddhas guide me upwards.
> Your pupil is here below;
> Converted to your faith;
> Converted to the law;
> Converted to the Master.'

Twenty-seven times she recited that mantra, and each time she did so she drew closer in spirit to her beloved Master; to the Maitreya, Tang Tsun.

When the verses were complete she felt cleansed and strengthened again. She stood and went to the bedroom and observed the naked slumbering man; despising him. What a horrid face and body the gwailo possessed, so hairy and gross, and the stink of flatus leaked from him.

And now you will go to him and touch him tenderly into wakefulness, and smile your yesterday smile. And if you cannot be happy then at least be proud, because you are a servant to the Master, in the service of the Master. Your faith is on high, Connie Tam. It is your impenetrable shield.

The man stirred in his sleep, sighed and muttered as about him his dreams dissolved. Connie hurriedly took off her headband and thrust it deeply into her gown pocket. Then she smiled her yesterday smile and knelt next to the man. She stroked his spine and kissed him with sweet greetings of the sun.

4

EAGLE'S GAZE, WOLF'S STRIDE

The death of Lulu Wong bled Charlie Lam of his youth at a stroke. His skin waxed and his features ran with grief. His bright eyes became coldly eclipsed and hardened with anger. Reven Forrester saw these changes in his friend, and he feared for him. He did all that he could to insulate Charlie from the day-to-day dolour of the murder investigation, and kept him prudently clear of their vital witness, Noona Cham. He watched Charlie's progress and drove him when he faltered. He demanded results in the investigation of the secret society activities of Tang Tsun.

'Go to Sai Kung, Charlie. I had a call from an ex-station sergeant, name of Fung Sham. He's been digging around for me; claims he's come up with some information on a temple society called White Lotus. Tang Tsun's father, Tang Ten-thousand Blessings, was a member of that society.'

'White Lotus? I don't think I've ever heard of them.'

'No reason why you should have, unless you're a student of Ching dynasty history. The White Lotus sect rose up against the Manchu emperor in Eighteen-Thirteen. They invaded the Forbidden City, but the emperor's forces crushed them. Four hundred thousand people died in the rebellion.'

'What was the White Lotus cause? Were they a triad off-shoot?'

'That's the most interesting part of all, Charlie; pure religious fervour drove them along. They had no triad connections. They believed that the decadence of the era was an affront to the

Mother Goddess, Hsi Wang Mu, and that the Middle Kingdom was soon to be destroyed; to be carried away by a Black Wind, sent down by Hsi Wang Mu, that would blow for seventy-seven days . . . Their cosmologists foretold the day of the Kalpa's arrival; they prophesied that only those who were converted to the White Lotus doctrine and who wore a special headband would survive the apocalypse. White Lotus assumed the responsibility of trying to win all of China to that cause, and they would have succeeded, too, if the Manchus hadn't put them down . . . Well, they didn't root them out entirely did they, or Tang Ten-thousand Blessings wouldn't have been able to be a sect member just twenty years ago.'

Mike Hempstead came into the office then, looking smugly self-satisfied. Unsighted by Charlie Lam he gave a thumbs-up sign. He set down a file on Forrester's desk: 'You called for this.'

It was a transcript of Noona Cham's statement. Forrester quickly flipped it into an open drawer. Whistling tunelessly, Hempstead withdrew.

'You don't have to hide that from me, Reven.'

'Hiding . . . what makes you think that, Charlie?'

There came that flare of anger; quickly controlled: 'I am perfectly aware of your conspiracy to isolate me from the *only* case that I should be working on . . . Why have you done that to me?'

'You know why, Charlie. It wouldn't be good . . . '

'While clumsy fools like Hempstead are put to work on it. Is *that* good? . . . I want that murdering bastard, Lonnie Huang, brought in. I can do it. Let me do it.'

'No.'

Charlie Lam slumped, and the fire left his eyes. He said: 'I think of Lulu so often, Reven . . . her awful death. It haunts me, day and night. It drives me crazy to think that my darling is dead, and her killer escapes punishment. And here I sit . . . '

'If there was any way I could draw you into that case, I would. Don't think that I don't know how you feel.'

'Let me question Noona Cham, at least.'

'And what would that achieve?'

'There's no answer to that question as things stand.'

'Can't do it, Charlie . . . I'm sorry.'

Charlie Lam sat quietly, reflectively, for a while. Then, as though in answer to some unvoiced observation, he sighed dismissively and nodded, then went on: 'You were saying, Reven, that Tang Tsun's father was a member of White Lotus.'

'We can assume that, yes.'

'So Tang Tsun would naturally as a boy have been exposed to White Lotus doctrine; whatever that is.'

'He went to study at the monastery of Chai Tin Dai Sing – the Monkey God, after his father's murder. Evidently that temple society teaches White Lotus meditation . . . But this is all conjecture, Charlie. Go and have a look-see. Hear what Fung has to say. He was a "caterer" as a station sergeant, so his information will be excellent. Ask for him at Fat-boy Shum's seafood restaurant. He's known as The Fixer. Fat-boy will find The Fixer for you.'

'Promise me this, Reven: that you will keep me updated as to your progress in the search for Lonnie Huang. It's so hard for me this way.'

'Yes, I will do that. There are good men on the case.'

'I know . . . I'm sorry I insulted Mike Hempstead. I'm not myself. Hempstead's OK. MacNaughton is first-rate. He won't rest on it.'

'None of us will, Charlie.'

'Thanks, Reven.'

'Now go to Sai Kung; investigate White Lotus and ascertain if there is a triad connection. Research any possible link between Tang Tsun and the sect. And Charlie . . . we'll get Lonnie Huang.'

'Yes.' Charlie Lam tried to smile; his mouth creased vaguely, bitterly, at the edges. Again he said, 'Yes.' Then he walked away.

'We'll get Lonnie Huang': that was not what he had intended to give Charlie Lam as his departing message. He had wanted to tell Charlie that his grief was a burden that they all shared; that he

111

was haunted by the horror of Lulu's death too. But he'd been unable to express these simple, kind words; he had thought them too maudlin and pulpitish. Now he knew he was wrong. The interview with Charlie Lam had left him depressed. As if there wasn't pain enough for Charlie, he had contrived to intensify it by denying him active engagement in the case. On an impulse he lifted the receiver of his telephone and dialled the number of Caroline's flat. A voice, very young, and excited with curiosity, came to warm him:

'Hello. I'm Shannon. Who are you?'

'Someone who loves you.'

She screeched delightedly: 'Daddy, Daddy!'

'Is your Momma there?'

'Do you want to hear me say a rhyme? . . . Old Mother Hubbard . . .'

'She lives in a cupboard.'

'No, I'll say it . . . you listen . . .'

Caroline's voice, distantly: 'Give it to me, Shannon.'

'It's Daddy. I'm telling him a rhyme.'

'Hello, Reven.'

'Caroline . . .' He could hear the lines of Old Mother Hubbard being recited. 'Determined, isn't she?'

'Well, you know where she gets that from.'

'I've just had Charlie in my office. I could have wept for him; he's going through bad times.'

'Were you able to do anything to help him?'

'That's it; that's the exact problem. He wants to be on the case . . . he needs to be on it for the sake of his own sanity. And I can't allow that. I feel so rotten. Everyone avoids Charlie here; they don't want to come near him in case they're infected by his bad luck, you know what the Chinese are like.'

'Why don't the two of you come home for a meal. You could talk freely here. That might be what you both need.'

Clairvoyant Caroline; how remarkably often she was able to tap into his moods. By home, of course, she meant *her* flat – that was home, as far as she was concerned, for Reven and Caroline and their child. And at that moment he was grateful for her inclusion of him in that familial bond; it gave him a good feeling.

'Charlie's gone to Sai Kung. I might not see him for a day or two.'

'Well, then, ask him when you see him. Perhaps you could induce him to take us to the opera. That might do him good.'

'Yes. I think it would.'

Shannon's voice again; insisting: 'Want to talk to Daddy.' Caroline acquiesced.

'Hello, Daddy.'

'Hello, cutie-pie.'

'When will you come and kiss me?'

'Soon.'

'I've got a new dress with *big* pockets. I'll wear it so you can see it. You'll like it, Daddy . . . Lotta killed a cockroach in the kitchen.'

Caroline again: 'She'll chat on for ever if you give her the chance; never comes up for breath.'

'Tell her I'm coming to see her new dress.'

'When? She'll ask me when . . . Why don't you come to-night? Lamb stew's on.'

'*Love* lamb stew. I'll be there.'

'He's coming tonight, Shannon.'

'*Yea!*'

A chuckle of pure pleasure spiralled in him as he set down the handpiece. He glanced at his watch, which informed him that he was ten minutes late for his last appointment of the day: MacNaughton's briefing for a surveillance operation that night. The inspector had delayed proceedings. When Forrester was seated, MacNaughton began:

'The target as you all know is a Cantonese male of medium build. Name: Lonnie Huang. You have all been issued with an identikit.' MacNaughton held up this item of issue. 'But we will not have to rely on the picture. Accompanying the surveillance team will be one Cantonese youth: Fish-boy Hua, who is extremely anxious to assist us, having been unkindly treated by Lonnie Huang. Now the area of operation . . . '

So Hempstead had found Fish-boy. Little wonder that his earlier mood had been so buoyant. Forrester looked around for the chief inspector; saw him leaning against the rear wall, looking modestly heroic. Forrester nodded: well done. Hempstead wiped his moustache in two smug strokes.

Amazingly, Mike Hempstead was showing signs of becoming a first-rate detective. Or was it so amazing: did one not reflexively just assume that all drunks were unfailing and unmitigated fuck-ups? At the conclusion of the briefing Forrester went over to Hempstead, bathed yet in his told-you-I-could-do-it glow.

'You've gained a lot of face with that arrest, Mike. The AC will be dead pleased.'

'Thanks, Ging Si. I guess we had our share of luck.'

'It's a break-through, Mike. It's going to make a conviction that much easier. Tell your team that.'

'I will. Care for a drink on it, Ging Si?'

'Not tonight, Mike. I've got a date with the cutest girl in Hong Kong . . . I'm going to visit my kid.'

'Some other time then . . . Things have changed for me in a big way . . . In a *big* way. You'll never believe . . . '

Mike Hempstead rode the lift with him to the ground floor, effervescing all the way: a new life; new horizons . . . A new, most extraordinary woman.

'It's Connie Tam. We're whacko about each other. It's bloody great.'

'Connie Tam? The exalted Connie Tam of stage and screen . . . You don't say. Well, now I'm heavily impressed.'

Hempstead beamed: opened the driver's door of the Merc and waved a grand salute. As he drove, Forrester wondered how Theresa Hempstead would react to the news of her husband's outrageous adventures; probably with outrageous fury. Perhaps she knew of the affair already. Mike, it seemed, was not being at all discreet. Still, such dazzling publicity would gain Mike awesome status amongst the rank and file of the RHKP.

114

Forrester laughed aloud as he swung the Merc into the parking lot beneath Caroline's flat . . . Mike Hempstead and Connie Tam; my God, life did produce its amazements.

Shannon was waiting at the door. She sprang at him as he came out of the lift. He squatted and hugged and kissed this warm, joyful bundle.

'Kiss me again, Daddy.'

He kissed her again, then bussed a raspberry into her neck. She wriggled into the bend of his arm – her favourite place. He wrinkled his nose at the drifting aroma of lamb stew, and she imitated him.

'Pick me up, Daddy.'

He carried her into the flat.

'The Bisto Kids arrive.'

Caroline was decorating the dinner table with red napkins folded into wine glasses, and red candles. The neck of a bottle of Dom Pérignon protruded from a silver ice-bucket. The table-cloth was white, and she wore white – a languid voile toga that lacked the will to conceal the points of her breasts, and hinted here and there at expensive underwear. An excellent garment. He stood and observed the entire tableau with an air of unequivocal approval, then drew comfortably into its snugness. He entered this woman-made sanctuary with the warm weight of his daughter on his hip – glad to accept this, his protectorate – champion of it all. She led him to the cool of the veranda, and immediately presented a massive glass of whisky and ice. He sat upon loose-cushioned cane furniture.

Amah Lotta arrived to carry off Shannon, wriggling like a hooked trout, protesting every step towards her nightly bath.

'She's quite a handful, Reven. She grows by the day. The play-school teacher says she's very bright. She's well ahead of the other girls of her age.'

And she's mine, Forrester thought, I'm the father and creator of this perfect super-intelligent creature.

'She can dress herself, you know, not totally but she can pull her knickers on in a crooked sort of way, and do up buttons, and brush her hair . . . '

Forrester leaned comfortably back and listened; happily imagining his daughter at these tasks.

'And she's quite the Miss Bossy-boots with her dolls.'

Forrester said: 'I love that child, Carrie. Do you know how good it is for me to be around her?'

'How good is it, Reven?'

'It's hard to put into words . . . You see, my world is a dirty place. Every vicious, sordid thing that could possibly happen to any human, can be expected to occur in Hong Kong. And the worst of all crimes are brought to me. The most bestial murders, Caroline, and it's impossible to stay remote . . . impossible. The grime seeps through the skin of my hands, and it impregnates, deeper and deeper, from one case to the next, each with its unforgettable horrors. I talk shop to my team-leaders over coffee and biscuits about things that would make you hurl up. I find myself thinking almost as brutally as the men I hunt. And then . . . as if by magic I come to little Shannon, and her absolute innocence is so cathartic, so cleansing that I'm proofed once more against all that.' He gestured widely towards the sparkling lights. 'All that . . . It's a very sick city that the Chinese will inherit from us, it really is.' He drank deeply.

Caroline said, 'Hmm,' in distant agreement. 'It's because you see her as your exclusively devoted angel, and she has ascribed to you the role of the complete hero, that she's able to scour you so miraculously of your work-a-day grime . . . But it won't go on for ever. She'll outgrow her little wings. Little girls become big girls, and big girls look beyond their father's shoulders, however broad, in search of perfection.'

'I realize that . . . of course.' Did he?

'I don't think you do.' She read him without rancour. 'We must start thinking about our daughter's future, beyond the darling days of lisps and podgy kisses . . . Her education, for example. It must be planned, properly. I don't want her to be a boarder at Roedean or Cheltenham like so many of the ex-pat kids, flying out to visit Mom and Dad three times a year, spoiled rotten with a vast expense account. Those kids grow up with warped values. My daughter will have a proper home, and I will be in it to personally see to her upbringing. No one could see to that better than I, and so she will not be fobbed-off with second best . . . I'm going to leave Hong Kong.'

Forrester sat forward rigidly, distressed. He said, 'That would be a sad day for me.'

'Not if you came too . . . Come on, why not? What's left for you, come the first of July? How many times have I heard you say: "I couldn't work under a Communist boss"?'

'Shannon could see her primary education out, here . . . she's still so young.'

'Standards are dropping in Hong Kong, Reven; they'll deteriorate further, faster after the Chinese take-over.'

'This is obviously not some off-the-cuff decision of yours, Carrie. You've thought the thing through; I haven't. So tell me about your plans.' He drank, aware of perplexity.

'Perhaps at the end of this year, or early next, we should go. There's lots to be done still; arrangements to be made, here and abroad. It will take time.'

Forrester said bleakly, 'Whatever is right for Shannon has to be, of course. I should have thought about it myself, I suppose . . . It's come as a shock.' Now he was slightly drunk.

Shannon, in a white cotton nightie, came skipping on to the balcony. Her display of vitality was in vain.

'Time for bed. Kiss Daddy good-night.'

She presented red cherub lips all pouted out to her father. He loved the damp, clean smell of her.

Caroline took her away to tuck her in. And Forrester went to the balcony rail, numbly musing on loneliness; not liking the prospect of it at all. He stared down to the neon-gashed darkness of the great city and wondered: what are you to me? So many years a Hong Kong belonger, good years, bad years, memories at every corner. It's hard to leave.

Caroline came back and leaned on the rail beside him. A

swirling mist was gathering, slowly glazing the sharp neon. He said:

'A century and a half of British rule . . . look at it. If Captain Elliot, RN, in cocked hat and breeches could stand here, right here, to confront the critics of his day with this massive view he'd be a vindicated man . . . "Behold, gentlemen: your small, unhealthy, barren, valueless island, Hong Kong."'

'His critics would say, "Listen and you'll hear the sound of the soul-wind of China. It's come to blow it down, Captain Elliot, as we knew it would."'

'The soul-wind of China. It blows away every thread of complacency, doesn't it . . .? I agree that Shannon should go from here, there's no point in her putting down roots in this uncertain place. As for me: I'll have to think the thing through. I'll take leave – my long leave is due. I'll come with you, and then make up my mind.'

'Shannon needs you, Reven.' She put her arm about his waist. A girdle of warmth. 'She loves you just as much as you love her; and she's yours, your blood. That is unchangeable, and the consolation for all other transitions and sadnesses. And if all that isn't enough to reckon with your obstinate heart, then you deserve to be alone.'

'Obstinate.' He frowned at the word. He disengaged from her, wishing he hadn't.

'Unforgiving might be equally as good a description. You'll "think the thing through" and then exhume those old and ugly, bitter memories – much loved, though, for their ability to hurt. Someone must be hurt. Hurt is essential. Life does not make sense without it.'

'If I'm that bad, Caroline, that bloody-minded, why persevere with me?'

'You know why. You know exactly why. I've made it plain to you in countless ways, countless times . . . So now you want it straight; unadorned? Here it is then: I love you. I always have, and doubtless always will. I bore your child because I loved you, and wanted to have a part of you as my own. But the story of

118

Reven and Caroline is older than that. It goes back to the time when she stupidly warned him against pursuing a vendetta. "Stupidly", I say, because no warning would have stopped him anyway; an eye for an eye, was his absolute dictum . . . Caroline did not realize how totally Reven was dedicated to that battle-cry; or how deeply he was merged in his culture of distrust . . . So she was kicked out, and with her, the unwanted warning that the vendetta would bring tragedy . . . And then there *was* tragedy on a grand scale, and as though in foretelling it, Caroline had precipitated it too, he slammed the door on her, for ever. And that is how things have stood for a long time.'

The clink of crockery told of the arrival of food. They went inside and sat at Caroline's fine table – an exhibit of love. He prized at the champagne cork which flew off with a festive pop that seemed quite out of place.

'Make a toast,' said Caroline.

He thought for a while, then gave: 'To forgiveness.'

'A wonderful toast. I'll drink to that.'

He trapped her hand and held it, and said, 'You had a right to say those things . . . Yes. The things I did were destructive.'

She looked at him with suspicious amazement. He went on: 'I've always despised people who recant under pressure. I won't say I'm going to change. I will say I acknowledge my past mistakes, and will try not to repeat them. And I will think long and hard about the things you've said. God knows, I need a home too, and a family of my own.'

Caroline knocked over his glass as she threw her arms around him.

Carlotta the Filipino heard the sharp clink of glass against china and was startled. Were these two fighting again? She peered through the crack in the serving-hatch and her shoulders relaxed, and she sighed. What her diminutive slit gave her were the arms of her mistress wrapped in a stranglehold about the neck of Mister Reven. Lotta pushed further forward, distorting her nose painfully against the hatch doors, and her view expanded. She could now see the spilled glass. The tablecloth was askew and a plate hung in precipitous balance at the edge. Carlotta held her breath. The man now countered Caroline's hold with his own embrace, drawing her, and the tablecloth towards him. Over went a plate – *crash*. Thank God there was no food in it. Ignoring all, still tightly wound to each other, the lovers rose from their chairs. Now Lotta could see the passion in him. His hands roved over her breasts, her hips and buttocks, especially her good full buttocks, and she was as resolute as warm plasticine – she squirmed and sagged and gave wherever he pressed. It came as no surprise to Lotta when table and food were abandoned, and her mistress sighed her way, arm in arm with him, to the bedroom. Caroline came back for the champagne, and the glasses, though, and gave a helpless glance towards the serving-hatch. Lotta shrank back. By the time she dared to peep again Caroline had fled.

'Silly pumpkin,' Lotta breathed, 'don't you know that this man needs the fight?'

Superintendent Lam munched sparingly on salted cashew nuts and sipped tea, and gazed at the silently groaning, slow-eyed fish filling the fish tanks before Fat-boy Shum's restaurant.

'The Fixer should have been here by now,' Lam said to the other occupant of the table.

Detective Sergeant Wu glanced at his watch and nodded agreement, and reached for the last few nuts in the saucer. He thought that Charlie Lam didn't really care if The Fixer came late, or didn't come at all. That was how things were since Lulu's death.

A misty rain began to fall, and Wu hoped it would not intensify before the meeting with The Fixer was over. The canopy above them was holed and rotten, and his boss would probably remain seated there, oblivious to the wet. Consequently, he would have to suffer too. Charlie Lam had recently displayed a markedly indifferent attitude towards such modest comforts as dryness, sleep and food. Look at the man; his sunken eyes and cheeks: he looked like an aged opium addict. Wu thought: I've never seen death change anyone, inside and out, as much as it has changed Charlie Lam.

Thank God for Fat-boy who arrived then with a replenishment of cashews, some battered shrimp snacks and fresh tea. Which was, Wu thought, probably all the nourishment he would get that night.

And then it did begin to pour, and as the sergeant had predicted, the rain came through the canopy as though it were made of old muslin, and Charlie Lam did not seem to mind one bit. Wu shifted the nuts away from a puddle that was forming on the table-top. The chat at OSCG was that Charlie Lam was still a good cop – but not because he loved his work. He did it well because he knew how; just like a wounded well-trained dog. They could be right.

Ever smiling, Fat-boy came bowing; recommending that his honoured guests should come into the interior of his house, the better to enjoy their dinner while they waited for The Fixer. Charlie Lam did not budge, nor did he order dinner, and Fat-boy's smile thinned with bemusement.

A man dashed in from the rain, folded his umbrella, then, finding himself directly below a gushing leak, swore and walked hastily into the restaurant. Charlie Lam's eyes followed the man, further than that he did not move a muscle. In a most disinterested way Lam said:

'Interesting.'

'Interesting, sir?'

'The one who just went into the restaurant, Wu. His name is Rabbit-lip Poon. He was a long-termer at Shek Pik. I interviewed him there recently. He was due for release yesterday, and today he's in Sai Kung. Poon was a triad enforcer with Sun Yee On in Sai Kung, twenty years ago.'

Now that *was* interesting.

'Look through the windows, Wu, and tell me what he's up to. Be prudent; he's a clever boy.'

Wu peered through the glass and water, past the occupants of the fish tanks.

'He's come back from the urinal, sir . . . he does up his fly as he walks. Fat-boy shows him to a table. Mrs Shum brings beer . . . Now . . . it seems as though he orders food from Fat-boy. He pours beer and looks at the television. He lights a cigarette . . . looks at his watch . . .'

Fifteen minutes later Poon's meal was brought. Half an hour later he had finished eating and paid his bill. Then he came outside, and without glancing left or right he popped open his umbrella and walked into the storm.

Charlie Lam made an immediate decision:

'I'm going after him, Wu.'

'My God, sir, it's pissing down. Let me go after him instead.'

Lam glanced at him oddly, made to say something, and changed his mind, then tapped Wu's chest. 'You're the old woman, ha. You wait for The Fixer. Go get inside, can't you see it's wet out here.'

Charlie Lam's loose overshirt was quickly soaked; it clung to his thin body and moulded to the shape of the pistol handle protruding above his belt. And that was Detective Wu's remnant image of his superior as the grey, driving rain closed around him like a curtain.

Charlie Lam hunched into the rain, feeling each drop of the thousands that pelted him meanly, coldly, stiffening him. He walked quickly until ideally positioned, then slowed down to suit the pace of the quarry. And Rabbit-lip Poon walked on in ignorance of his pursuer, tilting his umbrella like a shield at the pelting rain, coddling himself into its meagre shelter. The wind drove hard, cunningly whipping sideways at every corner, wrenching at the umbrella. Once it succeeded in tearing the flimsy device inside out and Poon stepped into an alcove to do repairs. Then he pressed on. Along the praya that skirted the bay the wind grew doubly treacherous. Junks rode the gale untroubled, their lights making bright tassels of the rain, but for those who walked on shore it was a stiff fight. The hardy umbrella met ultimate destruction along that path; a gust threw Poon, umbrella and all, into a heap and when he arose again the thing was totally crippled. He tugged up his collar buttoning it to his neck, and went on. They had reached the old part of the town. The streets were narrower here, pressed in by tenements of unplastered brick. Some buildings lay tumbled, ruined and dead, but those that had outlasted the century sent trails of thudding water from their bowed roofs into the lanes below. Charlie Lam lost his quarry in that dull wet maze, then saw the ghost of a movement at the end of a lane and hurried to close the gap. When he reached that spot he found no trace of Poon, but nearby there was light, a window pearled with rain glimmered dully.

There was a yard to cross, with rusted metal and rotted wood underfoot, and cobbles that were meshed with grass. Lam sneaked and stooped across the litter and reached the lighted window. A chink in the glass provided a poor view – an empty room but for a broken crate and what appeared to be some hooped wooden vats, piled with rubbish. The light came from a deeper source. He thought he heard a murmur of voices.

Charlie Lam found the door to the old building; it was wasted with rot and it was ajar, so he went in and followed a trail of voices, welling, then suddenly splitting into laughter, as sharp as broken porcelain. It was Rabbit-lip who was so keyed-up. Charlie knew the sound of him:

'Twenty years, brothers, breaking rocks in fucking Shek Pik, ha. I paid the price didn't I, for our black hands? So here I am, brothers, back in the ranks, but out of cash. But that's all over now. I've come for the big shine.'

More nervous laughter. At least two celebrants were with Poon; triads, by the sound of their jargon. One said:

'Oh, you've got inch, brother. You faced the wind, ha. We watched you. We're proud of you. You'll get the big shine.'

Poon hawked and spat. 'What a joke to get me back here. This is the room. This is where Tang bought his passage . . . here . . . no . . . here. Yes I'm quite certain. I remember it so well, now. *Pah!* just like that. He went down like a tree.'

'Like a tree, ah. Did he see you at all?'

'Just for a second — then that was it.'

'Show us how you did it.'

'I showed you.'

'No, no. Be exact; from start to finish. Don't skimp on detail, brother.'

Charlie Lam reached a spot beyond which he could progress no further without being discovered. But he could hear all that went on in the next room, and gloomy shadows cast by the men spilled on to an adjacent wall. Poon said incredulously:

'You want me to act the thing through . . . All right . . . let me see; let me think back. I came with Crooked-boy Luk, who stood guard at the street . . . The old man was working. His chair was . . . there. If you were he, brother, you would be exactly on the spot. He didn't see me come in . . .'

Poon revived the murder as no one else could. He slung his voice low in pursuance of good drama. And Charlie Lam, who was denied an overt view of the action, was granted at least a flickering shadow-play re-enactment of the murder of Tang Ten-thousand Blessings. With cat-like tread the assassin stalked the victim; slowly . . . slowly he came on, arm poised, ready to deliver the fatal blow. Then *'Pah!'* he struck . . . So ended the pantomime.

It must have been a brilliant enactment, for, for a while, there was silence in the room. Then arose a patter of applause.

'Bravo, brother.'

'Yes, very good, brother.'

'Now, Rabbit-lip, you come and stand where the old man stood. And I'll take your part.'

'Don't light me up,' Poon sulked. 'I'm tired of this shit, brothers. I didn't come here for this. Where's my money?'

There was a further silence which drove Poon to say: 'Well if that's what you want, ah, I'll do it. Then cash on the table; no more to be said.'

'Oh, we'll square the account, brother; we're the paymasters. But this is how it must be done . . . Now stand there, brother, right where the old man stood.'

Stupid Poon, thought Charlie Lam, they're setting you up. They're Tang's men, and they, too, will grant you a second in which to realize your mistake; to comprehend, Mr Poon, in that terminal instant how foolish you have been. Or all this theatre will have been wasted . . .

And that was how it was. The stealthy advance of the murderer – the raised arm. Then Poon's awakening: 'Oh God, no – *no!*' The killer struck, and struck again and grunted with the force of his blows. A pulpy thud ended it all.

Charlie Lam who over the years had learned all the sounds of human mortality, knew that he had heard true murder . . . and *perfect* retribution. Poon in his shocked last gasp had given that he understood his fatal error.

Charlie pulled back, shaken, limp, as though it was he who had wielded the hammer. He had never felt so aroused by the rapture of violence as at that moment, nor less inclined to do a policeman's duty. It was as though he was floating in a dream where retreat from conscience was a merit. He knew what he should then have done, and did not do it. He felt deeply in sympathy with these men who had done no more than to perform a natural need. A noble act of killing. Charlie's next thoughts were a simple reflex: what if the death of Lulu could be as sweetly and accurately avenged as that? Would that not be justice in its most absolute form? Would that bring peace to the spirit of Lulu Wong?

The answer was immediate: yes. That would be an honourable act. That would end the ordeal of constant hate. That would bring peace. Yes. Yes. *Yes!*

The good cop, Charlie Lam, lifted then like a brown moth and flew away. The new man stood there listening, planning, sharply aware of the change in him – the arrival of new values. Now here was a vastly exploitable situation. He was witness to a murder; a murder committed, no doubt, to the order of Tang Tsun, a man of massive influence and power; was it not possible now to harness that power to the cause of Charlie Lam? Another resounding, *Yes*.

Charlie was cold and wet, and getting colder and wetter. A runnel of water was coursing silently down the wall against which he leaned. Still, he did not move. He waited until the 'soldiers' of Tang Tsun had passed him by and gone into the night, then he followed on.

Lonnie Huang had once sought amusement by holding a rat by the tip of its tail and dunking it into a bucket of water; the rat had paddled frantically towards the rim, but being securely pinched by the tail it had not made headway. Rat had grown tired, and it had seemed it might drown, but with tiredness had come wisdom. It had perceived that its heroic struggle was in vain, and to survive it had better conserve strength, and so it had slowed its rate of stroke to the minimum required to stay afloat. Lonnie had then harshened the rules of the contest. He had plunged his hand and forearm deeper into the water so that Rat became totally submerged. Possessing but a few seconds' breath before extinction, for Rat the situation was calamitous. Rat survived by twisting its body towards its tormentor's forearm and clamping its cutting teeth into the human flesh. This painful surprise had caused Lonnie to jerk his arm from the bucket, with Rat affixed. Clever Rat had released his grip, sailed through the air to a place of safety, then scuttled away. Lonnie had unknowingly learned a great lesson. It was that no matter how great are the powers arrayed against one, perseverance leads to escape.

Lonnie did not consciously consider himself to be cast in the invidious role of Mr Rat. He did, however, follow the survival rules of his rodent mentor.

After the shock of Noona's arrest at the Po Shai Bank, he had shrunk back into the crowd which had swarmed in to gape at poor, bewildered Noona, handcuffed and head-bagged, and shoved into a police car. He had known at once that Noona would break beneath the pressure, and that as from that moment he, Lonnie Huang, was in desperate trouble. He dared not return to the flat to collect his possessions, or to the Perfect Golden

Phoenix to collect his outstanding wages. He was a fugitive. Still, he wasn't exactly destitute. He wore a new leather coat on his back, and a good pair of jeans. He had a few hundred dollars in an ostrich-skin wallet. But this was just weeds and straw in comparison to his real worth. For he still had Grandmother Wong's incredible ruby ring. This he carried with him wherever he went; in the daytime, wrapped up in a remnant of an old serviette it occupied a deep safe place in the side pocket of his jeans. At night these jeans were bundled into a pillow on which he rested his head. There was thus no way (other than by overwhelming violence) of separating him from his loot. It was with him as he walked away from the bank. It was with him as he rode the serpentine Mass Transit Railway to the Sheung Wan terminal on Hong Kong, from whence he caught a bus to Little Fragrant Harbour – or as the British knew it – Aberdeen.

Lonnie had once worked in Aberdeen, as a porter in the Urban Council Market off Main Road, and in the shipyards as a handyman. He had some friends there, he knew the place. But these things alone were of minor influence in his choice of hiding-place. What made Aberdeen the perfect refuge was the fact that no one knew him by his real name in that part of Hong Kong island. Those who cared to use any name at all when addressing him, called him Blind-boy straight and simple, Blind-boy. He'd earned the name by romancing (if one could call it that) the daughter of a local rice merchant. Lustrous Jade was her name, and if ever there was a misnomer this was it, for Lustrous Jade was unquestionably the ugliest woman in the world. But Lustrous Jade had a father who owned several rice stores in Hong Kong, and was thus in a position to be quite decent to any suitor who saw fit to ignore his daughter's repulsive looks. There were no takers. Lonnie had stalwartly tried, and failed, and in the process earned his nickname. But as the bus drove down Aberdeen Praya, Blind-boy thought that benefits might accrue from a visit to Mr Tin's rice shop off Chengtu Road. So it was in that proximity that he alighted.

And there she sat in the open-fronted rice shop: as handsome as a bull-frog on a lily-pad. Her vastness overspilled the stool on which she sat contemplating a wailing pop-group on TV Pearl. There was no doubt about it, she had put on weight. The trousers of her sam fu bulged as tightly as sausage skin. A jade pendant that had once hung visibly at her breast lay now so deeply moulded in flesh that only the chain was apparent. Thick squabs of cheek squashed her eyelids quite shut. Which was probably why she did not recognize Blind-boy at once. He was appalled by what he saw, and puzzled for a while at a less odious solution to his problem. None became manifest, even so he was about to retreat when Lustrous Jade sensed the presence of a customer and wrenched her gaze from the TV.

'Come in, come in.' The wicker fan she held quickened its beat. 'The good Thai rice is at the back, don't you know.'

He might yet have escaped undetected had Mr Tin, in singlet and shorts, not come out then.

'Blind-boy?' He blew the rice dust from his spectacles and set them on his nose. He squeezed a cordial smile towards his visitor. 'Well, long time no see.'

'Sure.' Blind-boy felt quite dignified by this convivial greeting. 'Came to see how it's all going along . . . Hello, Lustrous Jade.'

Lustrous Jade's pudding of a face seemed flushed. She coyly said, 'Hello.' And flapped away with her fan.

'Drink tea?' said Mr Tin.

Lonnie went into the shop. Lustrous Jade lifted her posterior from the stool to provide Blind-boy with a place to sit. It was all exactly as he remembered it – as though only yesterday he had been part of Mr Tin's establishment. He walked past rows of wooden barrels (false-bottomed to give a picture of vast stock), each capped with cones of white rice of varying quality – twelve different grades; thirteen if you counted the cheap broken-kernelled rice, bought to feed dogs, ducks and chickens. Opposite the rice display ran a table with its top divided into compartments for dried beans and peas, noodle cakes of rice and sweet potato, seaweeds and ground nuts, and Mr Tin's speciality, little crisp black Jew's-ear mushrooms. At the back of the shop a gloomy, great wall of hessian rice sacks bulged up to the ceiling. Here all the smells of all the produce intermixed in a cosy musty mish-mash that drew out memories of this comfortable, safe place.

'Sit?' said Lustrous Jade, setting down the stool.

'Bring tea, Daughter.' Mr Tin pushed at the clutter of his modest desk-top to make space, and also to discover his packet of cigarettes. He rolled a cigarette towards his guest. Blind-boy lit up with his own match, then supplied the flame to Tin.

'Hm,' Mr Tin appreciated the situation aloud. 'So two years, and now you come back.'

'Yes.'

'Maybe you're looking for work?'

Lonnie shrugged non-committally, 'Maybe.' He smoked for a while, quite content with this answer. It was quite obvious that Mr Tin had as yet not managed to marry off his obnoxious daughter, and was just as keen as ever to do so. So Blind-boy had a card to play.

'You married?' Mr Tin asked with hooded casualness.

'No time for marriage.'

Tin made sounds that suggested understanding. His daughter brought tea utensils and set them down on the desk, then waddled off to serve a customer, a woman with a baby slung on her back. Lustrous Jade cooed over the baby, chucking its cheeks. Mr Tin gestured towards her.

'Very good with children . . . Some mothers just slap for this, slap for that. My daughter *loves* kids. You can see . . . Can't find fault with that girl if you look all day.' Mr Tin leaned confidentially towards his guest. 'Surprise me if some rich man doesn't snap her up, just like that.'

Hardly likely. Lustrous Jade was nearing thirty – an old maid by Chinese standards, and an ugly one at that. Lonnie, his eyes now well adjusted to the gloom, stared at the wall of rice sacks before him and wondered if Mr Tin still kept his supply of opium stashed away there. He sipped his tea, quite at ease, and thought: this is the last place that the police will come looking for me. So

129

what if the price of safety is to hold hands with fat Lustrous Jade. There need be no more to it than promises. Just string them along until the heat is off, then dump her and her wet fart of a daddy, and back to Kowloon.

'. . . a big dowry.' Those words pierced Blind-boy's reverie.

'What was that, Uncle . . . I was just thinking of something else.'

'I said; for a man with no family . . . any man with no family, big advantage in marrying my girl. Come in with me, manage a shop, ha.'

'About the dowry?'

'I'm not a poor man, I own five shops.'

'I'm quite rich myself these days.' Lonnie flicked an imaginary speck of dust from his fine leather coat-sleeve.

'A man of action. I can see that . . . As for the dowry, you and I would need to prop up the pillow, ah? Money is a serious business.'

'I might just stay on for a while; see how things go . . . and then, if Lustrous Jade is up to the mark . . .'

'Oh she's a fine, obedient girl; a virtuous girl.'

'That's good.'

'No talents that might spoil her. She's respectful . . . but I'm telling you things that you already know, or why would you have returned, ah? I tell you this Blind-boy, this girl has a soft spot for you. She was broken when you left; days of howling, aieya! So of course I suffered too. But that's all past now. Here you are; no more to be said.'

'The Yellow River,' Blind-boy said enigmatically, 'can never flow backwards.'

Mr Tin looked impressed. He said, 'Quite so . . . yes absolutely so.' They drank tea and smoked while Mr Tin exaggerated the prospects of the Aberdeen rice shop. Lonnie surprised himself, and delighted his host with his remembered knowledge of the trade. And Lustrous Jade lumped around the front of the shop serving customers with great and obvious efficiency, bearing out her father's proud assessment of her:

'She works like a plough-ox, that girl.'

Mr Tin glanced at his watch. It was time to eat. He said for all to hear: 'We men are hungry. We're going for dim sum. Daughter, you better be in charge here.'

Lustrous Jade beamed behind the wicker fan. Blind-boy was back.

It took Blind-boy but a few days to establish himself as manager of that shop, he knew all the work, it was easy. Mr Tin did the buying from wholesalers in Hong Kong, so he didn't have to know about that. Once a week Mr Tin drove up in his green painted truck, and coolies unloaded the huge rice bags and rebuilt the rear wall (the opium was not stored there any longer). It was Blind-boy's duty to see that the false-bottomed barrels were replenished with clean rice. 'Clean' meaning rice that had been disinvested of the population of repulsive little white-worms that might infest it. This entailed work. The entire bag had to be shaken out in front of an electric fan which blew the majority of the pests away, the remainder had to be picked out by hand, one by one, over a sifting tray. And the tedium of this, and the storms of rice dust, were more than Lonnie could take. So Lustrous Jade was elected to do battle with the worms. She was a strong girl all right. Beneath her exterior of blubber willing muscles were at work, and good, clean rice went on display.

It did not take long for Lonnie to effect a state of absolute ascendancy over his prospective bride. A desirable condition, and easy enough to attain. Lonnie did not have to change Lustrous Jade's thinking one bit. From girlhood, as was the custom in Chinese families, she had been seeped in the mystique of male dominance. Her purpose in life, her daily prayer was to marry and bear sons, and Lonnie knew it. And the fact that her ugliness had previously precluded such honour made her pathetically easy to manipulate by the man who might (let all the gods assist!) end her barren days. Her simpering obedience, however, drove Lonnie Huang to further extremes. He began to knock her about.

'Wah! Lustrous Jade, there is a worm here, look.'

That was worth a cuff on the ear.

'Move quicker, fat-girl.' Another stiff swipe.

She looked at him through her deep slitted eyes, and moved

131

quicker. Not a murmur of objection, not a gesture of dissent. He caught her day-dreaming at the worm-winnowing basket and kicked her in the breast. Her breath hissed out, as basket, and rice, and Lustrous Jade spilled on to the floor. That time she protested: 'Aieya, Blind-boy.'

Lonnie was scared then that he had gone too far, he was not married to the woman, after all. So he swore, and blustered, and laid on a lecture about the evils of laziness, all of which Lustrous Jade accepted stolidly, even gratefully.

'I just don't know what goes on in your head sometimes, Lustrous Jade. The profit is what your daddy asked for, ha.'

'Yes; Blind-boy taught me the great lesson.'

'That's what I want.' He went on in a more conciliatory tone. 'You just think about the job; that's good.' He would not go as far as to stoop to help pick up the scattered rice, though. That was woman's work.

Lustrous Jade might have felt that such husband-like behaviour was the precursor of greater things, and in encouragement of such she took to beautification, as she saw it. She began to wear lipstick, and perfume, and had her hair bobbed. She frequently sheathed herself in a recklessly pink dress, thus gaining the appearance of a large, punctured beach-ball. She did not go straight home (as had been her habit) after the shutter gates in the front of the shop had been drawn and locked, but hung around, discovering things to do.

Lonnie was perplexed. Neither by word nor deed did Lustrous Jade show inclination to contradict him. Nor had she made a single overtly immoral move on him. She was, as her father had promised, obedient and virtuous. She seemed as harmless as a washed-up jellyfish, and yet he sensed an advancing threat from her that he had no answer to; monkey tricks in the mind of the woman. He would not have it. He beat her up again, meanly and without pretext; and the next day she appeared, more radiant than ever. Frustration set in. He might have taken flight had his other circumstances been less idyllic.

Mr Tin had provided for him all the major necessities of life.

He had a key to the back door that opened on to a lane, and a communal toilet. He had a sleeping-mat to roll out at the day's end, tea, and a portable gas stove on which to boil water. And there was the TV. He would have been content to sit tight and wait it out, but for the subversion of Lustrous Jade. She was quietly driving him crazy.

Frustration ran to anger, and with anger every chance of understanding the situation dissolved. So he went his brutal way and Lustrous Jade withstood it; more than withstood it. She came on in her passive, glutinous way, smothering him, implanting in him horrific speculation as to her carnal needs . . . And Blind-boy suspected that crafty Mr Tin, if not the master-mind behind her strategy, was at least a player in the game. He must have questioned her unusual latecoming, if nothing else. It was certain that Tin knew exactly what his daughter was up to.

It was on one such evening, with Lustrous Jade wedged into the shop, counting rice grains, that Lonnie arose from a prolonged session at the squat latrine, determined to escape, if only for the evening from the presence of that terrible woman. He did not go back to the shop, he climbed a low wall, slippery with rain, and dropped into the service lane beyond. His feet squelched on garbage and the stench of rotten fruit came up. But better things were in sight: the bright streets of Aberdeen, thick with people, boisterous with sound . . . Policemen; they would be there too, dawdling inquisitively amongst the crowds; so easy to spot though, in their crisp khaki and shiny leather. No danger from them, he reassured, just stay alert.

Lonnie crept from the dark lane into the bustling street, nervous for the first block, sniffing like an emerging rat at the smells of the outside: greasy ducks hanging in rows, and bean curd on the vendors' woks, and as he came closer to it, the pungent niff of the sea. The roar of traffic, the rattle of abacuses and the din of voices and full-blast music; all these things clothed him in a feeling of well-being such as he hadn't felt for weeks, and very soon he was at full swagger.

*

Connie Tam held to a faith more fervent than love and more dangerous than hate. It ran through her like an overriding nerve transcending the input of all five senses, bringing special awareness, making all things bearable in the furtherance of the cause. Connie Tam believed that the Third Buddha – the Buddha Maitreya – had come to earth, and his name was Tang Tsun.

First there had been the Lamp-lighting Buddha on His azure lotus throne who'd ruled for 108,000 years. His teaching was the Azure Sun Assembly. When His light went out, the Sakyamuni Buddha came to sit on a seven-leafed red lotus platform and he ruled by the authority of the Red Sun Assembly. But he had long since returned to Nirvana. Then, exactly as it had been prophesied, so it had happened. The Buddha Maitreya had come; born at a place called Stone-wall Village, and with the sign of Ming, and he was amongst them. His authority was of the White Sun, and his followers were of the White Lotus Assembly. And the Maitreya would guide his followers to the feet of the Eternal Mother and splendid, spiritual paradise. *Ah!* but before such utopia could be countenanced there would be cosmic holocaust that would destroy the world. And only those who knew the Maitreya would survive it.

The Lamp-lighting Buddha was extinguished by ice and the Sakyamuni by flood. The Maitreya's epoch – his Kalpa, would end with storms, pestilence and war. That was the simple truth. For a Black Wind was gathering strength to sweep the world from the sky, and cast away the past. And in its path it would leave mountains of white bones and rivers of blood, and there would be no place on earth for man or God. Those who believed, those who had come to the Maitreya, would be protected from the Black Wind by the almighty hand of the Eternal Mother. They would be lifted to Cloud City, where they could look down on the catastrophes of the Kalpa in absolute peace and safety. Connie Tam was amongst the followers of the White Lotus Assembly.

She had come to the Maitreya, and she was saved. She had come to him when he was a young teacher with few pupils, and had thus received the Maitreya's personal instruction. From his own lips she had heard the readings of the Ancient and Precious Volumes; the *Comprehensive Manual for the Survival of the Kalpa*. She had been taught healing arts that were used to recruit new members. He had showed her how it was possible, with the use of secret words and the circulation of breath, to lapse into a trance that made one impervious to pain. There were other wonders that he had taught her too; ecstasies too bright to describe . . . Now the Maitreya's disciples were everywhere, gaining every day new members for the Assembly. But she would never forget the early days when she had sat with those few others in the circle of his light, and had been initiated into the true way of eternal salvation.

Connie had worked for the Maitreya tirelessly, and when the need had arisen she had lied for him without conscience, and cheated without remorse. She would kill for him if that was asked of her. Now she was just one of the thousands who marched within the ranks of White Lotus, silently, secretly moving along . . . and yet she remembered the days when they were few, and the dreams were many. And Tang Tsun's smile had been especially for her.

Connie Tam breathed in the essence of that dawn's sun. She bowed towards it until her forehead touched the cold floor of her veranda. Then she folded into the lotus position and began her strength-giving mantras.

> 'As you breathe out and in
> So the heavenly gates open
> And the soul leaves the flesh
> To go to the throne of Eternal Mother,
> To bow respectfully . . . '

So she sat like a Buddhist monk swaying slightly for a while, then became deadly still. Her cheeks went pale and her eyelids fluttered as she circulated her breath to the four gates of her body, building strength for her soul-journey. Then, when the four gates were closed, and her strength had begun to dart in her

135

like a stream of bright silver, she sped her soul through the dark pass at the junction of her eyebrows – to Heaven.

Mike Hempstead, more asleep than awake, reached out his arm to the warm place in the bed where Connie had lain. His penis was morning-massive, and pressed as it was into soft-giving mattress it was loading him with the most erotic thoughts imaginable – marshmallow breasts; black-velvet-haired pubes soaked with desire. He muttered and groped out for these delights, then awoke fully, dismayed to find no more excitement available than Connie's residual warmth, and the urgent need to urinate.

Mike swung his legs off the bed, modestly hid his erection, then padded to the bathroom. When he had done with his bladder, rinsed the mulch from his mouth and finger-combed his thick hair, he went in search of Connie Tam, and nearly tripped over her.

Shrunk to the size of a small heap of washing, she sat cross-legged on the veranda floor. Mike called out a cheerful good-morning, and received no answer. He bent over her and peered into her face, her eyelids seemed slitted, more closed than open. He smiled, she took no notice. He made a few passes before her eyes; still no response. Obviously she was having him on. Mike decided to enter into the spirit of things. He hunkered down before her. He inhaled air until his cheeks bulged like a trumpeter. Then, suddenly, and with full force, blew directly into her face. That did it, Connie gasped; shook her head. Her eyes started open, wide and bewildered as one who is shaken from a deep sleep. Mike knew he had made a grave error of judgement. His face puckered nervously, his hands wrung with regret. Words of apology were wandering towards his tongue when she hit him. A little fist, as vicious and quick as a truncheon-tip, shot straight into his throat. The force of it sent him sprawling, clutching his distressed wind-pipe; the surprise of it changed him for ever. The pain, the weighted violence and intent – these things were amazement enough. But what shook him to the core was the immenseness of her anger and its swiftness of arrival. From serenity to rage in one single, sustained hiss. Her pupils had withered until dense with hate, her eyebrows had gnarled – she had struck! It was this rearing, cobra-quick transformation that he knew he would never forget.

And as suddenly as all that, she was beautiful again, and caring for him as though she knew nothing of the attack that had felled him; or was the cause of his pain:

'Poor Mike. Oh dear. Let me help you up. What a terrible thing to have happened.'

She knelt by him and cupped him with soft fingers, and stroked at the injury, cooing sweetness, sharing his agony: 'Aieya, *aieyaa*!'

The blow had riveted his air-pipe shut, so that for a while he could scarcely breathe, but as soon as he was sufficiently repaired he peeled her fingers from his throat and backed away.

Connie Tam came after him, tenacious with tenderness. Sighing words – soft gestures; ploys that capsized him as effectively as had that one, incredible blow. She led him to the bed and ravaged him with kindness. But he could not expunge the memory of that moment of incredible hate; he was in awe of it. She'd astonished him that morning in everything she'd done, and now beneath her, locked in nakedness to her, he lay in bewildered submission. Like a worshipper at his totem of devotion he worked in disciplined, fervent ritual towards the achievement of pleasure.

Later that morning Mike Hempstead was finally gelded of all claim to freedom. When they had eaten breakfast Connie Tam placed her hand on his and said: 'I think we know each other now, Mike.'

He faced her and saw that she was in earnest, and though he didn't think he knew her at all he felt compelled to nod: 'Oh, yes.'

'So, if you asked me to do something for you, I would do it?'

'I'm quite sure you would.'

'In fact, even if you didn't ask me, and there was something that I could do, that I knew would please you, then I would do it without asking.'

137

'If it was in your power.'

'Exactly. I would do anything in my power to please you.'

'And so would I.' Now, where was this leading?

'I have done something for you, Mike . . . I know you're short of cash . . . don't deny it. I've seen the miserable car that you drive. Your clothes hang in my cupboard now and I've seen how out of date they are. I made some bets on your behalf. You know I have good information . . . Well, let me just say that you're worth quite a good deal more than you were when we first met.'

'Good God!'

She kissed him. 'I love it! Look at your face – like a schoolkid who's pinned the tail on the donkey. Would you like to know how much cash you're worth, Mr Money-Bags? I'm sure you would.'

'How much?'

'Would fifty thousand Hong Kong please you?'

Mike gasped: 'Fifty thousand Hong Kong dollars?'

'Would it please you?'

'Jee*zus*! . . . Would it *please* me?'

Connie laughed lightly. 'Well a hundred thousand would please you more then.'

Mike's jaw hung; he snapped it shut and immediately it gaped again. Little squeals of delight were jigging in the back of his throat.

'That's what you're worth, lover.' She patted his cheek.

'*One hundred* thou!'

'I opened a Telebet account for you, in your name. I didn't want to say anything until we . . . *you* had made some wins. Well now you have. You're on your way to becoming a rich man, Mike.'

'Rich. I'm rich already. Christ! One hundred Gs. Connie, how the hell did you do it!'

'My little secret.' She opened her purse, smiling. 'Here, this is yours.' She gave him a yellow slip of paper crested with the horseshoe, bit and whip emblem of the Royal Hong Kong Jockey Club. 'Your access number . . . It's all yours, Mike.'

'Pinch me, I'm dreaming.'

'No dream, Mike . . . Unless you bet without the right information. Then it all might fade.'

'I won't. I won't.'

'I'm happy for you, Mike. Be careful though. Your colleagues might get the wrong picture . . .'

'Good God! They'll never know.'

'Your boss sounds like a dangerous man.'

'Reven Forrester. Have I spoken about him to you? I didn't think I had.'

'Oh, he's well known. He's a big crime-buster, the Ging Si; always in the Chinese press . . . In fact, I have something that I'd like you to give him; a message from an acquaintance of mine.'

'Why doesn't your acquaintance just phone him up? Forrester's quite accessible.'

'I don't know why he doesn't do that. And I wouldn't ask him either. As you said, Mike: for some people one does favours without asking why.'

She had misquoted him, but he wasn't going to quibble.

'If that's how it is then.'

'Just an envelope, with a letter in it . . . But he mustn't know where it came from, or who delivered it. That is important.'

Mike Hempstead knew how to show unequivocal gratitude. He said at once, 'No problem.'

It was a good-quality manila envelope of roughly foolscap dimensions. Mike laid it in his briefcase, and that morning he took it to Police HQ in Arsenal Street. He was early. The CSO's office was locked. No one saw him stoop down and slip the envelope beneath Forrester's door.

'It is a fact,' said Charlie Lam, 'that we Cantonese are the finest connoisseurs of good cognac in the world. The humblest Hokklo line-fisherman on his junk will tell you, blindfold, whether it's Courvoisier or Hennessy or Martell that's at his lips. He'd kill for the brand of his choice. But he wouldn't give a nod for your whisky. It makes you impotent, you see. It's strictly a woman's

139

drink. You should change, Reven, you really should.' So saying, Charlie Lam took up his glass and drained it to the toast:

'Yum sing!'

Reven Forrester regarded his friend curiously. Charlie had changed. He had returned from Sai Kung that afternoon and come to the CSO's office, and straight away Forrester had noticed the change. Charlie Lam had firmed up, the ghost had gone out of him. His eyes were ringed with fatigue, but he was solid and touchable again – a face set with optimism and a speck of wit.

Charlie had been keen to talk about the Tang Tsun investigation. He and Forrester had spoken all afternoon; discussed the case until the windows had darkened with night. Then they had gone on to Charlie's uncle's small, but excellent, wine-house at Aberdeen, there to settle in a private back room at a table with menus wedged under its chipped glass top, some stools, a bottle of White Horse and one of Courvoisier, which Charlie thus recommended:

'Hair of phoenix, horn of unicorn.' He poured liberally, lit a cigarette, then looked up, deadly serious. 'Reven, can I ask you a question . . . a very personal question?'

'Go ahead. Maybe I won't answer. But, ask away.'

'What does it feel like to gain absolute revenge; perfect revenge?'

'Should I be able to answer that?'

'More than anyone I know. I remember you talking about a little refugee kid called Kit Ling who you were going to try to adopt. I recall thinking at the time how much you seemed to care for that girl . . . I never saw the two of you together, but I noticed the change in you while she was around, everyone did. And then she was killed, and that changed you too. God, you were bitter. I helped you search for the killer: Eddie Woo. I knew he had no chance.' Charlie stared at the table, musing, then came earnestly back to his query: 'You promised an eye for an eye, and sure enough he drowned, too. A perfect revenge, ha? . . . Did it cleanse you, Reven? How did you feel? Please, tell me.'

Forrester cupped his hand to the back of his neck and massaged at the ropes of tense muscle. How had he felt when Eddie Woo had drowned? He'd never really answered that question satisfactorily even to himself. Had Charlie Lam not sat there as earnestly expectant as a basset hound he would not have been drawn to answer: 'It was a long, long time before I felt as though I could go on – to step into the next day without the pain of hate. I was glad of his death, no more than that. I was satisfied.'

'What if he'd died in another way, a car accident say, or pneumonia. Would that have satisfied, do you think?'

'It didn't happen that way, so that's conjecture.'

'Indulge me, Ging Si.'

'Charlie, here's a question for you: What the hell is on your mind? If it's the madness that I suspect it is, then I warn you, don't think of it. If I was your brother, I would give you that advice.'

Charlie Lam hid his mouth for a moment behind the rim of his tumbler, but Forrester saw a wrinkle of guile.

'No, no. You've got it all quite wrong, Reven. The hunt for Lonnie Huang is in your hands. It's just that I'm intrigued by Rabbit-lip Poon's murder. I was so close to it, you know. If I hadn't lost him in old Sai Kung then I might have been able to prevent it. As it was, I was the first on the scene . . . It was the perfect revenge, the same room, an identical pounding-hammer. The body stretched out in exactly the same position. What sort of mind is it that seeks out such perfect retribution? Tang Tsun is my involvement; *my* case. So of course the psychology of it intrigues me . . . We all know he did it, or at the least, had it arranged. And we cannot prove a thing. Don't you think in that case I should interest myself in the concept of revenge?'

'I think Tang's motive went deeper than revenge. It was a display of power. Perhaps he purposely set out to display his triad connections?'

'No doubt now, Ging Si, ah?'

'Perhaps he meant to tell us precisely that . . . and that he is infinitely patient. Patient enough to wait twenty years. He is resourceful, and ruthless.'

'A perfectionist.'

'A purist . . . like your Hokklo cognac drinker. A connoisseur of violence. You can be sure that Mr Poon was left in no doubt as to the justification for his elaborate end.'

'Do you think so, Reven? . . . How macabre.'

'How Chinese.'

'There was no struggle, no sign of self-defence.'

'And yet Poon knew, I'm sure.'

'Perhaps in the final seconds, like the killer of Kit Ling, he saw through the terror of impending death to the elegant quid pro quo of his murder.' Charlie drank deeply. 'No random virus, or reckless taxi driver to cut him down; nothing as chance as that. He faced a unique and meticulously planned extinction. Might the victim in that instant feel comfort, even gratitude that his death was such a well-structured affair?'

'Interesting notion, Charlie. My hope is that all he felt was remorse, and despair.'

'Yes I hope so too; utter despair. Poon's life was worthless, his death should be the same . . . Yet Tang did give him some face in the end. He went to great trouble to secure the perfect revenge . . . For twenty years he paid the rental on that shop, and left it all the while untouched, exactly as it was. A memorial as it were to his father. I wonder when he first began to plot the murder. In the monastery of Chai Tin Dai Sing, perhaps.'

'I thought that all that the monks were taught was the benevolence of our Lord Buddha.'

'God knows what they're apprenticed in, Reven. It's all a big secret. Tang was two years there, that's a matter of record. The Fixer, Fung Sham, reckons that their instruction includes some serious martial arts, and what I saw through my binoculars bears that out. So it's not all taufu and chim-sticks. Between lessons in celestial love there's a good deal of chucking about. They train to absorb vast amounts of pain and not feel it, no punches pulled, I can tell you. I was impressed.'

'And Tang learned that.'

'According to The Fixer, he was more than a mere pupil. The monks held him in great awe because of the Ming stigma in the palm of his hand. He was encouraged to develop a following amongst the neophyte monks.' Charlie tipped the brandy bottle to his tumbler; the fluid gurgled hollowly, the bottle was quickly emptying. He said, 'If White Lotus was revived by Tang Tsun, then be sure that it happened during that time.'

'He was a dreamer; a visionary, and an orator too. All the right qualifications for the leader of a sect.' Forrester yawned, bluntly tired, yet too fascinated with this conversation to let it be. 'This man grows massive, doesn't he? What a mind he must have. From a peasant farmer to a Celestial Dragon-head. And we don't even have a proper file on him . . . Put down as secretive one of his major attributes.'

'The monks taught him well.'

'On the subject of monks' skills: they receive instruction don't they, in the art of paper-folding?'

'Yes.' Charlie drank. 'That is so.'

'They're taught how to fold paper models for sacrificial burning – cars and junks, furniture, clothing and suchlike, to cater for the needs of the ancestors . . . In the old days they were adept in the manufacture of paper riddles. The sort of thing, Charlie, that when received, looks almost like a sheet of paper that's been crumpled up in the palm of your hand, then ironed out again, so that it's covered in little ink marks that make no sense until you're able to reverse the sequence again. That's the object: to fold it pleat by pleat back into its original form. Then the message that was inked on it becomes legible.'

'I've heard of such riddles, Reven. My grandfather used to talk about them. The old Chinese loved to make mysteries.'

'Perhaps the art has not died. I don't know what else to make of it. A piece of white paper, folded in a hundred different ways, was

143

poked beneath my door, this morning. I don't know who delivered it.'

'White . . . ' Charlie Lam frowned as one might when assuming superior knowledge of such matters. 'White, ah.' Sensing intrigue he was a-wriggle with curiosity and trying not to show it. 'Perhaps you should give it to someone Chinese who could decipher it, Reven.'

'I was hoping you might be able to help.'

'Of course. Of course.'

Forrester set his briefcase on the table and sprang the locks. He handed a large manila envelope to Charlie Lam.

'Go ahead, open it.'

'It's bigger than I imagined.' Charlie withdrew the wrinkled sheet of paper, deepening his frown, puckering his lips. 'So many folds.' He peered at it, this way and that, one side then the reverse. 'Difficult . . . Look, Reven, there seems to be some faint design to it. A bit like a spider's web, would you say? Do you see the spiral creases . . . here, here and there. Perhaps if the light was better . . . ' He pinched it by an edge and lifted it close to the bulb.

'I can't see any design to it, Charlie.'

'The design is repeated at this edge too . . . I'm sure.'

'No, I can't see it. All I can see are hundreds of creases with little ink marks dashing everywhere. I'd like to know what's written there, though. Perhaps I should have a stab at refolding it.' He took the paper puzzle back.

'Perhaps you should . . . then perhaps you shouldn't.' Charlie urbanely disagreed. 'One slip and you've lost it for ever. A man's fingers could be too thick and clumsy for such a job. A woman's hands, a woman's patience, that's what's needed here.'

It was decided then that small and patient First Aunt should be approached to decipher the puzzle. Recommending her further was her scholastic background. She had studied library science at the Chinese University of Hong Kong.

Forrester declined further alcohol and stood.

'Won't you eat evening rice with me, Reven? Third Uncle has sent out for bor-laap bream; your favourite.'

Charlie's inducement amounted to no more than mild politeness. Both men knew that. Forrester said, 'Not tonight . . . Which reminds me: we're going to the opera. Caroline's laid on tickets so you can't back out. And what a coincidence – can you guess . . .?'

'Sandy Tang?'

'The prettiest songbird in Hong Kong. Well, Caroline will get hold of you with the details. Dinner first, I hear, barbarian fare, no doubt. Then if your offer still stands, you may educate me in the arts . . . And Charlie, if you really want to know: it would not have satisfied had Kit Ling's killer died of pneumonia, or been run over by a car. I would have felt cheated, and I would have been wrong.'

'Walk slowly, Ging Si.' The words dragged. Charlie Lam's bright spirit had departed once more. In the murk of blue-grey smoke he hunched so deeply he looked dwarfed and shoulderless; hopelessly, fearfully alone.

'Walk slowly, Charlie Lam.'

Forrester turned away.

Charlie Lam did not sit alone for long. Third Uncle, Foulmouth Lam, came to join him at his table. Foul-mouth smoked Chesterfields, tip to tip, and was a glutton for dragon-lice, water-insects, preferably deep fried, which he ate heartily at every opportunity, and the clogging qualities of which (according to good medical advice) were the cause of his chronically blocked bowels. Which condition was in turn held responsible for his rather bloated appearance, and awesome flatus. Uncle Foul-mouth also swore with the facility of a Fukienese trawlerman. Some people avoided Foul-mouth Lam. Charlie rather liked his unsavoury uncle. Foul-mouth was not without philosophy:

'Avoid gwailos as a swimmer would turds floating in the surf – they're unpredictable, and they're messy. And *that* one is dangerous.'

'*Wah!* Uncle; short memory. Not long ago Ging Si was paying out for Second Uncle's great learning at University of Hong Kong – three distinctions, and now in private practice, tenth floor, Swire House, ah! You should be proud to have Ah Reven as your guest.'

'Pah!' Foul-mouth spat. 'It wasn't he who paid up. It was his father, Fok Lik Tak. And that man had a debt to pay from here to the gates of Hell. Who do you think it was who kept Fok Lik Tak in rice when the fucking, shit-eating Japanese had him behind wire . . . Our clan did it. Old Uncle Paau used to sneak up to the wire and throw in rice packets for Fok Lik Tak and his friends. So he owed us, so he paid. And what has that helped? ha? Second Uncle has his fuck-fancy Swire House rooms packed out, and he still can't cure my guts.' Third Uncle tilted his buttocks and decompressed vastly in proof of this. He prodded his belly. 'I'm dried up in here like a winter nullah.'

Windy as the summer monsoon, Charlie thought. He said: 'Well, maybe their debt is paid, and maybe it isn't. But the Ging Si has helped me to gain rank, and so for me it's more personal.'

Foul-mouth conceded: 'Gwailos, in some circumstances, have their uses.'

A waiter arrived to call Third Uncle to the telephone: 'Electric talk, Uncle. Will you come?'

'Will come . . . You stay put, Nephew. We'll play some mah-jong later, and eat.'

And Charlie was pleased to comply, for as uncouth as Third Uncle's company was bound to prove, at least it was company. Better that, any day, than the deep winter of loneliness waiting, coldly, just beyond the door of his flat to shrivel him to his marrow. No, he could not take that. Every room killed him with memories. Every mat, vase and chair had something to whisper of his dead love. And he wandered there from room to room, from light-switch to light-switch, flushing the rooms with light – quick on, quick off. Preferring the dark to poignant vision. But the gloom could work its own special sorcery. She came to him in the darkness, on the drift of sleep: 'Help me, Charlie . . .

Oh come! Oh please come!' Her voice, her words, as truly spoken as though she was with him in that room, or at most one room away. And he would jolt upright and fumble for the light-switch. Then he would wander from room to room again, in search of what? . . . There were her woman things in abundance: cosmetic jars and hairbrushes, clothes, handbags, shoes. A pair of pink slippers poked out beneath the fringe at the mattress edge, exactly where she had left them on the final morning of her life. He fiddled with these things – he picked them up, and laid them down, slowly, tenderly; and always positioned as they were before. One day he would pack all of her belongings away, but he couldn't do it yet; it was unworthy even to contemplate such an act while Lulu still abided there in voice, at least, with such desperate tenacity.

'Mah-jong,' Third Uncle roared from the door. 'Come on, get off your litchis, boy . . . Come.'

Charlie played a guileless game; a dry and unimpassioned game – and won. It didn't seem to matter what chair he occupied, or how limited his strategy – he won. Third Uncle and his cronies plotted and strained to rob him of his luck, but could not do it. At midnight, Ah Tse, whose luck had been miserably thin all evening, called out: 'No match! *Aieya!* Not an honour tile to my name, I swear, not a triplet, hardly a pair. No match!'

Ah Tse was jeered, but all of them had lost heavily to Charlie and showed no great wish for more play. They drank the brandy out, then broke up. Charlie Lam walked alone into the streets of Aberdeen. Cars and taxis clogged the rain-wet shimmering black tar, rumbling. The reek of petrol fumes stung the damp air. Neon-pale faces, pink, green, blue faces, filled up the pavements and Charlie stepped into the tinted flow, in no hurry to be anywhere, allowing the press of humans to float him along. If Lonnie Huang was in Aberdeen he would probably be on the streets at that time, but would he recognize him? He had seen the man on only one occasion, and that was months ago. Still he searched the faces of those who passed and listened for Chiu Chau accents in the hope that he might find the ex-waiter from the Perfect Golden Phoenix restaurant. He came to the harbour. Camera-draped tourists walked here; sampan women gestured and beckoned for their trade. Here too, in his torn, black rags, squatted Mad Fu the beggarman. Fu, with the endurance of the demented, perpetually held out one arm, circling it at the elbow, like clockwork, round and round with finger extended, as though in never-ending warning of disaster. Charlie stood and watched him as he had done often before, hoping to see him wind down. Mad Fu went on and on, and Charlie would have walked away then had he not sensed that he was being scrutinized.

A young, keenly dressed man leaned against the pavement rails, smoking delicately, staring mistily; tilting back his head so his long neck showed, he stroked with languid fingers at the satin of his shirt collar. A full-moon boy on the trawl. This man, Charlie had definitely never seen before . . . Charlie Lam stood quite still, amazed by the thoughts that were coming to him then as naturally as one breath follows the next. He walked towards the gay, and they smiled thinly at each other.

As he knew she would, Lulu awoke him that night:

'Help me, Charlie. Oh! come. Oh! please come.'

'Lulu!' he called out. 'Lulu!'

'Come. Please come.'

'I hear you my darling.' He sat up quickly; sweat drenched. He jerked his gaze around the dark room.

'Lulu.'

'Help me.' The voice was small, and gasping, as though near death.

'Lulu I love you. I always will . . . Lulu?'

No answer, but he was absolutely sure she was still there, watching him intently – close, so very close. Charlie needed only to whisper to be heard:

'I killed one of them, Lulu . . . Yes . . . Yes I killed one of them. I didn't hurt him much. It was quick . . . You see I had to know . . . ' How could he explain it better than that ? 'I had to be sure I was capable of it.' A rehearsal for murder, as it were? 'Yes . . . I was afraid that my will would fail. Now I know that it won't. I couldn't go on without knowing.'

Now that was the marvel of it. He had feared that the task would be too hard for him, but had found it easy. The man he had killed was vermin – of less consequence than a cockroach that crawls from a gutter and is trodden underfoot.

'I can do it now, Lulu.'

Charlie fell asleep then. Unstained by guilt, and with all self-doubt erased, fair dreams carried him to the new day.

He arose feeling quite refreshed, and was at the office by 08.30. He signed the occurrence book with a flourish and prepared himself for 'morning prayers' with CSO Reven Forrester. Several other superintendents of equivalent rank to Charlie were there, as were the senior superintendents in charge of the intelligence and crime bureaux and some less senior men. The biggest thing was a gun-gang robbery that had taken place in no less exalted surroundings than the Peninsula Arcade. Forrester put five OSCB teams on the job, including Team Three of Charlie's division.

Peter Quin, who bossed the Crime Bureau, and who was destined for greatness by virtue of the localization programme, and by marriage to a cousin of the Deputy Director, did his thing on cross-border gun-running. An old, depressing story:

'There are going to be more and more such incidents. Shenzhen is Boom-City, Ging Si. Guns are as easy to buy as toothpicks, there. With Hong Kong bound traffic what it is – five thousand trucks a day through the Lo Wu border post, it's a gun-runner's paradise.'

Shit, they all knew that.

'Things are out of control on the other side of the border. The triads have expanded operations. Big-Circle Gang executions run at four to five a week. In the Shenzhen it's the last days of the Klondike, so naturally their troubles will spill over into Hong Kong.'

And what the hell were they going to do about that? With

resignations from the force at an all-time high, and recruitment at an all-time low. Quin had every right to voice his frustrations, but a few solutions would be more welcome.

Forrester spoke as a schoolmaster to his class; a somewhat hawkish schoolmaster; a somewhat intransigent class. 'We'll take each case as it comes, Peter. The Peninsula job is high-profile, so put on the pressure. Forty-eight hours or we've lost it . . . I'm aware that the gun problem is growing. AKs aren't the worst of it. You'll find an intelligence report on your desk today concerning grenades. An intelligence team observed grenades being passed out prior to a bank job . . . All of which reminds me that some people in this room, you know who you are, have not been on the firing range for specified target work. Rectify that.' He paused as one does confronting an odious chore. 'I am to inform you that Police Tactical Unit fire-power is being brought up to platoon level standards. There is to be a general issue of SMCs to PTU.'

This was a subject of controversy. Not everyone liked the idea of policemen wielding sub-machine guns, but most approved even less of villains with infantry capabilities.

'It had to come,' Charlie's neighbour, a chief inspector from SIU said. 'We've been hopelessly out-gunned. Now we'll show them.'

Superintendent Feng from Research and Analysis was a self-made man; a successful gambler; a prognosticator of note. These attributes engendered respect. So people heard him when he spoke, even if it was as now, with his head hardly raised, with unimpassioned regret:

'The People's Liberation Army garrison in Hong Kong is going to be bigger than PTU, Ging Si. With the British military gone, God help us if we have general disturbances and we're forced to call on PLA troops to do our job. What sort of example will we have set with our machine-guns? They're trigger-happy those PLA soldiers. If they start shooting it will be on full-automatic. There'll be panic in the streets, sir. Hong Kong will bleed for ever. Machine-guns . . . ' He shook his head tiredly.

If Feng wished to say more, now was the time; a deep and austere quiet had enclosed them. But he was done. Forrester stood, leaning his knuckles on the desk-top. He said, 'Well, it's our job to make sure there are no excuses for violence. We must identify potential hot spots. We must take incisive action to neutralize criminal elements out to exploit a situation. It is critical that we stay ahead of the game.' He distributed then some investigation files that he had been reviewing back to the superintendents of OSCB. Each file, and sub-file, and sub-sub-file, now had clipped to it small memo forms, mostly containing unkind comments. The SPs of OSCB were expected to do better, much better, than the regional crime officers.

Morning prayers thus concluded, Charlie stood up to go, but was signalled by Forrester to stand fast. They shared a pot of coffee and some chat while a girl from the typing pool delivered files. When she was gone Forrester said:

'You all right, Charlie?'

'Never better.'

'You look awful, as though you haven't slept for weeks. Why don't you take some leave?'

'None due, Ging Si. You know that.'

'I'll have a chat to the chaps at Welfare Branch. They'll play ball.'

'I'm not sick, Ging Si.'

'You don't look in good shape. PK Lo has commented on it . . . Have you looked at yourself in the mirror lately?'

'I'm OK. I won't let you down.'

'I know you won't let me down. That's not the point . . . Look, if you change your mind . . . '

'I won't.'

'Fair enough . . . Did you see the murder report from Hong Kong Region? It was on the teleprinter this morning; a homosexual, they reckon. Someone strangled him in the public latrine near the Aberdeen Praya sampan-piers.'

The reek of concrete swamped with urine; a row of dank little cubicles with a common central gutter, clogged with the reeking

151

black discharge of human bowels. That was Charlie's memory at that moment.

'Strangled?' Charlie said absently.

'Well, the forensic report isn't in . . .'

Strangled . . . Yes, he could vouch for that. Amazing how the strength had flowed. He'd lifted him clear off the floor and choked the life from him in seconds. That's what the pathology unit would discover. What they would never know was how sweetly easy it had been; how euphorically powerful the killer had felt as he had tightened his grip . . . Forrester was still talking.

'Isn't that a coincidence, Charlie?'

'Isn't what a coincidence?'

'You weren't listening . . . I said that after I left you at Third Uncle's restaurant. I went for a walk along the praya. I saw some full-moon boys trawling for tourist business there.'

'Oh really?'

'Before I forget; Caroline's got the tickets.'

'The opera?'

'*Havoc in Heaven*, at the Ko Shan theatre; tomorrow night.'

'That's fine. That's an excellent opera.'

'We'll meet at Caroline's flat for a bite.'

Charlie walked back to his office at a cheerful pace, passing a fellow superintendent from OSCB and his team at the lift station. They had with them a brown, canvas duffle-bag. A detective was peering into the neck of the bag, he took out a sledge-hammer: 'Shit, there's no crow-bar in here. We'll need a crow-bar.' They were anticipating a forced entry. He envied them; a lively morning ahead. Charlie had no more energetic task to perform than to clear his desk of accumulated paper. However, he had a lunch date of vital concern, with no less a man than the shrewd and hugely wealthy cousin of Tang Tsun.

If Tang Tik-kat had been born in a rice paddy and suckled on sweat, he showed no signs of such hardship. Smoothly, urbanely fused within a grey silk pin-striped suit, he walked with the sanguine, assured gait of the very rich. He wore thick lenses that puddled shrewd, observant eyes and his tone was resolute and manly, yet a prankish chuckle constantly hovered. He would, Lam judged, make a formidable mah-jong opponent. The staff of the Chinese Club did considerable face-work on Tang's behalf – twittering politely in verbal ritual, bowing and gesturing onwards this extremely rich man. Charlie Lam, in Tang's wake, was given face too, but clearly by association only. He didn't mind.

And so they sat down to eat, and assess each other. They debated subjects that might interest any Chinese man: money and horse-racing, and gastronomy. They tossed about Hong Kong's chances against the visiting Japanese soccer side; a subject on which Charlie could speak with authority as he had once toured with the police team, whereas Tang had only played rough and tumble village football on a mountain slope. But the tactics of mah-jong seemed indeed to be Tang's real passion:

'More than any game the psychology of mah-jong can be applied to successful living . . . Do you agree, Mr Lam?'

Mr Lam did not disagree. A further course was brought; vegetarian cutlets that looked and tasted like beef, with side plates of wild rice shoots, straw mushrooms, and celery, and during that taste experience Tang Tik-kat brought his mah-jong analogy to its conclusion:

'We're allotted our seats and we draw our quota of tiles. All that is simply fate, what we are dealt we must accept. But from there on in it's a different matter. Then we must judge whether luck is with us, and if it is, then any risk is justified . . . We may dare then to do anything, and boldly deal with the weaker who oppose us. But it is the man who is out of luck, who tenaciously fights his way back into the game, who must be admired. Agreed or not, Mr Lam?'

'I agree. To change the wind of luck is a feat to be admired.'

'If this were a game then, here and now, and you and I were players, how would you rate your prospects?'

'I did not draw well, but through keeping well hidden I have improved my position. The situation is still dangerous, but as I observe my opponents' play, I perceive their weakness too.'

'Well said, Mr Lam. Your point is taken. You have considerable skill, I see. Hold on to your hand for a while longer; it constantly improves . . . Now on to the game as it affects our mutual interests. I hear you were in Sai Kung recently when a certain event took place.'

Charlie said quietly: 'I witnessed a killing.'

'All right, straight talk; a man who deserved to die, was killed. A life for a life, that's the Chinese way.'

'But not the British way. The Queen of England pardons murderers.'

Tang pecked amongst the mushrooms with his chop-sticks, searching for a tit-bit. He found a morsel and took it. 'Do I detect a hint of bitterness against the law you've sworn to uphold . . . ah? And where have your years of faithful service brought you? Have you ever wondered what will happen to men like you, Superintendent, when the British have gone? . . . The Reds have got many scores to settle. You're on the list, be sure of it. No British passport to wave goodbye with. No Queen . . . Hare rising, Falcon swooping, *pah!* It's a sad betrayal, Mr Lam.'

'There isn't a Cantonese, man or woman, who would disagree with you, but there it is, and there's little to be done but to wait and see. I'm patient.'

Tang looked up sharply. 'Waiting . . . for what? Haven't you seen the madness of Communism yet? My God, they've wrecked everything they've touched so far. Now it's Hong Kong's turn. Still, what you can't change, don't cry over . . . So here are the facts. Her Majesty's Government is shortly to be replaced by the government of the People's Republic of China. A senior superintendent of police has witnessed a crime. He has possibly traced a direct participant of that crime . . . Agreed, Mr Lam. Am I right so far?'

'Yes.' Charlie said. 'That's it.'

'So then this superintendent sends a message to the head of our house, requesting a meeting . . . Now this is not how a murder case is usually conducted by the police, so I ask: what is it that this man wants of our great family? This patient man; what is it that we can provide for him that he cannot obtain for himself? Dare I think that a new passport, a new life would satisfy?'

'No, absolutely wrong, Mr Tang. If I'd had children, for their sake I would have been tempted to ask you for that. For myself, what does it matter? All I have is here.'

'Hm.' Tang's quick chop-sticks nipped at the contents of a bowl of deep-fried lotus roots. 'Try these, Mr Lam, good . . . very good. Yes the family is all that counts. I have children. You would have had children too . . . '

'My wife is dead.'

'I know that. I know all about that. A foul murder. Tragic, tragic. Death would not atone for such guilt . . . Is that it then: a life for a life? As it was in Sai Kung?'

'Lonnie Huang killed my wife. I need White Lotus's help to find him.'

'To kill him?'

'I think of little else. We were in love, Lulu and I. We knew each other since childhood. And he tortured her to death.'

A waiter brought hot damp towels and Tang took one and wiped his mouth. 'I see.' He tossed the towel back into the dish. 'Yes, I sympathize with you, Please understand that it is not for me to agree to or to deny your request . . . White Lotus, ah? Some day you must tell me what is known by your people about White Lotus . . . But I'll see that your request is presented at the right level . . . and it will be considered. That's all I can promise you. Do you understand?'

'Yes.'

'If it was up to me then I would say: "Here is a man we can trust; a man who is in a position to be of great service, not just today, but in the future . . . " Is my judgement of you close to the truth, Mr Lam?'

'I would have to think on it. If Lonnie Huang was delivered to me by White Lotus then I would be in eternal debt.'

'Good answer. Yes, exactly what I would have expected from a man of your skill. Yes, it's in times of need and great danger that allies find each other.'

Charlie said humbly: 'You've given me hope.'

'Tell me, why did this man kill your wife? What made him do such a terrible deed?'

'Greed. Murderous greed. It began with the theft of a ring.'

'Where? When? Describe the ring.'

'A ruby; a magnificent pigeon's-blood stone, more precious than diamond. She was loaned the ring on her wedding day, and lost it then, too. It was too big for any of her fingers, and she dropped it while changing at the reception. Lonnie Huang must have picked it up and smuggled it out of the restaurant . . . He contacted her a few days later, and told her to meet him outside a chai tong in old Yau Ma Tei. Then he took her to a building . . . And there . . . '

'Yes, quite,' Tang said consolingly. 'He would have had to do that in order to protect himself. She acted irrationally in going there, but there it is. And now Huang must be found. The ring is the key. That's obvious. That bauble would lead to Huang . . . But I can make you no promises.' Tang stroked his chin-tip magisterially. 'You said you are a patient man. Be patient now, in this matter. I don't blame you for your anger, but where has it got you so far? I can see it in you like a tiger in a bird-cage. Hold it back whatever you do.'

5

HAVOC IN HEAVEN

Havoc in Heaven. It was an appropriate name for the story unfolding on the stage of the Ko Shan Theatre before an audience of two thousand. Reven Forrester was there – third row back – constantly aware that his lanky gwailo physique was all but blocking off the centre-stage action from the minute Chinese lady in the seat behind him. In a vain attempt to gain her rightful view, she lay dismally drooped half-way across her neighbour's lap, and this contortion had caused a ripple effect eventuating in a wake of human suffering to his rear. Being the direct and obvious cause of so much discomfort did not make Forrester feel good about being there. Charlie made things worse. He felt obliged to explain the finer points of the symbolism of the actors' gestures as they occurred. As Caroline sat between them this meant that Forrester had to tilt sideways in order to attend these lectures, thus periodically ruining the vision of those in rows D and E and probably F. He could sense the glare of a hundred displeased little eyes upon his back. As involuntarily unloved, yet immovable as a root-stump in a paddy field, cheerlessly he endured.

The basic plot of the opera was of the fable of the Monkey King, which deity felt slighted by not having been invited to a cloud-feast laid on by the Queen of Heaven. So Monkey decided to wreck the function by drinking up all the celestial wine and eating the peaches of immortality and some other scrumptious stuff before the invited guests arrived. After clearing the table Monkey retreats to the Mountain of Flowers and dares the enraged queen to do her worst. Great armies are sent to capture the insubordinate ape, but Monkey is more than a match for them. His magic wand turns back myriads of swords. With incredible acrobatics Monkey rollicks weightlessly through the battle. The aficionados (bar those to the rear of Forrester) all roar with delight. The costumes blaze with gold, crimson and azure, and set the stage alight. The orchestra is stunningly brassy – shocking cymbals and booming drums burst over the audience, who love it.

There were moments of sheer visual brilliance that carried even Forrester's cramped rump on a magic journey from that place unto the celestial throne of the Jade Emperor, whose part was played by Sandy Tang. He had a rare voice all right – a pure and penetrating sound, as Charlie had described it. But that was not the most observant comment that Charlie Lam had made regarding the star singer, that night. He had also given the opinion that Sandy Tang was the weak-hinged gate to the fortress of his brother. And, my God, if that wasn't the truth . . .

Sandy Tang's hands had that trickle-quick quality of the magician, and while he sang the audience sat fixed in silence: and when he stopped there was a brief vacuum of all sound, a space of wonderment when nothing stirred, then came a deafening applause. Forrester's gaze was constantly active, and it flickered from the brilliant stage light to the features of his friend, but one seat to his right. Charlie Lam sat hunched slightly forward, his lips narrowly parted, his head obliquely cocked, and he was frowning. Forrester studied him and what he saw intrigued him, for Charlie's eyes were bitterly hostile. No mistake; no illusion; he had seen that look too many times on too many faces to misinterpret it. Charlie sensed Forrester's curious stare and turned to meet it, and in an instant the passion of hate was displaced by a smile – a prosthesis as obvious as the business that was being played out on the stage before them. Both men returned to the gaudily attired Jade Emperor, Sandy Tang, who with quivering cheek and martial strut, rendered in full throat the final passage of his role. Applause descended on him like sudden thunder, and he drank it up and swelled with it, posing gloriously with flashing eyes, and peacock chest.

And Charlie Lam clapped too, adding to the adulation as he did – crying out with the others; *good, good, good!*

Forrester was close enough to see the sweat trails that had sprung through the laminate of make-up on Sandy's skin, but his proximity gave him greater vision than that. Beyond the silk armour, behind the fleshy face, deeper than the exquisite self-love and swagger there hid a woefully weak man.

Charlie Lam, who must have known that all along, turned to face Forrester then, his eyebrows raised in question. And Forrester knew exactly what he was asking: had he, or had he not shown up the soft underbelly of Tang Tsun? The answer was a cautious, yes.

And what better bait to hook Sandy Tang than pretty Noona Cham.

'There is a story, a story of long ago, about the Emperor AiTi who dearly loved a most handsome youth called Tung. AiTi took Tung with him wherever he went – to feasts and dog fights, and they flew kites. No more perfect relationship could have existed than theirs. One drowsy afternoon in the heat of summer, the emperor lay listening to music with his favourite sprawled out at his side in deep sleep. Tung's face was pillowed on the sleeve of the imperial robe, and AiTi would have been content to lie there, gazing at Tung's beautiful painted face until the boy awoke. But this could not be. AiTi was obliged to attend to his imperial duties. It was unthinkable, however, that Tung's rest should be disturbed. So AiTi called for a knife, with which he severed the sleeve on which Tung lay. And so the boy slumbered on while the emperor slipped away. Well, AiTi arrived at court, but behold, one sleeve of the imperial robe was shorter than the other! This is how homosexuals acquired the name: "Cut-sleeves" . . . Did you know that story, Noona Cham?'

'It's a beautiful story. Is it true?'

Sandy Tang stared into his dressing-room mirror, pausing at his chore, poised with a dollop of cold cream held close to his

159

cheek. The reflection of his questioner was in the mirror, too. He addressed it:

'True? Come stand next to me, Noona . . . Closer, so that your face is next to mine. Now what do you see in the mirror?'

'Two faces.'

'Do you? Isn't it just the reflection of two faces that you see?'

'I suppose it is.'

'Is a reflection the absolute truth?'

'Yes. If I wink, I'm winked back at. If I smile that face smiles in exactly the same way, see . . . So it's the truth.'

'I wish I could be as sure as you. I sometimes think I'm deluded in everything; it's all a dream; whether this side of the mirror or not.'

Noona laughed. 'It's not a dream, unless we're both in it together.'

'Oh, I've had many a conversation in my dreams. How can you be sure it's not a dream, all those winks and smiles, and any other check you care to make might just be part of it . . . You do dream don't you, Noona?'

'Of course.'

'So, suppose then that this is your dream, and that these hands of mine, this fine clothing and this reflection are just representations; paintings, as it were, on the mirror of your mind . . . an invention.'

'But you are real, look I can touch you.'

'Only your senses tell you that. Perhaps your senses delude you, and this is your eternal dream world.' Sandy Tang slapped the cold cream on to his face and began to massage it vigorously into his cheeks. 'Two and two makes four, a wheel is round and capable of rolling, and elephants are bigger than chamber-pots – my senses tell me that. And whether I live it, or I dream it, it's the same. So I prefer to believe that this is my dream. In which case who is there to argue with me, excepting the gods who, in their wickedness, made me as crazy as I undoubtedly am . . . Pass me the tissues, Noona, so that I can emerge, as me, from this mask; like a flower from its bud . . . I love beauty, Noona.'

'You shouldn't talk like that, Sandy; it's bad luck to talk about the gods. I once knew a man . . . '

'Fuck the gods. Fuck them all . . . Am I clean, Noona? Here, behind my neck. Am I clean? Look closely, ha.'

As Noona bent forward Sandy reached up his hand and touched Noona's cheek in that special, unmistakable way. Noona shivered and tautened and his words trembled:

'It's all off, Sandy . . . all the make-up is off.'

He did not move as Sandy Tang turned his face from the mirror and kissed him fully on the mouth. He moaned very slightly as Sandy began to undress him. He knew that his body would please the man who loved beauty.

'Oh wonderful dream-child, prove to me then that this is you, and you are reality, and reality is pleasure unending. I'm drunk on you, Noona. I've wanted you since the day you arrived. Judge my passion by the size of me . . . '

Noona judged him to have a massive passion. But he could match it. Talk of the gods! Here reaching for him was a god, acclaimed and adored, and worshipped with pounding applause. He would give this man-god his soul if he asked for it. How insufficient an offering was his mere body. He came then, gladly into Sandy's deep embrace.

So Sandy and Noona became 'cut-sleeve' lovers, and swore to remain as close as the saliva and the tongue. They had dinner together that night then went on to Sandy's high-rise flat on the very peak of Shan Teng. Noona had never before shared in such a rich man's view – Hong Kong spread lavishly out like a jewelled, dark carpet down to the water. A moon as bright as a five-dollar coin in the west sky.

'Come to the bedroom . . . You'll like the bedroom.'

The bed was circular and draped with green satin. There were mirrors all around. Countless Noonas and countless Sandys swarmed together in amorous embrace. They drank cold champagne then, thronged with writhing reflections, fell together on to the green drapes and groaned with love. Then they lay in languid contentment in the lap of sleep.

Noona awoke with a snore caught briefly in his throat. A small headache throbbed at his temples, and he was thirsty. Moving lightly so as not to awaken Sandy, he slipped from the bed and went in search of water, and found a plum-tiled bathroom with atrium lighting and huge green ferns. He drank water from a brass tap, and discovered a box of aspirins. Of course, here was the ideal place for more mirrors, all filled with multi-faceted views of that room's occupant. Noona examined his slim perfect body; tossed his head, delighted with the swirl of thick black hair. He pirouetted, then sank into a Tai Chi stance, swaying his body – wave hands like cloud – golden cock stands on one leg – fair lady works at shuttles. The art he had not practised for years flowed back into his limbs, and his fine lean muscles slid beneath his skin as he danced in exquisite self-enchantment. Then he stopped, suddenly mindful of how tenuous was his handhold on happiness.

He remembered the towering, cruel gwailo officer of police – the one they called Ging Si. He remembered his frowning words. Noona's physique slumped then in a great sighing shudder.

After a while he went back to the bed, but he could sleep no more. His mind drummed, baffled like a hornet on a window-pane, seeking a way to escape from his predicament. But there was none; none but the route offered by the gwailo officer – the betrayal of beautiful Sandy Tang. It was an awful thought – but more terrible by far was the visualization of Noona Cham, alone and unbefriended in the dock at the High Court . . . and what might result from that catastrophe did not bear thinking of . . . No, tomorrow he would go to the Ging Si, as instructed, and though he might fabricate in a small, face-saving way, his narrative in general would bear the truth.

There was to be no face-saving for Noona Cham, no squirming lies or omissions. By pure intimidation Forrester intended to ensure that. He had the little faggot brought before him in a stark, grey room approximate to the detention cells at the Kwun Tong police station. There was a table, a tape recorder, and two chairs, and the only view was of a passageway that held four steel cell doors, tightly, threateningly locked shut.

'Sit down,' Forrester commanded.

Noona obeyed; somewhat petulantly, and nervous, but not in the trembling funk that Forrester had anticipated.

'These are the rules, Mr Cham. I will ask questions, and you will answer them. I want no evasions, no hesitations, no fucking about. I will know at once if you lie, and then I will punish you.' He pressed the recorder button. 'Do you understand, Mr Cham?'

'Yes.'

'What is your name?'

'My name? . . . Noona Cham.'

'I want your given name, your real name.'

'Cham Naam Tak.'

Cham Southern Virtue. What a travesty. 'Your age?'

'Eighteen years.'

'Where do you come from? What village?'

'Fukien Province, Chiu Chau District, I don't know what village.'

'When did you come to Hong Kong?'

'I came as a boy, to find work. I don't know how old I was then . . . ten, maybe.'

'Are you a homosexual?'

Proudly answered: 'Yes.'

'Is Sandy Tang a homosexual?'

'Yes.'

'How do you know that he's homosexual?'

'You told me . . . *You* told me, Ging Si. Don't you remember your own words?'

'Yes, I did tell you that. Something else that I told you was to refrain from smart talk. Don't waste my time, Noona. How do you know that Sandy Tang is homosexual?'

'Last night we did secret things together.'

'Secret things? Does that mean that you had sex with him?'

An instant of amusement turned the corners of Noona's mouth; then he nodded.

163

'I'm afraid you'll have to answer yes, or no. The machine can't pick up your gestures, Noona.'

'Yes.'

'Yes, what?'

'*Yes*, I had sex with him.'

'Do you know that in Hong Kong that is a criminal offence?'

'Yes. But you asked me to do it, so how can you prosecute me for it?'

'Bright boy, Noona. Now, I want you to tell me all that's happened between you and Sandy Tang since the time you met him. Consider nothing to be irrelevant; no detail too trivial to be mentioned. It's all important . . . Go on.'

The story straggled at first as Noona randomly tossed in his experiences. But progression brought order, and order brought description. And Reven Forrester, who had thought himself to be shockproof to any action by man, was shocked. The amazing, and innovative, perversions that Noona depicted had Forrester squirming – still he'd asked for detail, he could hardly reverse his request. And though Noona did not intend it, some of his descriptions were pungently funny. A giggle was sputtering around in Forrester's belly, threatening to erupt and wreck the façade of the stern and unforgiving cop.

'Sandy read to me from a book – *Precious Mirror for Gazing at Flowers*. All love-stories of men from the theatre of the old days. It told how apprentices, and dressers like myself, were graded and progressed . . . It was custom for the Master to deflower all his young disciples, and so, to ease the Master's way, the pupils at their classes embedded their rear chambers in pegs that were placed on their benches, and that became progressively larger as they approached the head of the class, until . . .'

Noona was parading his perversity on a banner now. Forrester switched off the tape recorder.

'Sandy said my rear chamber was of perfect dimensions; as if . . .'

Could it be that this brazen twerp was actually enjoying himself; perhaps trying to mock his inquisitor and all he stood for

164

with his septic humour? Forrester concluded that Noona was doing just that. He let the man twit joyfully through the tales of the *Precious Mirror*, and when he was done he called him back to an earlier admission:

'You mentioned just now that Sandy was keen to make a video of the two of you on the green bed . . . You must encourage that, Noona. And when it is done I want it for a while . . . Get that done, Noona. Understood?'

Noona sulked: 'Difficult, difficult.'

'No harm will come to you, or Sandy, from my side.'

'What for then?'

'None of your business, Noona. No prosecution for homo-sexuality; that's all I promise.'

Noona tossed his head in disbelief. Forrester went on: 'So, you will continue as before. You will 'phone me daily. And you will provide me with that video . . . A car will take you back to Kowloon now. Any more questions before you go?'

Noona had a question – one that he had phrased on countless previous occasions: 'When will this be over? When will I have done enough? Not fair you should never answer me that.'

'Fairness does not come into it. Just do as you are instructed, Noona. That's all.'

'Please . . . '

'Perhaps when I have copied that video . . . Yes, when you bring me that I shall reconsider your position. So it's up to you.'

Noona's eyes closed and his shoulders slumped as a man who rests from an awful burden. The joker was gone; this man was all in.

'You've done well, Noona.'

Forrester was appalled with himself for having said that; for his moment of belief in this perverse man. He walked from the detention block to the sunshine. Gilchrist MacNaughton stood on the parade ground talking to a uniformed inspector, who braced up into a salute as Forrester came on. MacNaughton hailed his CSO:

'Mr Lo sent me to find you, sir. There's been another poof

murdered, for want of a better term. This time in Kwun Tong. I knew ye was here . . . ' A car with Noona in the back seat drew away from the parking-lot. MacNaughton cocked his head towards it distastefully. 'Wi' that one.'

Forrester said, 'Shit.'

'That's right, sir. Aye . . . well Mr Lo wants ye to look at it; thinks there's a pattern developing. Some daft bugger is bumping off the poofs.'

'Sorry, MacNaughton . . . '

'I said, sir: "Mr Lo is of the opinion . . . "'

There were days when MacNaughton's pibroch burr made conversation an ordeal. Forrester had diagnosed the malady as recurrent, incurable homesickness. The man was a Scot, and needed to hear the pipes swirl and to do wild reels in a kilt, with no underpants. Whatever the aetiology, today was such a day . . . 'bumping off the poofs, sir.'

'I see . . . Well, lead on, MacNaughton.'

The flat was in King Yip lane; a sad, grey six-storey block, sustained by rusty air-conditioners; adorned with hung-out washing. It overlooked a concrete-walled nullah that was flowing quite steadily, but in the dry season might put up quite a stench. They climbed a dismal staircase to the third floor.

The victim was a youth. He was dressed in tight denims and a short-sleeved shirt, and lay sprawled, face-down on the floor. His trouser belt was coiled about his neck, and his nostrils were crusted with dry mucus and blood.

'A fucking full-moon boy,' said a detective sergeant who was wielding a portable vacuum cleaner.

'You're sure?' Forrester questioned.

The cop from the forensic lab pointed to a stack of blue magazines featuring sneering young men with oversized genitals pouched in leather.

'Broke his neck,' said the cop, with a nod towards the corpse, 'then strangled the turd. Same as the other two. We reckon the time of death to be midnight.'

'Any signs of sex . . . sado-masochism?'

'No. He was fully dressed at the time. We'll check him at the lab for lubricating oils and seminal stains. But I would say, no.'

'Any flat-mates? Witnesses?'

'We've took them in,' MacNaughton said. 'Four groon males, for want of a better term. All poofs, or I'm rycht fraoch gorm . . . Bloody sick.'

Forrester did not trouble MacNaughton for a translation. He had the gist of it. He took a brief look around the small flat. Two single beds, a melamine table, and a portable radio, that, more or less, comprised the furniture. The table held a few brandy bottles, all of them empty, and an ash-tray overspilled with cigarette butts. All that remained of the air-conditioning unit was a rusty shell upon which stood a chipped porcelain figurine of Kuan Kung, and a few lesser immortals, all in bad repair.

'None o' his mates were wi' him at the time. Just our stiff and the killer . . . Must ha' picked him up at Kwun Tong pier. That was this poof's beat, they say . . . Aye, well if there's anyone else you'd like to hand the case to, sir, I'd be more than . . . '

'Gilly,' Forrester interrupted. 'Not one of our three homosexual victims had intercourse just prior to death. I think Mr Lo is dead right. There *is* a pattern to the killings . . . Well get on with it, lad. I'm going to take a walk.'

'Aye, sir.'

'Someone's got to do it, Gilly . . . Be glad you're not on the pathologist's lab team, imagine what those poor buggers have to poke their noses into.'

'Yer right, sir,' MacNaughton said gravely. 'Terrible business.'

Forrester took the MTR underground back to Admiralty, emerging, umbrella-less, into a downpour that stalled him in the corner of a chrome and plastic coffee shop. Still, the cappuccino was good, and it was pleasant just to dawdle there and watch the rush-hour crush weave through the shopping-mall. Swarms of humans like termites in some meandering subterranean passage, flowing in and around each other, each programmed to his own special task, yet in some small way affecting the whole. He glimpsed Charlie Lam scurrying in the direction of Police HQ, a shoe-box clutched tightly to his chest. He might have called Charlie back had the crowd been less viscid, and good company guaranteed. But the truth was that Charlie's recent moods veered so uncertainly, and radically, it had become a risk to engage him.

Forrester took out his pocket-diary and checked his appointment list – no hurry to be back at his desk. He was about to re-pocket the little book when a mite of intuition, as small as one of those meandering termites, emerged and crawled across the paper. In following it, his pencil wrote:

Surveillance on Noona Cham/Sandy Tang, adequate?

He snapped shut the diary and slipped it into his breast pocket, then signalled for more coffee, and drank slowly, reflecting as he sipped on the temperament of Charlie Lam.

It was Charlie who caught up with Forrester when at last he arrived (rain-spotted) in the bleak corridors before the Organized and Serious Crime Group offices. Charlie came up quickly, gingered with excitement. He called out, '*Wai*, Reven . . . hold up a minute.' He held out the shoe-box. His news was that nimble First Aunt had solved the puzzle.

'Here, Reven.'

Forrester unlocked his office door, then took the box. Charlie Lam sat and regarded his superior officer speculatively as he lifted the lid. Charlie said, 'First Aunt folded it back into its original form . . . Amazing thing, ha? Whoever made it was an artist. Have you ever seen anything more cleverly folded? Look at the petals, you could fool a bee with this thing. It's a masterpiece.'

Forrester lifted a paper lotus from its protective bed of shredded tissue. He peered into the throat of the flower and there was his message. He tried to read it. There were four characters, all of them unknown to him.

'Ancient characters,' Charlie Lam said. 'Ming dynasty. First Aunt couldn't read it either. She 'phoned me and asked if she should take the flower to her professor at the Chinese University. You weren't available at the time so I told her to do that. I hope I did the right thing.' Charlie Lam held out a strip of paper on which four modern characters had been written. Forrester took it, and read:

'*Fung-tin hoi-tau* . . . Respected – Sky. Open – enter.'

'Try the Mandarin equivalent, Reven: *feng-t'ien k'ai-tau*: Entrusted by Heaven to Prepare the Way.'

'Neither interpretation makes sense. Why do you Chinese love to make everything so chronically profound? Couldn't the professor untwist the thing?'

'No. But he was full of admiration for the calligrapher. He said he had never seen greater skill.'

Forrester tossed the lotus back into the shoe box. In his pique he'd handled it too roughly and buckled several petals. A quake of frustrated laughter came, and Charlie Lam who would never completely understand the humour of the white race smiled too; he wondered if Forrester had discovered in that obviously luckless message a vein of wit.

'Crazy, ha, Reven?'

'Crazy. Yes.'

'Flower . . . paper flower, for a man. Crazy like anything.'

Both men looked down at the lotus – white, in its froth of limpid tissue, as though floating in some stagnant temple pond, and there was no doubt then in Forrester's mind as to its origin. 'White Lotus sent it to me, Charlie. And they delivered it right to my doorstep. Someone on our staff, Charlie . . . I don't know what to make of it.'

'Something not nice. The triads call this folded paper a Gall. It's less than a threat, more than gentle persuasion; it recognizes your power in an unsubmissive way. Do you follow?' Charlie cocked his head and frowned, intent on being taken seriously. 'One day, when you're away from here, you can laugh about it again.'

'If you weren't such a joker, Charlie, then I'd suspect that I'd just been warned that Hong Kong wasn't a good place for me to be.'

'Reven, your father was my family's father, and you are a brother as much as if we came from the same womb. So if you were hurt I would feel the pain.' For an instant Charlie's hand brushed his arm. 'Listen to me then. This is not the Hong Kong that we once knew; a long dark night has settled in, and many bad things could happen before the dawn. Don't ask me how I know; just believe me, as you would a brother. You are the natural enemy of White Lotus, and they realize your strength, so they try and warn you off. But just as they know your strengths, they know your weaknesses, too. Without laying a hand on you, Reven, they could cut you so deeply that you would never recover.'

'They would not dare to touch my child.'

Charlie brushed his hands irritably at that stupid statement. 'When you say that, my heart shivers, Reven. Guard what is precious to you, protect it, and never think for a moment that there are those who would not dare to destroy what is yours. You of all people should know that.'

When Charlie Lam had gone Forrester drew the telephone closer and dialled the number of Caroline O'Shea. It was Amah Lotta who answered. Caroline, she advised, would return shortly. She had taken Shannon to dancing classes . . . 'Dancing classes for a girl, barely three?'

'Oh, she's very good,' Lotta's tone swelled. 'Much better than all the other beginners . . . She's so clever, sir. You should see her do the teapot.'

Instantly appalled: 'You're not letting her fool around with the kitchen appliances, Lotta?'

'Oh, sir. It's a little dance, don't you know?'

'Of course. Of course.' For a moment pride flooded him. His daughter, the best teapot of all, imagine! Then he said sternly: 'Lotta, you have my 'phone number haven't you?'

'Yes, sir. It's written here.'

'Good . . . but I want you to memorize it.'

'Yes, sir.'

'If you have any problems . . . if anything should go wrong, even something small then I want you to 'phone me. Don't hesitate, just 'phone me.'

'Yes, Mr Reven.'

'I would never be cross if you did that, Lotta. Do you understand?'

He heard the brief melody, then, of Caroline's front-door chimes, and said, 'If that is Caroline, then call her to the 'phone.'

It was Caroline, with Shannon's bright bird-chatter alongside. There came the rattle of the handpiece being lifted.

'Hello, Reven . . . Hold on.'

Instructions were issued to Lotta, and Shannon's commotion diminished with distance.

'I'm here,' said Caroline, a little breathless.

'Everything all right?'

'We were at Dancing.'

'I know . . . Why didn't you let yourself in?'

'Well, Mr Nosy, I've mislaid my keys.'

'*When?*' Fear woke up, ravenous. 'Try to remember exactly when.'

'Some time this afternoon. I took Shannon to her class, then went shopping for dress material . . . Nothing to get excited about. The car's still parked in the parking-lot at the Peak. But I had to take a taxi to fetch Shannon and get home. What a bother.'

'Do you have duplicates?'

'Yes, in the telephone table in the den . . . right here.' She jangled keys.

He weighted every word: 'Don't go back until I arrive.'

'There's a taxi waiting downstairs for me.'

'Send Lotta down to pay him off. Stay where you are and keep Shannon with you.'

'Reven . . . what is going on?'

'I'm not sure. Please just do as I say without question, for once. Close your door. Bolt it. Then wait for me.'

He unlocked the drawer of a steel cabinet that was stiff for want of use. It held some personal files – an old-fashioned brown cardboard tied with ribbon. There was a wad of American hundred-dollar bills, some old letters and photographs, and an ivory chop that had served as a signet for his father. Behind all this in a grey, oil-stained cardboard box rested a revolver; a stubby little weapon that bore the Colt emblem on the grip, with

171

the word 'Cobra' stamped on the barrel. He broke open a box of shells and seeded each chamber. A small leather holster fitted the Cobra into the hollow of his flank. In time, the weight of it would become unnoticeable.

It did occur to him that he might have been spooked into over-reaction by Charlie Lam. He thought about this as he steered through the cloying evening traffic, but the truth of it was that Charlie had done no more than bring him face to face with reality. What had happened before could happen again.

He drew into the visitor's parking-lot and was waved towards a vacant space. He knew the code required to pass the lobby door – a glass and aluminium façade that would disintegrate before a single determined shove. There was an attendant in the lobby – an elderly Chinese gent as frail as alabaster. They greeted each other: '*Jo san*', as Forrester passed by. He noticed these weaknesses now and wondered why he had never done so before. The lift transported him swiftly to the sixteenth floor which gave on to a vestibule with two large wooden doors. Caroline's front door lay to the left. The whole thing quailed when knocked upon, as Forrester did then.

Caroline's immediate demand was to know why so much fuss was being made over a lost bunch of keys. 'I've lost them before, and you never went into such a tizz then.'

He told her he didn't remember that incident. She, deter-mined that he should, led at once into a protracted replay of the forgotten event – 'You remember the day . . . And it was when . . .' This gave him the time he needed to pour drinks, to find the sofa and to effect an image of composure. Then he said, 'Caroline, a secret society I have been investigating sent me a message – not easy to interpret, but, clearly, a warning to lay off, or suffer the consequences . . . In which case these people might decide that the easiest way to stop me . . .'

'The keys . . . So you think it's a set-up.'

'I've been complacent; tardy in recognizing the dangers to yourself and Shannon.' He sat back then and awaited her response, and thought that if she were to shatter him with anger, that would be pardonable. But, as Caroline had done so often in the past, she surprised him then.

'I will not allow the threat of some cruddy little criminals to drive my family out . . . No. I intend to leave Hong Kong, and I will, in my own time, and not with my tail between my legs.'

Now he could see her father in her. A Liffey River Dubliner as stubborn as Wicklow mountain-rock who had stayed on after his regiment had left Malaya, and had survived and prospered in that land of rubber trees and graves. But she did not know the risks. He said, very seriously: 'You see, it's different now, lass. I agreed with you before that you should go, but my heart wasn't in it. Now with all my heart I believe it would be the best thing. These "cruddy little criminals" have got so much power . . . You can not imagine how powerful the triads are, and how ruthless. Listen to me; pack up now, and go.'

'I will go in my own time. Run once and you never can stop. Fear generates its own momentum, Reven.'

'Neither is stubbornness a virtue, Carrie. I've seen too many things. Too many people who should have known better making too many irrevocable mistakes . . . '

'Thank you for being so straight with me, Reven. I do not blame you for all this, though.'

'Then you'll go?'

'Not as a fugitive of triad warfare. No. Listen to me. I understand your fear, Reven, and I know where it's rooted. It's strength is in the past, can't you see. Its cause is sorrow and self-blame for the death of a refugee kid whom you loved.'

'Carrie, you can't tear pictures from your mind as though from a scrap-book. I was there when Kit Ling drowned. I saw her go under in that scummy green water, and I was seconds too late to save her. I failed her, and that's the truth of it . . . And now I have my own child. But this is not just about Shannon, lass. It's about you. The thought that someone might harm you terrifies me . . . I love you, Carrie. And I offer no excuse for not realizing it before. Today it knocked me off my feet. I love you.' And where that admission had sprung from he did not know. He hadn't

173

realized he'd owned that emotion until it had grabbed his tongue. But in saying it, he felt good, and tall, as one does when delivering truth.

Caroline sat then. Her teeth gnawed at her lips in an uncertain smile. 'Thank God for the triads then. At last they've done something good . . . Well if you love me don't stand around. Do something. Show me.'

So he kissed her; a hurried affair because suddenly he had much more to say: 'Let me do it then, while my blood's up. Carrie, before you leave Hong Kong . . .'

'Well? What then?'

'Caroline O'Shea, will you have me as your husband?'

She closed her eyes, reached for his hand and squeezed it.

'Well answer me, lass. Is it to be yes, or no?'

She kissed him tenderly in that happy, maudlin mood that is love's irresistible infection, then announced sweetly and precisely: 'Oh yes, I'll marry you, Reven Forrester.'

They did not go to fetch Caroline's Lancia that night. It might break the spell, she whispered: 'Contentment's settled on me like a mist. I can't see anything but you, Reven, nor do I want to. If there's badness out there, waiting for us, let it skulk miserably. We're doubly strong now, you and I. We'll see it through.'

No fervent passion swept down upon them after that, but a voiceless sharing, a tacit yielding – a sighing groan, then infinite inertia. He lay then in the spill of her hair, and whispered strength-giving words. Then came silence. He watched her eyelids twitch in sleep and held her so that even in dreaming she would feel wonderfully safe.

With the passage of time Lonnie Huang's confidence built. His walks became more frequent, more daring and distant; his activities more diverse. His ability to escape from the viscid reach of Lustrous Jade improved his humour, if not his behaviour towards her. That remained absolutely bestial. And she still blossomed in the face of his violence like some great tuberous plant that would not die no matter how brutally it was hacked back. She might have perceived the change in him: he would attack without cause, but at least it was without anger. Also sustaining matrimonial optimism was the fact that Blind-boy always came back to the rice shop. Every morning he was there when she opened the front shutters. He would sit up on his sleeping-mat blinking at the light, then hawk his throat clear, spit, and at once demand tea and conjee to eat. During these perfect moments Lustrous Jade all but burst with love.

Blind-boy did as little work as possible, but his presence inspired in Lustrous Jade surpassing productivity, so that the shop of Mr Tin ran like clockwork. The rice was brought forth, cleaned, dewormed and presented to the customers in perfect little heaps upon the barrel tops. The various other foodstuffs were also offered with great style. As a consequence of superior leadership, and Lustrous Jade's sprawling vigour, profits took an upturn. Mr Tin was cautiously pleased with the state of affairs. He hinted that the managerial position of his entire chain might be applied for by the husband of Lustrous Jade.

Lonnie had no intention of becoming a husband to any woman. He was biding his time, playing the old fool and his elephantine daughter along, and living very well.

There was a mah-jong game almost permanently on the boil in the meat market along the road. There, beneath the obscenely hung carcasses of fat cattle and pigs, worked Ching Big-bui, a Chiu Chau native like Lonnie, and therefore a natural friend. Big-bui claimed that he had once been a cop; a Narcotics detective, in fact. And in that role had taken his first inquisitive whiff of heroin smoke – and found it 'nice'. Now he loved to 'chase the dragon' – a sport nowhere near as physical as the name suggested. All that was required was to place a few heroin granules in a small pod of tin foil, then to rock this over a lighted candle. The dragon is the blob of molten heroin, the chase comes in the pursuit of the little brown trickle – sucking at its fumes through a thick straw. The result, according to Big-bui – pleasure beyond this world – the peace and contentment of the gods.

Lonnie had once tried 'playing the mouth-organ', a variation of the game, wherein a matchbox lid is substituted for the straw. Nausea and confusion had been the disappointing outcome.

'First time is sometimes like that,' Big-bui encouraged. 'Try again.'

Lonnie was content, however, to let heroin be. Mandrax continued to serve as his bridge to heaven. Big-bui conceded that Mandrax was good, too, not as good as heroin, but good, and inexpensive. Not that Big-bui was ever financially constrained. Whether he won or lost at the mah-jong table, or at dice, or cards, Big-bui was always flush, and sometimes generously so. Lonnie was frequently the beneficiary of Big-bui's distribution of lucky-money. And Lonnie excelled at flattery, which improved the situation further. Lonnie, of course, was intensely inquisitive as to his new friend's source of income. A meat-market porter who treated hundred-dollar bills like so much straw was someone worthy of attention. So he watched Big-bui sharply.

One night when Big-bui stood back from an exciting game of pai kau cards (at the height of a winning streak, mark you), yawned, and dawdled off, Lonnie knew that something was up. The time had come to peel off the wrapper of this most well-inclined fellow. He followed his friend into the street, then onwards, and saw that Big-bui's lethargy was mere pretence. He walked through the crowds at a pace that exercised Lonnie considerably – up this street, down the next; hardly pausing to light a cigarette before darting onwards. Lonnie, inexperienced in this form of pursuit, managed yet to keep up, and his excitement heightened with every pace. This was the stuff that movies were made of. Lonnie cleverly deduced that Big-bui's rather erratic route would ultimately lead to the harbour, and so it did. He watched as his friend hailed a water-taxi. He waited for a moment, then did the same thing.

'Where to?' demanded the sampan woman; a surly gold-toothed Tanka who rattled off her tariff.

Lonnie pointed. 'That way.' And off they went; straight across

Aberdeen harbour, or as straight as its jostling, weaving boat community would allow, to Duck-tongue Island – Ap Lei Chau.

If Lonnie had been a fraction less sharp he might have lost Big-bui then. The boat-builders' yards where Big-bui came to shore were poorly lit and Lonnie's sampan woman quarrelled about landing there: obstructions in the water, she sulked.

'Fuck the obstructions!'

'You fuck them.'

'Look, that other sampan went in there.'

'Perhaps she was paid more for it.'

He pried loose a few more coins from his wallet which improved her night vision at once, and in they went. He called her a born-of-an-egg Tanka whore and she called him the product of a rat's anus, and on those terms they parted. Thankfully she could not have observed his ignominious glide into the harbour water from the slimy slope of a slipway. By the time he'd collected himself from that soaking he knew that the hunt was over. Big-bui could have been anywhere on Duck-tongue Island by then.

Lonnie felt for his cigarettes and found them to be soaked. He squelched miserably through the boat-yard towards Ap Lei town, cursing the darkness, the wetness, the lateness of the hour; a bruise on his knee that was beginning to stiffen; but most of all accursed was his so-called friend, Ching Big-bui, who was (let's be honest about it) the cause of all this indignity. Then he stopped and sniffed the air, his nose twitching and wrinkling as it worried at the odour that hung there. A gust of wind and it was gone. Lonnie walked on. A big moon swept out briefly, showing piles of timber and drums, and the bare ribs of an unbuilt junk. He saw the high hull of a fishing vessel up for repair . . . And there was that smell again, more pungent than before – a repulsive, ammoniac sort of stink that momentarily stung his nostrils. Not the sawdust and tar smell one expected from a boat-yard. A few paces to the right brought the reek upon him so harshly that tears welled blindingly up. Now he could hear the hum of an extractor fan – now he could see it spinning in its housing. Now super-bright pain flashed in his skull, and a thousand bits of thought instantly incinerated; burned into a single smut.

From this bleak fleck he expanded back to earth with a hiss and a rush into a shimmering pool of voices, and when he opened his eyes there was Ching Big-bui's inverted face amongst some others, all spinning above the man who'd fallen from the merry-go-round, whose skull was crammed with pain.

When the voices became coherent, and the faces more stationary, it occurred to Lonnie that he was in serious trouble. He heard some angry suggestions:

'Kill him now, ha! He's a needle, for sure.'

'Dump him in the deep.'

And kinder ones: 'He's Chiu Chau, like us. Never a needle. Give him a chance.'

Lonnie's recent experiences came tumbling helter-skelter back to mind. He certainly was not a needle; to accuse him of being a police spy was most unfair, and required instant, if respectful denial. He sought out some triad jargon that might impress:

'Sirs . . . I'm not a needle . . . May a thunderbolt strike me, if that isn't so . . . may a thousand swords . . .'

'What's your name, ha?'

'Blind-boy,' Big-bui supplied. 'I told you what his name is.'

'Let him speak for himself.'

Lonnie Huang said, 'My humble name is Lonnie Huang. And how could I be an informer? I'm on the run from the wind . . .'

'All horse shit.' The big man who held that opinion, held, too, an ugly cudgel which he whacked into his palm in emphasis of each word. 'Let's wash this little fart; no delay.'

As 'washing' meant instant demise, there was reason for alarm. Lonnie's voice squeezed back into the debate:

'Don't think me rude, sirs, but it's easy enough to check on my story. My name, and a sketch of my face, appears on every police bulletin-board in Hong Kong.' He didn't presume to add that there was a police station not a kilometre from there. Yet Lonnie knew precisely where he was then. Slow to catch up, yet with him now was his sense of smell. And between the legs of his captors he could see various bits of equipment to do with that awful stench. There were huge stainless steel pressure-cookers and some LP gas cylinders, there were trays mounted beneath bar-heaters, redly aglow. A huge glass funnel with some tubes attached to it stood on the floor, and next to this a small compressor hummed. The whole place looked like a rather weird, untidily cluttered kitchen, but Lonnie knew that it wasn't. This was a heroin factory, without a doubt. And knowing that made Lonnie feel distinctly queer.

'I'll check the police station.' Big-bui was being helpful again. 'I was once a cop. I know my way around that place. If the poster's there, I'll bring it back.'

'Too much heart,' trembled the prisoner. He thought: let there be a poster there for God's sake, or Mr Hit, here, will disintegrate me.

As it turned out, the wanted notice of Lonnie's imagination truly did exist. Their copy was badly dog-eared and punctured by the drawing-pins of the strata of more recent villains. But there it was, a humblingly ugly work of art, nevertheless sufficiently life-like for even Mr Hit grudgingly to concede:

'It's him all right.'

Lonnie was invited to stand. Shivering wet; swooningly sick from the pain that movement brought, but confident that he might yet survive, he stood . . . More questions:

'What made you come here?'

'Sirs, I was following Big-bui.'

'What made you do that?'

The truth, no matter how embarrassing for Big-bui, simply had to be said. 'I was inquisitive. He always had lots of cash on him. I thought I might find out how he got it.'

Eyebrows raised, eyes turned upon Ching Big-bui, who stared artlessly at his toes.

'Brothers,' Mr Hit's weapon went thwack into his palm. 'This is a most serious breach of discipline.'

Lonnie agreed with the brothers. Big-bui shuffled the sawdust

179

at his feet, and said, 'Just a bit of gambling at mah-jong, and dice. No harm in it.'

'Could have been.' A mope-eyed little man pointed with his spectacles at Lonnie and said, 'Point is, what's to be done with the nosy one?'

'Humble suggestion,' said Lonnie. 'Let me be of service to you. I'm Chiu Chau, so I'm one of you. End my life and you're only doing what the wind would commend you to do. Why do their dirty work? Why not employ me? Give me a trial at least. I could learn anything. I'm quick . . . ' Interrupted by the chatter of . . . a monkey! Lonnie gaped disbelievingly towards the sound. Yes, a monkey; perched on a high shelf, grinning, swaying and clicking needle-sharp yellow teeth. Then, with an agile bound, it sprang; bounced from Lonnie, who gave a startled yelp, to the shoulders of the bespectacled man who took no notice of it at all, but laughed at Lonnie. Everyone laughed at Lonnie, who depreciated himself cutely:

'Wah! Sure gave me the fright.'

The tension was broken. The incumbent of the ape introduced it: 'Name is Lucky-boy.'

'Lucky-boy,' Lonnie laughed. 'Seems to like me, ha?' He hoped that Lucky-boy's opinion might carry weight. He knew a Tarzan joke or two, but let well enough alone.

The whole troupe, excepting for Big-bui, who was appointed as Lonnie's guard, adjourned then to a deeper room, presumably to decide on Lonnie's fate. But the omens were good. Big-bui chatted quite amiably with his prisoner.

'Crazy thing you did. Could be dead by now.'

Lonnie, who was vastly unconcerned about what *could* have been, asked: 'Which one's in charge?'

'Ma Lau, the monkey man, is the chemist, so he's important. Mr Hit is a big-balls, too. He likes to kill, but don't worry.' He did not specify why Lonnie shouldn't worry, but it was a nice thing to have said. Big-bui accounted for the status of the others, concluding with himself: 'I'm just a courier, but it pays. You couldn't do that job with your black hands.'

'I could use a smoke. You got a cigarette?'

'*Wah!* You smoke in here now you'll blow us all to hell. Don't you know what's happening here? This is the factory for "red chicken", the best in Hong Kong, ha. One spark now, and *Paa!* no more factory; no more Lonnie either. Soon you can smoke.' Big-bui went to the closed door, behind which Lonnie's fate was under discussion. He cocked his head slightly, vaguely eavesdropping, then shrugged and came back to the prisoner. 'So you're the big-time murderer, ha? Never would have thought it. Why did you kill her?'

'Stupid woman,' Lonnie said, as though gender provided reason enough for homicide. 'She didn't have to die . . . I think she just wanted to die.'

'Some people deserve to die. I knew a man, once . . .'

An inopportune subject. Lonnie changed it. 'Never thought *you* were the master-mind heroin gangster, Big-bui, just like in the movies.'

Big-bui made modest throat noises in acceptance of such admiration. 'Ma Lau is the real tai lo around the factory. But he shows me some things. I'm learning. Some day, maybe . . .'

'Of course, you'll be the tai lo. No doubt in my mind . . . I could work for you then, ha.'

'You need to be rich to get something like this going.' Big-bui gestured towards the drying ovens and the stainless steel bins. 'This stuff costs a lot. But the recipe, ah, that's what you have to know, and that's locked up in Ma Lau's head . . . Do you know how rich that makes him?'

How rich? That question was never asked, for a sudden gust of panic overtook all other thought: *the ring!* My God! Did he still have it, or had these rogues stolen it? His hand flew to his pocket and dug through the stolid wetness. The door opened at that instant and Ma Lau, the chemist, and Mr Hit emerged. Lonnie was to live.

'But certain conditions must be complied with.'

'Yes. Of course I agree.'

Thwack went the cudgel. 'You must become Lo Chiu, a Chiu Chau triad, no delay.'

'An honour I don't deserve.'

'Obviously you cannot expect to go back to the rice shop.'

'Not even,' added Ma Lau, 'to fetch your belongings, or wages . . . or to say goodbye.'

'Absolutely agree.' One of Lonnie's probing fingers discovered the ring. It was hard going to remain crestfallen before such booming good fortune. 'No question of returning – No.'

'You'll serve as a weatherman, here.'

'A look-out. You'll find me suited to that.'

'It would be wise to be good at all tasks from now on. You will swear yourself to Lo Chiu with thirty-six oaths, each one upheld by the punishment of agonizing death.'

'Yes.'

'Enough said.' Mr Hit gave his palm one unflinching, final swat. 'You will be taught certain secret things. Be ready.'

Lonnie could not have been more ready. Yet two weeks passed before he and a score of other Chiu Chau initiates were presented to the Lo Chiu Incense Master, and put to the test. It was a let-down. Lonnie had expected something grander; more awe-inspiring.

He had come aboard a dim merchant junk at night and crouched in the stern with a group of nervously giggling fellow recruits. At a given signal (which he missed), they all stood up and trooped towards a paper-framed gate. A guard with a menacingly held wooden sword challenged:

'What is your purpose?'

The recruits shuffled to a halt, mumbling: 'We come to enlist, and obtain rations.'

'There are none.'

'We bring our own.'

There was a long pause; the guard had presumably forgotten his lines. Another wooden-sworded soldier arrived; the new man seemed more clued up. He intoned:

'The red rice of the army is sharp with grit and stones, will you eat this?'

'Yes,' they all agreed. 'If our brothers can palate it then so can we.'

'When you see the great beauty of our sworn sisters, will you be swayed to adultery?'

'We would not dare.'

'All right then, come into the City of Willows and swear your allegiance.'

So they crawled beneath the wooden swords and before two rows of officials made the thirty-six vows. Lonnie took particular cognizance of vow number twenty-eight:

'I must not covet or seek to obtain any property or cash owned by my sworn brothers. If I have such ideas, I will be killed by myriads of swords.'

There were other oaths of equal stringency, evoking various other unnatural, painful deaths, but number twenty-eight caused Lonnie the most serious anxiety, for he did covet another man's property: Ma Lau's secret formula for red chicken. God, how he wanted that. And regardless of any vow to the contrary he would try to get it. It would make him rich.

The ceremony wound down. There were secret handshakes and signals, and enigmatic poetry recitals. Then all the neophytes stepped through a wide bamboo hoop, over some burning joss-paper, then along a pathway of paper stepping-stones. A squawking cockerel was decapitated and its neck-blood, and a pinprick of blood from each of the recruits, was mixed with wine and the ashes of the thirty-six oaths, and everyone took a swig.

That was it. Lonnie Huang was a full-blown brother of Lo Chui triad society from that moment. He had always wanted to be a triad member and now he was . . . It was an anticlimax. The vastness of it, the glory of it had somehow passed him by. Yet he was changed. The vows he had made weighed heavily in him; stone-cold, they depressed him.

Lonnie's mind, however, stayed as busy as a basket of crabs, nibbling, nibbling towards that most irresistible bait – the formula. How to get it? He thought there was a way. Ma Lau by virtue of his ability as a chemist was a big-balls at the heroin factory. But in the overall context, contrary to what Big-bui thought, the man didn't amount to much. And that was the chemist's own fault. Ma Lau's problem was that he was small-minded. He had the knowledge to make the best heroin in Hong Kong, but was clueless when it came to the conversion of knowledge into cash. And that was an exploitable situation if ever there was one.

Ma Lau was addicted to his own superior product. Lonnie soon learned that. Amazingly, Lucky-boy, the ape, was also hooked. After the nightly quota of red chicken was complete they would sit together, those two; Ma Lau chasing the dragon with a rolled-up brown paper straw, while Lucky-boy wrinkled his nostrils above the fumes, coming in for a big sniff now and then, with eyes all glassy and slow.

They were at it when Lonnie and Mr Hit arrived back from the initiation; squatting side by side on an old coir mattress in the shine of a dangling light-bulb. Lucky-boy blinked stupidly towards them. Ma Lau, stripped to the waist, didn't appear to notice their arrival.

'Crazy,' was Mr Hit's only comment. The enforcer had a flat in Kowloon and a big Mercedes to transport him there, so he didn't hang around.

Lonnie on the other hand had nowhere else to go, no desire to sleep, and no one else to talk to. He sat on the lumpy mattress next to the chemist. Ma Lau turned his pinpoint pupils on Lonnie then, and gestured towards a small bowl of red. 'Ten times complete; ten times beautiful.'

'What's that, Uncle?'

Ma Lau sighed slowly. 'Plenty for you, plenty for all of us.'

'No mistake.'

'You're a good fellow, Lonnie. I'm glad you came to sit here. This ape of mine just goes to sleep; he's no friend at all . . . Do you like poetry, Lonnie?'

'I heard some once, Uncle.'

'Listen:

184

> "Take pleasure in youth,
> It fades soon enough,
> Don't believe me,
> Look at the grass
> where the frost has bitten . . ."

Did you like that, Lonnie?'

'The grass where the frost has bitten, ha?'

Ma Lau took a pinch of red from the saucer and reloaded the silver-paper pod. Lucky-boy sat forward expectantly. More verse was summoned up as they prepared to smoke:

> 'The scent of love fades,
> The vat cools,
> I board the boat alone,
> Wild geese return . . .'

The chemist wedged the straw into his mouth then, effectively ending the recitation. Both Lucky-boy and he bent to the candle flame. After that 'chase' ape and owner sat staring blankly at each other. Lonnie decided that the time had arrived to quote his values.

'What I like more than poetry, Uncle, more than anything is money. Money is good. Money makes a blind man see. Money is a dragon; poverty is a worm.'

'Mm.' Ma Lau pondered on that.

'So I ask myself: why are some people content to be worms, when they could so easily be dragons?'

Lonnie thought that his analogy had passed with the clouds. But after a while Ma Lau commented somewhat dreamily: 'A most absorbing question.'

'Do you see my point?'

'Ah, yes.'

'Don't you desire to be rich?'

Ma Lau's lucid moment had passed, he swooned out on the mattress, mumbling, stunned. Lucky-boy toppled sideways, too,

185

in a sprawl of furry limbs, twitching lightly in some sublime ape-dream.

Lonnie took from his pocket the small, cloth parcel of the ruby ring and peeled away the fabric. The big stone swelled ruddily in the raw light.

> 'The glow of fire,
> The flush of dawn,
> It twists my heart . . .'

Ma Lau had seen the ring through his dazed black eyes and he wanted it.

A veteran kung-fu fighter called Shrimp bossed up the weathermen. Shrimp wore a baseball cap and a T-shirt with a Lucky Strike emblem, but was a non-smoker. He demonstrated to Lonnie how the blaze of a match could burn away a man's night vision. He taught Lonnie how to use the light of the moon to best advantage, and how to cup the ears to pinpoint a source of sound. He trained the new man to move like a cat through the darkness. Indeed, Shrimp's entire curriculum was based on the temperament of the cat: stealth, vigilance, cunning and a kindredship with the night. For that was when the heroin factory opened its doors, and Ma Lau the chemist arrived to mix his odorous chemicals, and turn out yet another batch of famous red chicken. If the wind were to strike, then they too would draw in at night. So that was when the weathermen manned their posts, cat-like. Lonnie soon got bored with this tiring chore. It would, he thought, be so much more congenial to have money, and drive around in a sleek silver Mercedes, like Mr Hit, doing big business in air-conditioned offices. *That* was the way to go. And if that cretinous gorilla could do it, Lonnie could too, blindfolded.

In the morning the ship-builders' yard conceded to legitimate industry. Buzz-saws and planers screeched and threw out storms of wood dust. Strong-armed carpenters drove nails as thick as pencils into hardwood hulls. And the winch clanked to the deep throb of its diesel engine as it hauled a big junk in for scraping, or varnishing, or to be fitted with new propellers. In the midst of this great racket Lonnie slept, but not very well. He was bloated with discontent, and he was worried too. Ma Lau could cause Lonnie's ruin if he wanted to. If he told Mr Hit about the barter Lonnie had proposed, there would be slaughter.

But Ma Lau it seemed had forgotten the episode of the ring, or if he hadn't, had seen no great wrong in Lonnie's action. He came; he made his marvellous drug, then coddled himself and his monkey in its forgiving haze and quoted dreamy poetry until the dawn.

But Ma Lau had not forgotten the beauty of the ruby, nor the insinuation that it might be traded. It was the ungracious Mr Hit who announced to Lonnie that he was in for promotion.

'Assistant chemist, boy . . . Ma Lau has quarrelled with his present assistant. Why he should choose you . . . still there it is. Just do as you're told.'

Lonnie promised that he would.

'It's a trifling job – fetch and carry. No more to it than that.'

He would be the best fetcher and carrier that ever a chemist had had.

'You've got inch, boy,' The infamous cudgel thumped hollowly upon Lonnie's breastbone. Mr Hit smiled unlovingly, and burped garlic in Lonnie's face: 'Listen, I'll be watching you. One wrong move is one too many.'

'No wrong move, Teacher.'

Lonnie began his new job that night. It was as Mr Hit had said – fetch and carry, scrape, scoop, pour and stir. The nose stung and the eyes streamed and a migraine kicked at the skull-bone. If he'd thought he might learn vital secrets in the doing of all this, he was soon disillusioned. At the night's end, when Ma Lau and his ape sat down to smoke, Lonnie's only gain in knowledge was that in the manufacture of red chicken, the assistant chemist suffered considerably.

Ma Lau smiled sympathetically and offered his cure: 'It leads

187

the dead.' Lucky-boy and his keeper bent to the fumes. Lonnie declined. And then the poetry came trickling from Ma Lau:

> 'A mountain
> Half-way to the moon.
> I sit and look up,
> And wonder in whose hand I sit.
> A boat
> Half-way home
> I hear the sea hiss.
> And wonder in whose tears I float.
> A window . . . '

And so it went; poetry, verse after senseless verse, and not a word of guidance for the new assistant, not a hint, not a trick. To hell with it. Lonnie crawled to his bed and wished his crushing pain on Ma Lau.

And the next night was the same.

On the third night of Lonnie's apprenticeship Mr Hit came calling: 'To see how things are.' From Lonnie's point of view they could not have been worse, but he overheard Ma Lau air quite an optimistic view regarding Lonnie's potential:

'Jade might lay hidden in a rough stone . . . Give time, Mr Hit. Give time.'

'Guard against . . . '

Lonnie was unable to hear more of Mr Hit's warning. It was bound to have been direful. Mr Hit was built from hate.

Ma Lau might have thought so too for when the enforcer was gone he beckoned to Lonnie. Secretively he said: 'Better you stay far from that one.' A new, conspiratorial tone that greatly intrigued Lonnie. 'Mr Hit gets bored unless he's breaking bone.'

'You would know, Uncle.'

'I could tell you stories, ha . . . never mind. The thing is to be careful.' As though they should both be so.

'Yes, Uncle.'

'So, there were things that you showed me that I would like to see again; a most elegant ring.'

'Oh, very beautiful . . . and *expensive*.'

'The worm and the dragon, ha . . . Well of course it's better to be a dragon, but not always possible . . . '

Lonnie undid the tiny parcel, Lucky-boy paused at his grooming, then came forward to see. Hungry-eyed as though some morsel of fruit was being peeled for him, he reached up his hairy, human-like paw, which Ma Lau smacked away. Mr Lau's eyes were just as filled with craving as his ape.

'Aah,' sucked Ma Lau. 'Yes, that would certainly cause me to think . . . Well, I might teach you some things, Lonnie, you seem to have the touch. I wouldn't have taught you if I thought you didn't have it in you. You can believe that. But I can't work for nothing. I'll never do anything for nothing. Do you mind if I hold it for a moment . . . Thank you, Lonnie.' Ma Lau found a finger to fit the ring and presented it to the bright light. 'Oh, yes . . . Oh yes . . . Is it then your wish that you and I should trade, Lonnie, the ring for the recipe? Red chicken for a red ring. Poetically, it's equitable. But my knowledge could make you a hundred times richer than the price of this bauble. Have you more to trade?'

'Uncle, it's the best offer you will ever get in your life. I'm not mustard green, ha. I've worked things out. Sure, *I'll* get richer with the knowledge than the ring, but *you* never will. You, Ma Lau are a slave to your own red chicken. That's all you have, and it's all you want, and Mr Hit and the other tai los know that, and they approve . . . more than approve. They wouldn't feel secure with a chemist who wasn't addicted. So here you are, Uncle, and here you stay, miserably paid, but able to soak up all the red chicken that your brain can absorb . . . Take the ring, Ma Lau, as you say: poetically, it's equitable.'

Ma Lau chuckled a bit, then pulled a wry face as though agonizing over the deal. He said, 'Well, you drive a hard bargain, but that's all right. And though I'm not as poor as you seem to think, yet I'm not insulted . . . You'll learn fast, Blind-boy. I can see that.' He began then to teach Lonnie as a pupil should be taught: 'At the beginning there is a morphine base.'

Morphine base came from Burma in the form of bricks; off-white, marked '999'. The bricks were crushed into small cubes, then steam-dried until pure white.

'Then the cubes are made liquid.' Dissolved in a bucket of acetic anhydride. This was the operation that caused the give-away stench of the heroin factory. Aieya! how the eyes streamed in the fumes that rose. 'Smother the bucket in wet towels but be sure it doesn't boil over . . . then pour in cold water and two pounds of chloroform. This mixture is called *pui*.'

Lonnie was the perfect pupil. His pencil skipped and darted, and the lesson flew to paper . . . 'Filtration next, through a funnel lined with filter paper and bone charcoal – four spoons of it. Pour the pui into the funnel.' (This was the big, glass apparatus attached to the vacuum pump.) 'Switch on the pump. Pour water, then alkaline solution over the pui (eight pounds American ICI soda). Then more fresh water to douse the pui – cold at first – then boiling – then cold again. Now take the pui from the funnel and dry it . . . '

Two hours to wait while it dried. During that time Ma Lau read happily to himself from some classical volume, while Lucky-boy wandered around, desolately gazing at the pui and scratching his buttocks. Two hours in ape terms was clearly an eternity. For Lonnie it was a long time too. He paced, abstracted with unreasonable fears of some calamitous event (a heart attack, an earthquake) that might occur and thereby prevent Ma Lau from imparting the final bit of knowledge. But at last, the chemist, without so much as a glance at his watch, announced: 'Time up.'

Ape and assistant came forward to observe the final steps. The pui had become a fine powder. Ma Lau said, 'Watch carefully. Three caps of ethyl-alcohol . . . then heat . . . then pour it into the basin. Now back into the funnel, and on with the pump, and when it's dry we add hydrochloric acid, ninety per cent . . . Then alcohol, five cups for this mix.'

Lonnie scribbled; Lucky-boy chattered and whooped, he knew that the chicken was about to hatch.

'Now is the critical point . . . I pour in ether . . . slowly, see . . . Observe now how it flashes with little golden stars – is that not a beautiful sight? Ah, but it's our signal. Stir, Lonnie, *stir*. If the crystals form quickly, add ether quickly; if they're slow to form then add slowly. Now that's everything. It just remains to dry this stuff.' Lau sighed grandly, and turned to face his apprentice. 'That recipe is older than I am, it was my father's. Now it's your's . . . Father wouldn't believe his eyes if he could be here now – all this equipment. What used to take a full day and night, I can do in minutes. Well that's progress, ha.'

Lonnie helped Ma Lau spread the crystals in drying trays; all of it but for Ma Lau's saucerful. This went into the microwave oven to be quickly dried. 'So that it can be tested by me, Lonnie. Not a batch goes out that isn't first tested.' A responsible attitude.

Master and ape fell silent then, they stared together through the oven door as the saucer of red revolved. *Ping*, went the timer. They took their precious ration with them to the mattress and from then on ignored the new graduate.

Ma Lau wore the ruby ring. He stared at it wistfully as he chased the opium dragon:

> 'The glow of fire
> The flush of dawn
> It twists my heart
> The flame dies
> The sun is transient
> Will you be mine forever?'

Ma Lau did not keep the ruby ring for ever, or even for a day. That morning he sold it to a Kowloon City jeweller whom he knew, for 30,000 dollars.

Still he was sad to part with such a thing – a jewel bright enough to light the way through the caverns of hell.

6

COMING DOWN LUCK

Charlie Lam possessed a crayon drawing that he had done as a child of an airborne green mouse, flying towards a splurged yellow sun with rays that projected from it like the spokes of an ox-cart. He had been a prolific young artist; he'd decorated every scrap of paper that had blown by. But the fantastic green mouse was the sole survivor of those vividly creative years. And the reason for the painting's longevity was that Lulu had preserved it. Her name had not been Lulu then, it had been Virtuous-fragrance, and he too had not as yet been church-christened, and his name was simply, Plentiful.

Plentiful had first met Virtuous-fragrance on the high slope of the wide ceramic gutter that served to drain the monsoon rains from the upper levels of the Ap Lei Chau Good Shepherd play-school. On sunny days, of course, the duet served as a high-velocity slide for the more daring kids. But it was also lots of fun to urinate at the top of the gutter and watch the golden stream speed away. The two activities were not compatible as a participant who was too slow upon the slide could easily be overtaken by the urine jet. Plentiful was aware of this, so why he did what he did when Virtuous-fragrance (a total novice to this sport) was in slow and giggly progress down the slope he did not know. In truth it wasn't an intentionally unfriendly act, and her bewildered frown had upset him. The next day, by way of apology, he gave her the green mouse. And she must have forgiven him for in adulthood she'd become his sweetheart. She had always kept that picture. So now Charlie owned the green mouse again. It was taped on to the inside of Lulu's cupboard door, and every time he saw it, he choked. Lulu was dead, and he was rooted immovably in sorrow.

Charlie Lam was yesterday's man. He did not know this grey and anguished stranger who answered to his name, who did his daily toil; walking bent; speaking tonelessly; eating when raw hunger drove him to food; waiting for the night. For the darkness was generous to him and to his dead bride. He would lie in their bed and she would come in slowly growing whispers, telling him of the agony of her death. He would tell her then of a love that would never die, and they would cry together. When she was gone he would arise with killing on his mind.

That night his hunt took him to Kowloon; to Temple Street; a midnight festival of rogues dressed as merchants robbing the unwary with broadsides of merchandise while shoals of pimps and pickpockets mixed in the tourist tide. Charlie did not care one bit what misdeeds took place in Temple Street. He sat at a table and sipped a beer and observed this endless, restless ravel of people, hoping that the face of Lonnie Huang would come along. It didn't. He finished his beer and moved on.

He walked through the littered streets of old Yau Ma Tei towards the harbour. Tramps, squeezed in like cockroaches beneath the Ferry Street off-ramp, felt him out as he passed, with antenna intuition, and fell silent, or coughed sickly in the smoke of small fires. He was empty of feeling towards them. His direction was set towards the distant amber lights that lit the praya, the godowns and the junks of the Yau Ma Tei typhoon shelter. He did not find Lonnie Huang there. Nor did he see him at the Jordan Road ferry pier. He felt too exhausted to continue walking, so he waved down a taxi, gave his destination: 'Hey-day Club,' then sat staring with sluggard eyes at the regiments of night-walkers. God knows, he would find Huang in the end.

The doors of the Hey-day Club opened to an explosion of music. The walls were midnight-black, and strobe-lights agitated the crush; jerking the dancers into slow flickering frenzy. All of them were men – none of them the object of his search. He

193

stayed long enough to be quite certain of that, then walked back into the night. And there someone called out his name the Fukienese way:

'Ah Lim . . . *Wai!* Ah Lim.'

The man was lounging against a parked car. He was lean and muscular and had the look of a fighter; the disdainful authority of a fighter.

'Ah Lim, you get in here.' He opened the car door.

'Who sent you?'

'It's coming down good luck, Ah Lim. We've found the ring. You get in now.'

'Where to?'

'Kowloon City. Dragon-ridge road. Come. Come.'

Dragon-ridge road, like most other roads of Kowloon City, was long and straight and hedged with grey tenements all hunched-up together, all gored and leaking with neon: Delightful Trading Company; Cheerful Marriage Service; Nice Dragon Investment Company . . . The sign beneath which their car drew up read, Fortune Jewellers. Charlie knew the shop. It had been there when he had been a PC on the beat. The question came naturally:

'Has he got the ring?'

'Not any more.'

The fighter was too vain to resist the smart retort, but Charlie couldn't draw him further. They walked in silence towards Fortune Jewellers.

Mr Chua of Fortune Jewellers sat on the high chair at the rear of his shop and sweated with fear, for he thought he was going to die.

The terror had begun a few minutes before closing time, when from that very same chair he had espied through the one-way glass that fronted his office a young couple walking hand in hand into his shop. They had asked politely, and in Chiu Chau dialect, for Uncle Chua. Now, nearly everyone called him Uncle Chua, but this young man claimed genuine blood-lineage. He said he was from Four Gates Village – Chua's ancestral village, and he named family names. The Chua clan members of Four Gates Village were as numerous as ants in a sugar-mill, so Uncle Chua was not overcome by any rash sense of amity, nor moved unreasonably towards charity. The boy seemed well off and was equipped with the ultimate status symbols – a gold Rolex and a portable radio-telephone. Chua, who not only saw everything that went on in his shop, but eavesdropped on all conversation too, observed and heard all this. He had not rushed forward of course, even though the situation had reeked of profit. He had awaited his shop assistant's diffident summons before emerging to attend to the prosperous couple. He wished he never had come out.

So honoured to meet Uncle Chua Pak Woh; humbly greeting – great Uncle One-hundred Harmonies. The man had said his name was Chua On-fat. He had come to buy a 'modest' ring for his betrothed.

Every ring Uncle Chua had shown them was a little too modest, however. On-fat described the stone he was looking for – a pigeon-blood ruby; square cut; three carats. Could Uncle come up with such a stone?

Uncle Chua had closed his shop doors at that, and as it was past closing time, had ushered out his staff . . . Oh, yes, how lucky for On-fat, he did indeed have one such stone. On-fat had smiled. His betrothed had smiled. Uncle Chua, who never smiled until a deal was final – cash on the nose, opened his safe and brought forth the ruby ring he had bought from Ma Lau the heroin chemist but a few days previously, for 30,000 dollars . . . Oh, they loved it. Her eyes had lit up and On-fat's handsome smile had effused. Uncle Chua was engaged in the happy process of calculating a price (family discount excluded) when struck suddenly down by a cudgel that burst whitely in his cranium like lightning from a clear blue sky. He was stunned – knocked senselessly on to his rump. Limply conscious, disbelieving his eyes, he stared at his assaulters.

The girl let two more men into the shop and they had trussed him, wrists and legs, to his stool. A sock was rammed rudely into his mouth and bound into place. And that was where he had sat nearly drowning on his unswallowable spit, painfully enduring the passing hours. Waiting for what? He feared the worst – robbery, then death. But what was holding them back? And why, for the past few hours, had Chua On-fat, if that was his real name, been sending, and receiving, hushed telephone calls on his radio-phone. Uncle Chua could not see the clock on his office wall but estimated the time to be well past midnight – for the big jets which practically skidded over the roof-tops of Kowloon City to drop in to Kai Tak airport had ceased their thunderous row. And they did that at midnight. Bound then, wrist and ankle, to the stool, Uncle Chua waited. His head wound pained and throbbed. He felt faint and sick, and totally unnerved.

Charlie Lam found Chua in that state and at once issued orders that the man should be untied; ungagged.

Chua gulped down the swamp of saliva that the sock had caused to well up in his gullet.

He was deathly pale. His eyes roved starkly about, glancing at those who stood around him, not daring to hold still on any one. Charlie took the ring from its blue velvet bed and laid it in the palm of his hand. He had forgotten how rich was its gleam. He said:

'This is the ring. Yes, this is it.'

He wanted to do something violent; something awful to this man. He couldn't hide his anger.

'Where did you get it, Chua?'

Chua's jaw was slack, his eyes pleading to be believed: 'I bought it for a fair price off the street.'

'Who sold it to you?'

Uncle Chua cupped his fingers over his mouth and thought: if this one doesn't kill me for lying, then he'll kill me for the truth. He decided he had a better chance with the truth. Then bluffed:

'A man I've never seen before . . .'

196

'It's no good,' said Charlie Lam to the others. 'He's too shit-scared to come up with the truth. I've got my ring back. Kill him.'

'Save life,' bleated the jeweller. 'Save life!'

'I think he should die slowly,' said On-fat. 'I like the idea of jamming the sock so tightly in his mouth that he chokes on his own spit . . .'

'Ma Lau sold it to me,' gasped Uncle Chua Pak Woh. 'Ma Lau, the heroin chemist from Aberdeen. I didn't know. How was I to know . . .'

Though the video was just a copy, it was of excellent quality. Sandy Tang appeared in a yellow flowing robe embroidered with the motif of a phoenix flying over the Island of the Blessed. Noona wore an equally voluminous green silk garment, and his embroidery was of a pheasant and flames. Green and yellow, phoenix and pheasant came together in a fume of fabrics; a joining of body parts in what the more libertine Chinese poets of old might decoratively have described as 'flower of the rear hall', which in modern, unadorned police terminology was simply expressed as buggery. Which breach of law, could earn both transgressors a considerable jail term. But, despite the fact that this video tape was in the hands of a most senior officer of the Royal Hong Kong Police, it would never be cause for prosecution, for several good reasons; the most persuasive being the gaping legal flaw in the evidence. The violator of Noona's most willing 'rear hall' wore such heavy and fantastic stage make-up over his features that he was totally unrecognizable. The man looked towards the camera now and grinned behind his red and purple camouflage: 'Sandy Tang,' Forrester said. But who else would acknowledge that? He switched the TV off and ejected the tape. Noona had played a fine joke on him; the tape was useless. He would never be able to put pressure on Sandy Tang with this high farce. Forrester chucked the tape into the wall-safe in his study and spun the combination lock. Then he stripped down for a shower, and then the 'phone rang.

A distant passage of jazz – that was all. The caller, whoever that person was, stayed silent. Forrester pressed the record button of his message recorder and waited, and listened. He thought he heard fear. Whoever was there intended to speak to him or he would have blocked the mouthpiece. Then came the rustle of breath, and the small sound that saliva makes as a tongue prepares for speech.

'Ging Si?'

'Yes.'

'It is Sandy Tang. Ahh . . .'

The voice melted with disquiet.

'I thought you might call.' My God, that was the last thing he had thought. More truthfully, he said: 'I'm glad you 'phoned me.'

'I must speak to you, Ging Si; urgent need. Whatever you want, I would be a fool to say, no. Believe me, I wish to be of help.'

'Perhaps this is so. Yes, I'd be glad to meet with you, Sandy.'

'I suggest we meet at the Ko Shan theatre, Hung Hom. When the public has gone home it's very private. I could wait for you there after tonight's performance.'

'Where are you now?'

'At home . . . Soon I must leave for the theatre. I perform there tonight.'

'Is Noona Cham with you?'

Sandy Tang sighed deeply before answering. 'Noona knows I'm 'phoning you. We have agreed that it's best . . . Yes.'

'He must not be present when we meet.'

'I wouldn't want him to be there, Ging Si.'

'What time would be best?'

'The curtain comes down at eleven p.m. and the theatre empties rapidly. The staff and nearly all the cast will have gone by midnight. I will wait for you. There is a side door that leads directly to the actors' change-rooms. I'll wait for you at that door.'

'Twelve midnight then.'

'I will be there, Ging Si.'

*

The Ko Shan theatre grows mushroom-squat upon a small ferny knoll that is the single green remnant of the foothills of old Hung Hom. The theatre is new and brash and unChinese but for a large, circular goldfish pond that has to do with the preservation of nature's harmony – the cosmic breath of feng shui. Forrester found himself at the pool's edge at twenty minutes to midnight. The east-bound highways had been less constipated than usual. There was simply no way of forecasting the motility of Hong Kong's traffic. Forrester disembarked from his car and walked onwards towards the stagedoor, hoping that Sandy Tang would be early too. Sandy wasn't there, but the glass door was unlocked. It opened with a click.

It was a simple matter to locate the stage; a wood-block was being tapped – *bong gwu* the Cantonese musicians call that sound, and that described it well. He followed the sound into a long corridor, screened here and there to provide lesser actors with changing cubicles. Fantastically embroidered gowns of crimson, gold, and deep sky-blue were hung here like the wardrobes of a hundred emperors. And everywhere there were stage props – tinfoil swords; long, fringed horse-whips, fans and lanterns and chariot-flags. A make-believe world, which at close quarters looked slightly fatigued, and lustreless.

The wings of the stage were bordered with long black drapes, and beyond that lay the stage; carpeted in red, and poorly lit. A fine net-curtain backdrop was pasted with willow tree boughs, and there was a pavilion with red pillars, and a bridge; all cardboard thin. That was where Sandy Tang stood, reciting prose to the pulse of the solo wood-block, as rhythmically as the beat of a metronome. Patter speech, it was called. Forrester listened, intrigued. Sandy had shed his majestic robes and wore instead street clothes – an overshirt and jeans and a tweed cap. Without the spotlights, the platform boots, the emperor's crown and brilliant silks it could have been a pallid performance, but Sandy's voice rolled strongly over the dust and the dullness and the empty pews. There was no one to hear him but the wood-block player at his single glowing music-stand, alone in the dark orchestra pit, and the watcher in the wings. Sandy Tang stood stroking his chin for a while, then called to his musician.

'That's better, Mr Meng, now there has been a coming together of pulse and voice. Perhaps there were times tonight when you and I missed each other, ha. A pulse-pattern for four beats on the large, and the rest on the medium wood-block is the requirement, *jet-ban-sam-ding*! Perfect.' He struck an arrogant pose – Ha! 'See, Mr Meng; the bold effect we've built up to. Well, enough for one night . . .'

Sandy Tang turned and saw Forrester and his arms flopped down. Forrester felt a pang of embarrassment. It seemed boorish to have been slyly peeping on this man while he cultivated his art. It was Tang, however, who apologized:

'So late already. I didn't realize . . .'

'The sidedoor was unlocked.'

'How rude of me to keep you.'

Squandering amicabilities, he guided Forrester to a change-room close to the wings that seemed more suited to a woman than a man, even one as feminine as this. There was a dressing-table, scattered with powder puffs and face-creams and black make-up pencils, and a teacup with its brim stained heavily with lipstick. A big mirror fringed with bare light-bulbs lit the room. Stout wardrobe-trunks of brown painted wood surrounded the walls. Sandy took a stool from beneath the dressing-table and gave it to his guest, while he sat down on the lid of a trunk. He poured tea from a flask as he spoke.

'My world, as you can see, Ging Si, is quite unreal. Never the same role for more than a week – now a beggarman, now a god; a prince or an emperor, you name it; I can produce the costume and the repertoire, I'm sure. I love it, Ging Si, in a way that I don't think you could comprehend.'

Forrester felt uncomfortable and lumpish in this butterfly-gay world, and he thought that Sandy Tang could sense it. He declined the lipstick-stained cup that had been proffered. 'Sandy, you're quite right. And if you sat all night explaining it to me, I still wouldn't understand. It doesn't matter though. I don't care what you are or what you do, however immoral I might believe you to be, your aberrations are your own business, and if you assist me they will remain as such.'

'But what if I can't help you? That's what I fear, Ging Si. What draws you to me? What attraction has the flower in the field to the passing tiger? You could crush me at a swipe, but what would it gain you?'

'I think we owe it to each other to be of service.'

'If only I knew how.'

'Your brother saved you and your great family from embarrassment once before. I wonder if he would do it again.'

'It's a question that has occurred to me too. "If heaven made him, then earth can find some use for him . . ." Do you know that Chinese expression, Ging Si? Elder Brother used to use it often when referring to my prospects in life. I think, though that he would rather have seen me die than become what I am; a "cut-sleeve" opera singer. But there it is. Heaven made me in a queer and unhappy mould – a god's voice in a demon's skin. That's how I'm seen, and that's my agony in life. People flock to the theatre to see me perform and be enthralled with song . . . then turn dead eyes on me elsewhere. How many times have I plotted suicide to revenge myself on them all; to rob them of the voice they adore – cruel, *cruel*. I despise those people so much that I'm one breath from suicide. It's true I tell you, splendid suicide that would leave them gaping and rotten with guilt, while my spirit soared . . . But, then, as though the gods themselves had repented, and plucked every blossom from the orchards of heaven and thrown them in my path, beauty arrives. Beauty and love sufficient for a thousand years of joy . . . Of course it's an illusion, and I'm a fool. Love's act is but a sip for a demented thirst, a punishment in its own way, and it must all end soon . . . But let it not be tomorrow. Let me have one summer with Noona. I beg you, Ging Si. I deserve that much.'

'Did Noona tell you of his past?'

'Everything . . . He's no murderer, Ging Si. You know that or you wouldn't have set him free . . . Yes, he's told me everything; even how you've used him to get to me. I forgive him for what he's done to me; how could I not forgive him for something that was forced upon him. Stupid boy; he took the video; he thought it wouldn't be missed. Well it was. I slapped him and he confessed. I cried when I heard what he'd been put through; we cried together. Yes, I know about Lonnie Huang and the stolen ring and the awful murder of that poor woman . . . Noona's not capable of such a terrible thing as murder. He told me how you'd shoved his face into the rot of her body . . . Oh my God! I wanted to be sick, I think of it now and I'm still sickened. Worse than death, such a punishment . . . How could you have done such an awful thing?'

'I don't intend to explain my actions to you, Sandy . . . There was a need.'

'"A need" – the rationale of tyrants.' Sandy Tang's quick little hands whisked with futile anger, then were still. 'So now control over me is your need. You have it. No more force. No more damage or outrage. I fear you, Ging Si. Is that not what you desired? I fear your great power and your ruthless energy. I am as frightened as is Noona of you. I would not *dare* to oppose you . . . You say that it's not your intention to bring the laws of homosexuality to bear against me. What is it that you want then?'

To abandon the persecution of this pathetic man; to close this sordid business and go home and soak in a hot bath until he felt distanced from the ugliness. And as none of that was yet practicable, let him at least be presented with straight answers.

'Sandy, you said your brother would rather have seen you die than allow you to sink to your present state. Let's talk about your brother. Tell me about the man, Tang Tsun.'

'I seldom see him.'

'Does he despise you?'

'Despise . . . Well, it never was his way to state his opinions so directly. Our father was murdered, did you know? . . . Yes, you would. I hardly remember Tang Ten-thousand Blessings. It was always Elder Brother who set the rules. It was he who guided the family. Like an old horse, he always seemed to know the way instinctively. And that is how he carried us along. But I couldn't be like he wanted me to be, obedient to Respected Elder — submissive, humble, self-abasing. I was out riding before the wild wind in a most unChinese way, doing what I wanted to do, trying to become a star. He warned me that my excesses would bring disgrace and hurt the family. Yes, that was one time when he spoke out, straight. But I had already sung my first solo and was deafened by the thunder of applause. I kept on, and our relationship was ruined.'

'Yet he stood by you when trouble did come. Or was that because the face of the entire family would have been lost if you were exposed?'

'The Chinese way. It's a curse I can't escape. Face. Moral face. Suicide would have been the right way out for me then. Yes, Elder Brother stood by me for the family's sake. But it was Tang Tik-kat who had the say by then. Elder Brother was out searching for the route to Nirvana, with his head in the clouds, and Cousin Tik-kat became the *de facto* head of the family. Ruthless, Tik-kat did all that had to be done at the time to expunge the messy stain of Sandy Tang. He sent me overseas, to cool down, and when I returned, walled me in with dire warnings. And I tried to live my life by his rules . . . Then came, Noona. I'm fed with the poison of love; I'm stupefied, I'm drugged. Too late, I see I'm helplessly trapped. Thus enters the Ging Si, cunningly schooled in the game of face, to remind me of family honour.' Sandy looked close to tears, his lip trembled. 'Where will it all end?'

Forrester, with mild concern, said: 'I don't know . . . You've been stupid and that's hard to forgive.' Further than that he was not greatly affected by Sandy's lament; which was, he presumed, no more than an extension of his repertoire. In fact, the time was exactly right for the imposition of deeper anguish upon Sandy Tang.

'Noona's immunity expires the moment he ceases to be of use to me, I think you should know that. His sole purpose was to connect you to me, Sandy, in a conducive state of mind. Now that's done I'll have to decide on his future.'

'Don't re-arrest him, that would be too cruel. Don't do it I beg you.'

Forrester plucked the skin of his throat, pretending to reason: 'What advantage would his arrest gain for me? That's what I must consider.'

'None at all,' Sandy Tang cried. 'Don't you see? If you took him from me I'd kill myself. Yes I would. And what good am I to you, dead? That is the question you must put to yourself.'

'I'm not certain that you're much use to me, alive.'

'I'll do what you want, Ging Si.'

'Your brother controls a secret society known as White Lotus. I know he's spoken to you about it, Sandy. Tell me what you know about White Lotus. Are you a member of that sect?'

Sandy blanched. 'My God,' he said over and over. 'My God. Oh, my God.'

Here was genuine fear at last. 'Ging Si, you don't know what you're asking.'

'A simple question for a start: are you a member of that sect?'

'I was invited to join. I don't have the strength to be one of them. I wish that I had such a passion for the after-life, but I'm not concerned with it. There's too much sweetness to be tasted on earth to be attracted by the honey of the gods.'

'You refused to join?'

'No.' He said desperately, 'How could I refuse Elder Brother? You see, I'm bound to the traditions that I hate so much. The Chinese way: there's no escape from it. And so I deferred to my brother's wishes, and joined, and even tried for a while to believe in it, and to be part of it. I was just too weak – too weak to refuse, too weak to stay on. And now, too frail even to stand up to you and make a fight of it.' He pressed his fingers to his temples, palpating his skin delicately.

Forrester gazed at this suffering; vaguely sympathetically he said: 'You should take off that cap – a headache, I've found, is worse when constricted.' Sandy took off the tweed cap, his forehead was beaded and dribbling with sweat. 'Better?' Forrester enquired unexpectedly. 'It's right that you should speak to me so frankly, Sandy. You could save your brother from the consequences of his actions. Beijing want to see an end to him. He's grown too powerful to manage, and he has the potential to cause huge problems. The PLA won't tolerate that. You know the Chinese. What do you think will happen when the British go? They'll kill him.'

'They won't do that.'

'Oh, they will, Sandy. They're ruthless.'

'You don't understand, Ging Si. He can do magical things . . . I won't talk about that . . . No, not even you can make me talk about that.'

'Well that's a disappointment, Sandy. You've done so well up to now.'

For a while it seemed as though Sandy would say no more. He sat bent forward, kneading the fabric of his cap, gazing at a distant memory. Then he raised his eyes to the Ging Si: puzzled eyes that gave no support to his next words: 'My brother cannot be killed. He can make himself invulnerable. There are meditations . . . I've seen amazing things. You wouldn't believe me if I told you.'

'Are there secret words? Is that it? I've heard of such mantras. I've seen men do incredible deeds – walk up ladders of sharp swords, that sort of thing. But I have yet to discover a man whose skin is bulletproof.'

Firmly now Sandy Tung avowed: 'Tang Tsun cannot be killed.'

Sandy had found strength at last. He closed on that statement as a man at the gate of his dearest property, and sullenly regarded the would-be intruder. Tang Tsun could not be killed. Forrester saw no advantage in battering on that conviction. Yet there was something valuable here; something worth knowing. So if he could not get past this barrier, how could he turn its very rigidity to his own advantage? He said:

'Only gods are immortal.'

Then Sandy hung his face into his palms and sobbed plump tears that plopped into his lap. Effortless victory. The ease of it left Forrester with the sense that he had achieved very little. He could only stare at broken Sandy Tung and wonder where things stood now. Sandy soon told him:

'There was a man called Judas, and I am his imitator. I could have been at my brother's side, do you know; at the side of the Maitreya. In madness I turned away from him . . . and loved a beautiful boy instead. What sort of a fucked-up imbecile am I? I lied to you. Of course I want the promise of Heaven. But I threw it away . . . I preferred a boy with buttocks like a peach, and I threw it away. I was tricked wasn't I? So fuck the gods . . . I'm here. I'll make my own heaven. You ask me does my brother despise me. No, he doesn't despise me. I despise him for what I did to him.'

Sandy Tang's hands trembled as he took a chain of keys from his trouser pocket and worked the padlock of a wardrobe-trunk. The inside of it was plain: unpainted wood, nested with drawers, many drawers. But Sandy knew exactly which one to go to.

The drawer held a book. It was bound in brocade as was the Chinese practice two centuries ago. Sandy held it up and opened it and on the first page was a picture of a radiant Buddha. He said:

'This is the *Comprehensive Manual for the Survival of the Kalpa*. It says here, Ging Si, that any man in whose family this book reposes, and who fully understands its meaning, will be guarded from all adversities and obstacles . . . I believe it. It also describes the coming of the Buddha Maitreya. It says he will come from a place called Stone-wall Village, in the hills of Ma On Shan, and that is where Tang Tsun was born. And it says that in his sixteenth year there will appear on the right hand of the Maitreya the sun-moon character, Ming . . . and that is the exact mark that Elder Brother has borne since his sixteenth year . . . But that's just the beginning. The book is mine but I don't want it any more. I bequeath it to you. Read it. You asked me about Tang Tsun. It's all written in there. If you want to stop him, then you have to know what's written there. But I don't think you could stop him, as powerful as you are. You see, a Kalpa is about to come. A Black Wind that will blow for seventy-seven days, and only those who live by the way of the Eight Trigrams Mantra will survive it. And that is God's promise, so how do you think you could stop it? Oh I would love to see you try. It would satisfy me to see you beaten, Ging Si. You'll not survive it, and neither will I. But let me survive long enough to see you fail . . . Here, take the book. I think you have the mind to understand it; perhaps even to see the truth of it. I saw it, and I cowed from it. You of course will try to defeat it.'

Forrester took the cloth-bound volume and opened it. It was a treasure of hand-painted Ching Dynasty calligraphy. He couldn't read more than a few scattered characters, but that didn't matter, he knew where the perfect translator was to be found.

'It's valuable,' Forrester said. 'I'll bring it back.'

Sandy Tang shook his head tiredly. 'No, it's yours, Ging Si. I've forfeited all right to it. I'm its betrayer, so for me it has no further value. Besides, I know every page of it . . . Will you leave me now? I've given you more than you asked for. Look, I'm wrung out, can't you see? No more of your torture, please.'

'It will all be over soon; one way or the other.' Forrester stood. 'Perhaps you're right, perhaps I won't be able to stop your brother. There isn't much time.'

'He is the Maitreya. You are on the side of the wrongdoers.'

'Then so are you, Sandy. You're firmly in my camp now. You and I and Noona will work together. There's more that I want from you. You must go to your brother. You must tell him that you've had a change of heart, and that you wish once more to be a part of White Lotus.'

'Please, no . . . I've done enough.'

'You've done very little, Sandy. Your employment by the "Wrongdoers" has only just begun.'

Chief Superintendent David Kwok, CPM, was of the class of '89 of Bramshill Police College, a year that had produced many commissioners in many different police forces. He wasn't a commissioner yet, even though there were times when he acted as though that exalted office was his. He certainly intended to get there by the shortest possible route, and it annoyed him when people stood in his way, even if such obstruction was inadvertent. When hindered in his pursuit of noble rank by a fellow police officer Kwok could become really nasty. He was a mason (District Grand Lodge Hong Kong and Far East) and he had friends who were master masons who could do incredible things with seniority lists. But as yet they had not been able to see to greater elevation for Kwok than Chief Staff Officer Narcotics Bureau. The stupidity of it was that Kwok was a very talented man; he could have achieved it all without any blood-letting.

Kwok was being exceptionally nasty that morning; but with good reason. And Forrester was on the defensive. Charlie Lam had, with God knows what objective in mind, blundered into Narcotics Bureau territory, and in that trespass had nearly wrecked a major operation.

'How could you allow it to happen, Reven? You've known about my operation for two weeks. Six months' hard work nearly went down the tubes because of that wally . . .'

Kwok had spent time in British pubs, where he had come by a taste for pork pies, bitter, and some admirable native invective: bloody, damn, bugger, berk, wally, wanker, etc.

'Your damn fault, Reven. Charlie Lam should never have been there. He really buggered up everything. What the hell was he doing hanging around the Aberdeen boat-yards at zero two-hundred this morning? Surpassingly bloody unusual, I'd say.'

Surpassingly bloody unusual, was an excellent description for the actions of the superintendent from OSCB. Forrester, however, still tried to protect his man:

'Highly sensitive stuff, Dave. Wish I could tell you more.'

David Kwok screwed down his brow suspiciously. 'What sensitive stuff? I should have been told. I don't agree that your operation should overlap with mine. That's not on.'

'It's hard for the man on the ground to be so exact.'

'Reven, that area was blue-pencilled for my operation by Director of Operations, and you know that. There is a substantial shipment of triple-nine morphine base on its way to a factory in that area. It was brought by Thai trawlers to the Paracel Islands where it was transhipped to a Hong Kong registered trawler. That fishing vessel is now approaching Hong Kong waters. They're a speciality syndicate, Chiu Chau run. I have been tracking these guys for years, and now, with any sort of luck, I'll have them. Don't let your boy fuck it up for me, Reven. That would piss me off more than I can tell you.'

'As I said . . .'

'This stuff was grown by Khun Sha Shaan; Shaan United Army. We've infiltrated their Burmese Command. We have a man who risked his life to get the news to us that this shipment was en route. How do you think my boys felt when this prat detective from OSCB appeared on the scene and started poking around . . . It's beyond belief.'

Forrester summoned up some placatory words and gestures, and hated himself for them: 'The important thing, Dave, is that your operation wasn't blown. It's still intact isn't it?'

'There are some old Chiu Chau villains involved with this syndicate, Reven. One hint of wind and that's it. They'll take off, and we'll never see them again.'

'I understand that . . . Charlie Lam is working on a highly sensitive case, too. If he intruded on to your territory, then it was for good reason. I expect to be briefed by him shortly. He knows that a Narcotics operation is going down at the Aberdeen boat-yards; all of my officers do. That's all I can say for now.'

'I'm sure it is.' David Kwok stood and squeezed off a patently malignant smile. He walked away, shaking his head, dismally reflecting on the trials of the deserving, thinking: what a hypertridimensional ass.

Forrester, hotly embarrassed, sent at once for the subject of his ire, who was not in. He therefore had time to consider the implications of the Aberdeen affair, and discover some worrying patterns. Charlie's only legitimate employment had to do with the Tang Tsun file, which requirement might take him any-where, at any time. But Charlie knew about the Aberdeen surveillance operation, so he must have known he was compromising it and coming under observation by the narcotics team at the boat-yard. Something vital must have occurred to cause him to do that. And yet, if the trail was that hot, why had he not come to his superior officer with such information? There were many possible answers to that, all of them most troubling. Rather than speculate, Forrester set the problem aside and went on with other tasks.

A new crime file had arrived on his desk from Kowloon CID. The case concerned a taxi driver with a penchant for preserving human female sex-organs in pickle-jars. The problem facing OSCG was to discover which jars held bits of whom. The taxi driver, dismayed at having his collection confiscated, wasn't co-operating. Forensic Pathology had thrown up their hands. It was up to OSCG. Forrester decided to hand down the 'pickled cunts' file to Super-stud, Mike Hempstead. Such a case might have a calmative effect on the man's libido. And even as he was plotting that, his 'phone rang and Tess Hempstead's anxious voice came to him:

'Reven?'

Forrester said: 'Ging-Si maybe gone out.'

She obliged with a giggle, unswayed from her serious mood. 'I've got to see you. It's really important.'

'What's it about, Tess?'

'Not on the 'phone, Reven.'

'How urgent?'

'Very, *very* . . .'

'Where?'

'I'm at Trixie's flat. You know it.'

'Can't get there until six; seven.'

'I'll wait . . . Goodbye.' She disconnected.

Charlie arrived. With the street sweat still on him he appeared before Forrester's desk.

'You wanted me, Ging Si?'

'Sit down, Charlie.' Reven Forrester willed: please, please don't lie to me: 'What the hell were you doing in the Aberdeen boat-yards early this morning?'

If Charlie Lam was shaken by the question he did not show it in any way. He lit up a cigarette, tongued a fleck of tobacco from his lip and tiredly slumped back. He knew who had reported him:

'The Narcotics team . . .'

'Did you think they'd be too sleepy to notice you; or too dull to recognize you, or what?'

'Nothing like that, I simply forgot about their operation . . . It went clean out of my mind. Can you believe that?'

Forrester found he could easily believe that. Charlie's eyes looked scorched for the want of sleep; his mind must be equally as wasted. He said, 'You've come nowhere near to answering my question.'

'I remembered too late . . . by that time I was in the boat-yard. How incredibly stupid of me, Ging Si.'

'Charlie, what were you doing there?'

'Ah yes.' And now he was a breath short of lying. But he didn't lie. 'I was looking for Lonnie Huang.'

'I thought so.'

'I had information that he was there, but it was wrong.' Now Charlie lied: 'I don't think he's there.'

'You're not on that case, Charlie; you never were. You were expressly forbidden to go near it. Those orders came from the Deputy Director, and they were relayed to you by me. And now this total mess . . . I'm not even going to ask you how you came by your "wrong" information. I don't want to know.'

Charlie said dully: 'Yes . . . It's a mess.'

'What the hell am I going to do with you? Kwok was in here, breathing fire. I gave him a story and he didn't believe a word of it. He'll go to the Deputy Director, and maybe it will stop there. But if it doesn't, if this is laid on the Director of Operations' desk, there will be an inquiry which could cause you to be suspended.' Forrester paused; leaned closer to his friend and said with irritated emphasis: 'Charlie, am I getting through to you?'

'I'm sorry for the problems I've caused you.'

'What about the problems you've caused yourself? You've done enough to ruin your career.'

'I'm ruined anyway, Ging Si.'

'I'm beginning to believe that, Charlie . . . Look, a while back I suggested that you visit Dr Sin, at Welfare, to request sick leave. You refused. You said you wouldn't let me down, but you have let me down. I had to sit quietly through a lecture on interdepartmental ethics by that arsehole, Kwok . . . And do you know what? He was quite right. His attitude was totally justified. One of my men *forgot* that a Narcotics surveillance op was going down, and nearly wrecked it.'

'I'll take the consequences . . .'

Forrester, sick of Charlie's repentant drone, slapped the desk-top. The noise was louder than intended; Charlie started; Forrester saw the advantage of briskness: 'You're too bloody tired to understand the consequences. You're so flaked-out that you can't even manage to disobey orders, and get away with it. Don't tell me about taking the consequences. Kwok would love to wipe the floor with you. But that's not going to happen . . . I've set up an appointment for you, Charlie, with Dr Sin, at zero nine hundred tomorrow. You *be* there. Sin is sympathetic – he'll fix it.'

'Fix it? What could he fix? Do you think a box of valium and three weeks at the seaside is going to help?' Charlie Lam shook his head; adamantly in opposition. 'I can't stop looking for Lonnie Huang. His death will fix it – it's the only cure, Reven. You've known that all along.'

'We'll get him, Charlie . . .'

'He'll get a life sentence. That's not punishment. That man would thrive in prison like a maggot in a dung-heap . . . Why should he enjoy a single moment of pleasure after what he did?'

'I simply cannot let you do this.'

'And you can't stop me either, I will disobey your order, Reven; as I have done all along . . . My only regret is the loss of face that I've caused you . . . So if the Commissioner sees fit to suspend me, I wouldn't oppose it.'

'You are making this very hard for me.'

212

'What would you have me do then, Reven?' Charlie ground out his cigarette angrily. 'Must I renege on my own conscience, because it is hard for you? Must I walk away from the killer of my wife because you ask me to? No, I refuse.'

'Charlie, Lonnie Huang is wanted for murder. The case against him is solid and he knows it. He's going to resist arrest, there's nothing surer than that . . . Anything could happen to him while resisting arrest.'

'That's not good enough. That would not satisfy.'

'Well, at least you've been honest with me.'

'I regret not telling you earlier . . .'

'I don't believe that you regret that one bit. Let's keep to the truth. I don't feel at all obliged to let you go and hunt Lonnie Huang . . . You listen to me carefully now, Charlie. You have an appointment with Dr Sin, and as far as I'm concerned, that still stands. And I'm content to wait, and hope that you will show up for it. If, however, Dr Sin 'phones me to tell me that you didn't arrive, I will consider our friendship to be over . . . I will take whatever action I consider appropriate in order to prevent you from interfering in the Huang investigation . . . Christ, I can hardly believe this conversation is happening. Get out of here, Charlie.'

'Only an Englishman could turn words into razor blades like that, Reven.'

'Get out.' He saw the wounds on the man before him, and judged them self-inflicted. He wanted no more now than to be rid of this man so persistent in error, so bent on folly. 'Get out,' he slapped the desk again.

He had calmed somewhat by the time he interviewed Gilchrist MacNaughton.

'Gilly,' he said to the detective, 'by an incredible stroke of luck Charlie Lam has located the whereabouts of your prime murder suspect, Lonnie Huang.'

'That's good news, sir. Aye.'

'The man's holed up in a boat-yard at Aberdeen.' MacNaughton scribbled in his notebook. Forrester went on: 'There is a complication to Huang's arrest. Narcotics Intelligence have it that a big triple-nine, morphine-base drop is set to go down in that precise spot.'

'That is a complication, right enough.'

'Well, yes. But maybe we can turn that to our advantage.'

'Aah.' MacNaughton gave a wise nod.

'You see, Gilly. The place is already under surveillance by Narcotics. So we can dovetail in our operations with theirs . . . The problem is that Lonnie Huang may not be there at the critical moment of the Narcotics trap. I will have to discuss the whole matter with the Deputy Director. He'll have to make some rules. That's what DDs are paid to do, Gilly; to make awesome decisions.'

'Who do ye think will get precedence, sir?'

'Narcotics have got the edge. You'd better pray that your boy is in the trap when it's sprung. I'm going to see PK now. So you stand by.'

'Aye, sir.'

'I want that bastard, Gilly; bring him in . . . a few degrees cooler than average, if there's no other way.'

'Aye, sir.'

'And, Gilly, I don't want this matter discussed with anyone; it's that sensitive.'

'What aboot Lam? Surely . . .'

'Not even Lam.'

'Ahm on to it, sir.'

Gilchrist MacNaughton was so reassuringly stoic: so utterly sheep-dog true. The perfect cop. An example to the entire fraternity.

The 'phone rang, and the call was from the office of the Deputy Director, Crime. Lo Ping-kin came suavely on the line:

'Could you manage ten minutes, Reven?'

Lo's thickly buttered mock-modesty could cloy at such a day's end. Forrester said shortly:

'I'm on my way.'

*

If Deputy Director Lo Ping-kin's wish of the moment could magically have been granted, then the two men who currently occupied the visitors' chairs in his spacious office would have found themselves propelled at great speed somewhere else; somewhere distant. Lo's morning had been benignly productive. He had then lunched sumptuously (and at his host's considerable expense) at a new Szechuan restaurant in Wan Chai. The afternoon had slid effortlessly by – now *this*: an interdepartmental squabble that had the potential to blow up into something nasty. Lo frowned across the desk at his two most senior officers: the ever canny, unpredictable gwailo, Forrester, and the hungry-as-a-shark David Kwok. Men of equal rank, but of the two, Forrester was the less dangerous. Kwok was Chinese, born of wealthy New Territories landowners. He was a favoured contender for very high rank; a prince in waiting who was capable of a great deal of mischief. But Lo was not without ambition either, and a wrong decision in a critical dispute such as this would reflect badly on him.

Kwok said:

'The trawler's name is *Tai Kwan*, and it's built on conventional lines. Two weeks previously it set out, with customs authority to trawl in Chinese waters north of Yu Lin. Its master, however, did not sail within a hundred miles of Yu Lin. He took his vessel instead to the Paracel Islands, halfway to the Philippines, and there, off an island called Passu Keah, he met with a Thai long-liner, and took on a cargo of no less than a hundred kilograms of triple-nine morphine base. The *Tai Kwan* then trawled for three days before setting course for Hong Kong. The trawler is currently two hundred nautical miles north of Hong Kong, making eight knots. Its ETA at Aberdeen is seventeen hundred, tomorrow. The narcotics will then be discharged on to a sampan after dark, which will run the stuff to the boat-yard. We will close in on them at that point. You can see, PK, how much trouble we've gone to to pursue this syndicate. They are a highly specialized gang, they use morphine and not heroin, and they've invested millions in this shipment . . . We know who

215

is involved. We know where the drop will take place. We've devoted hundreds of man-hours to the case. Our plans are set . . . Now OSCB wants us to delay our trap until their target walks into it . . . if he ever does. That is not bloody well on.'

It was a slightly exaggerated argument but basically sound. Forrester had not requested that the strike be indefinitely delayed; but that there should be leeway. And even that request, Lo believed, was simply a stratagem. What the wily gwailo really wanted was that which he asked for next:

'A team of OSCB detectives on site, specifically briefed to arrest Huang, should he be there when Narcotics go in . . . That should not present a problem to you, Dave. I see your point; can't argue with you. But I want my men there, too.'

'Too unwieldy,' Kwok disputed. 'My men are used to each other, and they work as a team. Your men would get in the way. If Huang is there we'll arrest him. Then you can have him.'

Forrester produced more argument. 'I don't doubt your men's abilities, Dave. But just as you have been putting in time on the *Tai Kwan* drop so assiduously, so OSCG have been sweating on the Huang case. We have a claim on him.'

'We'll nick him.'

'Forgive my doubts. You're after drug dealers. I'm after a murderer. Your trap will close on the big boys of the drug-ring . . . Lonnie Huang is not such a man. One pace outside of the perimeter of your trap and we'll miss him. What I recommend . . .'

'My God you want to saturate the area with OSCB detectives . . .'

'Not quite saturate – half a dozen teams.'

'I can't believe it.' Kwok appealed, open-armed, to Lo. 'An OSCB circus. Why don't we just dial nine-nine-nine and wait for the PTU to rock up with their sirens screaming.'

'Impractical,' Forrester said blandly.

'I think I see a compromise,' said Lo Ping-kin. And he gave Reven Forrester less than he'd asked for; more than was expedient; and quite enough to get the job done. 'One team of

OSCB detectives, under the command of the Narcotics task force leader.'

'They should act independently once the Narcotics trap is closed,' Forrester said. 'Huang might break loose. They should have their own vehicles and equipment.'

'Dave?' Lo gave David Kwok the right to object.

'I see no problem with that; providing it is left to the senior Narcotics officer to decide as to when they may operate.'

Forrester said: 'That will have to do.'

Supple, Mr Kwok had won enough to feel most satisfied . . . But it was Forrester who trotted off like the dog who'd got the bone.

Lo beckoned: 'A word with you, Reven.'

Forrester returned to his chair. When Kwok had gone out and the door was closed, Lo said, 'I expect you to exercise more control over your officers than you have done recently. I take a dim view of Charlie Lam's Aberdeen adventure.'

'I might have done the same in his position.'

'I'm going to have to speak to the Director about Dave's complaint.' Lo leaned forward, frowning – 'Very serious.'

'I would hate to see Lam burned, just to warm Dave Kwok's huge ego. Charlie made a mistake, but he's done some excellent work elsewhere. His initiative has steered us much nearer to White Lotus and Tang Tsun. I think we're close to a breakthrough.'

'How close?' His eyebrows kinked suspiciously.

'Tang's brother is working for me.'

'Lam turned him?'

'It was his initiative.'

'Excellent. Quite excellent. That weighs in Lam's favour; very definitely in his favour. He's a talented detective . . . So now do you believe that Tang Tsun is the new Celestial Dragonhead?'

'He's an extraordinary man, PK. He's more than a Celestial Dragon-head; much more. I'm drafting a report for you on my findings. You'll have it soon.'

Lo Ping-kin set his thumbs in his waistcoat pockets and drummed his fingers on his belly. Contentment had returned. He said:

'I knew it. I knew it.'

He smiled at the ceiling, day-dreaming of braided epaulettes; of crowns and laurel wreaths.

By the time Forrester reached his car he had brushed off the burrs and irritations of the day and was focusing on the forthcoming tryst with Tess Hempstead at Trixie Welldon's flat, where he would hear the secrets that she dared not transmit by means of the telephone. And what could they be?

Trixie's flat was one of twenty-four units that collectively raised that building twelve storeys from the ground. It had lots of windows that had once commanded a fine view of Hong Kong harbour but no longer did, as an even higher high-rise had come rudely between it and the sea. So these days there was nothing to commend the building, excepting for the fact that there were many civil servants resident there, which meant that the Public Light Transport route had been cunningly manipulated into a dog's-leg in order to pass its very front door.

Trixie Welldon worked as a housekeeper at Government House, so she had no need for minibuses. She was transported to and fro in a shiny black Rover with the Hong Kong coat of arms emblazoned on the doors. And it was this car that Forrester noticed leaving the parking ground as he arrived, and Trixie was in it. His Excellency's call to duty could come at any hour.

Tess Hempstead let him into the flat: 'You *just* missed Trixie.'

'I saw her,' Forrester said. 'We waved to each other.'

'Good . . . Do you want to freshen up?'

She walked ahead of him down the passageway. She was amazingly petite; and this was his immediate, recurrent, and invariable impression of her. Indeed this lack of stature was her very charm – her quick little limbs and miniaturized grace. To a small man this quality might not be so apparent. From Reven Forrester's height it could be delightfully appraised. She wore a pink and grey track suit and pink and grey gym shoes; cutely pink and grey, light and healthy and wholesome as pop-corn, she led on.

There were comfortable chairs to sit on in the lounge, and he was tired enough to sprawl, but sat pertinently upright. There was a bowl of caviar and biscuits at hand; no doubt from the pantry of the Governor; he refused that too.

'A sundowner then?'

It would have been callow not to accept so much as a drink. She brought him an excellent scotch. They spoke idly over the rims of their glasses for a while, then he said:

'It has to be a short visit, I'm afraid. I have a dinner date.'

'With Caroline O'Shea?'

There was a restless juvenescence about her; she crooked one leg over the other; her fingers twined fretfully with the laces of her shoes.

'Yes, with Caroline,' he said.

'There's talk that you're marrying.'

'It's true.'

'And that you'll be leaving for Australia.'

'It's for Shannon . . . the move.'

'She's gorgeous, that kid.'

'Yes, she is. I adore her.'

'Is that the reason why you're marrying?' she said quickly. 'Don't misunderstand me, that would be an excellent reason to do that; quite the best reason in the world, in fact, to get married to Caroline O'Shea.'

'That's only part of it.'

'Aah . . . So it's true. I saw you and Caroline looking in the windows of Tiffany's. You didn't look to me like lovers . . . more like an old married couple out for a stroll . . . So *old*.' She prolonged the l-sound, screwing up her eyes.

'Which,' he said, 'just proves once more that the eye is quicker than the intellect. Is this the subject that was so secret that it couldn't be discussed over the telephone?'

'No. But it is something that I wish to settle in my mind.' The elfin fingers stopped their twisting and twining, the legs uncrossed; the pink and grey shoes pressed together. Perfectly poised, she asked: 'That's fair isn't it?'

'I do love Caroline.'

'Well I've always spoken my mind, so I'm going to do so now. I don't think that that milch-titted bitch loves you. She wants a husband and you want a child. She saw the gap and she took it – clever; I won't deny that; she threatens to leave with Shannon, so you go into a decline.'

'Tess, this is no business of yours,' he warned with a smile. 'Don't interfere.'

'Quite right. I've told myself that too. I tell myself, Tess, this Forrester is no wonderful bargain – why bother. He's self-centred; he's incapable of foresight, and highly fallible. He will make a poor husband . . . Ah, yes, comes the reply, but you love him, Tess, you love the wretched man.' She said in a very measured way: 'Tell me that you have never thought of me, or hungered for me in your bed. Tell me that Caroline's love has melted away every sweet memory of ours . . . If you honestly can tell me these things then I will willingly get out of your life.'

Had he thought of her? Yes: on numerous occasions. Had he compared her sexual expertise to Caroline's? He had (more than favourably). Looks? Both of them were exceptionally good-looking in brilliantly contrasting ways: Tess – quick and petite: Caroline – voluptuous and bold. All this had nothing to do with it. Fact was that he really felt something for Caroline. He said: 'I do love Caroline.'

'You say that like a schoolboy learning by rote – repeat it enough times and you'll have it. Once you told me that love was a power for destruction – not Nirvana, but a hoax. A treason of the mind upon itself. Is that how you love her . . . ? Poor girl, does she know that?'

'I've changed.'

'That's good, yes . . . I haven't changed. Not since the day I first knew you. I loved you then. I love you now.'

'You married Mike. Not that anything would have been different today had you not. Yes, I've got memories of us that are unforgettable. But that's all over.' With stringent finality – 'It's over.'

Her voice countered coldly: 'It's Mike I wanted to speak about.' She stood and went away, and Forrester heard a cupboard door squeak. She held on return a sheet of white paper – a betting record of the Royal Hong Kong Jockey Club, a Tele-bet account record. The sums wagered were huge. The winnings drew from Forrester a hiss of amazement. There was no name on the sheet, just a serial number to nominate ownership.

'It's Mike's,' she said. 'I borrowed his car. It was in the glove-box.'

'It could belong to anyone who'd been in that car. There's no name on it.'

She said flatly, 'It's his. I checked.'

'Where could he have got these massive sums of money? Do you have any idea? God, there're some single bets here of over ten thousand dollars.' He folded the paper into its original creases and put it into his pocket.

'Mike is a weak man, Reven. You know that. He's vain. And he feels hard done by. He's always been jealous of people with money, but has never had the savvy to make it on his own. So whatever scam is offered he's likely to be infatuated with it . . . Please understand this, Reven, I wish Mike no harm, and what he's doing now is ultimately sure to ruin him.' She rested her hands upon his, and lightly squeezed, engrafting her earnest, sad mood. 'Get him out of this mess, Reven; please.'

'Maybe he's a step too far to reach, Tess. This place has a climate for corruption that's almost inescapable . . . If what you say is true, then it wouldn't shock me. It's like some creeping endemic disease that's bound to catch one in the end . . . Do you know, I wish you hadn't told me this.'

'I didn't know what else to do.'

'Dear God . . .' He gazed at the dregs of fluid in his glass, twirling it, watching something beyond that place. 'It would be the end of him, an investigation; break him; kill him. I suppose you know that.'

'I thought you could . . . You might be able to . . .'

'He has it in him to kill himself; he's just never been pushed quite far enough. This would push him far enough.'

'I had to tell you,' she said petulantly. 'Who else could I go to? You tell me what I was supposed to do?'

'Do you want him back?'

She made a soft, meaningless sound; shrugging.

Of course she does; she wants Mike back or she wants him dead. How feminine a demand. How dull of him not to have recognized her gambit earlier. He found no reply for the moment, beyond the comfort: 'I'll do what I can.' He emptied the glass, then stood.

Tess strutted pertly ahead of him to the door, and there on tip-toes pouted upwards to be kissed. Then she broke. She clung to him and her small body shuddered wretchedly. 'My God, Reven, it's all coming to an end. A different world, and I'm going to have to face it alone . . . I'm so scared to be alone.'

The telephone in the hall of Charlie Lam's flat chirped like a cricket, on and on, but no one came to answer it. The windows were shut, with the curtains scarcely fissured, entrapping firmly the heat of the day, encapsulating the encroaching night. Some goldfish lolling in a lime-algaed tank, gazed out at a small world – a room of unused furniture filmed with dust; scattered with litter; a hot and dismal place. The 'phone ceased its chirp. The emptiness of the flat expanded as its walls went dark.

Time passed, then came the soft knock, knock on wood of a cautious visitor waiting at the door. But no one went to receive him. There was the creak of a door handle being stressed, and then an inquisitive rattle of metal on metal, like keys, but looser. A cone of light spilled past the door as it opened and admitted the long shadow of a man.

Reven Forrester came into the flat, worked the light-switch, and frowned at the months of mess. He walked from the hall to the stale, hot lounge and stood for a while quite still, listening to he knew not what. Sorrow: it touched him mutely, feeling him all over, drawing him in. He went into the bedroom. Sheets, twisted and crumpled, draped the bed, and one pillow sagged on the carpet. The heels of a pair of silk slippers peeked out beneath the mattress; small slippers; Lulu's slippers. Lulu's photograph, shrouded with spirit-paper, guarded by a host of porcelain ornaments, smiled from atop a Korean chest. Her shower-cap swung from the bathroom taps. Her housecoat draped the arm of the bedroom rocker. Was he imagining the hint of her perfume on the cloistered air?

The built-in cupboard doors hung ajar, and on one of them was Sellotaped a crayon sketch, buoyantly childish, of some weird green animal flying to the sun; a huge yellow sun. And there was her brass-bound jewellery box – open-lidded. There was only one item set in the top tray; a square-cut ruby ring that gathered the dull light from all around into its red, red heart. He lifted it and frowned. His whole face wrinkled with doubt. 'My God,' he breathed, 'my God,' as questions stole from newly discovered seams of doubt.

What he had thought to be discarded wrappers, strewn helter-skelter on the floor, were not what they seemed. He lifted one up. It was a drawing, a crayon scribble as infantile and crazily garish as the picture taped to the cupboard door, and so was the next, and the next. And they were all imitations – scores of mouse-like green creatures, flapping their way towards bright yellow suns, and more, and more, and more in every room. He hunted for some that might be dissimilar – even a bold variation. He crouched and picked at the litter, searching for something to disagree with the kindergarten repetition that was otherwise certain insanity. But the sketches were all the same.

He went once again to look at the Sellotaped original and saw that there *was* something different about this picture. It was much older than the others. The paper was dog-eared and yellowed, and some untutored Chinese calligraphy decorated one corner. It needed the glow of his pen-light to make sense of the writing:

Plentiful gives sorry to Virtuous-fragrance.

A once-told story came back to him then; the need of little Plentiful to apologize for a playground prank he had played on Virtuous-fragrance. And from that had grown a devotion that had lasted for a lifetime. The invincible sadness now claimed Forrester, completely. He had at last arrived at the edge of the abyss in which his friend lay, broken, and all he could do was to stare down dumbly at the struggling, suffering man so far below. Charlie Lam was beyond his reach, he knew that now.

'Operation Chariot' was its rather grandiose code-name, and the final briefing for it was held in the main conference room at Police Headquarters, Arsenal Street. Forty men sat there, upright and razor keen, scribbling orders into notebooks. Gilly Mac-Naughton was there with his team of OSCB detectives: *Arresting Party H* was their designation – *H* for Huang. There was little to be heard but the rustle of notepaper, the hum and clatter of a slide projector, and the imperious voice of Mr David Kwok:

'This is an aerial photograph of the area of operation . . . These are the routes of advance . . . of team *A* . . . of team *B* . . . Team *C*.'

They were to converge from three directions; team *A*, being frogmen from Special Duties Unit, would emerge at the launching ramps, shed their rubber suits, then creep with great stealth upon the target building, and then raid the place. They were to neutralize all opposition, in other words – shoot people, bash down doors, and do any other violent thing considered necessary. And while this was going on teams *B* and *C* would be coming in unhurriedly. They comprised the experts; the Exhibits Officer – the fingerprinters, photographers, forensic chemists and other such sedentary types. Team *H* would also be activated at this stage of the operation. Kwok had a special message for the crass novices of team *H*:

'Do not smoke, or use a camera flash, or switch on any light until the chemist is satisfied that no explosive fumes are present . . .

'Do not taste any powder or liquids as many lethal poisons will be lying around . . .

'Do not come in until you're called in, and then *do not* get in the way.'

Heads turned towards the OSCB detectives, and there were smirks and sniggers. A surge of embarrassment arose in MacNaughton, swiftly followed by resentment, then pounding wrath and a muttered urge to settle accounts with the 'wee yellowish fella'. He sat there, glowering, remembering the clansmen of Argyle who'd killed for lesser insult.

MacNaughton did all that he was obliged to do at that briefing. He studied the slides and jotted down notes, and marked his field map with appropriate arrows and figures and dotted lines. He circled the point at Sham Wan floating jetties from whence the frogmen would embark upon their Zodiac inflatable dinghies, and the point opposite that, outside the Ho King market on Aberdeen Island, where the team *H* members would be located. He asked no questions of CSO Kwok because none that weren't entirely personal and grossly hostile occurred to him. He firmly believed that they would lose the elusive Lonnie Huang in the scrimmage of Operation Chariot.

The summer monsoon blew better than thirty knots all of that day, heaping up the deep blue water, whipping scarves of salty white froth across the deck of the stern trawler, *Tai Kwan*. Squalls of rain came pelting on the wind; fat droplets that beat the shine from the sea and shrank the setting sun, then passed on, freeing the sky. *Tai Kwan*, dead on course for Hong Kong's West Lamma Channel, took the slap of the big waves on its starboard quarter, but the trawler was made for these seas and it came through, easily.

Tai Kwan was big; sixty-six feet in length, and its draught owned almost six feet. It had a 200-horsepower engine, and a hold that, after a few good trawls, could easily swallow a fourteen-ton catch.

But what was caught from the sea was of little consequence on that voyage, and the fish in the hold were there to provide camouflage alone. Beneath the ice and cold silver corpses were buried many, many bricks of morphine base; all sealed up in cellophane and precisely marked with accounting numbers and weights.

At 15.00 hours *Tai Kwan* entered the calm waters, west of Lamma Island. An hour later the vessel was off Boulder Point and heading for the five tall smokestacks of the Ap Lei Chau power station. Shortly thereafter the chimneys came into line, and the master of the vessel had set a final course, with not a customs or police launch in sight.

At 17.35 *Tai Kwan* was off Remarkable boat-yard, manoeuvring towards the slipway. Rain came down heavily again, settling grey obscurity over everything, but this did not stop the progress of the master of *Tai Kwan*. He took his bearings on the blue-bright light of the yard's acetylene welders, and came on.

Hard-muscled workers walked through the downpour with ropes and poles, and mallets with which to hammer into place the heavy chocks that would support the hull. A pilot from the yard came to the bridge and steered *Tai Kwan* on to the submerged cradle lying beneath the slipway. A bump and a jolt and the trawler was bedded in its slippery cradle. The yard-men waded in with chocks and stays, and hammers thudded hollowly on the wet hull. A winch groaned and clanked and a thick chain drew *Tai Kwan*, on its cradle, up the concrete slope. At the blast of a whistle the winch stopped. By then *Tai Kwan* with its precious cargo embowelled stood high and dry.

Lonnie Huang, lounging in the shelter of a plank scaffold, observed the dry-docking of *Tai Kwan* with dejected curiosity. Security was at maximum, with every weatherman in the pay of the syndicate posted, and the whisper was that they would be out all night. He lit a cigarette and flicked the match into an oil-stained puddle and swore softly, without much flair or intent, being more or less disgusted with life in general (which was trailing sadly behind the expectations he had for it).

Then he swore again; this time with considerably more vehemence for now a definite target for abuse had appeared. Ma Lau the chemist, the man most responsible for his depressed state, had emerged from the factory and was walking through the yard. A ladder was propped up against the hull of the trawler and Ma Lau ascended it. Lucky-boy the monkey, restricted to the shed, pressed his ugly snout snottily against a window-pane with his little brown addict eyes fixed on the ship, keenly aware of the newly arrived bonanza. Lonnie sidled up to the window and rapped suddenly and hard on the glass. Lucky-boy started back, then stared stupidly at his tormentor, who sniggered with small satisfaction, and turned away.

Ma Lau, Lonnie reckoned, had cheated him; he had not given him full value in the exchange. The chemist had promised that he would show him how to manufacture his famous red chicken. And had indeed shown him how to do that – in theory. But one demonstration of such a complicated procedure, even when notes were simultaneously compiled, was plainly not enough. He needed to be able to practise the science in order to become proficient. There were techniques that could not be mastered by theory alone; things to do with litmus paper, and a mirror test for the hydrochloric acid solution, where the colour of the residue was critical. But rapacious Ma Lau would take him no further until he paid more: 'another ring perhaps, Lonnie – great sacrifice brings great reward.'

But Lonnie had nothing worthwhile left to sacrifice, so he hated the cheating chemist with an impotent hate, of violent imaginings and distant invective. There was not a thing he could do to retaliate against the man, so he punished his pet instead. Lonnie gained satisfaction by secretly terrorizing Lucky-boy at every opportunity. He injected Lucky-boy's apples and bananas with bitter quinine. He snagged the monkey's tail in the compressor pulley, thus adding a permanent right-angled kink to it. And when there were no volatile gases about (and this was his favourite torment) he flicked burning matches at the beast. Lucky-boy was quick to learn that Lonnie, by himself, was the

227

precursor of pain, and became adept at hiding. But then Lonnie became adept at searching. In the hunt for the cowardly monkey Lonnie made some discoveries that would have eluded a less persevering fellow. For instance, there was a Chinese-made pistol and a box of bullets hidden behind the god-box in the cluttered rear office, and in that same untidy room a ventilator unit was set into the wall, and this was hinged to swing outwards to provide a cunningly concealed emergency tunnel. There were other discoveries of some interest – a ledger filled with dates and numbers in a metal cabinet that the chemist sometimes forgot to lock, that proved that Ma Lau was capable of producing up to 3,000 ounces of heroin a month for which he was paid at the princely rate of ninety Hong Kong dollars per ounce. Lonnie multiplied the two sums. Hot shit! What was the man doing with all his cash?

That question was on Lonnie's mind even as the unloved chemist came to the deck-rail of the *Tai Kwan* with the enforcer, Mr Hit. It was darkening. Mr Hit peered down to the boat-yard and his eyes fell on Lonnie, who quickly looked away.

'*Wai!* You.'

Lonnie had to look up. Mr Hit was beckoning energetically.

'Yes, *you*. Come on, come on.'

Lonnie ascended the ladder.

'You were the clever one, ha, Blind-boy?'

Mr Hit's sneering tone warned that admission to cleverness right then might not be the smart thing to do. Lonnie tried to assume the look of one who is courteously vacant, yet willing. Mr Hit's every movement seemed calculated to terrify. His rock-knuckled fist shot out and Lonnie fell back – and all the man had done was to offer a sheaf of papers.

'Ma Lau says you're bright; that's good. You take these. You go down there, and mark off every brick; hear. You weigh them, you stack them, then mark off.'

Lonnie said meekly, 'Such honour.'

'Don't strike against the board, Blind-boy.'

'Won't disappoint, Teacher.'

'Better you don't. I'll check. I'll kill you half dead if you fuck up. I'll rip off your fucking head.'

I'm sure you will, penis brain, Lonnie dared not say. Egg of a turtle – bastard. He didn't share that either. Trying to look humbly pleased with his assignment, he clumped, weak-kneed, down the ladder, clutching the highly illegal cargo manifest of the *Tai Kwan*, then went to the room where the triple-nine morphine bricks were to be stored. There kink-tailed Lucky-boy sprang from the ground to a high shelf bobbing and chattering. His war with Lonnie took on a new dimension as a stream of pungent ape urine met its target.

Lonnie Huang gasped with outrage. A fighter called Bat-man arrived with the first consignment of bricks – his eyes widened; he burst with laughter; groped his ribs and roared until he staggered.

'Lucky-boy, oh my God!' Bat-man yelled. 'Did you see that. Did you see *that!*'

Bat-man was a malicious crumb-merchant – he'd tell the tale of Lonnie's indignity to the whole town. Lonnie (swearing awful revenge) stripped off his piss-stinking, wet shirt, threw it into a corner, then went about his task, which was not an easy one. All told there were 233 of those dull coffee-coloured, plastic-wrapped bricks, each of them was of a slightly different mass. Complicating matters was the fact that some of the inked serial numbers had partially worn off in transit and were illegible; these blocks could not simply be ticked off against the manifest. He built from the bricks two walls. One lot for those he was sure of; one for the doubtfuls – to be checked off by process of weighing alone. The scale that had been provided was of the old-fashioned grocer's type, which required a constant swapping of minor weights. But all of these adversities could easily have been coped with were it not for the sniggered insults delivered with the arrival of each subsequent load of morphine bricks.

'Nice perfume, Blind-boy; very exotic.'

'He's still up there above you, Lonnie. Watch it, he's aiming for another squirt.'

'Why don't you piss right back at the bastard, Blind-boy? Really get something going.'

How could a man concentrate in the face of such diabolical provocation? Lonnie worked on resolutely, but he made mistakes.

By the time Mr Hit arrived with Ma Lau and the master of the *Tai Kwan*, a little wizened-up man in vest and shorts, Lonnie's mind was panic-stricken to the point of vacuous incapability. Three bricks remained unmarried to the list. The whole job would have to be re-done, and he was in for it. That was, unless he faked it (a simple matter of three quick additional ticks on the manifest sheet), which would save him temporarily from the wrath of Mr Hit. So that was what he unhesitatingly did. He held up the juggled manifest before the eyes of the enforcer:

'All one hundred per cent accounted for down to the last gram.'

Mr Hit gave what was as close to a smile as his disgruntled mouth would allow. He took the papers and inspected them – or rather, pretended to do that. He glanced over the two stacks of bricks and ran his index finger down Lonnie's row of ticks, nodding dissatisfied approval, and at that juncture Lonnie saw Mr Hit for what he really was – a stupid, lazy bully, who had out-fought many other such bullies in order to become the Red Pole enforcer of a Chiu Chau triad gang. On the tide of this revelation Lonnie thought: how easy to trick this flea-brain. With Mr Hit in charge of security it would be kids' stuff to smuggle out a brick or two of morphine base.

Mr Hit prodded Lonnie with a finger, sharp as a bayonet, and handed back the manifest:

'So, smart guy; it's OK, or not?'

'OK,' echoed Lonnie, his mind away with some really good ideas. He thought of the secret exit hatch, and how it might be utilized to his advantage. He foresaw a cheerful improvement in circumstances.

Ma Lau said sourly, 'If we stand talking all night how am I to complete a new batch of red chicken before morning?'

Lucky-boy clicked his teeth in solidarity with his master and glared at the enemy below.

*

230

The plans for Operation Chariot lay in embarrassing disarray, and this was because of the unprecedented and unorthodox delivery technique that the Chiu Chau syndicate had adopted. It had been anticipated that they would tie up in the bay, then utilize sampans to run the drug consignment to the factory at Remarkable boat-yard; which to-ing and fro-ing of small vessels would have provided the perfect cover for the advancing SDU frogmen of the attack team. Instead, those rat-cunning Chiu Chau dealers had run their laden stern trawler on to the slipway of the yard, then winched it to dry land. And there it stood now, with its generators running and its 1,000-watt stern-deck lights blazing blindingly into the night-scopes of the police observation team, 'partying' in a private salon in an offshore floating restaurant, and illuminating the intended landing point of the A team frogmen . . .

'A potential bloody disaster.'

Those very words escaped the mouth of Chief Superintendent Kwok as he sat before the bank of radio-phones and maps connecting him to his distant operation. He enquired of his observation post:

'The whole slipway illuminated, you say?'

'Can't see a thing beyond the lights, sir. Our night-vision stuff won't penetrate past the dazzle. It's like gazing at the sun. Not a hope of surprising them from this side, sir.'

'What about the adjacent yards?'

'The southern yard has a few lead-lights burning, they seem to be doing welding on the deck of a tug boat. The northern neighbour . . .'

But even before the observation officer had completed his message, Kwok had come to the decision that to deploy team A from either flank would be a bad move. The yards were strewn with the rusting debris of a decade of broken ships. And that was where the Chiu Chau weathermen would be posted; an imposs-ible approach.

So if they could not come in from the slipway or from the flanks with stealth, that left only one possible alternative route of attack – full frontal with *élan*. Now here was the awful thought that had

Kwok sighing into his steepled palms: there was only one team that was ready – poised and capable of forcing such an aggressive entrance, and that comprised the detectives from Forrester's team *H*. Those cowboys had arrived with their own specially modified light delivery van with reinforced front bumpers that could knock down gates and shunt cars; that sort of wild behaviour . . .

David Kwok dithered on for a while in the hope that the drug-runners would decide to conclude their business in darkness. But that was not to be. The stern lights of the *Tai Kwan* did not waver. At last Kwok reached for the radio-telephone that would link him to the nefarious team *H*. He depressed the transmit button. It was best to speak to that Scottish haggis-head in his own language. Kwok sighed:

'Team *H* leader.'

And the reply was prompt and sharp: '*Sir.*'

Gilchrist MacNaughton did not believe in karma – but how else could one explain such a deserved shift of fortune. Gilly's face widened with delight. Here came the voice of the exalted chief super, now treacly sweet like golden syrup, agurgle with phrases like 'utmost support', and 'reliant on your judgement'.

MacNaughton guessed that there had occurred some monumental balls-up with team *A*. However he was more than willing to take over from them at the sharp end. Kwok said:

'Team *A* will be right on your heels.'

MacNaughton got in the last word: 'So long as they don't get in my way . . . Sir.'

It began to rain heavily again as MacNaughton's 'bakery' van roared off, to do battle.

The approach road to the target was new; so new that asphalt stuck to the tyres of the van, and as they accelerated, spattered against the mudguards. The first section of road fell sharply towards the harbour, curving slightly as it dropped. Then it ran straight, and parallel to the boat-building yards. MacNaughton tugged the straps of his seat-belt as they gathered speed. The problem that faced the police driver (as Gilly saw it) was one of having sufficient velocity at the point of impact to carry them through the gates of Remarkable boat-yard, for they would have to slow down in order to make a right-angle turn at the entrance of the yard. MacNaughton looked from the tarmac to his driver, Detective Constable Wong Kee, who had just returned from a refresher at Driving School, and was thus more than averagely keen on speed. The man's face was drawn into a silent snarl, in the best traditions of Kamikaze. The straight came up and Wong rammed the accelerator down flat. Two hundred metres of roadway, shanties and fencing and boggle-eyed pedestrians flew by. MacNaughton wondered when Wong would decelerate; he would need to do that very soon, for the entrance to Remarkable boat-yard was in sight, as was the end of the road, *and* the waters of Aberdeen harbour. Still the engine roared; still they hurtled on. MacNaughton stiffened, and flinched. They would go out of control now if they turned, and if they did not then they would fly into the bay . . . They turned.

As the tyres screamed, so did MacNaughton: 'Jay*sus!*' The van screwed and canted on two wheels and contemplated rolling extravagantly on to its head, but lacked the energy. They hit the gates with a jolt and burst through.

There was panic in Remarkable boat-yard. Men were running, men were shouting. The van collided with a small shed and then a larger pile of lumber, then stopped. The big green-hulled trawler *Tai Kwan* loomed over them. MacNaughton sprang from the van into the pouring rain. A man swinging something sharp and harmful came for him. MacNaughton shot him, but the sharp chopper didn't stop until it reached the bone of his shoulder. Gilly MacNaughton, in the full roar of battle, could not be seduced to weakness by one cut – he hardly flinched. He saw the direction he should take, and plunged on, yelling, and his men came on too, all yelling.

A rain-splashed window glowed. A locked door barred their way. They burst the door so heavily that it departed from its frame. The stunning reek of ether hung in the air.

In the next room they found two tall heaps of morphine bricks.

There were stainless steel drums and basins, and a large glass flask semi-filled with coffee-coloured fluid. A man who was too old to be Lonnie Huang, who had the sucked-away look of a heroin smoker, stood there, grinning with fear. MacNaughton thought he saw a monkey on the top of a steelframe cabinet.

The next door opened inwards, and wouldn't give way. Gilly would have shot the lock out but for the explosive ether fumes. He looked about for some kind of bludgeon. Wong came with a breaker's hammer and a pair of strong forearms. He smashed the lock and the door opened meekly.

Here was an office. There wasn't much to it: a cluttered panellite table and some rusted chrome chairs, two filing cabinets, with the usual pageant of red New Year papers decorating the walls. Lonnie Huang was not there. No one was there, which was remarkable as the door had been bolted from the inside, and there were no further rooms, passages, or hidey-holes. So there had to be an exit, somewhere.

Gilchrist MacNaughton attacked the filing cabinets more in anger than in hope, and flung them to the floor. But a numbing weakness was stealing frostily inwards, his left arm drooped, irresolute, thieving him of his quick, angry strength. His windcheater, he noticed, was gashed at the shoulder, and soaked with blood. More good red blood that should have been surging around inside him, furnacing his muscle, was trickling in a steady, useless stream to the floor and that was where he suddenly found himself, too.

It was while MacNaughton was trying to get up again that he spotted the elusive exit shaft. The ventilator fan was turning slowly as the night breeze caught it, but there was a gap between the housing and the wall. That was the way out.

Wong bent over him. 'The A team's here,' he said. 'The frogmen have come.'

'Too bloody late, lad,' muttered Gilchrist MacNaughton. 'Now gi' us a hand to get through that blasted hole. I'm havin' a bit o' trouble wi' me arm.'

*

It was coming down luck on Lonnie Huang; not just kick up a dollar kind of luck, but glorious, once-in-a-lifetime golden luck. Heavenly blossoms falling profusely. He had planned to knock off one brick of morphine base; at the outside two. But here he had no fewer than five such blocks in his plastic shopping-bag, and that was not all, the little black pistol was in there too. A fantastic starting-kit for any prospective heroin chemist. And to think of it, half an hour earlier he had been at the point of despair. After days of plotting and scheming he had all but arrived at the depressing conclusion that he'd underestimated Mr Hit; it had seemed impossible to steal this loot and smuggle it, and himself, past the Enforcer and his cat-eyed weathermen. But he had done it.

Of course the police had played a major supporting role in this achievement, and he would be a hundred years grateful to them for their timely arrival, but he had himself to thank mostly. He had done the brain-sweat that had allowed him to react with such devastating speed when the police had struck and the alarm shout of '*Wind*' had been raised by the guards. So while Ma Lau had been squawking and flapping about, Lonnie had grabbed five morphine bricks, dashed to the office and bolted himself in. And while the old chemist had been beating on the door, yelling, 'Lonnie, open up. Lonnie, open up!' Lonnie had been helping himself to the pistol then squeezing through the ventilator frame. Goodbye Mr Hit! Goodbye wind!

He had exited in the dark boat-yard that he knew so well, and run as he had never run in his life before. He had leaped and clambered and sprinted and dodged and slipped. '*Halt!*' they had shouted. '*Halt or we shoot!*'

Did they think he was crazy? He'd run. A gun had sparked flame and a bullet whipped by, which had only increased his endeavour. His lungs blew live coals – his legs became thudding lead weights. Still he ran.

Now, at the old Tin Hau temple on the dirt track at Lo Miu Tsuen, he stumbled, then skidded headlong in the mud. He raised himself and tried to run on, but his legs just wouldn't hold up. He had no choice then but to walk, and even walking was an ordeal. His rear thighs started to cramp so violently that he had to totter, with his knees kinked like an old man; short, shuffling steps that hardly moved him onwards. The night rain had the south wind to give it teeth, and it gnawed its chill right into his bones. But five bricks of morphine base was more incentive than he needed to keep going, and his mind crackled with the arithmetic of heroin manufacture. Sixteen grams of morphine would convert to twenty-six grams of number-three heroin. So five kilograms of morphine base (give or take a gram or two lost to experimentation) would surrender . . . my *God*! over eight thousand grams of best red chicken, at a street price of a hundred or so Hong Kong dollars per gram.

Lonnie hissed as ropes of pain twanged up his thighs; cackled and yelped; laughed at the agony in each step. The more it hurt the more he ridiculed it. Hell! He was a rich man; or he would soon be. He had the knowledge – almost. He certainly had the material. All that was lacking was a short-term backer; someone who would go out and procure the chemicals and equipment required in order to set up in business. And he thought he knew just the man.

Lonnie reached the fishing-wharf below the Ap Lei Chau housing estate in the grey of dawn. Sampan taxis floated there, bobbing and swaying in the swell. Tanka women perched on the sterns as hungry as early morning gulls for the scraps of trade – fisherfolk, disembarking from the trawlers, mostly. The wind staggered Lonnie as he shuffled along the jetty.

Ah Moon, the sampan woman, watched the shirtless man walking awkwardly through the rain with his yellow plastic bag, and assessed him as either drunk or demented. And this must have been the general opinion of the sampan owners tied up there, for as scarce as fares were to come by that blustery morning, some refused him a ride. Drunks were prone to topple overboard in such a blow, and mad men had no coin. But as he got closer she could see that this fellow was far from numb to his surroundings – he was quaking with cold, but his eyes were bright and shrewd. She took him on, and her charity brought

236

luck, for no sooner had she done so than out of the gloom walked another fare. This man was sensibly buttoned into a raincoat, and a peaked cloth cap covered his scalp.

Mr Shirtless's jaw snapped and chattered as he gave his destination. The other man just nodded that he would go there too. Ah Moon reversed her engines and they waddled away from the pier. Then she held the tiller fast, and steered them into the bay. Rough water – Number Three signal was glowing from the roof of the marine police building and fishing vessels were scurrying in to shelter. Ah Moon had to dodge a bit as the big green trawlers pushed in, and the sampan bucked and rolled in their wake, and the wind whipped the canvas canopy, thrashed it with rain, and tugged the lashing out straight. Ah Moon had spent her entire life on that bay, she'd been taught how to ply a yuloh-oar at the age of six, and was steeped in the lore of the Tanka. So she knew that such weather was brought about by some crochety dragons far out to sea. If those monsters really meant business they would turn on a typhoon, and the oceans would explode, but this stuff was just careless flatulence passed in Hong Kong's general direction, and all that was required was that she keep a keen look-out, and a firm tiller. So Ah Moon watched ahead. Which was why she did not notice until mid-harbour that one of her passengers was trying to kill the other.

Mr Raincoat had Mr Shirtless in a merciless grip in the crook of his arm, and was trying to break the man's neck. Ah Moon screamed:

'*Wai!* You stop that, hey! You *stop* that now!'

But when Raincoat didn't stop, but perversely improved his grip and increased his pressure until the muscles in his wrists showed like rope, what else could she do? Yelping: '*Save life! Save life!*' Ah Moon thrust her engine controls full forward and headed for the shore.

She nearly collided with an incoming trawler. Ah Moon thought she would just be able to scrape past its sharp prow, but at the last minute she realized that it was set to cut her beloved sampan clean in half. She swung her tiller blade hard right, and the boats came so close that for a moment all she knew was a great moving wall of green-painted planks and the thunder of diesel engines. Then the trawler drew past them and they were hurdling its massive wake, side on – pitching and rolling in a helpless wild dance.

At least these mad convulsions broke the grip of the strangler. Helter-skelter, the two men staggered about. Shirtless fell hard against the canopy, snapping a bamboo spar. The coated man sprawled backwards on the deck, but was first to regain balance. He rushed towards the man he would kill, and locked his arms on him again. Ah Moon yelled, 'No!' She heard a pop sound not much crisper than that of a dropped egg. And then, as Mr Raincoat fell back, a larger sound shocked the air – the stunning crash one would expect from a gun.

And there it was in the hand of the shirtless one. And he was still aiming it as they jolted against the jetty. Another flashing shot – this one came closer to hitting Ah Moon than its target. She yelped, and Shirtless sprang for the shore, and with his bag clutched and his frightful little weapon, ran, limping up the slope. She saw him reach the praya, then the grey-driving rain closed around him and he was gone.

The man who was shot lay on the bottom-boards, blowing pink bubbles filled with pain that trembled in the wind then burst at his lips. Ah Moon's sisters, who had heard the commotion, came running along the planks, then gathered around and gazed down at the man who was shot, and debated in awed tones as to what should be done.

Charlie Lam looked up at the ring of dark faces, and laboured to breathe. He knew that if they did not do something quickly, he would die.

Circles of silver came, like ripples spreading over a sunny pond. He saw Lulu, beckoning him to that bright place. And he thought it would not be so bad to die.

7

KING OF THE COCKROACHES

The summer sky was wide, and as bright as brass, and the ground was hot. Cicadas shrilled from the laurel trees and viburnums, as they shed their ugly underground armour and came forth, renewed. Brilliant winged butterflies alighted to a world of flowers, flicking long looping tongues into the heady nectar.

Tang Tsun sipped delicately from a thin porcelain cup of a drive-away heat brew of hibiscus leaves and orange-peel. He wore a flowing, saffron homespun robe, which quite tented the low rustic bench on which he sat. His smile was as beatific as though the blue and the green of the sky and hill, and all things graceless or beautiful that thrived in between, were beaming unto him a special, private, and entirely satisfying message. The ants that roved through the grass; the pair of magpies, circling; the silvery rustle of the trees; he knew more about these things than other men. He set the cup down on the springy, moist monastery grass and turned to the man who sat beside him. Some sadness wrinkled his eyes but the smile stayed on, and his voice was mellow.

'Seeing that you have asked, Younger Brother, I'll tell you. The tomb of the Eternal Mother is filled with emptiness . . . You looked puzzled, and so you may. Let me put it this way: there is a place that is neither dark nor light, nor air nor water nor earth. There is no hunger, for there is no food. There is no greed for there is nothing to possess; no hatred, for there is nothing to do you harm. There is no stopping, because there is no starting; or being born, or dying. That place is the Original Home; the womb of the Eternal Mother; Nirvana.'

'I wish to be part of it when I die.'

'There is no such thing as being part of it, don't you see? It *is* you. You may be it even now. There is no prescription of death — but to be born again.'

'Brother, you've lost me.'

'Then that's a good beginning. Now for you to lose yourself, as you are. Reject all desires . . .'

Sandy argued: 'But one of my desires is to be more like you — to come to White Lotus. So if I reject this, how can I succeed?'

'Simply follow the path of good deeds without looking ahead at your goal, or left or right, to see if the merit of your actions will bring you reward. Works of righteousness mean nothing. It is the attitude of mind that causes those deeds that will bring benefits.'

'And what will be the benefits?'

Tang Tsun said after a while: 'Bliss. You will know bliss.'

'Bliss, here on earth? It doesn't seem possible. Life's ebb and flow moves me, it's so strong. And it carries the grit of greed and lust. Perhaps it would be better to die, then seize another womb, and begin life all over again.'

'That would be the most unenlightened, unhappy thing you could do. Have strength. Let moral conduct be your primary virtue.'

'Easy words for one as virtuous as you to utter. I'm weak, Elder Brother. I have wants that argue against improvement.'

'Meditate in silence.' Tang Tsun stirred, as though about to rise. 'Silence admits to nothing. You cannot argue with silence.'

'Even in the deepest silence, I'd know it.'

'Meditation is pure observation — nothing less or greater than that. The precious gift of meditation is recognition, and the first thing you will recognize is the ubiquitous transience of all things . . . That is a feature of existence; as is sorrow and inadequacy. And seeing that in itself represents change, and so you will progress: and become stronger.' Tang Tsun stood up with a sigh that was not quite an admission of exhaustion. He took up a few old cloth-covered books that had lain on the seat unnoticed beneath the fabric of his robe. 'I must go. I've got so much to do.'

'One last question.'

'What is it?'

'My brother, are you really the Maitreya?'

Tang Tsun rolled up the sleeve of his full monk's robe and held up his desperately burned hand, palm forward for the doubter to examine. There was the sign of Ming, Sun-Moon, set amongst the grey cobweb of scars, as absolute as the most perfect calligraphy. Then he turned away, and walked in the direction of a tall terracotta pagoda rising from the trees.

But Sandy Tang was familiar with the Ming. He'd known that mark since childhood, and for him it had lost its wonder. He begged for more proof; he called after the departing figure:

'Show me something else. Show me a miracle.'

Tang Tsun stopped and half turned to look at his younger brother. He seemed to frown, as though Sandy had offended him. Then he beckoned Sandy to follow.

They walked for a while with the sun baking their shoulders. They came to the pagoda and passed it by. Here, statued, rigidly frowning sat Wen Shu on his giant blue lion, making all else around him seem very small. The terrace took them onwards to an avenue where the eighteen sculpted disciples of the Buddha Sakyamuni stood contemplating the daily parade of mortals, awaiting the advent of the Buddhist Messiah – the Maitreya. How miraculous, how incredible if this man in the saffron gown was he. Sandy almost swooned as the full force of that thought knocked on bone. In his chest there was a gathering of belief and disbelief, a-wrestle, so that at any time a champion of one side or the other might arise and cry, *'Victory! Here is the truth.'* But the battle was so constant, so intense and inconclusive that he longed for extraneous proof, one way or the other. Some vision or act that would lead his slug-spirited flesh away from conflict to a destination, any destination.

They passed the door of the temple of Ten-thousand Buddhas

and saw shelf upon shelf of bottle-sized, gilded Buddhas, and in the centre of this wall of gold three more Enlightened Ones sat, double the size of life. Tang Tsun gestured vaguely, but said nothing, and they walked on in the sunshine.

On a higher terrace were some temples of lesser dimensions. In one they found the remains of the amazing abbot Yuet Kai, embalmed and gilded and serenely sealed in a glass display case, and looming over this bewildering corpse the fifty-foot statue of the Amitabha, Lord of the Temple. They moved on then to the temple of Heroes, a small place housing Kuan Kung and Chan Ti, who had once put paid to an enemy by turning him into a one-eyed peacock. All very well, but Sandy had come with expectations of more vigorous and immediate marvels. The spectre of the man called Ging Si generated more fear in him than all these gold-skinned gods added together. The ruthless gwailo had clawed him to the bone, subordinated and recruited him. These lacquered effigies had no balls, no heat or power; no energy to face the snarl of that most puissant animal, the Ging Si.

The final temple that they visited was the most fantastic of all. This was the home of the King of Heaven, the God in whose role Sandy had been cast in his latest opera – the Jade Emperor. But it was the guardians of that deity who dominated that chapel – four of them, towering above the emperor, with splendid armour and martial frown.

And after that there was no more to see. They went outside. The sun still blazed from a broad sky, the cicadas still chirped. It was all as it was before. His brother had not proved what he had intimated he would prove, and Sandy felt flatly disappointed in him.

'No miracle, ha?'

'Not one, but ten thousand, Brother.' Here was the change. It was in Tang Tsun's eyes, the petalled languor had fallen away, and beneath it were thorns.

'Elder Brother,' Sandy said. 'I too dress up like an emperor, and go on stage. I do that nightly, and people pay to see me, and applaud. That does not make me anything other than what I am.'

'You still don't understand. But you will. It has to do with devoutness, love and reverence . . .'

'People revere me too.'

'Meditate. I will show you breathing exercises of great benefit. Things will become clearer.'

'I asked you a question, and you called me on. I thought you would show me things. I wanted proof of your claim to be a God, and you knew that. But what have you given me that wasn't there before? I'm sadder than I was. If that was your gift to me then I have it. Here there is no answer . . .'

'You're closer to it than you realize.'

'Yet, I have such faith in you.'

'Have faith in your own god-mind. The answers are there. They have always been there. This world is not the real world.'

'I must go, or the curtain will rise without me.'

'One day it will rise without you, no matter how great is your act or how many people adore you. Re-learn the condition of life. Nothing is permanent, my brother . . . We'll talk again. I too must go. I have to leave for Kowloon City; Master Shun Cheng's Kung-fu Academy. Do you know it?'

'Boxing is not my sport.'

Tang Tsun watched the man he loved turn away in lanquid disappointment, and walk down the terrace towards the Veda. He did not take his eyes from his brother until Sandy had walked beyond the figures of the eighteen disciples. Then a voice at Tang Tsun's side caused him to turn:

'How can you keep on with him? He brings you nothing but suffering.' It was cousin Tik-kat.

'Oh it's you, Cousin. I didn't see you coming.'

'Sandy hates you. I was sitting over there . . .' He gestured towards a shady tree. 'I could see it on his face. Beware of that man, brother or not, he has a traitor's eyes.'

'He can be changed . . . I've finished here, Tik-kat. I've warned these monks of the Kalpa, and instructed them in ways to prepare for it. I must move on.'

'Did you convert them?'

243

'Some will join White Lotus, and some will not.' Tang sighed deeply; sadly. 'Some, like my poor brother, require more proof than the stigma of the Ming and some ancient predictions can provide. Prophecies aren't trinkets to be sold prettily from a tray. It's difficult and unwelcome merchandise, the more so when the customers are monks – complacent and well-fed with home-cooked infallibility. Moreover, some think I'm dangerous, and my teachings will bring down upon them the anger of the Communist power-clique.'

'That is true.'

'Yes it's true. But they should easily be able to endure that hardship. They're too attached to comfort. Where did they learn that? They're vain men and untrustworthy. They too can be changed, but there's so little time.'

'They tire you, the doubters,' Tik-kat said. 'There is no time for such men. The Communist cadres will use them against you.'

'The enemy . . .' Tang Tsun massaged his eyelids, wearily. 'Keep reminding me of them, Cousin. Keep telling me how close they are to the gates. The Eternal Mother weeps as the tyrant rulers of China grind down the people and waste the motherland. The wolves of Beijing have scented us. Soon they will come howling and baying and stripping us totally bare. Yes, remind me of their coming, Cousin; in doing so you double my strength.'

'I'm interested in the reason behind Younger Brother's visit to you here.'

'He's confused.'

'I hope not so much so that he's forgotten where his allegiance lies.'

'He wants to be with us but fears that he has too much to lose. He has mistaken life for happiness; and happiness for virtue. He'll find his way still. Have patience.'

Tik-kat thought about patience, and the other virtues that he too lacked, or possessed in less than commendable quantities. For instance, he took short cuts with meditation, both in form and duration. He frequently allowed temptation to lead him into lustful situations. He had pride. He enjoyed making money, and was very good at it, and had no intention of changing. But despite all this, or perhaps because of it, he revered Tang Tsun.

There were generous earthly rewards for such devotion — financial gain for one thing. To Tik-kat there was not a single thing, ethereal or material, that could not be parcelled up and sold at a profit. Some triad dragon-heads of Hong Kong possessed every earthly comfort, but wanted an honest place in history. Tik-kat had that on offer . . . These same men knew too, that if they did not stop their feuding, the Communists would grind them under, piecemeal. Tik-kat had proposed an irresistible deal on intersociety unity. Pragmatic Tik-kat had seized the opportunity to provide for everyone what they required: to the triads he consigned internal peace, and respectability, and a tangible link with God the Eternal Mother. To the Maitreya's cause he welded an army. For himself he had gained some power, and a lot of money. That was good trading.

Of course the Maitreya, had he been aware of the total width and breadth of the dealings of his cousin, would certainly have cast himself adrift from these arrangements. But he did not know. And the reason why he did not know was because Tik-kat was a giantly skilful manager of the affairs of the White Lotus Assembly. The Maitreya was never exposed to triad executive meetings where decisions were taken that were less than pure. Tik-kat saw to that. Tik-kat had a keen understanding of the way life worked, and had the gift of being able to handle people – which he misused to great effect. There were some triad societies who for one reason or another (jealousy, or long-remembered grievances, mostly) would not unite with those within the White Lotus Assembly – notably the powerful, twenty-thousand strong Wo On Lok society of Sham Shui Po. But Tik-kat saw this as a minor problem. On the whole, the dragon-heads were pleased with the new alliance. They were getting richer, more powerful and more holy, all at once. Unity had proved to be an excellent investment.

When the Maitreya met with the dragon-heads it was to communicate to them on matters spiritual and inspirational. Some of the dragon-heads were old men, and all of them were sinful.

Some of them had faced death before, and all of them had thought of it. The concept of peace everlasting within the 'womb' of the Eternal Mother was therefore tolerable. One such meeting was scheduled for that very afternoon. In fact, if the Maitreya did not make immediate progress towards Kowloon City, they would be late for it.

'We'd better go now, Maitreya. It's a long walk to the car and a long drive to Kowloon. We have a meeting with the dragon-heads of the Chuen group and the Fourteen-K, and some others. It would be a mistake to be late.'

'So much to do.' Tang Tsun, with his Precious Volumes held to his chest, walked on. The sun was losing the contest for the sky. Shadows were stretching greenly, coolly over the gardens. 'You see, Tik-kat, how nothing is permanent and everything unfolds in permanent flux. The death of the day is the birth of the night. Birth, life, then decay and death. So it is with all things, and even a whole year of days is a blink of the eye in the universal master-plan. Can you imagine therefore how small and insignificant is the span of one human life; your life, or mine?'

Tik-kat thought: well, if it's that short, let's squeeze out every drop of pleasure that it holds. He breathed in deeply of the pine-scented air and quite enjoyed the burning in the front of his thighs that the down gradient was causing. Bamboo grew thickly on both sides of the descending track and the setting sun shot bright green through its tips. More and more steps carried them steeply downwards. Soon they were in the valleys. There was a railway line ahead, with a concrete underpass forged through it, and while they were there a train rumbled overhead; massive with its rhythm – *clank-clank, clank-clank*, it rattled the bridge and shook the ground. Tik-kat stopped, thrilled by the power of locomotion on such a grand scale. The Maitreya walked through the barrier of sound as though it did not exist. Perhaps for him, in his world of exclusion, it was too transient to be noticed.

A group of young monks en route towards the monastery came past Tang Tsun, and some of them turned their shaven heads.

They came through the underpass in a huddle, their clotted whispers amplified in the now still tunnel.

'He has the sign of Ming . . .'

'Even the abbot recognizes that.'

'Yet he works with the triads, it's said. Now, would the true Maitreya do that?'

Not with the triads, but *for* them – for their good. Tik-kat felt the urge to pinch that dull grey monk by the ear and shout those words directly into his brain. He works with love with those who by right he should hate. That is the man called Maitreya.

The monks, however, walked by, unscathed by this silent broadside of devotion. They did not condescend to notice Tik-kat, who hurried then to catch up with his cousin – energized by the knowledge that comfortable transport was almost at hand. His deep-maroon, chauffeur-driven Rolls-Royce awaited them in the parking-lot at the base of the hill. They would glide in its extravagant, cool interior all the way to Kowloon City.

Those monks had better come up with a bit more reverence if they wanted to make it through the turn of the Kalpa.

Tik-kat was immersed in such thoughts as that when he reached his cousin's side. Without turning his head the Maitreya said: 'You're mistaken, Tik-kat, if you think that my concern is for the triads, or for their good. My concern is exclusively for the motherland . . . For the suffering people of China. The triads are the only cohesive force in all of China that can be harnessed to oppose Communism. We must point them at the enemy.'

'How did you know . . . ?'

'The tongue is the trickster of the mind. I hear with my intuition. For instance, I'm aware that some of the dragon-heads we are going to meet are intolerant of White Lotus doctrine, and merely exploit it as a means to expand power and wealth. They're small men, but they're as big as I've got. They pretend infatuation with my ideals amongst themselves, and to me, in order to provide the tether for a fragile unity which serves a temporary purpose. But they may find that this belt

247

that binds them will require more undoing than they are capable of . . . What's your opinion then, Cousin?'

The Maitreya turned questioningly towards Tik-kat.

Tik-kat was almost too afraid to think. What if the Maitreya could really penetrate his cranium and fetch his secrets? . . . There were some dark corners, some very dark corners. Tik-kat bit his lip and concentrated on the pain. But thought is like a monkey in a banyan tree: impossible to tie down. Before very long ideas were bounding to some precarious reaches.

Yes, it was true that some dragon-heads would not deviate from the stratagems that had carried them to their present fortunate positions. They peered suspiciously from their financial fortresses, constantly on guard, and ready to take on all challenges: the puny Hong Kong police, other triad societies, traitors in their own ranks, they had fought them all in the past, and triumphed. Now these same leaders were prepared to fight off the perceived challenge of White Lotus.

Stupid, stupid men; they couldn't see that the enemies of yesterday were a pebble thrown against the door. The new enemy was a cataclysm. Unity was the requirement for survival, and those who would not unite should be removed by any means. Tik-kat said, 'It's just as you say, Maitreya.'

The room was large and cool by virtue of its ceramic-tiled floor. One wall was dominated by a thick teak sparring post, set firmly into a cement base. From this post there projected at different levels and angles three, wrist-thick wooden arms, against which the boxers of Master Shun Cheng's Kung-fu Academy were supposed to work up some calluses, but which at that moment served merely as a rack for the umbrellas of those assembled there.

Against the windows of the outside wall was placed the mandatory tank full of orange and pearl goldfish, to absorb the mortal shock of any bad feng shui that might emanate from the street, two floors below.

Master Shun was present, alas, in photographic form only. For he was deceased. Nevertheless he honoured the assembly, gazing expressionlessly at it over a stubble of burned-down incense sticks, from an illuminated red and gold shrine stuck to the wall.

The living participants of that meeting were seated at a circular linen-covered table that had been borrowed from a nearby restaurant. And though the table was circular there was no doubt in the minds of those seated there as to which was the place of honour. That chair stood facing the doorway, and it was unoccupied. Another chair in a lesser position also stood vacant. The rest of the places were occupied by men of various ages, physical conditions, and modes of dress; generally describable as unprepossessing.

Eel-eyes Chang of the Leun group was there, staring grotesquely through his super-magnified spectacles at his fellow delegates; his malacca cane pinched between his knees. Next to him sat the Vanguard officer of the same triad association, a quiet man. There sat Black-dog Heung, from Ma Kat association, in earnest and subdued conversation with his neighbour. Heung's skin was speckled and his eyes were hooded with age; a wet cigarette drooped from the corner of his mouth, and his wispy white moustache was smoke-stained. If Mr Tan of the Wo Shing Tong had a nickname, then no one knew it, or if they did, they did not care to use it. Mr Tan was thick-set and bristle-scalped, and his face bore the scars of a boxer. He could easily be provoked into anger, and seemed more than averagely scratchy that evening. In fact it was not his fellow office bearers that were giving him the fidgets; it was the new 'Vigor' men's panties that had arrived that very day (by courtesy of Leaping Tiger Mail Order Co.) that was the reason for his discomfort. The advert had guaranteed: 'Promotion of sperm production. Continuous cool and refreshing feeling.' And, most importantly: 'Prolongation of sexual intercourse.' He had been delighted to receive so thoughtful a gift, and had donned them at once. The contraption had an inner panel with a hole in it through which to dangle the penis and press it against a patent, hemp rubbing-cloth which, by its abrasive action presumably, caused the glans to grow dull (thus prolonging the time of sexual intercourse, distinctly). The sperm count, moreover, was improved by means of an insulator pouch which maintained the entire scrotum at an even 33 degrees C. He had put the panties on strictly according to instruction: (1.) Put your seminal vesicle into its pouch . . . (2.) Hang your penis on the band type ring . . . (3.) Pull up your Vigor panties tightly. Perhaps he had pulled them up over-tightly. His penis felt as though trapped like an otter in a noose. Still, if the panties proved true to promise it was worth the discomfort. Mr Tan entered conversation with a young gentle-man from Lo Cheun:

'Did you know that many young men nowadays are suffering from decreasing of the sperm count on account of propensity of wearing tight jeans?'

'Wah! don't say.'

'I think I might recommend something good for that.'

Mr Tan was prevented from enlarging on his thesis on cramped testicles, for at that moment someone announced the approach of the maroon Rolls-Royce that bore the leaders of the White Lotus Assembly.

Now, here was an astonishing sight: a room full of typical Cantonese businessmen (a little more avaricious than the norm perhaps), whose collective attitude towards gods and ghosts and religion in general was that to muck around in such matters made for abysmally poor luck, preparing to receive in their midst a Buddhist Monk.

'Aieya,' sighed Eel-eyes Chang. 'Times have changed, brothers. Kneel down to feed the mother pig.' Which comment just about summed things up. The British were packing their kit to leave; the People's Liberation Army were packing to come in, and for a very long stay. Now, no one doubted that the new masters of Hong Kong would prop up the pillow with the triad leaders; the Chinese were even more corrupt than the British. But they were also a lot more exploitative, cunning and ruthless than the departing gwailos. So, unless there was unity amongst the triads, they would find they were being played off against each other, and not in a small way. Some of them would be wiped out.

Then there was the matter of the predicted Kalpa. Now, mendicant monks who wandered the countryside with a begging-bowl, predicting the end of the world, could be derided without a qualm. Monks, on the other hand, who arrived, chauffeur-driven, in late model, ultra luxury cars should be taken very seriously. But there was more to it than that. As Eel-eyes put it: 'There's something about the man. He's . . . different. He has a way.'

Shrewd, Chang had once again drawn from all of their minds. Tang Tsun had a way. He was as unlike a monk as the bamboo is to the river-reed. In his humbleness there was persuasive spirit. In his courtesy there was steel. And somewhere in the shallows of his eyes there was war. It was easy to believe him when he spoke of Heaven, Earth and Man in disarray. Starvation and civil strife in China was everyday news. The PLA generals had turned loose their armies on their own people, while aged madmen clung to power in the Great Hall. Earthquake and flood ravaged the country as never before. These things could not be denied. Perhaps they were one step away from the end of an era; perhaps the Kalpa of the Third Buddha *was* at hand.

Mr Tan saw things differently. He conceded that Tang Tsun was an amazing man. But that was as far as he was prepared to go. The Kalpa was nonsense; patent scaremongering, so comically naive as to be laughable. In his opinion Tang Tsun was a highly intelligent opportunist whose reputation had been faked in order to gain power. And for that fine con-job he could admire him. The point was that Tang Tsun had caused the triad factions to come together, as one of them had put it: All sleeping in the same bed, but with different dreams. He had no argument with that. So he was prepared to sit there in his extraordinarily disconcerting underwear, and listen. He also had a point or two to make. But he was in no hurry.

There was no great ceremony in the welcoming of Tang Tsun. He was announced by name, as was simple courtesy, and he and his cousin took their seats. Tea was poured for him, but he didn't drink. Those deep and troubling eyes of his stilled the room. Then he began to speak:

'In the earliest writings of the triad it was recorded that one hundred and thirty-one monks left the perfect tranquillity of the Sui Lam monastary and came down from the Kaolin mountains to fight the Ching invaders. Those monks were highly skilled in war and Chinese boxing. But through treachery they were defeated by the Manchu-Ching soldiers and the monastery was burned to the ground.

'Only five monks survived. They prayed to the Buddha for deliverance, and the Enlightened One came miraculously to their side and they fought their way free.

'Weak, and bleeding, they made their way to the Long River and fainted on the bank. They had a dream, and it directed them to a place where they discovered an incense pot with this message written on it: "Overthrow the Ching: Restore the Ming." And, "Act according to the will of Heaven." They decided to worship heaven for this sign.

'Five men cannot defeat an army. They continued to flee. They came to the Black Dragon River which could only be crossed by a two-planked bridge, heavily guarded by Ching soldiers. But three stepping-stones appeared, each bearing one character: Calm – Sea – Floating. So that was how they crossed.

'They were helped by some peasants, who fed them and led them to the Wai Yeung district of Guandong province where they found shelter in Po Tak monastery, and began to raise another army. On the twenty-fifth day of the seventh moon of the Kap Yan year these Five Ancestors and all their new followers swore an oath to overthrow the Ching and restore the Ming, and they became the Ming Eternal Society – the first triad.

'But the Manchu-Ching dynasty was still too strong to be deposed, and our forces were defeated at Nanking, and in the

White Tiger Pass, and a hundred thousand triad brothers died in battle.

'In Eighteen Thirteen a great battle was fought by the triads under the banner of White Lotus Society. They called it the Eight Trigrams rebellion. Again the Ching army was victorious; eighty thousand triad brothers died for the cause. But still the ideal lived. Manchu spies were everywhere, and so in order to survive the persecution, the brothers split up into the Five Lodges, and spread right across China. To the south, and here in Hong Kong there came the second Lodge. In Fukien the First Lodge made their headquarters; the Third Lodge went to Yunnan and Szech-uan, and the Fourth to Hunan and Hupei. The Fifth Lodge, known as the Forty-Seven Tai, formed in Kiangsi and Chekiang.

'And that was how things stood when early in this century Dr Sun Yat Sen united the banners of all Five Lodges under the Kuomintang generals and drove the last Manchu emperor from the Dragon Throne.

'So an empire fell; the Ching Dynasty was defeated. But was the Ming ever truthfully restored?'

Oh, this priest could talk the fish right into the wok! You didn't realize how deeply he'd enmeshed you in his tale until he paused, as he did then, and in eagerness to hear more, you leaned towards him in mind and body. Then he gave more, and so you came on . . .

'No, the Ming never regained their rightful place. China was in turmoil and war-lords ruled. Even the wily Chiang Kai-Shek could not unite the armies. When the Japanese first invaded there was little resistance, but abundant treachery. Brothers, let me tell you about treachery. From the hills disguised as the saviour of the motherland came the evil genius Mao Tse-tung, open-armed, and draped with promises of a new dawn. He showed the people a new religion – Communism. He wrote about a new god – himself. And into his embrace flocked the hungry, the foolish, the hopeful and the weak, and he closed on them with a grip that at first seemed loving, but never ceased to tighten, tighten . . . tighten.

253

'He squeezed until they were no longer people, just straw. Then he gave the straw to his successors, and said, "Do what you like with it." So they burned it, and they are still burning it. And *who* is there to stop them?'

No one asked. But their minds shouted – who?

Tang Tsun would only tell them who would *not* be able to stop them:

'The once proud triads, high on the rungs of noble purpose, no longer exist. The once proud generals who hoisted their battle flags at Nanking and in the White Tiger pass are dead and gone. What remains of that heritage of heroism? What I see is a cowering huddle of leaders who've lost all sense of destiny. When the books are written of the history of this period, and the eyes of those, yet unborn, look at the deeds of today's men, whose names will they see written there?'

Questions that impaled the soul. Who would not give his last breath in the struggle for a place, however feeble, upon the scrolls of history? Cunning, cunning, Tang Tsun, what impossible prospects now?

Tang Tsun would only tell them what was not his guarantee: long life and a lenient death. And was there amongst them a person so unChinese that he would take such terms? Amazingly, it seemed that there was more than one. Amongst the elder leaders, especially, there were those whose every inflexion showed approval for Tang Tsun's predictions.

'The spirit of a true ideal cannot be severed by one, or many deaths. It cannot be cut down by sword, or bullet. So the Ching-Manchu failed, and were swept away, and the man who posed as god – Mao Tse-tung, failed too. A thousand shouted quotations lie like a thousand shattered shards from a broken bowl, and his successors have nothing to hold to but Mao's fading ghost, and no power beyond the range of a bullet to preserve their monstrous tyranny.'

'True,' Tan interrupted, 'but many bullets from many machine-guns make for many dead people.' He felt the time had come to open the windows of common sense. 'Dead people:

that's all this Maitreya can promise. I'm a businessman . . . Forgive me, but I should like to remind you all of the number one rule of mine. "If it won't sell, don't buy it." . . . There's *no* market for martyrdom.'

Black-dog Heung disagreed with old-fashioned politeness. 'Much to lose, yes . . . but possibly more to lose by letting the enemy grasp the throat. We all know that the Communists are liars; they treat vows like eating so much lettuce. They'll break the agreement they signed with the British, quicker than the hop of a locust. They'll ruin Hong Kong, if not deliberately, then because it's in their nature to destroy things. It's true what the Maitreya says; their policies are distant echoes of a failed ideology . . . To follow such a path is to confine the lessons of history to the ash heap. We should make a stand.'

There arose a sudden din of voices:

'A stand: how?'

'With what? Where are the guns?'

'They'll mow us down!'

And through this uproar the voice of the Maitreya darted brightly, and keen as a needle mending sackcloth. Then he drew the edges together:

'Brothers, there is a way.'

'Then,' Mr Tan shot up from his chair, 'please make sure that "way" does not include me.'

Stiff-backed Mr Tan strode out of the Shun Cheng Boxing Academy. Not until he had reached street level did he slacken, and glance over his shoulder to see which other triad leaders had had the good sense to follow his initiative. There was no one behind him but his bodyguard. That was disappointing. Still, he had not lost face. The others would come around in time.

'Crazy,' he said to the bodyguard. 'All of them just fucking crazy.'

When Mr Tan was in such a thundrously bad mood, the wisest course was not to say a word. The bodyguard opened the rear door of his silver Mercedes, and Mr Tan climbed in and settled, and thought about where he should go from there. His thinking was consciously influenced by the tortion being imposed on his private parts, no doubt about that – the time had arrived to put to the test the claims made by the patent-holders of Vigor men's panties. He gave instructions to his driver.

'Shouson Hill.'

The driver knew exactly which address to take his boss to in prestigious Shouson Hill Road. Mr Tan had owned a luxury apartment there for as long as he had been his chauffeur, and that was for many years. The occupants of that apartment had come and gone. The single condition of tenure was that they should be female, young, very beautiful, and ever ready to lay out for Mr Tan. Even so he tired of each of them eventually. Mr Tan's current number-one tsip's name was Harmony, and she had long, lustrous hair. Her amah had told him that she was summoned to brush it five hundred full strokes, morning and night.

Mr Tan 'phoned Harmony when the Mercedes emerged from the harbour tunnel and was disgruntled to find her number engaged. He 'phoned again on passing Happy Valley and became further frustrated with her non-attendance. By the time he was able to make contact with her, they were almost at the gate. He shouted into the mouthpiece:

'. . . there in a minute, fuck!'

And, give or take a few seconds, that was how much longer it took to reach her driveway. Frangipani dappled the moonlight, and scented the air, and an outside light flicked on to guide Mr Tan swiftly to the front door. By now, despite all other discontentments, he was certain that the Vigor panties were all that they were cracked up to be. He had the good heavy feeling in his balls that signalled a quality erection.

Harmony wore a bare-shouldered dress in two shades of red. She was petite and golden-skinned, and had small pearly teeth that gleamed a smile of pure pleasure at her 'Adopted Father'. That was what she called him: Kai Ye.

'I'd hoped with all my heart that you'd visit tonight, Kai Ye. All prayers answered.'

How could he retain anger in face of such an amicable welcome. Still, he wagged a hefty finger under her nose. 'Not good to talk on the 'phone so much . . .'

'Aieya, Kai Ye; just chit-chat to girl-friends.'

Mr Tan sucked at a brandy and ice and flopped his substantial frame on to a long couch. Harmony took off his shoes and socks and applied ten-happiness massage to some pressure-points on his feet, which caused Mr Tan to clench his teeth and hiss with delight.

'Chase the demons from your temple,' she said. 'Good, ha?'

It was more than good. Little thrills of exquisite pain squirmed through him. This woman was a rare find. He watched her at her work; firm little arms, strong fingers. Her long hair swayed past her cheeks, and one button-loop of the dress had opened, providing a gap with a blissful view. Mr Tan gave a great sigh, and Harmony looked up and showed him her excellent teeth.

'Ah, the demons escape, Kai Ye.'

'Fools . . . I should tell you, Harmony.'

'They made you angry?'

'Crazy I should say . . . A mad monk on a suicide mission; he fills up their heads with wild promises and those fools lap it up like mother's milk . . . He wants to fight the Reds; to bring down Communism. Dangerous talk. Madness. I walked away.'

'What will you do, Kai Ye?'

'I must think.'

Harmony did not lift her gaze when she said: 'A man stood alone once in Tian An Men Square before a column of advancing tanks. Even when they were about to crush him he did not break . . . And he stopped them. Is that the kind of madness of this monk?'

'There will always be fools and heroes, they are made in the same mould. And to be near them is dangerous. The driver of that tank was just as much a fool, for stopping as the man who stood in his way was, for standing there. And I detest them both.' He reached for Harmony then, caught her by the hair

257

and hauled her upwards. 'Sometimes you should watch your tongue, little one.'

'Yes, Kai Ye.'

'You'll see that I'm right . . . Yes.'

Now should have been the time for him to give this woman the full lesson in masculine arrogance, and other stern stuff. There she knelt with her head bowed and her eyes downcast, her pink mouth trembling with the pain of his grip. But supplanting raging desire a wave of nausea came burgeoning from his abdomen to his throat, and cold sweat chilled him right through. His stomach suddenly boiled and heaved. He staggered towards the lavatory and leaned into the bowl and vomited, yellowly. That granted no relief. The pressure and gripe in him built and built, bending him double, and out it shot in an endless foul gargle, again and again.

Beyond the open lavatory door Mr Tan could see Harmony. She had one hand pressed to her mouth, but there wasn't a wrinkle of concern on her face. As the truth of it came to him, his limbs, his whole body began to shake and convulse, and his vision broke into little whirling pieces. There was a red piece and that was her, and he forced his eyes to hold it and centre it. He knew he was looking at his poisoner, and that he would die an awful death.

Harmony knew that Mr Tan would not suffer for very long, and that pleased her. He had never done her any serious harm. Now the vomiting would cease and a great languor would creep over him; a stupor that would blunt the final minutes. His kidneys would bleed and his heartbeat would rapidly slow down and then stop.

Mr Tan, for his part, decided that his end should not be as passive as all that. He drew away from the latrine bowl and stood up, then swayed towards her. Harmony retreated towards the stairs that led to the first-floor bedroom, and on he came, frowning and blinking as though dazzled by a great light. He barged into a small table, and a priceless porcelain figurine crashed. He grasped the banister rail and hauled himself onwards, upwards, while Harmony backed away. Sixteen steps made up that staircase, and every rise seemed that it might defeat him, yet did not. He reached the landing, and found her with his stunned, slow eyes, and came on.

Harmony fled into the bedroom and would have slammed the door, but his weight came against it and he burst in. Then he fell, and the floor shook with the weight of him. He should not have been able to rise, but he did. He hauled himself up and lunged at her, and though she darted back he snagged her dress and tore it clear away. His other hand gripped her hair, then closed on her neck and his fingers bit into her windpipe and tightened as though he would tear out the core of her neck.

He toppled on to her and they fell together as drunken lovers might, upon the marshmallow softness of the satin-sheeted bed.

Dr Savoury sucked mournfully on an old, chipped briar which made unclean, wet noises and issued clouds of acerbic blue smoke; which odour was preferable to the stink of chloroform and dead things that otherwise took over his laboratory. He was a wrinkled man, from years hatless beneath the Kenyan sun, and as slow as a tortoise. He picked up a test-tube and gave it a patient shake; held its pinkish content to the light for a moment, then set it gingerly back in a rack. He said to Reven Forrester: 'Abric acid is a seldom-used poison, though I can't for the life of me think why. You can knock a horse down with a minute dosage, it's child's play to make, it's practically tasteless and there is no antidote – none whatsoever . . . Why don't you and I go and sit in my office; more comfortable there.' He tamped down the bowl of his pipe with his fire-proof thumb, and jammed the apparatus into the top pocket of his lab-coat. There were burn marks all over the garment. The doctor was a walking incendiary.

Savoury's office was very small. The walls were cluttered with old photographs of himself in various poses, mostly with a background of African thorn trees; one with a bi-plane aircraft, and one with a woman in a pith helmet who had a lovely smile. The furniture was as hard-bottomed and primal as only the PWD could supply. The comfort factor lay in a small off-white refrigerator, which, besides slides of human tissue and other various effluents, contained a shelf full of frosted bottles of beer. Dr Savoury drank as though just returned from a week in the Sahel – one full bottle, and half of the next before he spoke again.

'Abric acid, yes . . . The Kikuyu tribesmen used it to kill the settlers' livestock during the emergency in Kenya, and for one or two murders, but generally they preferred to use pangas for that; energetic people those Kikuyu . . . Abric is not a commonly used poison in this part of the world, though I can't see why not. The toxin is contained in the seed of the Rosary Pea, and that's easy enough to obtain. It's a creeper. I've seen it growing wild all over the show in the New Territories, and especially on Lantau Island . . . Have another beer, Reven.' Savoury took time for another life-saving swig. He burped with polite energy into his fist, then carried on: 'Well, as I was saying it's a toxin that should appeal to the Chinese mind. It gives the victim just time enough to work out who is killing him, and why, before he falls off the perch. And even supposing he had strength enough to summon medical help, there's nothing any doctor could do but watch the poor bugger die.'

'Yet our Mr Tan got up and killed his lady-friend . . .'

'Sheer bloody willpower, Reven. Amazing. He must have reckoned she'd done it to him . . . Do you think she poisoned him?'

'It looks that way, doesn't it. The question that intrigues me, is why? She was well provided for by Adopted Father, so why do him in?'

'Jealousy perhaps. Who's the investigating officer?'

'I've given the case to Mike Hempstead.'

'He'll need these then . . .' Savoury shuffled the papers on his desk, muttering, 'Damned if I didn't have them a minute ago.' He patted the pockets of his lab-coat. Not finding what he was looking for in either of these places, he went back into his laboratory, returning after a while with a small clear plastic bag which enclosed some pea-sized red and black seeds. 'Here . . .

Those are the seeds of the *Abrus Precatorius* – the Rosary Pea. Pretty little things, aren't they? That's what Hempstead needs to look out for. Poisoners are careless, that's my experience. They never seem to rid themselves of the evidence. Fascinated by it, I suppose.' He gave a mordant laugh. 'By the way; those homosexual murders. You wanted to know if there were signs of anal intercourse . . . There were no lubricants and no seminal fluid present, so I should say, no. A case of selective, cold-blooded murder. Had a rash of such cases in Kenya in '52 . . . Never solved them.'

Savoury took his briar from his pocket, and tampered with it until satisfied that it would smoke well, then clamped it between his teeth. He walked with Forrester to the door of the lab. By way of farewell he said: 'Anything else I can do . . .'

It was close to the end of the day and the lifts were crowded with those who kept well-regulated hours. Those cops who still had duties to do went about them in that tired, stubborn way that comes from years of chipping and picking at the unaltering cliff-face of hard crime; Forrester's day was not yet over. There was Charlie Lam to visit. Then he would go on to Shouson Road; to the site of the double murder. Mike Hempstead would meet him there.

The hospital to which Charlie had been admitted was sited on lofty Pok Fu Lam Hill, a place well washed by healthy wind. On that cloudless day its windows gave a view, as clear as a postcard, across the blue waters of the East Channel to the islands Lamma and Cheung Chau and distance-hazed Lantau. Queen Mary Hospital should have been a good place to get well, but Forrester regarded its intentions with suspicion. Perhaps there were just too many damaged people to cope with soundly. The passageways were beset with stretchered, bled-out humans waiting for whatever medical fate was to be served up.

Charlie's rank entitled him to a two-bed ward. His form lay small, dismally still, crisped by sheets, bandaged and betubed, but definitely no longer at the door of death. Flowers of every hue (Caroline's prescription for a rapid return to health) surrounded the bed-space. Charlie appeared to be sleeping, but no sooner had Forrester sat than his eyes opened narrowly and turned upon him; pained, beaten eyes that wished his visitor was not there.

'Hello, Charlie.'

Charlie whispered, 'Ging Si.'

'They dug two slugs out of you, nine millimetre, eighteens; made in China . . . I'm profoundly grateful it's such an undeadly round. Still, one in each lung could have caused some grief.' It hurt to talk to his friend; even to look at him.

Charlie Lam turned away again. He gave a barely perceptible nod.

'Who shot you, Charlie? . . . That question I need an urgent answer to. The sampan woman gave us an incomplete description, but what would you expect: "dark", she said: "raining", she said. Still, we got a bit out of her; enough of a description to make me think it was Lonnie Huang . . . Our same old sampan-foo said that you started it; you were trying to strangle him . . . Why did you do that, Charlie? You've got a pistol, why didn't you use it, if not to arrest him, then to kill him straight off?'

Charlie offered nothing. Forrester went on:

'The raid on the boat-yard was a success as far as Narcotics are concerned. They made some good arrests. An important Chiu Chau chemist and some fighters, as well as the entire crew of the trawler that brought the stuff in . . . And a bloody monkey, can you believe it – a total dope-head . . . Well, Dave Kwok has been soaking up all the kudos; photos in the *Post* and all that, but the real hero of the day was Gilly MacNaughton. He went in at the sharp end, and nearly got his arm lopped off by a triad chopper . . . Lonnie Huang got away though . . . Oh, he was there all right. Your information was valid. He was employed as the chemist's assistant, they knew him also as Blind-boy. Am I telling you anything you don't already know? . . . We believe he took a Makarov, type fifty-nine pistol, and some blocks of morphine base, and made a run for it. I believe that's the weapon that he shot you with.'

Charlie Lam, wary of pain, shifted his torso to be able to observe his visitor better. Of course, the visitor's view of him improved, too. Dry, yellow mucus was pasted to his lips, and strings of the muck, stuck at the corners of his mouth, moved elastically as he slowly spoke: 'Ging Si, don't play cat and mouse with me any more, and I'll be straight with you. It was Lonnie Huang who shot me, as you already know. You also know that I tried to kill him . . . and why I didn't simply shoot him. The point is, what are you going to do about it?'

'I'm not sure, Charlie. You've a gift for putting me in a hard spot. Can I give you some water, Charlie?' . . . A glass with a bent straw. He looked so thirsty, yet hardly sipped. A moist cloth was needed to clean the muck from this poor man's lips. Where was such a cloth to be found? Blasted nurses, where were they? . . . Forrester said, 'Well, it wouldn't do any good if I asked you to stop your vendetta against Lonnie Huang, you've already turned down that plea . . . I've done a lot of thinking since last we spoke. I also visited your flat while you weren't there. I saw the ring; Grandmother Wong's ruby ring . . . and I saw some drawings.'

Charlie Lam flinched as though stabbed by sudden pain. Forrester wished this interview was done. 'Scattered all over the place were dozens of those bizarre drawings. I took one, Charlie. I gave it to Doctor Sin.'

Defencelessly he protested: 'You had no right . . .' He coughed, and grimaced with pain.

Forrester said, 'I'm not concerned with legal niceties. I had a right, as your friend, to do what I did, and I have no regrets. I had a long discussion with Sin about you, too, but when it came down to it he couldn't tell me anything that I didn't already know . . . These bullet holes are mild wounds when compared with the fury let loose in you when you were forbidden to join the man-hunt. That decision was right for the Director and right for the Bureau, but for you, old friend, it was a massive blow, and a crushing injustice. It took the good cop Charlie Lam and changed him to a night assassin . . . That's what you've become, though no one knows it but me.' He stood and went to the window. Clouds had swept a weepy film over the postcard view. Charlie's voice came dawdling from behind:

'What will you do, Reven?'

'It's what you must do, can't you see. You must get out of the force.' He turned, irritated with himself. So hard to look at this hurt man; a penitent pain that he wanted to avoid. His friend's voice questioned, thinly:

'You want me to resign?'

'No, then you'd lose everything that you've built over twenty years. I'm going to have you boarded, Charlie. I've already made arrangements for you to go before the Medical Board. I want you invalided out on full pension. It's an honourable way to go.'

'Honourable dishonour. Too hard for me to accept that, Reven.'

'There are other ways to force you into early retirement. That is your best choice.'

'It's take it or leave it, ha?'

'I'm afraid so, Charlie.'

Charlie stared inwardly, bitterly. The stringy mucus stretched to permit bitter, slow words: 'There is no other way, is there? I've thought about it too . . . I knew that you'd find me out, Ging Si. Sooner or later, I knew we would have this conversation.'

'It's not a question, Charlie, of what I found out, or didn't, don't you see. It's a question of sanity. You've taken the blame for Lulu's death fully upon yourself. God knows why; but there it is. That's what Sin believes, and so do I. The guilt of it has built into an incinerative blaze which is more than your mind can take. Your flat is scattered with apologies to a dead woman; dozens of outpourings of sorrow; just fuel, more fuel for more sorrow . . . I can't do any more for you now. There was a time when I was prepared to defend you, but that's past. Knowing what I now know, I cannot let you stay on as a police officer.' Forrester paused; Charlie seemed to wish to speak, but nothing came of the silence, so he claimed it. 'Whatever happens after today, must happen. If you cannot alter your course: if you continue to hunt Lonnie Huang, then so be it.'

Two red circles of heat flushed Charlie's cheeks; he seemed enlivened. His speech was quicker: 'I would rather be dead than to go on like this, too. I'll admit there are times when I cling to normal thought by a very frayed thread . . . Reven, there are nights when it's all I can do to stop myself from screaming out loud. There's a huge blackness, I can't describe it better than that, it threatens me constantly and I fight it off. It's easier to keep it away in the daytime, but at night it's overpowering. I'm not sure whether Lonnie Huang's death will drive off this black beast. But I know there is no other prescription that's any good. It's right that we've spoken like this, Reven. I tried not to let you down. I think you know that. It's been a fine friendship; yours and mine . . . Would that have to come to an end?'

'Don't make me answer that.' No more such questions, please. As though to crush a broken-winged sparrow, a storm-crippled bird, there needed to be a quick and merciful end to this hopeless conversation. Charlie's voice trailed, broken-winged:

'Yes. Wrong to ask that.'

'It's over for me here, anyway. I'm getting out of Hong Kong. I've decided that. Caroline and I are going to get married . . . Start again.'

'It's what Lulu always wanted . . . and predicted. That's good news; it's really great. Shannon needs both of you.'

'We're going to have a look around Australia. We both like Australia . . . I'd better get along, Charlie. There was a murder in Shouson Road.'

'It was on TV.'

'Good luck, Charlie.'

'Walk slowly, Ging Si.'

Charlie Lam raised his wrist and gave the smallest of waves, and Forrester's gesture was not much larger than that. Sparse movements that sheltered vast emotions; for both men knew that here and now they were cutting away the past. And both of them wished it were not so.

Mike Hempstead knelt on the soft giving mattress. He pinched the slippery silk corners of the pillows on the bed; an admirer of such succulent prodigality. He gazed at an intricate pen-and-wash painting that crowned the large headboard – a masterpiece of Japanese pornography that depicted a writhing octopus obscenely guzzling at the crotch of a well-fleshed and hairy Nipponese lady. It was described as 'the dream of the fisherman's wife'. The fisherman's wife seemed quite relaxed about things. There were some further assorted erotic *objets d'art* in that room but none quite as raw as that Japanese painting. Mr Tan had entertained some unusual sexual notions, yes indeed. But how meanly death scooped out all secrets, debased dignity and dispensed with privilege. Never die wearing funny underpants. Mr Tan for all his wealth and power had last been seen in these luxurious quarters, with trousers clinging at half-mast, and a long pencil-thin pathologist's thermometer protruding from the brown bud of his rectum. It hadn't seemed right to guffaw so heartily, but the detectives had done it just the same.

Harmony's corpse had invited softer comment. Such a beautiful girl; a poisoner? It was hard to believe. As the morgue attendants had transported her on their aluminium trolley her long black hair had trailed on the floor. Someone had gathered it, and put a twist in it, and stored it beneath her shoulders. That seemed the decent thing to do.

The investigating officer, a Chinese detective inspector from regional CID, had surrendered his notes to the man from OSCB who would take over from him, and seemed more than happy to be off the case. He stood around chatting with the CIB detectives while Hempstead copied the notes. Then he left. The specialists, with all their paraphernalia, were next to depart. Hempstead and his team then searched the flat and made an inventory of everything in it, large or small. And this had taken them all day.

Now, apart from the uniformed PC who stood guard at the front door, Mike was alone there, with little to do but wait. So he perused the pornography and drifted from room to room, making further observations and worrying at the crime as a good detective should. A grey cat stalked in from the small walled garden; it rubbed and purred on the toes of his brogues, then trotted off in the direction of the kitchen, mewling for food. He ignored the animal and went back to the bedroom – the most interesting room by far.

One side of that room was panelled with mirrors, and another with louvred, built-in cupboards. He hadn't personally searched these cupboards, a subordinate had, and the inventory list was large. He counted, eighteen pages. My God, the woman had owned half a hundred pairs of hose; seven housecoats with slippers to match, and six racks of shoes of ten per rack. There were some trays in that cupboard that were laden with perfumed underwear of every hue and variety of style. Mike was swooningly overcome by the urge to delve into that filmy soft and thrilling store, and thus discovered amongst Harmony's panties an item that seemed out of place: a white, calico scarf embroidered with a lotus flower and some Chinese characters, of which he could make no sense. He referred to the inventory, and found that the item had been recorded simply as, 'one white headband'. A headband . . . of course. He folded it into a strip as it would be worn. He had often seen demonstrating workers and students wearing this sort of thing. He was still puzzling at the characters; and had all but decided that they must be of ancient Han script, when Forrester's image came into the mirrors.

'Hello, Ging Si.'

The cat had attached itself to the new arrival. Forrester nudged it with his foot. 'Does this thing belong here?'

Hempstead shoved the headband back into the drawer. He said:

'I was thinking of taking it myself. It seems a pleasant animal. Connie likes cats.'

'Check that it is the property of the deceased before you cart it off.'

Forrester seemed to be in a black mood. He strode from room to room, flinging questions as he went.

'Were the french doors locked?'

'Yes, they were.'

'The front door?'

'Yes.'

'Any signs of forced entry?'

'No.'

He walked into the lavatory and wrinkled his nose at the stench of vomit.

'Have the chemists taken specimens from here?'

'Yes.'

He flushed the cistern, then walked to the lounge. The cat trotted after him. He sat on the couch where Mr Tan had last sat, and trailed his arm to the glass table at its side.

'Is this where the brandy glass was standing?'

Hempstead pointed to the exact spot. 'The photographer took dozens of pics. I've made sketches too. Everything is thoroughly recorded.'

'Did you serialize the photographs, and note the photographer's position at each frame?'

'I didn't think that was necessary.'

'Well it is, Mike . . . I've already seen the photographs, they're fine. But you must add to that record a sketch of where the man stood for each picture, OK?'

'Will do.'

'At the inquest the jury will return an open verdict on this one. You can bet on it. You're going to have to stand up there and give your version of the event. It had better be faultless. Tan was a wealthy guy, so there's going to be publicity, and a lot of speculation in the press. The total truth about Tan will never be known though . . . Now, this is for your ears only, Mike. Tan was the dragon-head of Wo Shing Tong . . . On the night of the murder he attended a meeting at a Kung-fu academy in Kowloon

City. He argued with certain other triad gentlemen of equal rank, and within the hour he was dead. I'm telling you this right at the outset of this case because it's almost certain that Wo Shing Tong will retaliate, and the case will expand. In which event you will be the investigating officer . . . Do you understand the significance of what I'm saying?'

'I . . . think so.'

'Mike, it's the sort of opportunity that is delivered once in a lifetime to one in a thousand cops. And you have it. Triads, like cockroaches, there will always be in Hong Kong; they're endemic. They're part of the Chinese landscape. The secret is to subjugate them, to sever them from any real power, and pick them off at will.'

'A form of pest control.'

'A close description, but more than that. They must be fed, too, and rewarded when reward is due. They must feel content with their lot, so that their crime is rational and predictable.'

King of the cockroaches, thought Mike Hempstead. He said: 'Do you really believe that this case will provide such opportunities?'

'Not immediately. But in the end it will. I've a feeling about it.' Forrester stood. From his jacket pocket he brought a small plastic packet containing red things – beans, small red beans, blotched blackly. 'Let me give you these before I forget . . . They're from Doc Savoury's collection of noxious things. They're seeds from a creeper called the Rosary Pea, and according to him, the poison that killed our Mr Tan is an extract from this type of seed; abric acid . . . Looks quite harmless, doesn't it? But it's deadly, and there's no known antidote.' He jiggled the packet and the beans whispered about. Then he handed it over. 'Dear, pretty little Harmony, she looked inoffensive too . . . God's world abounds with sharp deceptions. Few things are as they appear. And now I must go. Give my regards to Connie.'

Give his regards to Connie; why? What earthly reason existed for Forrester to issue such a cliché? He closed the front door on his superior, then returned to the lounge and sat down. The cat came, purring, and he held it beneath its forelegs and hoisted it up. It had a surprisingly long sleek body and yellow glowing eyes, it mewed silently, and he said to it: 'Cat, what shall we call you? . . . Harmony. Yes, that'll be your new name.'

It had been an excellent day, so far. He saw no reason why things should not continue in that vein. Life, despite its sharp little deceptions, was what you made of it, and the new Mike Hempstead was turning it into an unqualified success. He did some more sketches, as per the pedantic Forrester, then, with the cat clutched under his arm, went to his car. Connie would be delighted with this furry, purry creature.

Connie, of course, was not at home, but as the time was approaching eight she would in a few minutes be radiated into that lounge by courtesy of ATV Newsdesk. He deposited Harmony, and the cat, sensing the luxury of its new quarters, settled down straight away in uncomplaining fashion. The signature tune of Newsdesk came up – its chrome-like logo assembled like bits of magnetized space-debris on the TV screen. And there was Connie; an initial smile, then attentive and serious as she worked into the lead item: a pronouncement from the White House that the inhuman repression of Chinese democratic movements was unanimously disapproved of by the American people; and that, if the Chinese military was not ordered to desist from further unacceptable acts, then financially punitive action would, however regrettable, be unavoidable. She emphasized the word's 'further' and 'unavoidable' . . . Meanwhile in Beijing, at a press conference at the Hall of the People a uniformed general of the PLA gave the true picture. That was, that reactionary political bandits, and other hooligans, financed by overseas warmongers, were engaged in acts of terror, rape and destruction in Guandong, Fujian, Jiangxi and Hubei provinces. Heroic and loyal units of the PLA had put down these contemptible insurrections. The peace-loving people of China were united in praise for the PLA. China would not bow to foreign pressure. All was well in the Motherland.

So, you could take your choice of scenarios. It seemed that the vast majority of the Hong Kong Chinese did not see the People's Liberation Army as saviours and heroes, though, as evidenced by the next news item: there was an unprecedented rush on to liquidate assets in Hong Kong. Property values had tumbled to a fifteen-year low. Business confidence had evaporated, and with it hard cash . . . Goodbye Hong Kong, hello Xianggang.

Mike, who was as financially conscious as anyone these days, took a vital interest in such bulletins. In his previous life, as a pauper, there had been no need to attend to such matters – to gear up for every jig and wobble of the Hang Seng index. Well, times had changed. Now, thanks to Connie's incredible (clairvoyant, you might say) predictions as to the quickest horse in any given race, he had become a rich man. Not stick-it-to-the-Colbys rich, you understand. But well heeled enough to write a six-figure cheque at any time he felt so inclined. It was an exhilarating feeling, but there were attendant problems to great wealth that he had previously not appreciated: *what* to do with it all? Not that he wanted to join the Sunday yacht-set, or to apply for stewardship in the Jockey Club, or even to decorate himself with any affectation. But, hey! It would have been nice to trade in his rusty, third-hand Nissan Crown for something more respectable. There were, however, dangers in even so modest a purchase as a new car. The Independent Commission Against Crime waged a constant vendetta against all cops, whom they considered to be natural criminals. And he had some particular enemies in their ranks who would just love to bust him.

Mike, therefore, secretly bought gold. Solid chunks of gold, the price of which seemed to improve with every fresh execution. Last week China Central TV had screened a Beijing public execution – a whole lorry-load of 'bandits and hooligans' had been taken to the field adjacent to Marco Polo Bridge, where policemen of the Public Security Bureau had drawn the shaven-headed condemned into two cowering rows and made them kneel. A public prosecutor had said a few words, including, 'Justice must be seen to be done.' And so it was; an executioner of the PSB, pistol in hand, had walked along the rows of skulking prisoners, providing each with a bullet in the skull (in some cases two) . . . The gold price had rocketed by three dollars an ounce. Now you couldn't call that bad. Bullion was the thing to be into, in these times, at any cost.

The rest of that night's news was tame stuff. Someone had said that the loss of the Amazon rain-forests was tragic. And a Zulu with an unpronounceable name had been elected as State President in South Africa.

Mike drank four large brandies; the cat finished a bowl of tuna fish, then both man and beast fell asleep in a symphony of contentment on the sofa. And that was how Connie Tam found them.

'*Where* did *that* come from?'

That sudden, and sharp-toned, question quickly returned Mike from pleasant sleep to less pleasant wakefulness. Where did he get what? He followed the angle of her irritably pointed index finger . . . 'Oh, the cat. Nice isn't it?'

'Where did you get it?'

'This is a better cat than any in the building. It comes from a good home.'

'Which home?'

He didn't understand why that should matter, and said so. He picked the animal up, the better to display its niceness, and held it out to her. Instead of adoring it she retreated from it. He said: 'Its name is Harmony.'

Connie gasped. Her hands flew to her mouth. Her eyes widened and her voice pressed past her fingers: 'Why are you doing this?'

However gaping was the divide between Mike Hempstead and sharp intellect at that hour, the intercept of Connie's raw fear was instant. Nothing he had done in the past had caused her fear. This was something unique; something intriguing, and possibly exploitable.

'It's just a cat,' he said. 'If you don't like it then I'll get rid of it.' He made, however, no attempt to withdraw the animal.

'Harmony,' was all she said. 'Harmony.'

'You could change its name . . .' Mike scratched the cat under its chin, and immediately it purred. He discovered then that it wore a thin gold chain. He pulled it outwards from the fur so that Connie could see it too. 'Look how well-bred it is; gold around its neck.'

She said with a choked voice: 'Take it away.'

Mike lowered the animal. It was fun to bend the mainspring of this woman's emotions, but it was hard to know when it was at full stretch. Anger could hurtle from her without warning. He shook his head: 'Well, I really thought you would like it.'

'The cat must go at once.'

'I'll take it down to my car. Tomorrow I'll find a home for it.'

Mike did not do as he had said he would do. He gave the animal instead to the night watchman in the foyer of the building. He showed the man the slim gold chain: enough reward to take the beast away and drown it. Then he dawdled with a cigarette and a mind clogged with bewilderment at the vagaries of the opposite sex.

When he arrived back at the flat Connie was still clothed in her dress. She hardly looked at him when she said: 'I think we should talk.'

'Yes . . . Fine.'

There was no obligation on him to begin the conversation, so he sat opposite her, in silence, more puzzled than expectant. Then she looked up; piercingly serious. 'I think you know why I reacted as I did.'

He, just as studiously, nodded affirmatively: 'Yes.' In truth he had not the vaguest notion as to why.

She nodded, wryly, and said, 'Hm,' as one might on observing a subtle move at chess. 'Well, what are you going to do now?'

A vague thought dragged itself to the front; he dismissed it. But it came back doggedly, stronger.

She went on: 'How did you find out?'

The question was premature since he had, as yet, found nothing out. But Mike sensed that he was hard on the heels of discovery. He thought of the white headband he had seen in

273

Harmony's drawer and he remembered a similar if not identical band that he had seen Connie wearing at her morning meditation. Then he said: 'She was your friend.'

'A beautiful and pure woman.'

'Beautiful? Pure? Ha! She was a poisoner.'

'He was filth; body and soul.'

'Harmony and yourself; you're of the same sect.'

'It's wrong to call it a sect . . . It's an Assembly; a great Assembly.'

'I've been a cop for too long to be bothered with semantics. A rodent is still a rat.'

'My people are not triads. You're inferring that they're gangsters. They are not like that at all. Their employment is to further a just cause.'

'Mr Tan was a dragon-head, a very senior man. Did he oppose the Assembly? Is that why he was killed . . . ? You hang about with pretty ruthless people.'

'We have ruthless enemies; we *must* survive. It's vital that we survive. Mr Tan was part of a great evil; and he knew he was evil.'

'So he was killed. That's a bit harsh. Tell me, by whose standards was he judged to be so evil as to demand death? If all the evil people in Hong Kong were "washed" there'd hardly be a soul left alive.'

'It's hard for you to understand . . .'

'Yes . . . What *is* hard, is to approve. Would you kill for the sake of the Assembly, Connie Tam? Would you take abric acid and sprinkle it over my brandy and ice?'

'Are you evil? Are you an enemy? Are you set to destroy the Assembly? The reply to all that, and your question, too, is, no.'

Mike said subduedly: 'You understand, I was shocked.'

He engaged her no further on the matter, for truthfully, the concept of killing for ideological gain was too radical for him to personally accept. And as feeble as his grasp on the subject was, it was all he wanted. She was right, he would never oppose her, because such opposition would be contrary to his vital needs . . . There was comfort in knowing and acknowledging something even as feeble as one's own fallibilities. For a while he had been in authority over Connie, but he hadn't liked it, really. It hadn't brought him any reward for its own sake, but had lain upon him threateningly. If he'd dared to admit his thoughts then, he would have said, 'Woman, you frighten me. You really frighten me.' Instead he sighed: 'I'm just plain tired. I want to sleep.'

'Come to bed then.' She stood up and held out her arms and cooed: 'I would never harm you, Mike. You're mine.'

It occurred to him that people frequently hurt the things they owned. They abused their children, and drowned their pets. But for now, she offered peace. So he made himself small and likeable, and came across.

He dreamed that night that something of intense evil was hidden in the room . . . It was a man, and he could see his furtive form in the drape of the curtains . . . He was afraid yet he felt impelled by a will, not entirely his own, to approach and identify the hidden danger. So he did. He advanced, slowly and fearfully against the radiant evil. He reached out, not wanting to, but willing himself to do so, and jerked the curtain back. There was nothing there . . . The dream awoke him and brought restless, troubling thoughts. Thoughts of a murdered man; judged too sinful to live; and Connie Tam whose creed was that murder, in special circumstances, was a virtuous act. What dreams was *she* dreaming now? Forrester's warning stole in: 'God's world abounds with sharp deceptions. Few things are as they appear.' The Ging Si should know; he was the master player of such ingenious hide-and-seek, and this man had offered him power such as he'd never thought attainable. Why should Forrester do that? There were inner deceits that were camouflaged with such masterly brushstrokes of light and shade and dappled innocence, that even the stern critic Conscience might pronounce them meritorious and good. Yet others might see the fault. Had Forrester seen the fault?

So the bad dreams came, and the spine fearfully stiffened and ached, and acid punctured the entrails.

Mike slid his body slowly away from Connie Tam. He padded

to the bathroom in quest of Alka-Seltzer. A stiff brandy on top of that, and he would sink the full distance to the dawn.

Reven Forrester did not sleep that night at all. Wearing nothing but jogging shorts he squatted cross-legged at the low teak table that was central to Caroline's study. A big Nagra tape recorder occupied the table-top, its reels slowly turning as it passed its secrets, low-voiced, to the man who sat there listening. Forrester had foolscap at his elbows and a typewriter before him. He typed till his wrists cramped, his eyes ached, and the muscles in his neck and shoulders staged brutal mutiny. When it was nearly dawn he gathered the papers, set them in order and numbered them. Then he headed the first page:

Subject : Tang Tsun
Analysis of tape recordings made at Ten-thousand Buddhas
Monastery and at Master Shun Cheng's Boxing Academy, Kow-
loon City. Facilitator: Tang San-kiu.

Forrester tapped the papers to square them and secured them in a spring file. Then he took the tapes, the file, and the many pieces of discarded paper; the spoilage of his night's work, and locked everything into his briefcase. Rubbing at the horribly sore muscles of his neck he went to bed.

Caroline was drowsily awake. She said: 'That was a marathon. Do you want to sleep now or shall I make some coffee?'

'Coffee,' he chose.

She turned on the pedestal lights and in their amber glow welled from the down duvet. He loved to see her like this; her hair awry, slow and yawning, and creased in fine satin. He stared until she'd wrapped herself into her gown, then with a great sigh he coddled himself like a foetus into her vestigial pod of warmth. She returned with coffee and crispy bran-muffins, and a pot of Fortnum and Mason's strawberry jam, and cream. Caroline was little concerned with sensible dietary conventions when it came to midnight snacking; deliciousness was the only criterion. They ate, messing the covers with crumbs. She said,

'I've been hearing the mutter of that typewriter in my sleep. Is it all done?'

'If you mean; will that be the last of it, I doubt it . . . I've done what I was asked to do – a report to the Deputy Director about a man who either suffers from delusions on a massive scale, or who is the long-awaited Third Buddha, the Maitreya. I find it hard to see the gold beneath the mud.'

'But what does your instinct tell you?'

'That he's sincere.'

'But that doesn't answer the thorny question, does it?' She smeared a muffin redly and set upon it a turban of cream. This she presented to his widening mouth. 'Craziness doesn't preclude sincerity, or vice versa. A wobbly mind might still be a holy one . . . I've heard some whispers about this man, I think. Some Chinese journalist friends of mine were chatting about such rumours . . . What's he done wrong that the greatest of all sleuths is on his trail?'

'He could be prosecuted under the Suppression of Secret Societies Ordinance, I suppose. But that would be stupid, for several reasons. You see it's of little consequence whether he is the true Maitreya or not; or whether I believe his incredible claim, or whether such an event will ever occur as the coming of the Third Buddha. What counts is whether there are people who are prepared to recognize his divinity. For then, at least in their eyes, he *is* who he says he is. What counts, is not whether his claim is pure myth, but whether this moment in history is opportune for such a myth. And if there are believers, and if the time is right, then it would be folly – utter stupidity to oppose him. And I tell you, there are believers. To them he is perfection . . . to me, an enigma. The Tang family, of which he is nominally head, is fabulously rich from land sales near Sai Kung. He wears homespun and is driven in a Rolls-Royce. He cries peace, and prophesies apocalypse, and people who oppose him die in strange ways . . . What the hell am I to make of him?' The last muffin was eaten; the last sweet crumbs pecked with the beaks of their fingers from plate to mouth. Caroline took away the tray, then came to sit on the edge of the bed, frowning:

'I've never heard you speak so frankly about a case.'

'I've never been so unsure about a subject.' He said, 'I've got yards of tape of him preaching his brand of liberation doctrine. He passionately loves China, and hates the Communists. He accuses them of deliberately destroying the Motherland, and Mao Tse-tung of posing as a god. He would unite China to stand against the Communists if he could. Caroline, I'm moved in sympathy towards his grand dream.'

'If you know all this then you can be sure that the Chinese Intelligence Service knows as much, at least. They'll kill him if they can.'

'And he knows it . . . He preaches to those thick-skinned triad dragon-heads about the coming of the Kalpa, a millenium philosophy of a Black Wind that will blow for seventy-seven days, and sweep the world from the sky, and destroy all evil. Only those who have accepted the ways of the White Lotus Assembly will survive to join the Eternal Mother in Purple-Cloud Heaven. And Heaven and Earth will be restored to harmony . . . Oh yes. He's got followers; some very committed people are in the Assembly. Agents of the Eternal Mother, their dictum is to respond to the Kalpa; to see to the destruction of the Communists; to make known the way. I have one of their most ancient books of prophecy. It's called *A Comprehensive Manual for Responding to the Kalpas of Three Buddhas*. I know therefore their innermost secrets. It's a repeat of history; the Eighteen Thirteen, Eight Trigrams rebellion served up again. And I'm sure that it will fail again, in just as bloody circumstances . . . But perhaps some good will come out of it. He will have caused the triads to stand up for an honourable cause.'

'And they will be obliterated. Do you think they realize how pathetic their chances are?'

'I don't know. The Chinese can be incredibly brave, and incredibly naive. Tang Tsun made them repeat a mantra . . . He told them it would protect them against all adversities, and in the end would carry them straight into the arms of the Eternal Mother . . . Unbelievable stuff.'

Caroline was still for a while; deeply reflective. Then she said: 'I've never felt so troubled by anything anyone has told me before. You've pointed to a monstrous destiny; is there no way of preventing its oncome?'

'If your question is: could I alone stop it, then the answer is, no. To stop this man I would have to do the work of the Ch.I.S.: to send out assassins to kill him in the night, or have him arrested and thrown into a cell to await the arrival of the Communists . . . Those are the current options.'

'That's unthinkable.'

'I've no real power to alter this thing in any way, Carrie; but others have. There is a full report in my briefcase, and I shall lay that, and all its attendant problems, on the desk of my superior, the Deputy Director, this morning. That's my duty. Lo Ping-kin must decide what to do. He's Chinese; these are his people.'

'No harm must come to Tang Tsun, Reven. Make that your duty too. The Chinese people are spiritually famished. There has never been a time in China's sorrowful history when the Maitreya was more needed than now . . . And this man could be the Third Buddha. I would rather never have been born than to have stood by while they shot the God of Hope.'

The Urban Council Market Complex was a place of frenetic energy. From basement to roof it was thronged with eager humans – buying, selling; of feather or skin or scale or shell, of breathing or still or incurably comatose, there was little that couldn't be traded here. On the escalators children played daring screech-filled games, while mothers shoved and shouted in a search of the bargain they would smugly brag about over tea. Lonnie Huang helped Big-bui, the meat porter, to impale an obscenely pink pig's carcass on a hook. He had to raise his voice more than was prudent:

'Sixteen grams of morphine base makes twenty-six grams of

number three heroin.' Lonnie took up a piece of brown wrapping paper and wiped his hands on it. 'Don't know how you can work here, Big-bui . . . Now look.' On the same scrap of paper he pencilled the sum: 'Five kilos of morphine base gives eight thousand one hundred grams of red chicken . . . OK? Wholesale price, ninety Hong Kong per gram . . .'

'Won't get ninety,' said Big-bui, slinging a carcass. 'Who do you think will pay you ninety? Seventy dollar, maybe. No more.'

This pessimism did not deter Lonnie from completing his sum: 'Seven hundred and twenty-nine thousand Hong Kong . . . Fuck! . . . Of course we'll get ninety. I saw that figure written in Ma Lau's diary.'

'So he was the expert; he had the dirt under the fingernails. What do you think; one lesson and you can make red chicken like the old man? Crazy days! The guys that bought Ma Lau's goods have got "nose". You won't fool them.'

Lonnie firmly believed otherwise. But this was neither time nor place to further that argument. A pair of patrolling policemen had just strolled on to the floor, arrogant-eyed men, they knew how to seed guilt in the purest heart.

'Wind,' Lonnie swivelled the pig's carcass so that he was hidden, then whispered urgently, 'you better tell me now, are you interested in the deal or not?'

Big-bui was not one for precipitate decisions. He let Lonnie wait for an answer while he hung up some meaty red rib-cages of beef. What Lonnie had offered was forty per cent equity in his proposed new heroin factory. Lonnie owned the basic raw materials – Big-bui's share was dependent on his ability to provide the necessary chemistry apparatus. A not too difficult task other than for the cumbersome, glass Büchner flask, which would have to be specially blown. But he had once been a narcotics cop, and he knew on which doors to go knocking. He would also be expected to distribute the finished product to the freelance sellers in Kowloon City – a job in which he was well experienced. What was causing Big-bui major unease was the element of risk involved – not from the police, whose form of retribution was kid-stuff – but from the Chiu Chau syndicate who were the real owners of Lonnie's morphine hoard. Their enforcer, Mr Hit, had not been netted in the police raid. Sooner or later he would hear about Lonnie's bright enterprise, and he would come calling. And Mr Hit's revenge would tend to be extreme.

'Fifty-fifty.' Big-bui dusted his hands as one who has made his final offer. He was half expecting a refusal, but Lonnie accepted at once:

'Partners, Big-bui; roots deep, stem firm.'

They went in search of premises that very afternoon, and found an excellent spot – a vacant third-floor flat in an old but roomy building with the most auspicious name of New Prosperity Mansions. There was one minor drawback; Mr Tin's rice shop was located close by. In fact a section of the view provided from the south windows was of Mr Tin's extremely mucky shop-front awning, beneath which Lustrous Jade sat, despondently stirring the heat with her heart-shaped straw fan.

The great, and unmistakable, advantage of that site was that the finished product – Lonnie's brand of red chicken, could be transported swiftly, and with minimum risk, to Big-bui's butcher's truck, after it had been unloaded at the market. Clearly, the benefits outweighed the single problem. They negotiated a rock-bottom price with the landlord, a tricky Shanghainese, who insisted on a deposit, and two months' rent in advance. A paltry sum when considered in the light of Lonnie's previous arithmetic, but in the meantime, as Big-bui pointed out, they were a few dollars short of broke.

'No problem,' said Lonnie strutting about the new premises. 'Practically the gold-mine here.'

Big-bui was not so optimistically propelled: 'You got the overheated brain, Lonnie, or what? You haven't even made one gram of red yet. Maybe you never will.'

'I will,' Lonnie avowed. 'Solid truth!'

'Five kilograms of base isn't going to make bigtime heroin tai los, either. It's a one-shot job, and then what?'

'Once we've got money we can buy more morphine base. You think maybe I walked around for the last few months with my eyes stuck up my shit-door. I've made contacts. I know where to go for more.' Lonnie almost believed his own lie. He challenged Big-bui to do so, too: 'You think I'm not the master-mind, ha?'

'Everyone said you were clever, Lonnie.'

'We've got to plan.'

Lonnie planned, frowning through a cloud of cigarette smoke at the peeling paint of the walls, while Big-bui went out for take-aways, and beer. By the time they had eaten Lonnie had committed to paper a full list of requirements, including such mundane domestic items as a mattress to sleep on, light-bulbs to fill the empty, dangling sockets, soap and toothpaste. He had good reason for such thoroughness:

'I'm going to eat, sleep and work in this flat. Your job, Big-bui, is to go out and buy the chemicals and stuff that's written here . . . Please, Big-bui, just please don't ask me the unintelligent question: "How do I pay?" . . . You just go and get the stuff, ha, like I got the morphine base. You want to be equal to me, fifty–fifty. Well then you can't fly kites under the bed.'

After that inspirational message Big-bui picked thoughtfully at his teeth for a while, then sallied forth in search of the required products. Despite the considerable shortage of cash he did well. On the first day of the new partnership he arrived back with a commercial pressure-cooker, some stainless steel basins and a suction pump. On day two he came up with a jerry-can full of acetic anhydride, 'moused' from a New Territories acrylic factory; two polythene sacks of ICI soda powder, and some odds and ends: wooden spatulas, plastic tubing and bowls. And, on that same day, in the sulk of the afternoon drizzle, Lonnie climbed the wooded green hill beyond the Chinese cemetery.

A mat of dead leaves, wet and mulchy, hid the yellow shopping-bag with the morphine base blocks, and the gun. He had not told Big-bui about the gun, his partner might want to sell it.

By day seven Big-bui had filled the list, but for the glass Büchner flask. They had to wait for a further week to pass before that vital piece of equipment was ready. Big-bui delivered it as a flower-vase, complete with long-stemmed, orange and yellow tiger lilies from Kwai Fong market; an extravagance that totally wrecked their finances. They would not eat that night, but you couldn't fault Big-bui's sense of occasion.

The stinging odour of acetylating morphine soon filled up the flat. They smothered the cooker with wet towels, still it rose up; it scoured their nostrils and punched bluntly at the brain. They opened windows, stuck their heads out and gasped at the night air, as wind-driven rain lashed their necks; then back to the stench. But this was the sort of punishment that a man might learn to crave, it was the reek of prosperity.

The long-awaited confection of the novice heroin chemist came from the ovens at 3 a.m. in the morning. It disappointed at first glance. It didn't possess the crisp, pink look of Ma Lau's esteemed product. Instead, it lay ashen gray and sickly on the drying-tray. Lonnie stabbed the granules around with his finger dejectedly, not wanting to show his depression, and thus showing it all the more. Not a hope that this lot could be passed off as vintage red. He couldn't work out where he'd gone wrong. He frowned down at the tray of pasty granules. A blighted crop; and yet he had followed each step according to the teaching of the master. Naturally the thought occurred to Lonnie that Ma Lau had held back some vital segment of training, a pinch of this or that chemical – barbitone, caffeine or scopolamine at just the right moment. Well, if Ma Lau had short-changed him, it was too late to shout, thief. The miserable cheat (may his family die out) was locked away in Victoria Remand Centre. Lonnie produced a satisfying mind-picture of the old heroin-addict, drooling, rattling the bars – screaming for a fix.

Big-bui seemed less perturbed by the insalubrious appearance of their product. He argued that it did not matter what the heroin looked like, it was how it smoked that counted, and there was only one way to discover that.

He'd brought the full test-kit with him in readiness for this moment – a strip of silver paper which he folded into a little pod, a candle end, which he lit, and a gay red matchbox cover, which he fitted squarely between his lips. He placed some heroin granules in the silver pod and held it to the flame. The granules melted quickly, popping about like spittle on a stove.

Lonnie felt compelled to ask prematurely: 'Good, or not?'

'Hm,' muttered the tester through his exotic square beak. He leaned into the smoke and expanded his lungs and sucked until his cheeks hollowed. After the pod had burned dry, he spat out the matchbox lid and giggled, pin-eyed. He gave a great, slow sigh, and without looking up reported:

'Lonnie, aah, good, good . . .'

'Seventy dollar, or not?'

'Maybe more than ninety, Lonnie. This is better than red chicken . . . better than Hong Kong rock, or even spider brand. This is angel-food.' His features then slackened into a stupid grin.

A surge of excitement filled Lonnie. 'Angel-food.' Like the artist who discovers some unique and pure new colour, brighter than anything known before, or the sculptor who finds that his chisel has shaped a fourth dimension, Lonnie was dizzily propelled to the pinnacle of creative joy.

While Big-bui slumped on the mattress, beatifically stunned, Lonnie paced about in a ferment . . . Possibilities, amazing possibilities zoomed about in his mind. With such a superior product he would soon be able to shove open the gates of trade of all of China. 'Angel-food' would be the perfect trademark.

Whirled then in such a current of elation, it took Lonnie a while to steady himself to the cold facts of that dawn . . . They were dead broke. Their product had yet to be acclaimed by anyone other than Big-bui. It lay in the drying-trays, unlovely, unpacked, unready for distribution. So while his partner slumbered, Lonnie measured the Angel-food into half-ounce plastic packets, which he sealed with Sellotape. Ten half-ounce packets made up a stick. And it was by that measurement that the Kowloon City wholesalers contracted to buy. By seven o'clock, Lonnie had neatly packed the entire consignment. Nor did he forget the principle of brand-name loyalty. He endorsed each packet with a felt-tip pen with the Chinese characters: Tin-shan leung – God-spirit rations. There was no more he could do; now it was up to Big-bui to make things happen. He woke his business partner up with an impatient shake.

The Angel-food sold dismally. In fact it took all of two weeks to move half of the initial batch. And in the end it had to be discounted, not in sticks to the Kowloon City wholesalers, but in half-ounce purses to the small-time freelance street operators, who retailed directly to the addicts. The price that the manufacturers received was not ninety Hong-Kong dollars, not even seventy; but forty miserable dollars per gram. Still, as the raw material had cost nothing, and most of the equipment had been 'moused', this represented a net profit in excess of nine thousand Hong Kong dollars. It was a moderate start. A moderate celebration was therefore in order.

They visited an apartment in Yau Ma Tei where they shared a bottle of brandy, and the rather overblown vagina of a 'family girl' who called herself Candy. The whole evening (drinks included) cost less than 300 dollars.

During the following week things cheered up: repeat orders began to trickle through. They tentatively increased the price of their product by five dollars an ounce, which didn't cause the slightest drop in demand. So they raised it by twenty. Business improved substantially, even so.

That weekend they returned to Yau Ma Tei, and this time splurged on two bottles of brandy, and a packet of MX tablets for Lonnie. They negotiated with 'Elder Brother' for the hire of two girls (under-age Vietnamese sex-kittens), who were hot rub specialists – 700 dollars for an evening that left Lonnie with a serious abrasion on the acorn of his penis.

The days that followed embraced them in golden arms – bright fortune, ten times complete. The demand for Angel-food rocketed. Lonnie worked as he had never worked in his life before, and had he been able to work at twice that capacity, he still would not have been able to fulfil Big-bui's indents. They raised the price. That just increased the clamour for their product. Hong Kong in its last unhappy days of Foreign Barbarian rule had lurched into a happiness binge of every kind of narcotic known to man, and Angel-food was heading to top the list.

Of course their stock of raw material quickly dwindled to a precarious level. Within the first few weeks of trade they were down to half a kilogram of morphine base. And that was not the only problem caused by the escalating demand for Angel-food. As Big-bui put it:

'When we were shrimps, I could move about as a shrimp from the Wo Shing Yee enclave in Yau Ma Tei, to Hei Shui territory in Tsim Sha Tsui. The triad fighters didn't notice me . . . quick in and quick out, with a few hundred dollars in the hip pocket. Who would bother with such a small catch? But things have changed, we're fatter and they want their share. Selling Angel-food is getting dangerous, Lonnie.'

'Dangerous? Of course it's dangerous.' Lonnie, however, was more inclined to see the shortage of base as the greater threat. It would be easy to hire a freelance fighter or two to accompany Big-bui on his rounds, such men hung about in the boxing academies looking for someone who would pay them to knock someone else's head off. Lonnie said, 'You go get yourself some guys like that, Big-bui, we can pay. How to get more morphine base; that's the problem we should worry about.'

'Don't think me rude, but just the other day I'm sure I heard you say that you knew where to go for more.'

Lonnie had hoped that that rash statement had been forgotten. He complained: 'Some people could pick fault, but look how much money I've made. I would like you to remember that.'

'Tcha! Lonnie. You got annoyed for nothing.'

'You see, Big-bui, there's technical stuff that you don't know about. For instance, I could buy heroin base, just like that – cash and carry. Heroin base is what most of the chemists buy, because it's so easy to get, and to use. But to make Angel-food we need Thai morphine base. Not many chemists use it because it takes longer to break down. So there's not much around.'

Big-bui, chastened-toned, said, 'We better think of something clever.'

'That is exactly what I was saying.'

They passed a couple of hours in studious thought and serious conversation, but what came out of it was not very encouraging. Big-bui had a cousin in Yau Tong who had once been a close friend of a dealer, who knew a lot about the trade, but who had subsequently been shot dead in a drug bust. That was as much as Big-bui had to offer. Their business had reached a crisis point; these were the options: they could continue to manufacture at their current rate for another day or so, or they could slow down and stay in business for a week, or they could join the common herd and start up in manufacture of an inferior product made from heroin base. Well, the choice had to be made there and then, and they decided on a slow-down. Then it was time for dinner.

'Something will turn up,' said Big-bui as he departed to buy food.

The 'walk-with' food shop they patronized was hardly a street away, and yet two hours passed before Big-bui, smiling enigmatically, wafting polystyrene-packed aromas (Lonnie's was fried pork and bamboo shoots with rice), arrived back. He was also carrying a plastic shopping-bag which he staged in the middle of the floor in a way that was calculated to draw Lonnie's curiosity, and then did not open. A most childish man was Big-bui when the mood took him.

Lonnie refused so much as to glance at the enigmatic bag. He worked his chop-sticks with concentrated energy, leaving Big-bui totally deflated.

'You didn't want to know what I bought us, Lonnie?'

'What did you buy, ha?'

It was a scowling plastic deity (Guan Ti) complete with red god-box, double-sided adhesive tape and a length of flex. When plugged in to the mains, a chain of fairy lights around the gate-arch of the box winked on and off in clock-wise rotation – a truly state-of-the-art bring benefits kit for those who'd worn thin on luck.

'It was just what we needed.' Big-bui found a place on the wall, at the limit of the flex, from whence Guan·Ti could best observe, and do helpful and right-minded things.

Lonnie drained the juices from his moulded food bowl: 'So now we've got the third partner in the business . . . Do you think he knows where to discover some morphine base, maybe?' He slapped his thigh and exploded with laughter, and rice pellets in most directions.

Big-bui ate on with stone-faced dignity.

The following day Big-bui came back to the flat, buoyed up with hope. He had heard of the existence of a store of triple-nine morphine base in Shenzhen. Twice a week Big-bui drove his truck through the border at Shenzhen, laden with pig carcasses. If the reports were true, and he could locate the dealer, then they would be in full production in no time. Lonnie saw a fault:

'The customs officers. What if they search the truck?'

Big-bui laughed: 'Wah! Five thousand trucks drive through Man Kam To every day, Lonnie. You can't breathe for the fumes. They don't care, they smoke your cigarettes and stamp your papers, and wave you on: "Hurry-up. Hurry-up."'

'I can't believe.' Lonnie had the makings of a smile on his lips. He eyed the frowning Guan Ti in its twinkling red shrine. The potent little god of war (and police and prostitutes and pawn-shop owners, and other thieves) glowered back at him, daring him to pass another asinine joke.

8

HARD ROAD TO HEAVEN

The people of old China used to call this day the Feast of the Fifth Moon. They didn't do much more in celebration than to go out and settle up outstanding bills, and if the weather was clement, and there was energy to spare, they'd dress up and go down to the bay and throw rice cakes into the sea. There they would watch an amusing event in which slim sampans, with carved dragon-heads affixed, raced over a short course, making a lot of noise and waving banners. At nightfall the dragon boats, lantern-lit and languidly rowed to a melancholy drum, came again and sorrowed the water, hills, and heart.

It was such a poignantly beautiful sight that the British could not resist altering it. They had seized the day, knocked out the dents of rustic charm, polished it to a gleam, and renamed it as the Dragon-boat festival. Now rowers arrived from the four corners of the earth, with boats of polished camphor (thirty-eight feet ten inches, with sixty-seven inches of dragon's head and an equal measurement of tail). Grand, striped pavilions of canvas draped the East Tsim Sha Tsui waterfront, while out to sea huge triple-decker ferries and harbour lighters tied nose to tail laagered the course. These days, it was a famous event, and though the British had made it so, it was the Chinese who bore the strain of this excess. For the gwailos might row, and do so with all their muscle, still it really was a colossal joke – *Dragon-boat races!* . . . The Shun De teams from the Chinese mainland, on the other hand, rowed with only one purpose in mind – to win. How could it be otherwise, when in the next lane a team of barbaric, cud-chewing Yanks were aligned, and twenty thousand roaring spectators lined the course. A foreign tiger, as you are aware, is not equal to a Chinese worm. So it was a matter of face; and not just that of the participants, but of the very Motherland. So they dug in their paddles, and sent their boats skimming, and won, year after year. There were those gwailos who quietly, cynically chuckled behind raised glasses at all this forced labour, and considered the whole show to be a specifically invented, diabolically subtle, white man's revenge.

Reven Forrester strolled down to the East Tsim Sha Tsui waterfront with denim-dungareed Shannon perched on his shoulders, steering him by his ears. This would be their last Chinese festival, and its worthiness lay in that very finality. It seemed right that Shannon's three-year-old memory cells should be bathed with this bright and splashy spectacle, lest they never again encounter it. As for himself, he had seen enough of dragon-boat races; had in fact rowed in one on Sai Kung bay one murky day when boats and crew and all had sunk beneath the waves, five strokes from the finishing line. Today's skies were blue and clear, still a gutsy wind was rocking the big boats at their moorings, and there was talk of a number-ten typhoon down Manila way.

They arrived in time to hear it announced that the Hang Seng Bank team had taken the Oriental Daily News Cup – second prize to the University of Hong Kong. Now the women's teams were lining up. There was money on the Canadian girls who'd sped over the course on the previous day in less than three minutes, but Forrester knew that the red-vested little-titted Shun De girls would thrash their heftier opponents. And they did, by all of eight seconds.

But this was petty stuff, and not essential material for subliminal absorption by his offspring. The stern and unforgiving final would be the event towards which he would direct Shannon's attention. That race would lift the spectators en masse to their feet, cheering. In the meantime Shannon wanted an ice-cream. He bought her one and conditionally promised another, later.

Loud-speakers whined, then with the stridency of mortar-fire announced something, in Cantonese, to do with the arrival of someone, probably His Excellency the Governor. Forrester hoisted his daughter, who by now was stickier than before, and set her once more on his shoulders. It was the only sensible method of manoeuvre through that seething crowd. She squeaked in his ear:

'Looka boats, Daddy. Looka there.'

Another race was underway. The drums from each dragon-boat pounded, pulling – *boom-boom*, *boom-boom*, at the passion and blood of the rowers. Ten oars a side dipped and hauled and shot the arrow-slim hulls through white spray.

'Hai ya!' yelled Shannon. 'Hai *ya!*' She was becoming Chinese this little girl. If only she could have seen the dragon-boats of old Sai Kung, they were a sight to remember. They'd had movable heads that bobbed with the momentum of the bows, and red and gold banners, and not just drummers but cymbal men, too, who'd cracked the heavens with their brass. Today was just an exaggerated echo of a past, and better, time. But Shannon was up in the saddle with excitement, 'Hai *ya!*' New times, new sights and sounds that chased at mossy memories.

He discovered then what he was searching for: a vacant seat upon a stand as bright as a flower stall with rowers in colourful track suits, or vests, all open-faced and cheerful. A buxom girl in a Freemantle vest gave a hand to Shannon.

'Now what will happen?' piped Shannon.

'Cute,' said the heavy lady from Freemantle. She nudged a beery question at Forrester. 'She yours?'

'Very much so.'

'How old is she?'

'She's three and a bit.'

'Yer!' said the lady, in mock disbelief. 'And a dinkum heart-breaker already.'

Forrester glowed with pride.

'What,' demanded Shannon, 'is going to happen now?'

Forrester said, 'Right . . . This is the final. And all the winners of all the other major races are going to race each other . . .'

'What's "major", Daddy?'

'It means, sort of, grown up.'

'Who will win, Daddy?'

'Well that's why they're going to race, you see . . .'

'But you always know.'

'Shun De . . . most probably.'

'Cute! Couldn't ya eat'r rup?'

Forrester said, 'Look Shan, they're lining up at the start . . .'

But Shannon had lost interest. Her Daddy, who was *never* wrong, had already declared the winner. The distant dragon-boats held little further appeal. However, there were other interesting things going on all around. Daddy had now glued his eyes to his binoculars:

'Any second now . . . There they go.'

'Go Austr*alia*,' screamed the friendly lady.

'Go Philadelphia!'

'Go Vancouver!'

Silly people, thought Shannon. Didn't they just hear Daddy say who would win? All muggled over nothing. She swallowed the last deliciously soggy remnant of ice-cream wafer, then turned her attention elsewhere. Behind the stand an old man with a kind face, and short cropped grey hair, walked slowly, bent forward as though walking against a wind. He wore a baggy suit, buttoned to the neck, his trousers were rolled above his knees, and he was carrying a bird-cage of reed-bamboo, inside which perched a little green-feathered, white-eyed bird, as beautiful as could be. Then the old man stopped, as if caught by the strings of her eyes, and he looked through the barrier of noise and saw between the slats of the trembling structure a small girl's grinning face, and he smiled back at it, and held up the cage so that she could better observe his pet. Bird-like in her own way, the nimble-limbed child slipped between the seat-slats and lightly dropped to the ground. Hop, hop, hop, she came up to him with delighted eyes. The bird man held the cage to her. She poked one little finger past the bamboo splits, and as it was accustomed so to do, the white-eye perched upon the offered digit.

Shannon felt the matchstick feet grip, and giggled with joy, a sound too tiny to live at all in that jabber of amplified commentary and human roar.

The old man, too, tried words. He told her the name of his bird: 'Green Lucky . . . You like?'

She wrinkled her face, not understanding. Of course a little ghost-girl like this would not speak Hakka. He chuckled at his own stupidity and turned away.

Shannon, fascinated by this most wonderful of all birds in its reed-fence home complete with minute flower-vase and flowers and porcelain tableware, and sure that she had made a friend for life, followed unhesitatingly on.

Forrester watched the boats come on – the wicked snarling dragon's heads – the drummers flailing full-force, raging, pumping madness into veins and muscle. The Canadians had a lead as they made for home, the Indonesian team was challenging; while slick as a water-snake, the Shun De boat kept pace . . . Twenty metres to go, and still the men from Vancouver had it, with Shun De riding second, straining, straining . . . The crowd rose, roaring. Forrester bent to lift up his daughter, and found that she was not at his side, nor was she near at hand.

Hard panic, that starts in the midriff then burgeons hollowly upwards to the mind, shot through him – a hideous, giddy, ragged-breath funk that sent him pushing blindly at people who stood in the way of his search. She was not on the stand – not anywhere on the structure.

The race was over and people swirled into his path. He chose direction by some coarse instinct – west, and set off, dodging, at a fast jog. She could not be far. He had taught her, when lost, to stay in one place and not to trust anyone but a policeman. 'Peaceman' she called them, but she knew the uniform. He ran for a while, and then stopped, agonized by the thought that he

293

might be moving in quite the wrong direction, thereby compounding his problem . . . But, no . . . this was the most natural route for her to have taken.

But all this rationalizing was just chaff in the storm, and was no real barrier to the cold and naked, deepening, fear: little Shannon could have been kidnapped.

He was approaching the end of the esplanade when he saw her. She was seated on a flower-box next to an old Hakka gentleman, and both of them were peacefully gazing into a birdcage wherein a little white-eye hopped and trilled. The old man saw him coming and gently flicked Shannon's attention towards her father . . . Did she come running into Daddy's tremulous arms – no she did not. She gave a grin and kicked her heels against her concrete seat, and said, 'Daddy, can I have a bird, just like this?'

Of course she could. She could have a dozen little white-eyes, in a cage five times as tall. He picked her up and kissed her. He said to the bird man:

'Thank you.'

'She followed me, I had no knowledge of her presence until we were here. I thought you would come along soon. No need for thanks, I'm a father too. Look at this grey hair. I'm only thirty-five, but look at me.' He screwed up his age-freckled face and quaked with laughter. 'You take good care of her. She loves birds. She's like one too. Keep her wings clipped or you'll lose her.'

'If ever I can do anything for you . . .' Forrester took a card from his wallet and gave it to the man. 'My phone number . . . Don't hesitate to phone if you're in need.'

'*Hou Hou!* A *tai lo* policeman, well, you're still young, your luck may change.' And he laughed again. 'But seriously, I may 'phone you yet. My humble name is Loh Man-tseung from Man Uk Pin Village. These days, I keep a bird shop in Kwun Tong . . . Take good care of that girl now, I've grown to like her in this small time.'

'She likes you too, Ah Loh.'

*

Tang Tsun's view of the dragon-boat races at Tsim Sha Tsui was unplanned, and unsatisfying. He was standing on the deck of a lazy-engined *kai-to* ferry, bound from Peng Chau Island to Sai Kung bay, when he heard the booming drums, and was drawn towards the familiar sound. He saw quick flashing episodes of the long boats dashing up the straight, but a line of big vessels, hobbled stem to stern, blocked any good view. What those fragments of vision did was to unwrap memories: lamp-lit boats in waters so warmly rich with phosphorus that the paddles churned fire with every stroke, and every ripple ignited with trembling chains of flame . . . Tang said to the man at his side:

'When you and I were very young Grandpa would take us to Sai Kung to see the dragon-boats, do you remember that, Tik-kat?'

'I've bits of memory of those days.'

'The best time was after dark, when most people had gone home. The drums had a different sound then, as though all the rage had been beaten out of them, and all that remained was peace.'

'That was a good time, but the races were best for me. I liked to hear the drums as you hear them now, banging like cannons.'

'I remember the cool sand of the evening, and the warm misty smell of the night sea.'

'You're older than I am. I don't recall such fine details . . . I liked the brightness, the processions and the gongs.'

'I liked that too.'

They spoke about such things as occurred during the fifth moon, and especially those things they could mutually recall: one year Sixth Aunt, Jiu Ling, had, despite her yellow paper charms, and garlic amulet, been bitten by a king-cobra and died; and Ah Shek had developed pig's hair disease and had lain for a week with thick bristles sprouting from him. It was generally considered to be an evil month, of either drought or flood; a month when nature shows how indifferent it is towards the welfare of man. It was a time for keen prayer to the God of Healing, Yo Shih Fo.

When the *kai-to* reached Easy Dragon Island it met the south-westerly swell of the open sea, fat green rollers capped whitely by the wind came along, and the simple act of standing became a clumsy dance that nudged at the contents of Tik-kat's stomach in an ugly way. For he was no sailor. His knowledge of the sea was that, though ships could sail in it, they could, with equal facility, sink in it. And this creaky *kai-to* they sailed in was a very small, frail-bodied thing after all. He stared longingly towards dry land, and hoped that the Maitreya appreciated how he had put himself out to take the sea route to Sai Kung with him. He also felt that a warning was in order:

'The fishermen say that the water has risen in an ominous way, Maitreya.'

'In what ominous way, Cousin?'

'I heard them talking. They say there's a bad typhoon building out there.' He waved towards the South China Sea. 'Personally, I think those Hoklo rascals like to bluff like that when a landsman is in earshot, in order to make an impression.'

'Oh but this time they're not joking. The sea *is* building. It's angry. Can't you *feel* it? Everything is out of harmony . . . It's the force of the Kalpa, Tik-kat, it's on the turn. And even if it wasn't predicted in the Precious Volumes, I would know it. It's an agony of all the elements. My body tingles with warning . . . The sea is impassioned with the knowledge, and it's written in the sky.'

Tik-kat followed the Maitreya's upwards pointed hand, but could, in all honesty, see no more than some strands of cottony cirrus hanging in the everlasting blue. Of course he didn't doubt that something was in the air – there had better be. He'd die from loss of face if nature didn't throw down something huge and horrible to mark the Maitreya's predictions. Secretly, however, he hoped that the event would be considerably less cataclysmic than forecast. He had some profitable real estate deals in the pipeline, and it would be a shame if they came to nothing. He said:

'When . . . When do you reckon it will come?'

'Very soon.'

'Can't you be more precise?'

'The stars are aligned; this is the fourteenth – Male Clown year of the sixty-year calendar. The animal is the Ox and the element is Fire. This is the space in time given by God . . . What more can we ask Her to provide? What is vital is to be totally prepared,'

'I say my mantras, morning and night. I work constantly to further White Lotus objectives . . . Dare I remark that it might be overly harsh to simply wipe out everything; to flatten the skyline, as it were . . . if that, indeed is what the Eternal Mother intends.'

'The non-believers will be eliminated. That is all that's sure.'

Tik-kat wanted more clarity on that point: 'By eliminated you mean, gone – totally vanished . . . like steam from a kettle?'

Dart-winged sea-birds skidded on the wind and raked the green waves, plunging then lifting, whitely. Tang Tsun watched them, considering, then said: 'It will possibly be that complete.'

'Tell me what happens to the believers, then, men like me.' Tik-kat said with greater emphasis, 'Men like *me*.'

'I've told you before; you will be unharmed. That's the promise of the Eternal Mother.'

'Maitreya, the Kalpa has always seemed a great distance off, but now you say it's practically here. Taking a long view I was content to be taught in metaphors: Cloud City . . . The Great Way of Long Life . . . The Seven-treasure pools and Eight-virtue streams. These concepts I grew accustomed to over the years, without really understanding them. There was no urgency, but now that's changed. Tell me bluntly what to expect when the day arrives – where to go, what to do?'

'Right up to the last minute, Cousin, your single responsibility is to gain converts – men, women, young and old, there will be place for them all in the new order.'

'How will I know which are the last minutes? When must I look only to myself and my family?'

'Wear the White Lotus headband. You will be identified as a believer by it. "Entrusted by Heaven to Prepare the Way", those words are written there. Just wear it and have no fear. You will be spared.'

'Spared?' Tik-kat raised his arms frustratedly. 'Spared how, and from what? I need to know more, Maitreya. I've got faith. I've got more faith than all of them. I've worked for the Assembly, night and day. It's time I was told these things.'

'All I can say is that there are symbols that are beyond human expression, and I am human. I've tried to build bridges of understanding and clear meaning between man and god, but I've lacked the materials. Forgive me, all I have is the Ming, here in the palm of my hand, and the certain knowledge that I am who I say I am; and the promise to you, Cousin, that you, and your family, and all the other members of the Assembly will be spared. These things are *written*.'

'As truly as *that* is sea, and *that* is sky, I believe that you are the true son of the Eternal Mother, the third Buddha. I know it.'

The cousins watched the hissing, rolling green sea, pondering on its everlasting energy, its fathomless, bottomless energy. After a long while Tang Tsun said, 'It's a time destined by Heaven. The mysteries are too vast to fit into our small skulls – the ants can't know the aspirations of the elephant.'

'If there's confusion I don't want to be amongst the confused.'

'Meditate. Meditate, Cousin. That is what I shall be doing.'

Tik-kat felt disinclined towards further conversation. The *kai-to* was beginning to roll horribly, making swill of his thoughts. On any other day they would have used the regular passenger ferry to get from Peng Chau to Hong Kong, and then have travelled the remaining distance to Sai Kung by road. This mode of parochial transport was fine for peasants, boat-people and other lesser humans, pigs and ducks. But there it was. Indignities were sometimes unavoidable; especially when evading the police.

'Big Seed Island,' Tang Tsun pointed, 'where Uncle Ah Lok made his home . . . Do you remember?'

What Tik-kat remembered was that Big Seed Island marked the entrance to the bay, and that smooth water lay beyond it, and at that most pleasant thought he perked up immediately.

Well at least they'd achieved what they had set out to do – to transport the Maitreya secretly from Lantau Island to Sai Kung. Tik-kat said, 'How long will you stay at the monastery of the Great Sage?'

The answer seemed far too stunning for such a commonplace query: 'Until the Kalpa has come.'

The *kai-to*, seeming far less stressed now, came into Sai Kung harbour and found a place at a sleepy quay. Sai Kung, as always, seemed more comatosed by the narcotic pill of the sun than any other town. The sea was a spent force here, torpid and greasily reflective of a skyline of fatigued stunted buildings. A thin, tawny dog was the only creature to show interest in their arrival. It came and sniffed at the skirts of the Maitreya as he ascended the paved steps of the jetty, then it too went back to the shade where it flopped, and lolled its sleepy tongue . . . Surely the forces of the millennium would by-pass this enervated spot for fear of contracting its malaise.

Tang Tsun had only one piece of luggage; a leather satchel for his books. He slung it on his shoulder and made the strap comfortable, then smiled at Tik-kat. 'If only I could have shown you the picture you asked to be shown.'

'You did,' Tik-kat brooded. 'I just wish . . .'

'I tried . . . I'm as awed by the mystery of this thing as you are. Perhaps in the stillness of the monastery . . .'

'It will be as though God whispered in your ear. You could practically feel the breath.'

'Perhaps She has a use for me, as yet undisclosed.' As though agitated by some sceptical inner audience, he said sharply: 'We will win. We *must* win.'

'Stay strong, Maitreya. We'll meet again soon.'

Tik-kat watched the figure of God's earthly general walk from him. No eagle's gaze or wolf's stride, but a gentle, slight man, nudged with cheerful dimples, armed with nothing but ancient books and correct teachings. It hardly seemed sufficient to carry the day.

What if the Maitreya had misjudged? 'What,' he asked of the

departed monk, 'if heaven's forces are insufficient to gain victory?'

The street was short, but before it turned and finally hid him Tang Tsun glanced back, and seeing his cousin still standing there, raised his arm in farewell. Then he quickened away.

Tang Tsun looked up to the rich green hills that shouldered in Sai Kung. And they would have to be climbed, and their pinnacles would reveal still higher mountains; the hunchback ridges of Ma On Shan. The night would have coloured them black before he arrived at those slopes. But there lay his destination – the monastery of the Great Sage Equal to Heaven, who knew all the secrets of the universe, and who would, hopefully, share a few.

Deputy Director Lo Ping-kin sat behind his mighty desk, drumming his fingers on his waistcoated chest, as a man of plenty. A single, open file lay before him; its contents a credit to the investigative ability of the men under his command. Notably, CSO Reven Forrester . . . but let it not be forgotten who had prognosticated this exact end result:

'I knew it, Reven. I never had a single doubt from the word go; Tang Tsun is a seditious little shit-stirrer. Now we've got him.' He pursed his lips approvingly. 'I must say, you've done an excellent job; as thorough a job as I've ever seen.'

Reven Forrester said blankly, 'What do you intend to do about the situation, PK?'

'Well, that must be obvious. I'm going to give you the honour of seeing to his arrest . . . Do I detect a furrow on the brow of the Ging Si?'

'The man isn't a criminal; not in the true sense of the word. There's no hard crime been committed that you can charge him with.'

'His membership of a secret society is now provable.'

'As is the membership of every freemason in the force . . .'

Lo's insistent, skinny fingers tapped the file before him,

successfully interrupting Forrester. 'The freemasons, as far as I know, don't advocate the murder of enemies. And even if they did, *theirs* is not the case under discussion; Tang Tsun's is.'

'I'm not happy with your decision, PK. I don't think Tang Tsun is guilty of ordering anyone's death. Someone else made those decisions. Cousin Tik-kat, most probably. *He's* the one I'd go for if I were you.'

'Reven, for God's sake, the man is a common criminal. A dragon-head . . .'

'A celestial dragon-head.'

'Exactly; and thanks to you we can prove it . . . So why are you bearing a torch for him?'

'It's a wavering torch, PK, on a frail standard . . . Here is a man who believes himself to have been provided by God, the Eternal Mother, to do her work on earth, to recruit people into a religious assembly, and thereby save them from a heaven-sent catastrophe . . . You propose to arrest this man.'

'Absolutely so,' Lo said blandly.

'He will be incarcerated to await the arrival of a new commissioner of police, a Beijing political appointee, who will, doubtless, kill him.'

Lo Ping-kin's eyes widened. He gave a sort of flustered hissing noise, then leaned across the desk. 'Hey man, you shouldn't talk like that. No, I don't want to hear that sort of loose talk.'

'I've considered, very carefully, every word that I've said.'

'I will never understand you gwailos.' Lo threw up his hands. 'You mystify me. You seem to enjoy complicating everything in life. This *is* your report isn't it? . . . You've written here that Tang Tsun is capable of causing problems on an awesome scale. Allow me to read back to you, your own words.' Lo flicked irritably through the pages of the file. 'Yes, here it is:

'"The religious beliefs that inspired the Eighteen Thirteen White Lotus rebellion were never totally expunged . . . remained as a millennial vision to be revived generations later . . . In consequence, this could pose a threat to Government . . ."

Now do you wish to recant anything you've written here, Reven?'

'No.'

'So we have here a man who poses a threat to Her Majesty's Government.'

'That is improbable . . . I also wrote that Tang Tsun sees Communism as the greatest, most virulent and destructive plague ever to strike China; and that the country was in its death throes and could not be saved.'

'And that he saw himself as the Maitreya . . . A sort of Moses of Mong Kok, do you suppose?'

The rejoinder was as obvious as was its need to remain unsaid: 'You may suppose that if you see yourself as the Herod of Hong Kong.'

'Very humorous, I'm sure.'

'The analogy is worth reflecting on.'

'Your brain is overheated, Ging Si.'

'PK, will you at least consider having him deported? The Taiwanese would gladly provide such a potent enemy of the People's Republic with asylum.'

Lo Ping-kin leaned back in his chair and stroked sapiently at his moustache ends. Then he wagged his finger in final judgement: 'We can hardly deport a man who is *not* in our custody. Do you get my drift, Reven? . . . Thank you for the argument; one can always count on you to provide a stimulating argument. Now, in order that we may sleep tonight, peacefully, and in the secure knowledge that violent revolutionaries will not drag us from our beds . . . *please* go out and arrest the bloody man.'

'It will be a most sensitive operation, PK. Arresting a Buddhist monk is bound to create some awkward political problems; and what is there really to gain by it?'

'Our problems will get worse if we don't stop him now. I'm satisfied that we have a case. I want you, personally, to conclude the matter, Reven. Where is he now?'

'He's on Lantau Island, I'm advised. We have him under twenty-four hour surveillance, or as nearly as possible under the circumstances. He's been proselytizing amongst the monks at the Po Lin monastery. I'll get Marine to lay on a launch for me, and go out there at once.'

'Practically like old times for you, Ging Si; you were ADC Islands, if my memory serves me.'

In the event, Reven Forrester did not make the sea-trip, or the arrest. He did not even progress to the extent of assembling an arresting party. The subject, Tang Tsun, had departed the Po Lin monastery, to a place unknown. A message that said approximately that, emerged from a fax machine in the operations room, soon after the interview with Lo. The signal had originated from Mui Wo police post, Lantau Island.

At lunch-time a further message came; this one from Peng Chau: a man, who fitted the subject's description, had arrived, by means of *kai-to* ferry, upon that island, that morning. Unfortunately he had also left that morning, by similar transport – destination unknown. The canny monk had slipped away with the dawn. Forrester broke this news to the Deputy Director.

Lo Ping-kin showed his displeasure by thumping the edge of his desk with the palm of his hand. 'Crass incompetence . . . I expect you to come down on these men.'

Forrester said: 'We're obliged to make do with detectives of less and less experience, PK. The police force is the least desirable of all vocations in Hong Kong now. I'm having to recruit detectives from the Districts, whom I would have rejected as totally unsuitable in the past . . . How hard, do you suggest, I come down on these men?'

Lo growled, 'Hm.' Then briskly said: 'And, on that very subject: Superintendent Lam's post will have to be filled.' He passed a thickish file to Forrester. 'The verdict of the Medical Board. Read it, sign where you have to sign.'

'Which way did it go?'

'Oh they've invalided him out on full pension with all increments – a fair decision I think. A notice to that effect will be gazetted, and posted in orders. But if you'd like to, you can break the news to him. You were his superior . . . and his friend . . .

Funny isn't it; as close as you were to him, you didn't perceive that he was going under. I remember you telling me that Lam was fine; that he was coping . . . Well thank God he had the good sense to come forward in the end and admit that he was not.'

'Yes, thank God.'

'I wonder what finally brought him to the realization that he just couldn't carry on . . . Doesn't that intrigue you too, Reven?'

'No.'

'Well there it is; all neatly phrased and documented, and set between cardboard covers. The end of an almost memorable career; a good cop . . . Let me tell you something about good cops, Reven. There are two kinds; two distinct species. There are those who rely on judgement to get their work done; and there are those who are supported by insight.' Lo pushed his finger about on the desk-top as he spoke, drawing imaginary diagrams of squares and lines in support of his thesis. 'Those with good judgement are fairly common; those with insight, on the other hand, are a rare breed; a somewhat dissident lot. They cut across the grain, and they solve more cases than their counterparts . . . I far prefer to work with men of judgement, which you, Reven, are *not* . . . However, you have incredible insight – far more than was needed to have thoroughly assessed Charlie Lam. I hope you warned him to stand well clear of police business from now on.'

'He understands that well.'

'Good . . . Excellent. I had to know that, Reven.'

'Now, you should know this too, PK. Our decision to totally exclude Charlie Lam from Lulu Wong's murder investigation was thoughtless, almost immorally so. However enlightened our reasoning might have seemed, we were wrong. We sent him a message of absolute distrust, and that was the first cut.'

'What could we have done, for God's sake?' Lo raised up his arms then flopped them on to the desk.

'*I* believe that the ethos of the good cop is founded in a spirit of dogged unforgivedness. That's what truly marks the elite. Charlie had it, and we forced him to forbid that instinct . . .

Poor, bewildered Charlie Lam, was instructed to pervert his ingrained sense of right. That angered and frustrated him, twisted him, then made him sick, very sick. And with all my alleged foresight, I didn't see the warning until it was too late. I'm deeply shamed by my part in his misuse. What we could have done is now irrelevant. What finally brought him down is irrelevant . . . As you say, there it lies, all neatly phrased and documented, and set between cardboard covers. The end of an almost memorable career.'

The dimensions of life closed down on Charlie Lam as one who is walled into a mine – a journey within a tunnel, which didn't seem long, as he could clearly see the end of it, yet was indeed very long, because he never reached the end. There was nothing, no feature, grim, or pleasant, to interest him along the way, and even if there had existed some break or place of exit, he wouldn't have noticed it. The stunning, sudden wounds had thrown him back but briefly from his determined course. Now he was ready to start again. He did not care how he had come to be so entrapped; he scarcely remembered the beginning; it didn't matter how darkly, unendingly miserable lay the middle distance. The concentration of all his energy, of eye and mind, of sinew, bone and spirit was focused on the single, glowing, ever distant exit . . . which he *would* reach.

The Medical Board examination was a pale interlude of white halls, white-coated doctors with serious, drawn faces, who captured his breath in plastic tubes, took X-ray pictures and warned him not to over-exert for a while, and to quit smoking; then faded away. And when they were gone he forgot them in an instant, and returned to the tunnel.

His feng shui protectors, the goldfish in the tank in his hall, expired one by one. He flushed their slippery corpses down the lavatory, and did not replace them. When the last fish died, he switched off the light in the tank and left the creature to rot.

When people knocked on his door he didn't respond; he had no curiosity. One day a brown manila envelope, postmarked OHMS, slid through the gap. He knew without opening it that it contained his discharge papers. He was now a pensioner. A note was clipped to the envelope, and it was in Forrester's loping handwriting. He didn't read it.

When he was able to breathe again, full-chested, without bracing against the pain, and the smoke of his cigarettes curled into his lungs in a snug fit, he made a journey. He took the MTR all the way to Lo Wu station on the border with the People's Republic; 'Business,' he told the customs men, 'hardware business.' They stamped his papers and pronounced him, 'Admissible to China'.

But this was not really China, this was China's pretence at capitalism, Hong Kong's less nourished, more neglected, disgruntled twin sister: Shenzhen. Shenzhen's heart was made of tall concrete, but its extremities had crumbled into slums. Charlie's taxi ran him westwards to a destination that he knew only by repute.

In a market street called 'Near the Enclosure of Rushes' there was a building that had once belonged to a rich and educated man, but was now home to a dozen squabbling families. It had four great pillars to front it and support a second floor with shuttered windows that had in better times been painted red, but now were all sorts of colours. Where noble palanquins had once waited, a clutter of bicycles now stood, and every other space was hung with drying washing. Away in a corner, beneath a sign that read: 'A good place to bring broken thing', an old man in vest and shorts sat, tinkering with the body of a rusted electric fan. Charlie offered him a cigarette, and the old man offered a chair. After some chit-chat of the day there ensued the strangest conversation:

'I'm looking for Iron-man Pang. I hear this is his address.'

'Oh,' said the man. 'Well let me thin' (ornate thought). 'Is it or isn't it his address? . . . I suppose that would depend a lot as to who it was who was at the door.'

'Humble name is Lam.'

306

He slitted his eyes inquisitively. 'And what would Ah Lam want Pang for?'

'He's come to buy a gun.'

'Wah! dangerous talk.' The old man looked up from his work and grinned nervously with a stockade of mouldering teeth. 'Ah Lam should know that dealing in guns is illegal . . . the death penalty, ha. On the other hand it's not illegal to talk about guns. Nor is it illegal to sell promises. Would you be satisfied to buy a promise, Ah Lam?'

'I've heard you can be trusted.'

'Yes, I've built a reputation.' With a sly, one-eyed grin. 'Of course, the money would have to be up front; Hong Kong or American dollars, and not just a few.'

'Money should not be considered as a problem.'

'Yes, I can see by the fit of your cloth that you're no peasant.' Pang cackled, pleased with his proven perspicacity. 'What sort of gun would you like to talk about?'

'A revolver, thirty-eight.'

'Very costly; a rare weapon. After the US aggressors were defeated in Vietnam there were a few available, but very few. It wasn't their basic weapon. Perhaps there are still some to be had. On the other hand a type fifty-one as used by the victorious People's Liberation Army in that same war might be more easy to locate.' Pang gave his comrade-to-comrade wink, and leaned closer to whisper: 'But let me say that the ultimate assassin's weapon is the silenced type sixty-four. There's nothing quite like it; but *very* expensive.'

'I'm prepared to pay a lot of money for an American thirty-eight.'

'The *promise* of an American thirty-eight, Ah Lam; that's all I can sell you, remember. Do you have Hong Kong or American dollars with you?'

'Hong Kong.'

'Do you have eighteen thousand Hong Kong?'

'Yes.'

'Leave me with two things, Ah Lam: that exact sum of money,

307

and your address.' Iron-man Pang plugged the cord of the fan into a wall socket. The blades did not revolve. 'It doesn't work. What does it matter? When you're old nothing matters. I was with the PLA, Ah Lam, I shot Americans at Da Nang. It was a different army then, we were proud. Now the Chinese army shoots the Chinese people. How can they hold their heads up?'

Within three days Iron-man fulfilled his promise. A Colt, calibre thirty-eight revolver, wrapped in newspaper was deposited in Charlie Lam's post-box. An old weapon – perhaps twenty years old. The butt-plate bore the engraved logo of the Macau police. The cross-hatching on the wooden handle was worn smooth, and bright metal showed through the blueing. This was a weapon that he could shoot expertly with, and that would place him on equal terms with Lonnie Huang.

Charlie went by ferry to Cheung Chau Island. On the sports-field there a giant shed of bamboo poles clad with rust-streaked shed-iron, had been erected. It squatted, four square across a concrete pitch, and glistened dully in the afternoon drizzle, exporting sound throughout the village. He bought a ticket and climbed the bamboo steps that brought him amongst a scattered audience in the huge theatre.

Charlie sat down, first in one spot, then in another. His final seat benefited him with an angled view of the brilliantly lit stage right into the wings, and also beyond the open-sided auditorium to the wet puddled street. It was perfect. Bathed then in the boisterous sound he shrank to stillness. And like a spider on a log, his eyes missed nothing.

Interval came. A vast crimson curtain swirled downwards to cloak the stage. It was emblazoned with the name of the star of the Tung Wong Opera Company, who would sing that very evening: *Tang San-kiu*.

Now a hawker of Chinese cure-alls patrolled the aisles. He must have seen some prospect of trade in cadaverous Charlie

Lam, for he came across with some marvellously salutory tips . . . But you can't flog music to an ox.

Charlie Lam's gaze, and complete attention, was fixed upon the street. Sandy Tang had appeared as he knew he was bound to . . . and there, at his elbow, as sleek as a pigeon, strutted Noona Cham. Charlie stirred forward.

The journeyers paused beneath the dripping awning of a restaurant. They seemed to be in a light mood; flashing secretive smiles.

Charlie Lam got up from his seat and walked quickly out of the theatre.

'Hai, *Shee*!' called the huckster. 'I'm selling wings of lightness; I'm selling garments of sunshine . . .'

'You are our great hero,' said the schoolgirl.

'We follow your every word,' said her companion.

'We love you with pure hearts,' said the third girl as she bent in *ta-him* before Sandy Tang.

'May we take photographs?' This timorous plea came from the teacher of the group: 'Something to keep to remind us of this heavenly moment.'

By way of an answer Sandy Tang struck a pose with riding-whip forthheld, and haughty chin, and the schoolgirls chirped and giggled and rushed like day-old chicks to gather in the folds of his lustrous robe. Dazed to stupidity they grinned towards the flash: '*Aieyaa*.' Another pose, a passive one with delicately pointed little finger and downturned gaze. Then it was Teacher's turn to be captured for an immortal instant. Sandy gave his last (and without a doubt most impressive) pose with blazing eyes, arms wide and knuckles bared. The girls clutched on to one another as their knees collectively failed. Noona then shooed them all from the change-room. Sandy still had lines to study, and he would certainly want to drink tea before the curtain rose.

Sandy drank from the spout of the teapot so as not to mess his immaculately painted lips, but he didn't bother with his lines.

'I've played this role so many times . . . I'd rather talk to you, my dearest. You looked so down when you came in; so piqued with worry. And I watched you as you dressed me, your fingers were trembling and cold. What is it?'

'Unforgivable of me to worry you, Sandy . . .'

'What nonsense! Did anyone touch you? Tell me . . . Did that filthy sex-wolf Sup Yee try to fondle you again? I'll break his neck. I'll twist off his mangy yang and . . .'

'No, no.'

'I can tell at once when you're lying, boy.' Sandy swelled into his military pose.

'I'm not lying, Sandy . . . A man came into the restaurant while I was buying cold drinks . . . I didn't recognize him at first . . .' Noona lumped down on a wardrobe-trunk then, gracelessly leaking tears, soaking Sandy's proffered handkerchief, quite unable to do more than mutter: 'Oh God. Oh God.'

Sandy stood close to his lover, grim-faced, pressing Noona's wet cheeks to his embroidered breast. Intuitively he knew what had occurred:

'He's found you then . . . at last.'

'He said he'd always known where I was.'

'Why? . . . Why?'

'He wants me to bait his trap. He's after Lonnie of course. I feared this would happen, Sandy; some day, someplace. There's been a hidden trap-door forever beneath me, no matter where I stood . . . Well, now it's sprung.'

'The Ging Si gave his word. He promised me to my face that he'd safeguard us from Charlie Lam. I'll reach the Ging Si at once. Don't you worry, Noona, I'll have him stop this . . . Do you think I'm powerless? I'm not powerless.'

'His eyes are so filled with suffering, Sandy. I dared not look at him, I couldn't face him. Yet I could feel his bitter vision hurting me. I told him it was not I who'd killed his wife, I told him how her terrible death had tortured me too . . . Do you know, he said he forgave me, but that I had a debt to pay, and that was my sole identity and total reason to exist . . . *he* is Lonnie's death; his inescapable executioner. And he's honed me into the sharp edge of his plan.'

'I'll stop this outrage.'

'I don't think anyone can do that. He hasn't a thought left that isn't related to death – Lonnie's, and even his own. It's written on his face.'

'I *will* stop him.'

They heard the squeak of pulleys then as the curtain lifted. Zhau Zong, a waggish mandarin, opened with poetry:

> 'The Ming Dynasty hangs
> Like a leaf on an autumn tree.
> The Manchus are a storm wind,
> Blowing through the Middle Kingdom.
> And I am Zhau Zong . . .
> A high official of the Ming court,
> But, oh, how ambition eats
> At the crust of loyalty . . .'

The orchestra adhered to his final phrase. The opera was truly on. Sandy shook Noona's drooping shoulders to jerk him to full attention.

'Listen to me, boy. It's going to be all right. I promise you that. Charlie Lam can go to Hell . . . Now I must go on . . . Did you *hear* me, Noona.'

'Yes, I love you, Sandy.'

'And you believe me, don't you? I will not allow this to happen.'

But Noona's despair was too concentrated to be mended by such dilute promises. In the dark cave of his mind someone was keening with such piercing anguish that he capped his ears from it, learning then that the sound was real enough, born in his own throat, and held back there by force. If he loosened his clenched jaw it would explode. He sank down on to his knees and knuckled his fingers tightly against his teeth and held on, and when he was sure that he would not scream, he stood, then searched around

311

for a pen. On the back of an old programme he wrote more vicious lines than he could have, had shabby fiction been his lifelong profession:

San-kiu, I never loved you. How could I have loved you. I'm going back to Lonnie. How much better he is than you.

He left that note on Sandy's dressing-table, then he walked to the wings where he stood amongst some extras (Manchu soldiers in fur-trimmed tunics, with tinfoil swords) smoking a last cigarette before going on. This was a favourite spot of his – one step short of the glare of the stage lights. It was a border that his feet dared not cross, but which, in splendid fantasy, he traversed nightly to sustained applause. That night he stood there, drained, held by the pull of the limitless art of the only man he'd ever loved with all his heart. It was a cruelty to draw himself away. Yet that was what he did.

Noona came out of the stage door, walked down the bamboo steps, and stood uncertainly in the street. Someone was making an awful din, banging on a drum. Once his vision had adjusted to the darkness he perceived that the sound was being made by a kid, thumping, flat-handed, on a metal bin. He looked around for Charlie Lam, and was startled by the dead, flat voice, almost at his shoulder:

'Did you do it, Noona?'

'I wrote the note . . . Surely, Ah Lam, surely there's a less hurtful way? Sandy's done no harm to you.'

'You can go back to him, Noona, when this is all over. There is no way left other than this. I've been weakened by many blows, and you're all I have left. Come now: we've ten minutes left in which to catch the ferry.'

'I told Sandy I'd seen you.'

Charlie Lam thought about that transgression: 'Well, what's done can't be undone. But from now on you'll do *only*, exactly what I tell you.'

'Yes, Ah Lam . . . Sandy knew, though. We have a way of becoming part of each other's sorrows that you would never understand.'

312

Noona's bicep was taken in a painful grip; he was pulled away from the theatre, drawn down the puddled road towards the ferry terminal. Ah Lam spoke as they quickly walked. 'Your future happiness means nothing to me, Noona. You are my implement. If you prove to be useful, then I'll treat you well. If it turns out that you have no value, then I'll break you. And I'll destroy Sandy too, as though he were part of you. That is my promise. Do you believe me, utterly?'

'Please don't hurt Sandy. That's all I ask.'

'Don't be so sad, boy. You're alive, and so is Sandy. My wife is dead . . . Ask me about sadness; I'm its true connoisseur.'

'It is a terrible thing that Lonnie did. He always told me he had no reason to harm her, and I believed that. He lied to me with every breath.'

They scurried through the hull-door of the ferry just as the whistle blew. The gangplank rattled closed behind them, and the impatient ship slipped away from its berth. They took seats on the unfilled upper deck. Its glass panes were frosted by cool-pumped air, so Noona went on to the open stern deck to watch the lights of Cheung Chau fade, then wink, then die in the suffering dark mist. When there was nothing more to be seen but the churn and foam of the ship's wake, he went back into the long cold coffin, wherein sat deathly Charlie Lam.

'Sometimes,' the cut of Ah Lam's mouth opened haggardly, 'sometimes the sea has a luring voice, not so?'

'As though it calls you, Ah Lam.'

'Yes, just as though it calls you. Did you think of jumping, Noona; to become a hungry ghost?'

'I've thought of it before.'

'So have I . . . Were you ever really happy, Noona; filled up, as it were, so there was space for nothing else?'

'I'm not sure,' he learned as he was saying. 'I'm not sure if I've ever been truly happy.'

'I was happy once – to the absolute brim. But it was so long ago, I can't remember how it felt.'

They said no more to each other until the lights of Hong Kong's bright waterfront sequined the rain-specked windows. Then Noona asked:

'Where will you take me, Ah Lam?'

'To Aberdeen, boy.'

'So that's where Lonnie's hiding.'

'Every crab has its crevice,' breathed Charlie Lam as he stood. 'Come, boy; the tunnel's end can't be far.'

As Big-bui had predicted, the customs officials in their white-coated uniforms were far too harried to undertake a search amongst the raw pig torsos hung up in the back of his truck. On the first trip through Man Kam To he brought with him not only a full consignment of pork, but twenty Ks of best Thai triple-nine morphine base. The Hong Kong customs officials were just as cursory in their search. There was, thought Lonnie, something about a row of swaying pink carcasses that caused most men to shrink from contact.

The meat-porters at the Aberdeen Urban Council market had no such inhibitions. Once there, Big-bui was exercised considerably in the secret, quick transfer of the twenty morphine blocks from the rib cages to a big Union Jack patterned hold-all. It was an almost successful operation; block number nineteen, as fate would have it, slipped from his fingers, and fell with a resounding *clunk* on the metal floor. As Big-bui stooped to retrieve it he was aware of curious eyes. Tak-on, the meat porter, saw him retrieve the cellophane-wrapped brick, and drop it into the bag. Big-bui made certain that Tak-on was elsewhere before he groped for the final block, but the damage was done.

At the day's end Tak-on stopped him with an emollient smile: 'Wai, Big-bui . . . Wait-up for a moment . . . Cigarette? *That* was some delivery, *hey-a!*'

Big-bui took the cigarette and lit it, and said nothing. His silence forced Tak-on to come to the point quickly:

'That was something special you brought in today. *Wah!* My eyes nearly shot right out of their holes when I saw that.'

'When you saw *what*?' Big-bui said coldly. It occurred to him that Tak-on probably thought he was a big-syndicate courier, and that was why the man was treading so tenderly.

'Look, I know how to keep my trap shut . . . I just thought . . . Aah . . .' He conjured his arms around to adorn his incoherence. Big-bui let him stumble on: 'I'm a decent sort of fellow. You know me . . . a wife and four kids . . . Well, I could use some extra cash, you know. Things are tight.'

'Extra cash?'

'Yes, I swear, I'd work like crazy.'

'You're looking for a job?'

'Yes, yes. I thought you could put in a word for me . . . upstairs.'

Big-bui felt a giggle coming up, and converted it into a cough-like snort. But why treat the matter as a joke? Here was the situation: Tak-on believed that he was in a position to apply squeeze on Big-bui in order to obtain employment in a big-time syndicate. Well there had to be some advantage for the manufacturers of Angel-food in that. Big-bui spoke hoarsely from the corner of his mouth:

'*Wah*; you crazy or something, Tak-on. You talk stuff like this in the street you'll get us both killed.'

Tak-on swivelled his eyes; impressed. 'I always thought I'd make a reliable triad forty-nine.'

'You, a fighter?' Well, they needed a fighter. But this guy didn't seem to have the aptitude.

'I can box, Wu style . . .' Tak-on demonstrated, whirling, hissing, jumping around with his arms pumping with bone-snapping speed. 'I can kick, too. I'm fearless.'

He kicked. '*Ha!*' And again, '*Ha!*'

By now a small circle of onlookers had gathered. Big-bui had to give credit: here was a really stupid man – probably the perfect material for a fighter. Tak-on was as good as hired:

'I can see, straight off, that you'll be OK.'

It was coming down luck. Not only had he returned with the morphine they so desperately needed, but with extra staff, too. They were now in a position immediately to expand the Angel-food operation.

And so they did. Big-bui, with Tak-on glowering at his side, daringly penetrated new markets in Mong Kok and Castle Peak, and thereby doubled the uptake of their product. Lonnie slaved over his pressure-cookers and ovens, and stoked his Büchner flask to full capacity – night and day. But, faster than he could make it, Hong Kong's addicts burned it up.

It wasn't long before the partners realized that even more staff would be required, and it was agreed that a further two fighters from Tak-on's redoubtable school of boxing would be taken on.

'We,' said Lonnie, 'have become tycoons . . . Look, a shit-house full of money.' A slight exaggeration; what they had was two drawers of a wardrobe, stuffed with 500-dollar bills. 'It's time we took it a bit more easy.'

'Agreed.'

'It's time we did something with this mountain of cash.'

'Absolutely agreed . . . Yes. Something spectacular.'

'What's the good of being rich men, if nobody knows it?'

'No good at all.'

'We could buy some gold chains.'

'I have an uncle . . .'

'New clothes. A fancy car.'

'And there'd still be plenty left over . . . Lonnie, we've been too hard on ourselves.'

And so it was resolved that funds – a lot of funds in fact, should be set aside for the pursuit of pleasure. Big-bui went out and bought an almost new, red Mercedes. Lonnie, shackled neck and wrist to weighty gold chains, rode with him. They went together to Happy Valley race-track and bet prodigiously, and laughed at their losses. They sailed to Macau where they played fan tan. They ate expensive food and drank a lot of good brandy, and fornicated with whores of excellent quality.

But Lonnie had needs that had been gnawing with growing insistence for a long time; needs that a whore's crotch, however well manipulated, however much semen it drew from him, could never satisfy. He wanted a beautiful boy.

Of course, he dared not admit to this hybrid appetite to anyone. Big-bui would have thrown up his hands in horror had he known of his partner's weakness, but there it was. There was nothing to be done about it, but to go out and find such a perfect youth.

There were gay bars on Hong Kong Island, and in Tsim Sha Tsui, that cracked the skull with sledge-hammer sound, then spilled and dashed and kicked the senses across mirrored dance floors. He liked those places, but had in mind something less hectic, more romantic. The Upside-down Cloud in steamy Shanghai Street would suit his mood nicely. So that was where he went.

'*Dar*ling, long *time* no see.' Mr Puk, whose hair was waxed flatly to his scalp and who owned the longest cigarette-holder in all of Hong Kong, threw wide the front door, and kissed Lonnie on both cheeks. 'Well, what a *brilliant* surprise . . . Don't tell me . . . Don't *tell* me . . . I know *just* the boy for you.'

Lonnie allowed himself to be drawn by the hand into an interior of couches and curtains and tassels of purple and pink. Accoutred in waiter's silks, a row of talon-eyed youths leaned at the bar . . . Lonnie let them all see his new gold.

'And here, darling, is a special place for you . . .' Mr Puk pressed his hand to Lonnie's knee. 'You just lean back and let your troubles float away.' His face came close to Lonnie and his moist hissing breath whispered. 'May I recommend David? Oh! he's got quite the most divine body . . . a butterfly tattooed on his saucy, sweet tail, I ask you . . . and practically a virgin . . . Are you comfortable there?'

'Outstanding.'

Puk set a cigarette in his wand-like holder and giggled so that all of his corn-yellow teeth showed. Then, with a fluid little gesture of fingers and wrist, he called up David. Embraced in self-love, cutely stepping, David advanced.

'Such perfect form, such grace, don't you think?'

'The pupil outshines the teacher, Mr Puk.'

A pianist began to play soft rag-time and Puk went to the foyer to lead in another client.

'*Darling*,' Lonnie heard him say, 'well *what* a *su*-per surprise . . .'

Lonnie stared, and heard himself mutter: 'It can't be . . .' But it was who he thought it was. The man whom Puk now led by the hand was his one-time lover, Noona Cham . . . and Noona was perfection; he was all that Lonnie wanted.

'Fuck off,' said Lonnie to David of the butterfly bum.

Lonnie Huang led whimpering Noona Cham to frenzied stunts upon a purple velvet couch in a back room of Mr Puk's Upside-down Cloud Club, and knew from that moment on that there was no other lover for him. Here was his sole and everlasting mate, and never again would they be separated. A table was set for them, and Lonnie ordered a feast, and when they'd eaten they danced to romantic music. And so for Lonnie the night sped away. He thought Noona had changed and said as much:

'You seem a bit caught up. Not relaxed like the old Noona.'

'Understand, I've been through some tough times. I was in prison, you know. You can't imagine how bad that is until you've been there.'

'Poor Noona. I'll look after you now. I'm rotten rich now, can't you see.'

'All that gold, aieyaa. What did you do; rob the bank, or what?'

'Do you like it? It looks great on me I think.' Lonnie waved his arm about, loving the weight of his bracelet. 'I might buy you some gold too.'

'*Too* generous.'

'I'm serious, Noona. I've got to make up to you . . . I caused you hell. But I've changed, honest truth. I'm a big shot dealer . . . I've got a factory.'

'I always knew you'd be the big success story.'

'Noona,' Lonnie whispered. 'What would you say if I told you I've got a heroin factory?'

'A *what* factory?'

Lonnie leaned right up. 'Heroin; Hong Kong rock.'

'I'd say it was a good joke.'

'It's true.'

'You mean it . . . ? My God, yes you do.'

'Not the biggest, but the best in Hong Kong. I'll take you there. I'll show you. We could go there now.'

'Now?' Noona stiffened. 'Why so soon?'

'Noona, it's morning. Look . . . We're just about the only ones left in the club.'

Indeed even the indefatigable Mr Puk seemed quite worn under. He came to their table: 'So good to have had you two darlings; wonderful, *wonderful* . . . You'll have to come again, soon.'

'An excellent facility, Mr Puk; always the best. We've had a good time, right, Noona?'

'Yes, quite marvellous.'

Mr Puk conjured their bill on to the table.

Lonnie captured it with equal largesse: 'Three thousand dollars,' he announced to the near empty club. From his back pocket came a wad of brown 500-dollar notes. Mr Puk gathered up the scattered currency; a smile that stretched to his molars gave testimony to his faith in the selfless altruism of man.

Five in the morning; there had been heavy rain during the night; water trickled in the gutters, and you could hear its thrum in the deep storm drains. The air wafted mistily, pungently eructed from a sickened sea, and the grume of the gutters was banked up at the street corners. A straw-hatted Hakka woman swish-swished her broom at the litter, stooping now and then in search of treasure amongst the trash; a matchbox with some members left unburned, a ten-cent coin that clinked beneath the bristles. Noona stared about, searching. He couldn't see him, but he knew Charlie Lam was there; he could *feel* him . . . At last a taxi passed. Its wet tyres hissed to a stop.

Lonnie patted Noona into its interior; Lonnie who was marked for death.

They drove quickly through the empty streets, while the wiper-blades slapped dismally at the mist, and Lonnie gabbled on about his marvellous factory – not the biggest, but the best. 'You'll see, Noona, how well I've done.' He was as happy as Noona had ever known him to be. Tired Aberdeen, but for its fishing fleet, was still aslumber. They stopped before a block of flats: New Prosperity Mansions.

On its steps Lonnie warned: 'My partner is a straight sort of fellow. You'll like him. But he might frown on the male custom . . . So we'll just say that you're a friend of mine, and that you've got troubles, and you need somewhere to hole up. That will be our story when he comes.'

It didn't matter one way or the other what lies the partner was told, Noona thought. This nightmare would be over soon, and then he would go back to Sandy, and beg for forgiveness, and Sandy would take him back.

Flat number eleven was on the third floor. The door opened into a stark and acerbic-smelling room, more like a kitchen than anything else. Lonnie must have noticed the resemblance too, as he gestured towards his implements:

'Here I'm like a great chef. Only I know the recipe for the stuff I make. We call it Angel-food. Do you like the name, Noona? Angel-food; because Heaven is just a puff away . . . I don't smoke it, though. You know heroin makes me ill . . . I have to work now. Noona, you just sit there and watch. Play the radio, if you like.'

Lonnie took off his smart clothes; stripped down to his vest and boxer shorts and put on an old pair of slip-slops. He took off his gold chains and gave them to Noona to hold. He opened some windows and switched on an extractor fan: 'The fumes make your eyes run, but so what: we'll cry all the way to the bank.'

While Lonnie prepared to make his Angel-food Noona sat quietly in a corner, wondering when, and from what quarter, the attack would come. And what murderous technique Ah Lam would use . . . They were playing one of Sandy's arias on the radio.

Lonnie had not overstated the stench-power of his chemicals; pungent fumes rose to submerge all, tapping snot and tears as though the very brain was dissolving in the stink, and leaking away.

Ah Lam came without warning. The door swung open, and there he stood with his gun outheld and pointed: '*You!*' The word was fused and burning with deadly accusation. '*You!*' That's all he said. Lonnie held up a heavy glass flask, as though to deflect the bullet when it came; snarling, flinching, whimpering, and sheared of all courage.

For a moment it seemed as though Charlie Lam would not fire. Then he shouted, '*Bastard*,' and the gun barrel flashed.

Noona had little recollection of noise, or of the explosion that wrecked the flat; burst every window, and split the furniture to matchwood, but of a huge and stunning force that struck like a hammer blow driving him a massive distance to a black disorganized place where he lay quite still, while his mind crawled fearfully about trying to find something that it could distinguish and grasp. Pain; it grew slowly and insistently within him, nagging at him; drawing him away from the darkness. There was a distant sound, coming ever closer, calling, 'Help me, help me, *help* me' . . . At the place where the voice joined the pain, Noona opened his eyes and saw that the owner of the voice was Lonnie, who was shuffling on his knees with his hands pressed to his face, moaning: 'Oh God . . . help me someone, help me.'

Noona imitated the movements of his friend and grovelled towards him, and said, 'Lonnie. It's all right, Lonnie, you hear . . . It's all right . . .'

When Lonnie dropped his hands from his face, Noona ceased to say that. Lonnie's skin was puckered with pearly raw blisters. He was frowning and blinking, and his eyeballs were blistered too. Noona heard himself say, 'Oh no. God no.'

'Oh God, I'm burning . . . Do something, Noona. Do something for my eyes . . . Do something, Noona.'

People with shocked faces began to edge into the room, staring around at the destruction. Slowly more of them came, the rearmost craning their heads to get a better view. When they saw money scattered amongst the wreckage they surged forward.

Noona knew what he must do. He hoisted his damaged friend to his feet, and with one arm supporting him led him to the door.

Ah Lam lay on the landing, pulped and crumpled like a spider that is hit by a shoe. Dead, thought Noona of the one-time connoisseur of suffering – how nice for him to be back with his bride. They had to step over Lam's body in order to reach the stairs. More people came to stare at groaning Lonnie. Noona pressed through them:

'Be quiet,' he hissed at Lonnie.

'My eyes; such pain; I can't see. Why can't I see?'

'You're blind, Lonnie. There's nothing to be done. Your eyes are burned out. I saw them.'

'Oh no; oh fuck . . . Why, Noona, why?'

'You killed his wife. Do you blame him?'

'Where is he now . . . ? For God's sake.'

'He's finished.'

'That's good . . . Where are we, Noona?'

'A few more steps . . . Now we're in the street.'

Noona could hear the bleat of distant, but fast-approaching claxons. He gave the blind man terse instruction:

'Walk with me, Lonnie, as straight as you can. Take your hand away from your face. I'm going to barely hold you; just to steer you . . . you understand.'

'Yes, Noona . . .'

'We don't want the police to spot you, ha.'

'Yes.'

A woman's sharp voice cut across the street: 'Wai, Blind-boy . . . Hey-a, wait up there.'

She was preposterously fat; a planless, amorphous collection of huge body parts, each portion more absurd than the next. Two strapping arms dangled widely; two billiard-table legs bowled her surprisingly swiftly across the street. A bright red, jumble-sale shift united these appendages to a many-tiered jowl and ruddy, dimpled visage. A very ugly sight.

'*Wai*,' she shouted again. 'Wait up, Blind-boy.'

Noona contemplated flight, but the creature seemed more eager than dangerous. Lonnie said angrily: 'Fuck,' then desolately: 'Fuck,' then slumped.

'It *is* you, Blind-boy.' She caught up with them. 'I thought it was . . . You're *hurt*. Aiey*aa*.'

'Badly hurt,' Noona said. 'An accident.'

'Aieyaa,' she cooed, 'I can help. That's my shop over there. Come with me.'

'You'll help?'

'Oh gladly.'

It was a rice shop; clean and stocked with quality merchandise. Noona had no hesitation in leading Lonnie in. And no sooner had he done so than two police cars sped by.

'I knew you'd come back, Blind-boy.'

'My eyes,' Lonnie pleaded. 'Help my eyes.'

'Poor Blind-boy.'

The name was appropriate, still Noona had to ask: 'Why do you call him that?'

'Because that's his name, don't you know . . . What's *your* name?'

'Noona. I'm his friend; Noona Cham.'

'My humble name is Lustrous Jade.' She floundered into a little bow. '*I'm* his fiancée.'

'*Fiancée?*'

'Yes. Of course . . . You look so surprised.'

'I see . . . Well it's just that . . . Lonnie, *this* is your fiancée.' Lonnie whispered, 'Oh God, no.'

'Amazing,' said Noona. 'Well then I'll go . . . You'll see to him, Lustrous Jade.'

'No more to be said.' She placed a flipper-like hand on Lonnie's defeated shoulder, bowing him further still.

Noona walked briskly away. He caught a bus to Central then walked to the Outlying Districts ferry pier. Next to the Cheung

Chau ticket-booth a poster was adhered – an advertisement for the current opera season. Noona pointed to the central figure: 'Sandy Tang,' he bragged to the ticket-seller. 'I know him well.'

'Have you not heard?' said the man. 'Don't you listen to the news . . .?'

That joy is as vagrant and mutable as mist was a truism well bedded in the experience of Sandy Tang. But nothing in his history had prepared him for this sudden and awful change; from inebriate love, to sober, bitter emptiness in the blink of an eye. There had been no warning; no time to prepare; where all things had been perfectly complete, now lay a shattered mess. No poetry was too sad to relate his absolute grief; nor did it seem possible to bring order to this chaos.

The Ging Si was unreachable. Sandy left a score of pleading messages with a mordant-voiced secretary: 'Desperate, sir. Yes. I've written that down. I assure you, sir, he'll receive your message in due course . . .'

Sandy tried in his nightly art to gather in his fragmented being. Music was the glue that he could trust to connect the discordant and weld it into harmony. If so, could it not counter this destruction? It failed him. His agony poured from him in song, and gave him nothing but more agony – no order; no logic – just deep, sobbing, everlasting grief. He began to reckon with the possibility that it would be with him for as long as he lived. And his next thought, of course, was of immediate death.

Suicide . . . No sooner had that potential taken root than it spread its tendrils to every corner of his mind, and not a minute passed when it wasn't working through. When on the platform waiting for the train, he'd shuffle to the very edge, and gaze at the shining silver rails, and stand there, faint and sweating as the coaches thundered by . . . Suicide. An honourable Chinese institution; and a fine means of laying guilt at the door of the guilty. In this case the lying, manipulative and unforgivingly cruel, Ging Si. Had ever a man deserved to carry the remorse of another's death more than that terrible man? . . . On his ferry trips to Cheung Chau Sandy gazed into the churning shuddering sea, and wondered what it would be like to drown beneath that ceaseless hiss . . . Too ill-marked and lonely a grave, he decided.

He was, after all, a star, and so his ultimate leave-taking from this earth should be an event of dignity – yet not so dignified that it went unnoticed; of drama – yet not pretentiously so. An end that pointed its bloody finger unequivocally towards its cause.

The solution to this quandary, so perfectly fitting, so elegant and rewarding that it made him cry, came to him during the penultimate performance of the tragedy, *Princess Cheung Ping*, that night.

Here was a story of disenchantment and sorrow; of unsparing love, and the ultimate triumph of good over evil: the perfect analogy on to which to suffix his own tormented tale. The Ming emperor's forces are subdued by the evil Manchus, and the princess, to escape dishonour, plots double suicide with her husband, Prince Zau Sae Hin.

In the standard production, the couple, having sung 'The Fragrant Passage to Death', fall on their swords and end their mutual misery – and are later seen dressed in god-like robes, dancing in heaven. Sandy's reworked final coda would be different. There would be no reincarnation for Prince Zau; no arising from his sword at all. He would be truly dead.

Suicide . . . Those who have not contemplated it in seriousness as a means of revenge, have no idea of its potential for bright ignition. The twisted and blackened wick of Sandy's spirit took joyful flame . . . There was much to be done in preparation. There was poetry to be written. The ultimate stanzas of Prince Zau's final aria needed new words; a narrative that would, however studded with allegory, quite clearly spell out the epitaph of Sandy Tang.

Some lines danced up immediately:

A blackened pool
Of waters, cool
A fallen sky
Beneath my feet.
Is this your lair
Your fine disguise
Oh God of Lies?

In my cupped hands
I raised a star
Briefly I loved
This glinting speck.
Then I beheld
Your fine disguise . . .

And so the words came tumbling and turning – filling him up with poetry . . . Why, this was the clay from which folk legends were moulded. He must do a thorough job in all respects . . . Of course, Prince Zau's normal, tinfoil sword would not do. It would have to be the real thing. And though he personally did not own such an implement, there were many actors – acrobats in the main, who did.

He had twenty-four hours in which to prepare for his final exit. Time enough, if he worked exceedingly quickly.

He 'phoned Cousin Tik-kat with the message of his renewal:

'Will you tell the Maitreya, that in the end I turned to the correct teachings. I have converted to the beliefs of the Assembly . . . And I beg that I may be allowed to be at his side in the Hereafter . . .'

'What are you gabbling about, San-kiu? I'm a busy man.'

'I wanted Elder Brother to know that finally I converted. I don't know how to reach him now, other than through you.'

Tik-kat was quiet for a while, then said: 'The Maitreya commanded me to gain converts . . . But you San-kiu are deformed and powerfully diseased to your soul, and there could be no hope for you. I reject you as I would a sewer-rat.'

'Will you please just tell my brother . . .'

'Not a word of this conversation will he hear from me.'

'I've changed.'

'You are merely disguised.'

'No, Cousin . . . I'm nearing my end.'

'San-kiu, I wish you nothing good.'

'You have had your wish come true,' Sandy said to the dead 'phone. His vision blurred. 'You bastard,' he sobbed. 'You utter bastard, Tik-kat. How could you reject me, now?'

Sandy borrowed a long curved sword from a traditional *Kimshut*, a fencer – a truly graceful blade, and as reflective as a mirror. 'Just for one night's work,' he told the fencer.

'Take care not to cut yourself, Sandy. It's sharp like a razor. What will you use it for?'

Sandy invented his final lines at that precise moment:

> Exit, bright truth
> From silver cut
> Strengthened by death
> Damnation flies
> Oh God of lies.

The fencer, a simple fellow, nodded and said, 'Well just be careful, ha.' Then gave him a velvet-lined case in which to transport the sword. And with that case as his only luggage, Sandy boarded the evening ferry to Cheung Chau. A roughish passage; a dull sea and sky. On that trip he wrote out his final script – polished it, and learned it. He added some dramatic ornaments to the musical score, paying particular attention to the percussion patterns of the prelude and the finale. After those orchestral instructions had been clearly written out there was no more to do. He opened the sword-case on his lap and contemplated the length of sharp metal that he would cause to end his life. He pictured the puzzlement on the faces of the cast as he launched into his amended aria; the glances they would exchange: 'What's all this about; and a real sword too? What the hell is Sandy up to tonight?' . . . He rehearsed the bitter-sweet smile he would offer in those final moments . . . Then, pandemonium as with both hands he thrust the sword into his vitals and awful pain momentarily flushed him. 'Why, Sandy, why . . .?' 'To celebrate an iniquity.'

Cheng Chau ahead. Rain was spatting; the air was sulky, warning of a blow. Sandy walked with his fellow passengers across the gangplank to the shore. He felt more distanced than ever he had before from the crush and jabber of the common herd; adorned with hair and filled with teeth, he despised them. More than ever he wanted to be freed from his bondage to this miserable, bigoted race.

He ate a meal, then went to the theatre and issued his instructions to the orchestra leader. He expressly beseeched that the lute players should stroke such sweet music from their strings that night that the sound would stop the sailing clouds.

Then he closed himself off in his curtained changing-cubicle and began to apply make-up, to rouge his cheeks and whiten his forehead and the bridge of his nose. He slanted his eyebrows and taped them into immovable anger. When his stand-in dresser arrived, Sandy forbade him entrance. There was one more thing that had to be done, alone; that was the recital of the all-powerful mantra that was the key to Heaven, no matter where Cousin Tik-kat stood on that issue. This was what the Maitreya had taught him to say:

> 'As there are eight trigrams in Heaven
> And eight rivers on earth,
> So my body is of eight houses.'

It was a long and complicated mantra, and Sandy had only been instructed in it once. But the lines came readily enough:

> 'My white breath rises to the Imperial Heaven,
> My Original Home in the World of True Emptiness.'

Distantly he heard Zhau Zong launch into his patter-speech. The orchestra began to play. The opera had started, Sandy realized, and he was not yet dressed. He dashed through the magical words:

> 'There to prostrate to the Eternal Mother,
> And prepare for wonders that are to come.'

Yes that was right, but now bare seconds remained in which to dress, and the mantra was not completely said:

> 'As I breathe out and in,
> The Heavenly Gate opens . . .'

His dresser, in desperation, threw back the cubicle curtain. Sandy pliantly availed himself of his robe, while still silently reciting:

> 'My soul takes essence
> As it . . .'

As it, what? For God's sake how did it go after that? No more time, he'd lost the key to the gates of Heaven. Sandy strode towards the wings, then straight on stage.

He stunned them with his genius that night; he lifted them on his wondrous-winged voice to rarefied heights, then flung them down to Hell. Cast and audience alike clung to his passion as though they knew that this was art in its purest and most consummate form, beyond which pinnacle it was impossible to reach; and there was nothing left for this master to achieve now, nothing this side of the grave. A squall-driven storm arrived, drumming hard rain at the metal-sheathed hall. His voice subordinated the grumbling, jealous sky.

For the final scene, the aria of the Fragrant Passage to Death, Sandy changed into his most resplendent red robe embroidered with twelve dragon medallions. He stood before the implacable barbarian soldiers with Princess Cheung Ping, who also had donned her most gorgeous ceremonial robe with fringed cloud-tippet, and peonies. And together they vowed suicide.

They sang their way to the Imperial garden, and there drew their swords. The princess was first to die (side-on to the audience), with her tinfoil sword thrust (under her armpit) right through her slim body, she collapsed in a heap.

Sandy Tang knelt face-on to the audience, and drew his sword, and the flash of true metal carried to the last hushed row.

> 'Exit, bright truth
> From silver cut
> Strengthened by death . . .'

He poised the sword point at his abdomen. It pricked sharply through his silk breastplate. 'Damnation flies. Oh God of Lies . . .' He tensed his arms and commanded them to do it; but they wouldn't. He cursed his disobedient limbs. He pleaded for resolute and pitiless action; one mighty heave, a single convulsive thrust and it would all be over. Do it. Do it now! The order thundered from his brain, and died with a whimper at his wrists; his trembling, recreant wrists. They would not kill him.

Sandy dropped the sword and fled blindly from the stage. In full operatic regalia he dashed into the darkness beyond the theatre walls. A strong wind drove rain at him and caught at his long robe. He tore away the gaudy cloth, and it billowed and sped with the moaning gale, then dropped into a sodden heap. His pavilion-cap blew off on its own. In boots and flannel under-clothes; inwardly screaming, Coward! Coward! he ran into the face of the storm.

Sandy found a place where bare-teethed waves cannoned by the mad wind pounded the shore. He crept up to a gully where the sea boiled blackly, sucking, swirling, then crashing forward with a thud and boom that shook the ground and cascaded hissing spray, as hard as hail. And there it was that he remembered the final phrase of the Maitreya's mantra – the key to Heaven:

> 'My soul takes essence
> As it rises into Her arms,
> Protected from all chaos,
> I will weep no more.'

And he cried that as he fell into the waves.

Sandy Tang's body was discovered by some Cheung Chau kids, out combing the rocks at Pak Kok Tsui for usable storm debris. Though abraded and dented by the pounding it had taken, and somewhat wrinkled from its immersion, the corpse was remarkably intact, and easily recognizable. So that Tik-kat, when summoned to the Kowloon police mortuary, had but to take a single distasteful glance before nodding his affirmation:

'Yes, it's Tang San-kiu.'

'My condolences,' said a coroner's officer. 'Now there are some documents you must sign . . . And if you could oblige with a short history . . .'

Tik-kat said curtly: 'Is there any reason why I should have to remain in this dreadful room any longer?'

'None at all.'

They went to the waiting-room. A young Hakka woman sat in a chair there, her upper body rocking in the impulse of sorrow, keening. The coroner's officer waved affably to a vacant chair, and Tik-kat sat, shrinking from all contact, hardly daring to breathe this grief-laden air.

'Now,' said the coroner's officer, unclipping his pen. 'When did you last hear from the deceased?'

'Months ago,' Tik-kat whispered.

'Can we put a date to it?'

Tik-kat gazed, unanswering, at the officer. He thought: Even in death San-kiu you drag your blood-relatives to disgust and hate.

'No . . . date,' wrote the officer. 'You look a little pale, Mr Tang. Would you like to drink tea?'

The thought of touching the porcelain of this ghoulish place to his lips brought emphatic response:

'No tea.'

'We're almost certain that death was caused by drowning. But there will of course be a post-mortem examination. I'm telling you this because it may interfere with funeral arrangements . . . Mr Tang . . . where are you going, Mr Tang?'

'Out,' said Tik-kat. 'I'm going out.'

It was raining and Tik-kat turned up his face to it until thoroughly, gladly wetted. Then he walked to his Rolls.

He could not face lunch that day, and sat staring at his computer screens, not daring to buy or sell while still permeated by the mortally bad feng shui of the morning. He made several 'phone calls. The first was to a Kowloon feng shui professor whom he summoned immediately to his office. The second was to his wife, advising her to remain indoors until further notice. The third was to Connie Tam, to whom he said:

'Sandy Tang has gone away.'

'So I heard, earlier; a tragic death. We'll run the story tonight.'

'Yes . . . There must be no disgrace for him.'

'Of course. The Maitreya's only brother. I will use influence.'

'If he's disgraced, then so is the family.'

'You may rely on me, teacher.'

'You must give him face; a brave suicide . . . Yes, an act of outstanding courage . . . Portray him as a Cantonese, Hong Kong patriot; an artist who saw no future for his art under Communist rule. He wrote some poetry before his death; it's being delivered to me. It seems he totally changed some words and music in the score of his opera.'

'Perhaps his great patriotism is set down in those words.'

'That's what I expect. I'll keep you informed.'

'The Maitreya, is he well?'

'I'm sure he is.'

'I think of him every minute.'

Tik-kat concluded resolutely: 'We must be strong.'

The feng shui professor arrived then with a young apprentice who bore his baggage. He quickly took command of Tik-kat's office. Masses of incense was lit, as well as some small, but lively fires in brass crucibles. A tripod was set up and to its platform a geomancer's compass was affixed, then spun so that its centralized, little, demon-chasing mirror took in every aspect of the room. While Tik-kat's defences were being thus revitalized, a woman arrived who said that her name was Lotus-bud, and that she had been a friend of Sandy. She wore a simple cotton frock, and was astonishingly beautiful. Tik-kat noticed that her eyes were rimmed with grief. Surprisingly, it seemed that someone had loved Sandy Tang:

'He was a great artist . . . *very* great.'

'Yes, quite so.'

'When Noona disappeared Sandy was broken. They were so happy those two.'

'Would you care for tea. My office is in a mess, feng shui all wrong, you understand, but we could find some chairs.'

That was what they did. While the feng shui professor warred with the forces of evil, they sat and sipped high quality heung-pin from Tik-kat's best porcelain. He was captivated by this elegant flower. She claimed to have often sung lead roles opposite Sandy:

'He had the ability to lift the performance of all those around him . . . And never more so than on that tragic night. He altered the score for his final aria.'

'So you said on the 'phone.'

'I've brought his orchestral instructions.' She handed him a sheaf of papers, indecipherably scrawled upon. But there was a page of lyrics that was legibly written out in Sandy's unmistakable flamboyant script. Tik-kat read silently.

'Beautiful words,' Lotus-bud said quietly, 'are they not?'

'The God of Lies . . . He's titled his new aria, "The God of Lies".'

'Yes. That's how he expressed the song when he sang it – laden with bitterness . . . one voice raised against a malicious and phenomenal power. It was so, so sad. We, in the cast, all realized that he'd reached the breaking-point, but what could be done to help? We're in a strange community, as insular as a one-name village clan. So if one person pains, in an instant all of us know. And we whisper about it, but, like true Chinese, do nothing more.'

'Do you suppose this "God of Lies" refers to some living person, or that it's simply an allegory: a fist waved at the perversity of fate?'

'He *was* being harassed . . . Several months ago at the Ko Shan theatre a gwailo came backstage; dark-haired, and tall; a Cantonese speaker. One of our percussion instrumentalists saw him clearly, and overheard him threaten Sandy.'

'My dear, if this is true; if this man is the cause of my cousin's tormented end, then it places on me the burden of retribution. A matter of honour, you see . . . This musician; you must bring him to me. I want to hear more about this gwailo, and his threats.'

'I knew that I was doing the right thing in coming to see you, Mr Tang.' Lotus-bud's eyes flashed, then tightened into tiny buttons of hate. 'You should see him punished, that "God of Lies". You should bring him down for what he did to Sandy.'

'I should, and I will.' He pressed her hand in his. 'I'll bring him down.' But not because of Sandy's feeble lament. This gwailo, whoever he was, had wounded the Maitreya by his actions, and *that* was his unpardonable sin.

9

BLACK WIND BLOWING

In Kowloon, on the edge of tumultuous Nathan Road, bestrode by tenements, and within the drift of aroma of a large Mc-Donalds, there stands an old red brick church with a steeple and high-pitched roof, and leaded cusped windows that glow grimily with the hallowed disciples of Christianity. On Sundays, when the good bell tolls to draw in the faithful, a hundred or so perspiring, ex-patriate Anglicans plod in and take up their places upon teak-benched, wicker-backed pews, where they beg for the remission of sins, and life everlasting. They sing, pretty raggedly, as Englishmen tend to do, and say the prayers they have been taught from youth to say. St Andrew's Church stands like a twig caught in a stream; the colonialists are going home, the gaudier religions of the Orient will one day, quite soon, sweep it away.

In the meantime this venerable church would serve as the venue for the marriage of Caroline Catherine O'Shea, to Reven Forrester. So that was where they met before the event, to rehearse the promises they would make, then go on to take early lunch in an equivalently colonial preserve: the Peninsula Hotel. It was not a good morning for any such excursion; a mature typhoon was skulking about in the South China Sea, close enough to deluge Hong Kong and cause some nasty land-slips in the hillside cottage areas. Forrester was in a dispirited mood. Sandy Tang's pathetic suicide brought no honour to him. He knew the surly wave-clapped rocks at Pak Wok Tsui – total desperation must have driven Sandy to life's end at that grim spot. A wretched way to die.

Caroline had somehow found out about his late evening visit to Trixie Welldon's flat, where 'seductive' Tess Hempstead now 'lurked'. His bride-to-be had prodded him with deliberate and pointed innuendo, then retreated behind pretended good humour.

An abbreviated explanation would have been perceived as a sign of cowardice; a lengthy explanation as a sign of guilt. So he declined to excuse his action at all. Bluntly (somewhat sullenly, even by his self-forgiving standards), he snapped:

'Leave it!'

'It was supposed to be a joke.'

In retrospect he could see that. It was also just as plain that he did feel more than a little responsible for Tess Hempstead's current plight, though for the life of him he couldn't figure out why he should.

They ordered food, and some drinks, and might have got on well after that, had one of Hong Kong's more pestilent investigative reporters not chanced by. Bertie Humphries wrote for *Time* magazine, and some respectable Chinese Hong Kong dailies. He had learned his trade with the *South China Morning Post*, which made him an ex-colleague of Caroline's. He was fat – so fat that the lower buttons of his shirt could not take the strain, and a segment of his coir-matted belly was constantly exposed. Bertie was aglow with his usual beery bonhomie; he saw them and waved, then waddled towards their table where he leaned over a vacant chair.

'My God, is it true what I hear, the great Ging Si and Caroline O'Shea are to be matrimonified at last?'

Piss-off, Bertie, Forrester willed.

'Sit down and have a drink,' said Caroline.

'Don't mind if I do.' The wicker chair winced pathetically, and expanded as Bertie jammed his massive stern into it. 'It's on me.' He patted Caroline's knee and laughed for no reason.

Now he would tell a dirty joke, Forrester reckoned. Bertie, Forrester knew, had a notebook filled with dirty jokes which he kept in his blazer pocket. Whenever he heard something original he would whip out his little book and write in the key words – he had seen him do it. Presumably he dipped into this lexicon of smut as the day progressed in order to refresh his repertoire. Bertie had other things on his mind, though; he waved down a waiter, ordered drinks for all of them, then leaned, as best he was physically able, towards Forrester:

'I've heard from good sources . . . *good* sources, that you people expect trouble in Statue Square this Saturday; that the Pro-Democracy movement is planning something . . . something more provocative than Beijing would tolerate.'

'Bertie, you know better than to try and pump me. I trust you less than the lamp-post trusts the dog.'

Bertie was undeterred. He listed even further, and said even more confidentially, 'I've also heard . . . just a rumour mind you, that some tractor-trailer drivers from the container port may decide to block off the main roads and bring Hong Kong to a grinding halt.' He waved his podgy hands about. 'Don't even think of asking me where my information comes from. Don't even *think* of it.'

'I wouldn't think of it, Bertie.'

'I would,' said Caroline. 'Who told you that?'

'Freddy Chong.'

'That little thief,' she laughed derisively. 'And you believed him!'

'He's in the know.' Bertie sounded offended. 'He's on the Urban Council, crissake.'

'He's the biggest crook in all of Hong Kong.' Caroline expanded on her calumny. 'He's been siphoning off millions from his own bank for years.'

'Not to mention the Lo Wah building scam . . . *But*, that doesn't mean his information isn't prime.'

Forrester sat stunned before this avalanche of slander – a few million dollars' worth, at least, in less time than it took him to fill his beer-glass. And, mark you, this case was supposedly one of ICAC's currently most secret investigations. Forrester knew about it because ICAC's Director of Operations had appealed for police assistance. Nine hundred million dollars had been skimmed from the bank's loan balance and sent overseas – a sign of the times. Bertie re-aimed his focus at Forrester:

'I hear that you people are preparing to charge the poor fellow on eighty-three counts of fraud . . .'

The figure was exactly right.

'. . . Freddy is therefore deeply in the shit.'

Forrester said, 'Whether that is so, or not, I couldn't tell you. It looks to me as though Freddy Chong is trading for some sympathetic press. That's a smart move; he could use it. What are you in the market for, Bertie?'

'Here and now, not much. You've never given me anything in the past, Reven. It would be naive of me to expect you to break down now . . . You never know though, I'm the patient type . . . For instance, I hear that Hong Kong's top Cantonese opera star went for a dip during last night's storm and never came back to shore. The inside story on that queer hawk would make quite a scoop.'

Caroline's eyebrows arched: 'Sandy Tang's drowned? . . . I didn't know that.' She looked shocked, and said to both men, 'What happened?'

'That's exactly what I just asked the Ging Si . . . Our Sandy gave a rather unusual opera performance, according to his colleagues. He wrote a new score for his last aria, then produced a long and hell-a-va sharp cutlass, with which he proceeded to not kill himself. Then he rushed out of the theatre, howling, and went for a midnight swim . . . Weird. And to cap it all, this guy's brother turns out to be a Buddhist monk; some sort of prophet; and *he's* vanished. What a headline I could make out of that . . . Hey-a! Ging Si, how about it?'

'I wish I could help you, Bertie.'

'Sure you do . . . What the hell, let's have one more drink.' The occasion called for a poof joke. 'Have you heard the one about the Yankee sailor who wakes up, hungover, next to this little Chinese bloke. "Shit," he says, "I must have been tight . . ." "First time tight," says the Chink, "second time not so tight."'

338

Bertie's colossal girth showed modest signs of laughter.

When the food came fat Bertie departed. Caroline said: 'You didn't tell me about Sandy Tang's death.'

'He committed suicide by jumping into the sea near Pak Kok Tsui Head on Cheung Chau Island. Bertie's version was pretty accurate. At this stage that's all I know.'

'I just thought you might have told me . . . And the Maitreya; has he really disappeared, or is that mere disinformation, put out by the police?'

'Why should we do such a thing?'

'Well, if you had arrested him, you wouldn't want anyone to know it.'

'You have a more devious mind than I gave you credit for.'

'Don't try and dodge the question, Reven. Have you arrested Tang Tsun?'

'You know, Caroline, when you've had a few drinks on an empty stomach, as now, you tend to verbally overexert, as now.'

'You prissy bastard . . . No. Oh no . . . I'm not going to get angry with you. That's exactly what you want. I know your game, you want me to start apologizing, so you can lapse into angelic silence. Well, I'm on to you. So I want an answer. I deserve one. You involved me in this, remember, and it's worried me ever since.'

Forrester stood. 'I have to attend a briefing at Arsenal Street in twenty minutes – less time than that, in fact. I've timed things rather badly. I'm sorry. I must go at once . . . You know, Carrie, it's your colleagues, like Humphries, with their subtly damning pens who you should carry the battle to if you wish to see Tang Tsun survive. They're the king-makers, and the destroyers. If I could trust Bertie, I'd gladly have him on my side . . . Yes, Tang has disappeared, as Bertie said. I've no idea where he is, but I'll find him, and I think, quite soon.'

*

Grey rain pelted against Reven Forrester's office windows, drumming so trenchantly on the glass that small leaks sprang through the joints, trickling over the sill to the floor; there expanding darkly into his carpet. Amongst the messages he found on his desk was a cryptic note from Fung Sham – The Fixer.

Ging Si. The bird who flew is back here in Sai Kung. Phone me.

Forrester dug Fung's number out of his computer and dialled it, and was confronted with an engaged tone. There was a message from SSO Criminal Intelligence; they wanted an urgent meeting. Forrester locked on to Fung Sham's line, then called his subordinate from CIB, on the intercom.

CIB's news was that a police 'needle' who'd penetrated Wo Shing Tong Triad Society was warning of an imminent truckers' strike. The ostensible reason for their action was a grievance over parking facilities; the truckers were obliged to back-up for hours on end whilst en route to the warehouses at the container terminal, inching forward, wasting costly fuel – correlation of the amazing Bertie Humphries' earlier tip-off. Forrester said:

'Sounds like a good reason to strike.'

'I'd agree, sir, if it wasn't triad motivated. The drivers have all been warned not to scab.'

'Right, I'll pass it on to the Tactical Unit.'

Fung Sham's number gave a ringing tone at last. Mrs Sham came on the line. Through a deafening rattle of mah-jong tiles, wife of Sham said curtly:

'*Hai!*'

'Mrs Sham, it's the Ging Si. Is . . . ?'

She screamed, 'Husband, the man is Ging Si. Pick up electric-talk next time yourself.' She dropped the receiver.

Forrester pictured Mrs Sham, in curlers and a shapeless shift, a wiry, cantankerous Hakka peasant, whose only redeeming feature was the phenomenal fruitfulness of her womb. She had produced nine sons in eight years. The receiver rattled; Fung said apologetically:

'Only my pig-faced wife, ha. Don't notice her . . . How things, Ging Si?'

'It's pissing here.'

'Same here; ten times extra . . . You got my message. The man you asked me to keep the look-out for turned up, just like you thought. He went up to the old monastery of Monkey God – Great Sage Equal to Heaven.'

'Good work, Ah Fung.'

'It was nothing . . . when you're coming Sai Kung?'

Forrester's wrist-watch gave him that the scheduled briefing of the Director of Operations was about to begin. He said: 'I'll see you soon, Ah Fung,' then disconnected. He dialled Organized and Serious Crime Bureau and established that the team on stand-by was MacNaughton's. He requisitioned two Landrovers from the transport pool, then simply had to go and empty his aching bladder. By the time he reached the office of the Director of Operations, Forrester was rebukably late.

Senior Assistant Commissioner Mark (Xi Zing) Long was a man of unflagging energy which he released in spirited bursts, as now, as with pointer vigorously in hand, and overhead-projector loaded, he spoke of Sunday's big operation. A map of Happy Valley Race-course and its environs shone brightly on a screen, as well as the shadow of his pointer, skidding this way and that.

'. . . Right then, this is it in a nutshell. The demonstration has been called for Sunday at zero nine hundred. An accurate forecast of numbers is impossible. Count on at least five hundred thousand people. If the rain continues, it might dissuade the less enthusiastic from attending. So pray that there's no change in the weather. Right. The rallying-point is to be Happy Valley, where the crowd will be addressed by Pro-Democracy student leaders, and some of Hong Kong's other more militant gentlemen. When the speeches are over, they will then all march along Wong Nai Chung, following the tram route all the way to Central, where they will disperse . . .' An upside-down map of Statue Square was juggled by an aide into proper perspective. The pointer rapped. 'Here . . .

'I don't foresee any insurmountable problems occurring at Happy Valley. The subsequent mood of the crowd will, however, be unpredictable, and will depend on how softly, or hard, the orators have played it, and how capable they were in welding the crowd into a single-minded entity; and, of course, how efficient we are in keeping a firm overall control on things. As usual, our motto will be minimum force. Right. Our Tactical Units will be totally extended, but they have been well trained, and they have modern equipment . . .'

Mark Long spoke on about the need for this demonstration to be contained without violence; for senior officers of the People's Liberation Army would be on hand to observe the efficiency, or otherwise, of the Royal Hong Kong Police. A day later, and Hong Kong would become part of the People's Republic, and a PLA garrison would be the new tenants of Her Majesty's Dockyard, Prince of Wales Building; a Beijing appointee would sit at the Commissioner's desk, and they would all be shorn of their 'Royal' entitlement, and simply be known as the Hong Kong Police. Mark Long concluded:

'We *have* to show them, gentlemen, how very efficient is the dictum of *minimum* force . . .'

As Mark Long lectured, Forrester wrote on a note-pad:

(1) *Int. report – we can anticipate a strike by the Allied Truckers Union, a blockage perhaps of main arterial routes.*

(2) *I have located Tang Tsun.*

This message he folded and addressed to Lo Ping-kin, who was seated several rows before him, then passed it on. By return of post he received this instruction:

Go immediately and arrest Tang.

The word immediately had been underscored so drastically that the paper was gouged through. Mark Long gave over his lectern to the Deputy Director Operations, who, after some face-gaining waffle, gave over to the man who would run the show on the day, the head of the Tactical Unit, an unnecessarily tall sort of fellow with an engrossingly active Adam's apple; Ruddle was his name. As Ruddle began his briefing, Forrester slipped away.

Gilly MacNaughton was waiting in Forrester's office.

'I heard ye' was after me, sir.'

'Gilly, I want you to make up an arresting party of six men, including yourself. I have requisitioned Landrovers. We are going into the hills beyond Sai Kung.'

MacNaughton raised his eyebrows.

'It won't be so bad, Gilly. There are village paths that were cut into those mountains by the early Hakka stonemasons, that are still perfect. We'll use them.'

'Right then, 'ahm on to it, sir.' He half turned, then hesitated; clumsily tentative: 'I've just had a thought. There's that wee kink-tailed monkey up on the roof, sir. The one that adopted us after the Aberdeen thing . . . The boys put it in a cage and fed it daily doses of methadone. Well, we've cured it, you see. We offered it to the zoo, but they refused to adopt an ex-drug addict. They said we'd best release the wee fella' out Sai Kung way.'

'Very well, Gilly, make up a party of seven including yourself. And, Gilly, let's move on it. I want to be there and back before nightfall.'

Tang Tik-kat believed that, in a spiritual sense, he had come to himself, and identified the man he saw, and was pleased with him. Here was a naturally wise man; a person gifted with lofty intellect, sufficient to presume morality in all actions. The Ging Si had been unambiguously warned that his attacks on the Assembly would provoke stinging retribution. He had received the folded White Paper Gall and had chosen to ignore it. Tik-kat felt not the slightest qualm therefore when pronouncing sentence on this wilful, destructive man:

'Hurt him. And let the wounds be as deep as any inflicted on our Maitreya. For it is written in the Book of Rites, that with the slayer of his father, a man may not live under the same sky; against the slayer of his brother a man should find an immediate weapon . . . You, Connie Tam, are the Maitreya's immediate weapon.'

Of course, Tik-kat realized that true wisdom put him beyond such simplistic ancient dispensations, but it was useful on occasions to quote from such well-accepted sources. He had used such punitive adages before when reckoning with wickedness. It sounded impressive. And on that note he concluded:

'Hurt him in any way you can.'

The meeting was over. Connie Tam arose from her chair, unawed by her assignment. In fact she was elated by the metaphor of the Maitreya's 'immediate weapon'. She felt privileged to be thought of as such, and she was well prepared.

She went to her flat and waited for Mike Hempstead's arrival, and when he came in, sodden and miserable, she was on hand to towel him down and provide him with numbingly beneficent quantities of brandy. She knew this man well; only the chemistry of alcohol could separate him from his fundamentally morbid self-pity, and bring about a state of amenable, if hazy curiosity. When she judged him to be sufficiently unfastened from his melancholy, and comfortably well-settled, she said to him:

'Do you believe that there is an authority; a power that one must answer to, and heed, and give thanks to, as the source of all good things?'

Mike Hempstead closed his eyes, and for a moment she thought he'd gone to sleep. Then he said: 'Like a god; is that what you mean? . . . I go to church once a year. I don't know why I bother at all.'

'Yet you do have faith enough to make that single journey . . . so in that way you and I only differ by the degree of our convictions.'

Mike Hempstead sat forward, as though disposed to follow this avenue of conversation. 'Yes . . . I suppose so. But you're a Buddhist, and I'm a Christian. So that makes us entirely different.'

'Not so different. We both have a capability to believe in something that is intrinsically good; that is capable of favouring us in an after-life. Mike, you've seen me meditate often, you must have sometimes wondered where it is that my mind takes me, and what I see.'

'To tell you the truth, more often than not I'm asleep . . . But, yes. I confess to some curiosity. You seem so at peace; does it give you peace?'

'Boundless peace, Mike. It enriches me. I spin into a world of bright eternity.'

'I envy your happiness.'

'I use secret words and special breathing techniques to unlock me from my earthly body. Then I feel no pain, and nothing could possibly wound me . . . A buddha taught me how to bring about this state.'

'Hell, I've got my own Nirvana. It comes out of a brown glass bottle. God knows who taught me about it, but no one can hurt me then, either . . . Pass the bottle.'

'Don't mock me, Mike.'

'I'm not; honest to God. Frankly I'm too tarnished with booze to ever catch up to you, and I'm just envious I suppose.' Satisfied with this fluid lie, he said, 'I follow, but with envy.'

'I'm telling you these things, not to make you envious, but in order to show you how vitally important they are to me; so that you might know how zealously I'd be prepared to defend these ideals.'

'I've had that demonstrated to me before.' He stroked his neck and smiled wryly. 'Oh yes, I remember it well. I need no further convincing of your adherence to your cause.'

'I would kill for it, Mike.'

'As Harmony did.'

'Exactly as Harmony did. We were born of the same womb, and on the same day, Harmony and I.'

Mike, who had spent most of his life in concealment of one thing or another, was a master fabricator of nonchalance. He paused with his glass at his lips and raised one eyebrow in a measured show of surprise. In fact he was astonished by Connie's confession.

'She was your twin sister?'

345

'Yes. And we followed the same paths right through life. Our parents were Taoist but we became Buddhist. By different routes we both found our way to the same teacher: the Buddha Maitreya. And both of us became members of White Lotus Assembly on the same day. As Christians may be born again, so were we. Harmony and I have the same karma. We learned the same truths . . . I will share one of the immutable truths with you, Mike. It is that the Kalpa of the Third Buddha is on the turn; and a Black Wind is about to arrive with a force that will blow the earth from the sky – an apocalypse is at hand, and those who know the teachings of the Assembly will survive it, but those who are enemies, and those who stand in the way of White Lotus, will perish in it. But the soldiers of White Lotus, who die in the cause, will live on in the arms of the Eternal Mother. Harmony is in Her arms; in Cloud Heaven. I'm prepared to follow Harmony's example when called upon to do so.'

Mike Hempstead, who had never believed in anything with sufficient fervor to suffer for it, shifted uneasily before this avalanche of zeal, unable to find any common feeling, or even a single sentiment that he could match to one of his own, and thereby honestly admit to. He felt compelled to lie: 'Yes, I know what you mean.' Her colours were too bright for him. He would have preferred to have turned away. But then he might never discover what it was that she wanted from him. For here was something more than aimless chatter. 'But I'm not even a Buddhist. So what could I do?'

'You've done so much already, Mike. You warned us of the imminent arrest of Tang Tsun; and so he escaped the net. But his persecutor is virulently set against him. Because he could not destroy the Maitreya, he attacked the Maitreya's family. He killed his only brother.'

'The Ging Si? . . . He *killed* Sandy Tan?' Mike doubted this information. 'I heard that it was suicide.'

'Sandy called the Ging Si "the God of Lies". It was the God of Lies who hounded him to his death.'

346

'The God of Lies? . . . No, Forrester's mortal enough; a cynic, more than a liar. And if he lies, it's the consequence of some deserving purpose of his own invention. Like a knight in slightly rusted armour.'

'He has willingly made himself the eternal enemy of the Assembly; and he's your enemy too, and *you* have made that so.'

That was not quite factual, Mike thought. His actions had made of Forrester a dangerous antagonist, but Forrester had yet to discover that. Which he might do at any time. It was natural to fear the man for that reason; and so of course to hate him too. Now here was someone proposing, if he was not mistaken, the elimination of the Ging Si. This project was certainly worth listening to.

'He should,' she said, 'suffer wounds equally as deep as those inflicted on the Maitreya . . . Against the slayer of his brother, a man should find an immediate weapon.' Her eyes flashed proudly. 'I am that weapon, and so are you.'

With all the rhetoric peeled away, the core requirement was that Reven Forrester should suffer in some awful, and equitable way. The rogue of irony was at work here. Forrester had told him that this case would expand dramatically, and provide him with power to manipulate the triads. He'd said the triads must be subjugated, like a colony of cockroaches, but that they must be fed too, rewarded when reward was due. They should feel content so that crime might be rational and predictable . . . Well here was a reward for them; the Ging Si himself.

'The God of Lies, eh?'

'He was warned; you brought the Gall to him yourself. We have been scrupulously fair, and he has cut us at every opportunity. So now he must suffer; he must be hurt in any way we can.'

'Did the Maitreya demand that?'

'He's above such things.'

'So you don't know if the Maitreya would approve. I was of the impression that Buddhism was a religion of peace.'

347

'This is the Kalpa. It's God's war on Her subjects, lost in sin and vanity in the red-dust world.'

'Let me warn you against any thought of harming the family of Reven Forrester. If that is even your remote intention, then I want no part of it, for many reasons. But, from your point of view it would be a colossal error. *That* is an immutable truth. He'd tear your heaven from the clouds, I promise. Don't even think of it.'

'Against the slayer of his brother . . .'

'That proverb leaves me cold. Hear this one: Money makes the Devil turn the millstone.'

'Mike, your rewards would be beyond your wildest dreams. The Eternal Mother . . .'

'I don't want anything beyond my wildest dreams, or any promises of salvation from your apocalypse . . . Nothing as wonderful as that. I have a specific and very earthy sum in mind.'

'Dear Mike, you have been paid, and paid, and paid. The time has arrived for you to show gratitude, and faith. The Assembly expects that of you now, and so do I. You're part of me.' She came to him then, all languid limbs and pleasing, darted kisses. She whispered:

'Do you know how much I love you?'

As much, he thought, as the fire loves the fireplace. He was the hearth of her aspirations, no more than that. He licked his tongue into her mouth and his penis became alert. They ground their hips and roved their mouths and shuddered and heaved and made noises of love.

Opposing sleep, as always, was his laborious quagmire of trials. He listened to the hiss and sough of the high wind at the windows, and heard as well the soft purring breath of Connie Tam. He thought about Reven Forrester – the God of Lies, and this woman, the instrument of his destruction. He pondered on the tyranny of ambition, and the elegant sophistry of religion – of morals, and money, and survival of the fittest. Dilemma after dilemma, inseparably binding him to the woman at his side. Perhaps the time had come to cut the knot.

The dawn was grey and late in coming, and hardly made its way past the heavily curtained windows. But Connie sensed its arrival, as he knew she would, and she arose to greet it, as she always did. He pretended to be asleep then, and watched her through hooded eyes as she bowed to the east. By then he'd planned his actions of the next few days in a most inventive and self-serving way.

The solid, stubborn Land Rovers of Reven Forrester's convoy of two met the rains of Cyclone Dora with plough-horse equanimity, and the men contained in these good vehicles seemed equally untroubled by the storm. They joked, and passed sweets, and told dirty stories about impossible sexual exploits, and smoked, and generally spurned the view beyond the runnelled windows. Dora was not expected to do more damage than it had already done, which, according to the commentary they were picking up on their police radio, amounted to some blown-off roofs, flattened squatter shacks, and flooded basements – minor stuff. The heart of the cyclone lay to the south-east, some three hundred kilometres away. It was forecast that Dora would now lift her skirts and depart to the north. It was the typical nuisance weather of that time of year.

Detective Constable Fok was the only man in the foremost vehicle who was prepared to bet on a deterioration of the weather:

'Fifty dollars that it gets worse.'

There was a clamour of takers.

'Even the monkey would bet with you, Fok, if he had some cash . . . I'm taking up a collection for the monkey . . .'

'Here's five dollars for the monkey.'

The monkey, caged within a small bamboo structure, reached out and took the proffered cash, sniffed it, tasted it then dropped the coin.

So much for Cyclone Dora. The next wager was based on the time, to the nearest second, that it would take for their convoy to reach the dog-leg at Razor Hill. Sai Kung was known to be five kilometres beyond the dog-leg, so that computation was a natural additional bet. In the event, no one came near to a correct guess.

It was at that point that the rear vehicle flashed its lights, and limped to the side of the road. Its front right tyre had met with a large nail, and was deflated to the rim. As it happened, the spare was equally as flat, and as a further complication they could not find the jack. The uniformed driver was adamant that both jack and tyre had been available, and in perfect condition when recently checked.

Forrester, wet, and getting wetter, swore quietly and raised the hood of his oilcloth storm jacket. Both jack and spare tyre of his vehicle were brought into use – half an hour's delay. That bet was called off and a new one was mooted by that incredible pessimist, Fok:

'Fifty dollars that there's more delay.'

Two kilometres further down the road, at the outskirts of the village of Pik Uk, the engine of the lead vehicle, without a jot of warning, died. Fok began an immediate collection of his winnings.

While Forrester, MacNaughton and the entire arresting party gazed gloomily down at the inert machinery beneath the bonnet, the drivers tinkered about with wires and bolts and long pieces of pipe, giving the impression of doing something useful, but with no salutary effect.

'It's dead, sir,' they finally admitted.

Neither driver had brought rain gear. Their uniforms clung sodden dark green to their bodies. Dismally shrunk and bent by the prospect of immediate retribution, Forrester's man spoke:

'A thousand apologies for this ignorant fucking engine, sir.'

With the optimism of the mechanically ignorant, Forrester instructed: 'Try it once more.'

This the drivers hurried to do. Once – twice – thrice, the starter motor groaned – the diesel engine clattered and wobbled, then rumbled into life. Thoroughly wetted, disdainful of their aberrative transport, they clambered back into the Landrovers. They drove on in silence for a while; just for a while.

'Fifty dollars . . .'

'Mr Fok,' MacNaughton said sweetly. 'Have ye heard the story aboot Jonah and the whale . . . No? . . . Well it goes like this. There was this here chappie, and his name was Jonah, see. A Heebrew, he was; a rather pestilent mariner who God didn't care for one wee bit; so much so that He sent down a storm to wreck his ship . . . Well, the long and the short of it is that his shipmates, realizing that this Jonah fella' was terrible bad luck, chucked him overboard. And Jonah was swallowed, Ahm, no' kiddin' ye, by this huge fucking fish . . .'

MacNaughton's version of the Old Testament fable carried them without further incident (or wager) all the way to Sai Kung. There they scraped and shrugged through alleyways invented for rickshaws and wheelbarrows, and found a gap called Get Honours Street, which was where Fung Sham, The Fixer, lived above a bean curd and snake-wine store. The rain had sluiced all humans from the street, but the sky seemed lighter now. There were some streaks of silver in a dome of gloom.

Forrester went on from that point on foot. He mounted a sharply steep staircase, and knocked upon a doorway that was sternly guarded by two peeling posters of the warrior-gods, Chin and Yu. Defeated by the clatter of Wife of Fung's mah-jong tiles, which carried to the street, he rapped again.

'Crazy days.' Fung Sham flung open the door. 'Only madmen out in this sky-time.' Three smallish, pug-featured sons came to observe the madman at the threshold.

'I told you I was coming, Ah Fung.'

'Yes. Yes. Good to see you. Come in; let's drink and forget why you're here.'

Wife of Fung squawked, '*Sik!*,' as she made some devastating play at the mah-jong table. Then she too came to stand lumpishly at Fung Sham's side. 'Get worse,' with up-pointed finger she warned of the weather. Which presumption obliged Fung to more or less contradict:

'Won't get worse; won't get better . . . not today.'

'Tomorrow,' said Forrester, 'will be too late. I can see you're comfortable, Ah Fung . . . It's no problem for me to go alone. *No problem.*'

'Aieya,' breathed The Fixer. 'Wife, bring me my raincoat.' To Forrester he said, 'It's easier to get there than it was in the old days. Now, there's a paved track through the valley from Water-waves Shelter to Golden Bamboo Village. From there on it's a steep walk up the final slopes to the monastery . . . Are you sure tomorrow would not do? . . . No, I see it would not . . . An ideal day for arresting tricky monks, and suchlike. Who would expect the police to come calling on such a day? . . . Age, does it slow us, Ging Si, or merely make us more cunning?'

They took Fung's recommended route from Sai Kung to the turn-off at Water-waves Shelter, then kept to the track as it wound and crept towards the mountain called Ma On Shan – Horse Saddle Mountain. Grey rain pelted them, and all hope of kinder weather died over that distance.

Golden Bamboo Village could not be seen through the wetly shot air. They knew they'd reached it when the road abruptly ended and the lead vehicle sank into an old rice-terrace. Here they dismounted into ankle-deep water; blank-faced, they huddled, stoically, like cows with rumps towards the weather, staring dully at the man who'd brought them to this sorry destination. Forrester prodded them with taciturn authority:

'Mr Fung here will lead us. He knows these mountains well. Stay close to the man in front of you. Stick to the paths. Do not take any short-cuts. I expect to be back here well before last light . . . All right, let's go.'

Thus ordered, they began the steep climb up Horse Saddle Mountain. Snug-fitting stone pavé ascending never-endingly, worn by the peasant tread of villagers long dead to gravestone smoothness, took them on and on, and up and up. And as they walked, there came to Forrester a rapture of *déjà vu* that sped a twenty-year divide like an arrow flight; the crusty station sergeant and the wet-eared gwailo inspector tramping the timeless pathways of Ma On Shan. This was where his duties as a policeman had begun. His thighs burned nicely with the exercise, and his lungs expanded. He thought it was almost a pity that the climb would be over so soon. Before the road to Golden Bamboo Village had been cut there'd been some decent adventure to this hike.

They had progressed at a pace-count which by rough calculation positioned them half-way from bottom to top, when a sharp curse of pain brought the patrol to a shuffled stop.

A man lay on his back in the slick shrub on the verge of the path, snarling at his ankle: 'Shit . . . *shit!'*

Some men stood tiredly where they were, others came to huddle around the injured man. Forrester was hard put to bolt his anger in the back of his throat.

'You took the short-cut at the loop.'

'Yes.' The man looked up, frowning against the wash of the rain. It was Koo, recently promoted from Uniform Branch.

'Can you walk?'

Koo tried, and failed. It took two men to hold him upright. Fok spat an opinion:

'It's the monkey that caused it . . . Bad luck that monkey, I tell you. Why must that thing stay with us?'

Every face turned towards MacNaughton's caged ape. The rain came heavier. The furry-faced primate huddled wetly in its bamboo prison and gazed evenly at its accusers. Fok pointed: 'Bad luck as long as that thing stays with us.'

'Nonsense,' said MacNaughton. 'That's absolute mumbo-jumbo,' and he looked around for support, but none was forthcoming.

Of course it was mumbo-jumbo, what else. But this was the kind of maleficent gunge that clogged the Cantonese brain from birth. Here was a troublesome situation, a stubborn, angry Scot set against a knot of ensorcelled Chinese males.

'Gilly,' Forrester said, 'call up our drivers on the beat-radio, and inform them that we have a casualty; and I'm sending him down with two escorts.' Of course, one of those escorts would be their self-appointed Shaman.

'The radio's no' doing a bloody thing,' was MacNaughton's reply. 'We're off net.'

Once more they gazed balefully at the sinister ape.

Forrester immediately appointed Koo's escorts. 'Well,' he patted the damaged man in a way that couldn't be mistaken for sympathy, 'you'd better get going then . . . And Mr Koo, you are on report for contravening an order.'

Forrester did some face-work on behalf of MacNaughton. He allowed the Scot to transport his pet a few hundred metres further along the track.

'Let him out here, Gilly.'

'A good place.' Fung the Fixer lied his way into Forrester's debt. 'I've seen monkeys about here before.'

MacNaughton said, 'Aye, sir.' He unpicked the knot that fastened the bamboo door. The ape in one elastic movement bounded out then sprang back inside and clung to the bars, as if this humble structure was all it had ever wished from life.

'Move on,' came Forrester's order.

So the patrol moved on, with MacNaughton snatching mournful rearward glances until the pelting rain had drawn a grey shroud over cage and contents. Then he marched stoically forward. It wasn't long thereafter that Forrester began to suspect that they had trailed too far to the west. They were descending steeply, and they should still be on an incline. He called a halt.

'Yes,' said Fung without being asked. 'We've missed the turn-off and come right over the Saddle. I was about to stop and turn around. It's the rain, Ging Si. Can't see a thing.'

It took an hour to discover the north-leading path that led to the summit of Ma On Shan, and in that time the storm built up a howling savagery that shoved them about and tore at their jackets. And the rain did not simply fall now, but pelted from the south in wind-driven sheets that flogged their necks and backs; that hissed and danced in whirled white patterns over the paving, and chased deep swells into the thick sword-grass. The track became a gushing, foaming stream of runnels and waterfalls, alive with stealthy tricks.

On the summit MacNaughton stumbled into Forrester with shouted news:

'The typhoon, sir . . . It's tracking at speed towards Hong Kong . . . I had radio contact for a few seconds, but it's gone again. They said we should turn back, at once.'

'We're closer to the monastery than we are to base. We've no choice but to go on.'

'Go on,' MacNaughton nodded. 'Right, if the set comes on again, I'll gi' them that . . . I saw the monkey, sir.' MacNaughton gestured towards a looming cliff.

'Crazy,' Forrester would have said had a rush of wind not emptied the sound from his mouth.

'What!' shouted the inspector.

Forrester just shook his head and waved the man onwards. No insult had been intended. The word had ridden to his tongue in a vein of disbelief. For into his mind had come the thought: This is a Black Wind.

He hadn't been seeking a description for this storm, his past had fetched it up, unasked from some arcane crevice where such notions lurked, and there it was; A Black Wind.

'The angry breath of Hell, that will blow the sun from the sky . . . and cut away the past . . .'

'Crazy!' As though that shout might chase such absurd prose from his skull . . . It did not.

He could recall worse storms than this. Once he'd seen a typhoon through on the prancing deck of a police harbour tug, flinging cobweb lines into the heaving water, hauling half drowned fisher-folk from the demon sea. Once he'd seen grown trees plucked from the earth and blown away like feathers in a gay breeze. This storm did not possess such terrible force, but it did have power of another sort: a deep, and entrapping, dark passion that he'd never sensed in any wind before. And he watched it with a frown.

They clung, whelk-like, to their small friend the pavé track, slowly advancing as the eboned sky swooped wildly, swirling, coiling, flinging harsh stinging rain. Then they found the last turn-off that led to the monastery of the Great Sage – Chai Tin Dai Sing – the Monkey God. Here was a forest; and from it a new sound arose – a drawn-out agonizing howl of trees and foliage, lashed and bent, hissing and cowering. The path wound steeply upwards now, through this tortured wood, then crossed a salient and descended into an arbour which dammed the south wind and the driven rain. From there they could see the mountain they'd crossed, shouldering hunchbacked against the storm-driven sky, breaking it as a rock-line breaks the thundering surf. Great dark clouds tumbled and rolled and spat their rain, but the venom of the sky was spent on the peaks, and puny humans could walk here, unafraid.

One square of yellow light shone from a single window into the grey drenched afternoon. They walked along a neat path lined with jessamine hedges and viburnums, then over a bridged pond, its green water roughened.

A great red double door opened before they reached it. Monks with shaven heads, as nervous as grey mice in a field, squeaked about, asking questions by the hundred of each other, but not a word to the travellers. Then an old fellow came, an open-faced man who said words of welcome and showed them towards a room of a raw wooden table and benches. A gaslight hissed and threw white light against white walls whereon one picture hung – Kuan Yin. 'She who hears all prayers' gazed serenely from her black-wood frame at the arresting party as they shrugged out of their raincoats (to find their inner garments as wet as any they removed), and massaged their bruised flesh, joking, filling the white room with lithe shadows.

Forrester came closer to the picture and saw that it was not a painting, but an exquisite tapestry of fine silk. And while he was there, a grey-robed monk came in bearing a tray of small cups, and a teapot, and a message: humble and pitiful accommodation was being prepared. This was not a monastery which was designed for visitors, but under the prevailing inclement sky, and in the name of All Merciful Buddha, whose light never dimmed, all wanderers and those in need were welcome . . .

There was more to it than that, but that was the gist of it; a speech drawn from stock, Forrester guessed. He wondered how the reverend brother would have related to the true purpose of their mission. Not in an obliging way. And this was Forrester's quandary: it was nearing last light. If he made clear his intentions now it might precipitate failure. Tang Tsun might slip away in the dark. Yet the alternative was to stay cast in the false cloth of 'wanderers and those in need', and that was an unthinkable deception. He drank the tea, insipid pale-coloured stuff which imparted no benefit beyond warmth, and reflected on his options. By the time the monk came back he had made up his mind:

'Reverend brother, at the abbot's first free moment, I must see him . . . urgent need.'

The monk hesitated in his gait for a bare instant, and that was all the acknowledgement Forrester received that his request had been heard.

MacNaughton said: 'Are you going to tell him why, sir?'

'What would you do, Gilly?'

'It's a predicament, right enough.'

'That it is, Gilly.'

'If the storm, had nae' closed in . . .'

'And the vehicle had not broken down, and Koo had not bust his ankle, and the track had not disappeared . . . It's been a day of acute unanswerable delays. We're here to arrest a man who is believed to be the Maitreya. But it must be clean, or not at all.'

'The Maitreya, sir?'

'A buddha, Gilly. In fact the long-awaited Third Buddha.'

'Good grief, sir. I knew it was someone important.'

'A God come to earth, if you can believe it.'

Gilly MacNaughton thought lengthily on that, then said: 'If I may ask an impudent question, sir . . . ?'

'Go ahead.'

'Do you believe in the New Testament, sir?'

'You're asking if I'm a Christian?'

'There is a Christian comparison to such an arrest . . . It's a weird turn isn't it, sir, to be the ones to strike at someone else's religion. I reckon I know how those Roman soldiers must ha' felt.'

'Our employment, Gilly, is to uphold the law. Tang Tsun, no matter how good-inspired were his motivations, broke the law. So here we are, you and I. But we'll do what we have to do in a humane and honest way.'

'And if honesty fails, sir?' MacNaughton squeezed off a cynical lop-sided grin. 'I've found it sometimes does.'

'Have you, Gilly? . . . Well, I'm not sure how I'd feel if I failed. This Tang Tsun is an uncommon man, and he has a vision that, were I Chinese, I would share with him. Let's wait and see.'

Fung Sham, the Fixer, who had been listening to all this, put in, 'Ging Si, these monks are full of tricks. They sit up here and think their thoughts and forget that they are just humans – bone and skin like you and I. They mumble Sanskrit gobbledy-gook that not even they themselves can understand, and pretend to some or other profound knowledge gained by enlightenment. Enlightenment – show me some – sell me some. I don't know anyone who's got. Ah! what's the good of it?' He whisked his hand in dismissal of such credulity, 'You gwailos are too easily impressed by monks and priests and suchlike, and where does it get you?'

Forrester said, 'And what is your religion, Ah Fung?'

'Religion, *religion*?' He plumped the word up pompously: 'Who forced upon the world this grovelling dependence? I believe in all the Chinese gods – the *lot*. Kuan Yin, Kuan Ti, the Five Sages, and the Eight Immortals. Buddhist–Taoist–I've got a shelf full of them. So if one doesn't work for me, there's ten others to step in and do the job. The more of them that I employ, the less chance for error, ha? . . . I spread it around, but the best of them all is Kuan Di . . . Religion? *That's* religion. And one day, when I die, then Buddhist monks will see me off, but I've no need of them until that day.'

'Here, Mr MacNaughton, behold the original Chinese zealot. If you were to believe him you'd be likely to think you had more godly fear in the pickings of your nose than Fung has lodged in his entire body and soul. It's mere bravado of course, like all Chinese, he's petrified of the great unknown . . . Tell me, Ah Fung, truthfully, what if you knew you were fated to die tomorrow?'

'Then I'd go out and buy the most expensive coffin in Hong Kong, and park it in my flat then put my feet up on it, and wait.'

'So much for the apocalypse.'

'Apocalypse, sir?'

'The end of the millennium, Gilly. It's due.'

'*Tcha!* Ging Si. You don't want to believe that shit.'

'I'll tell you what I believe, Ah Fung. On Monday at the stroke of midnight the Communists will take over Hong Kong. And then they will ruin it, as surely as they have ruined every other thing they have touched. They're finished breaking China; there is no good thing that they haven't perverted, wasted, or totally destroyed in that once magnificent country. Why should Hong Kong receive any better treatment? There is no power on *earth* that can prevent that iniquity. So why not a millennium? If I was God I would have shot the lot away, and begun afresh.'

'Aye, right enough,' MacNaughton agreed vigorously; that's what he would have done too.

Two monks came then, bearing large wooden platters, piled with bowls of good-smelling cooked vegetables and sauces. They set them on the table, then placed chop-sticks. Fung Sham, MacNaughton and the two young Chinese detectives set about the food straight away. Forrester, despite the hardship of the hike, felt little hunger. He made slow work of some bean curds and rice.

When every morsel was eaten the monk who had welcomed them came back. He said with politely pretended anguish:

'A poor meal . . . Too little food.'

'A feast,' said Forrester. 'Enough for an army.'

The monk took up the pressure lamp by its handle. 'We have prepared a sleep-room . . . Please, will you all follow behind me.'

He took them along a corridor where the lamp cast long, swaying shadows, stencilling their presence on dark brick walls. There were some statues: two pop-eyed demons glared at the passing men. And there was a wall-rack of staves crested with brilliant gold insignia. They by-passed a moon-gate which led into darkness and rain, through which could be heard the chant of prayers. Then the passageway turned sharply, and they mounted a staircase.

'Here,' said the monk. He led them into a room where five rough beds had been made up with quilts.

The lamp hissed and the rain drummed and the men stood languidly, warily regarding their leader. If he told them to rest now he knew they would be asleep in an instant. He thought about mounting a watch, then discounted the idea. He chose a cot for himself, then gestured for them to do likewise . . . He was proved right; except for MacNaughton who lay staring at the ceiling, making occasional faint 'tsk-tsk' sounds as though at some reprobate thought, the others grew quickly limp.

Forrester made a cushion of his quilt and squared his spine against the wall so that if he slept he would topple, and wake up. He sat like that watching the moths and insects of the night come to the lamp, to flutter and butt at the hot glass until, stunned, they fell, then rose again, then dropped, continuing choicelessly until the marvellous light, at last, killed them.

He saw a hundred minute suicides before that blue-white orb benumbed him, too, and he withered and drooped and toppled on to the cot, but did not awake. He did not wake up until tugged and nagged from a deep and dreamless sleep by a voice that called, 'It's time . . . It's time.' His awakener was a monk whom he did not recognize: an old fellow, fantastically wrinkled; casting sighing courtesies:

'A tragedy to draw you from such peaceful god-given rest, a thousand regrets for such an intrusion, but was it not you who requested to see our abbot?'

He arose heavily from his rough wood cot, disoriented, sore and stiff. The old fellow seemed as spry as a bat. His grey robes swirled as he walked ahead, and he didn't stop jabbering:

'He'll cure you, don't you worry, no matter what the ailment. The calf comes to the mother, does it not? . . . Solitary among solitaries, and source of all healing light. You need look no further . . .'

They passed through the moon-gate into the yard from whence the chant of the monks had earlier emerged, and the yard gave directly into a pompous palace of brilliant red pillars and three golden Buddhas, serenely enthroned and glass-encased. Huge, writhing dragons breathed fumes at each other, thus forming a proscenium over a deep alcove of intense mystery. Here, crowned, bejewelled and silked in emperor's robes, sat the prankish, grinning, golden-faced ape – the Monkey God – Great Sage Equal to Heaven, Chai Tin Dai Sing.

Dwarfed before this virile altar, cross-legged on the floor, two monks sat, one dressed in saffron robes, one in grey. Tang Tsun, the more splendidly dressed of the pair, seemed distanced from that time and place. His eyes were shut; his face deathly pale and still. His hands rested openly on his knees; the right one, terribly scarred, bore the famous Ming.

The grey-robed abbot, though not young, had lean handsome features and a strong neck. His eyes were distrusting, and he fixed them unmovingly on the gwailo in his temple.

Forrester's escort did kow tow, then whispered to his gwailo charge: 'Strange things may happen to those who show no respect to Monkey.'

'Forgive me,' Forrester said. 'So astonished by all this greatness . . .' He bent the knee, and took a faggot of incense to a candle flame. A serpent of smoke, grey sweet smoke, coiled. He planted the fragrant sticks in a brass censer.

'Sit now,' whispered the old monk.

Forrester did that, arranging himself on the floor near the abbot, who had not lifted his gaze from him all the while.

'Are you the one called Ging Si?'

The man had a mellow, husky tone, and a commanding way. Forrester had heard that voice before:

'Master Kaan . . . ?'

'I remember you too now, Ging Si . . . Twenty years? Well, time thins the cord of memory, but now it's all come back.' He gestured towards Tang Tsun. 'You came to talk to the Maitreya in those days about his father's death . . . That's right. You were the one who arrested the killers.'

'This time I've come for the Maitreya.'

'We were warned that you were on your way here . . . Ah, I see you wondering, If that is the case, why didn't the Maitreya flee? Quite simple, Ging Si: this is not the Maitreya, this is his mere earthly shell. His soul is elsewhere . . . I don't know where. He's sat here for three days in meditation, as you see him now, and still it hasn't returned. How could he escape without his soul?'

'Yet I must take him with me, Master Kaan. That is essential.'

'You would be taking nothing but a relic of flesh and blood. And then, when his soul returns here, as it will, it would find no body to inhabit. You would have killed him. Let me dispel the disbelief that marks your face. See, here are lighted candles. Take one, Ging Si . . . That's right, now feel the heat of it; pass it beneath the palm of your hand and see how long you can stand the pain . . . Not even for a second, ha? Well, that's understandable; it's very hot . . . Come closer, Ging Si, bring the candle, closer . . . closer. I want you to sit right in front of the Maitreya.' He patted the appointed spot. Forrester sat close enough to touch the man he'd come to arrest, and obeyed the following instruction:

'Place your fingers on his eyelids, and press with slight pressure . . . Is there a tremor of movement?'

'None at all.'

'Is there a hint of the warmth of breath?'

Forrester waited, then admitted:

'No breath.'

'Be absolutely sure. Hold the flame close enough for the smallest breath to bend it.'

'There is no breath from his nostrils or mouth, Master Kaan; none at all.'

'Do you believe me then that here before you there is nothing but a husk, a thing uninhabited by life?'

'Master Kaan. I know of your techniques. There are parallels in nature for such mimicry. There are snakes that when scared, crumple as though dead and dried out . . . I've come for this man for good reason. The Communists are too powerful to oppose. They will grind all opposition down; they are prepared, and easily able to do this, and yet you plan to stand against them in open rebellion. It's madness, you must realize that. It's a hopeless cause; and therefore meritless. Where are your battalions? Do you think you can turn bullets aside with sweet meditations? Forget such nonsense; brave dreams are no more than that.'

'We have brave men, Ging Si . . .'

'You have false generals and commanders whose interests waver between White Lotus doctrine, and insatiable greed. You believe that the Eternal Mother has closed the millennium, and sent down a Black Wind that will blow for seventy-seven days, to strip the flesh from the bones of the disbelievers, and carry the earth from the sky . . . Master Kaan, it's a fable. I've come to tell you that.'

Kaan's eyes sharpened with anger, nor could he hide it from his voice: 'You think all this is a fable . . . an invention? It's you who's wrong, Ging Si. You compare our Maitreya with a frightened snake, how dare you? What do you know of us but what you've gleaned from one stolen book. A few pages of history, and you storm us with omnipotent knowledge . . . Your mind is worm-eaten with conceit and ignorance, and your errors are heinous. Still, I believe there is some speck of good in you. So I say again: you may not take the Maitreya. You will kill him if you do.'

'There is no alternative. Time is running out.'

'What good is this soulless thing to you? He will not answer you no matter what torture you apply . . . Look.' Kaan snatched the lighted candle from Forrester's hand, and advanced the flame towards the Maitreya as he spoke on:

'Enlightened one, here is the man called Ging Si, at last . . .'

The flame progressed to within an inch of Tang's face.

'What should I do to cause this man to depart from his wrong course?'

'Stop that.' Forrester delayed Kaan's arm for barely a second.

'He says, Precious One, that I should not do this. What he believes, of course, is that you are prepared to endure any torture to impress him . . . What he does *not* believe is that you are impervious to pain.'

Kaan thrust the candle flame so closely beneath Tang Tsun's chin that the dancing yellow tongue forked upwards on to both sides of his cheeks and touched his nostrils. Tang did not flinch; he made no move to avoid the flame. It was Forrester who winced. But more shocking than his surrogate anguish, more wonderfully awesome than he was prepared to credit, was Tang Tsun's immunity to injury. He saw no sizzling burn, no blistering. No scar was visible when Kaan withdrew the torch.

A breath that Forrester had contained for too long, escaped with a sighing hiss.

'Now,' Kaan turned questioningly towards the gwailo; '*now* do you believe me? . . . Now do you see that we practise no deception on you? Now are you prepared to stand out of the way of the millennium of the Eternal Mother?'

Forrester searched hard amongst the debris of his argument for the remnants of logic: 'Master Kaan. I read the Precious Volumes, and I read them well. To my mind they brought a serious question. It's this: If God, The Eternal Mother, gave holy men the vision to write such predictions, then she herself foresaw the exact date of exhaustion of her patience with man, and sent warning of it. Is that not true?'

'It's a fair assumption, Ging Si.'

'And therefore it's logical to assume that she knew ahead of time, that she was powerless to stop this march of Evil . . . or she would have done so?'

'There could be some truth in that.'

'It must be as clear to you then as it was to Her that there exists a tyrant who is stronger than She – a God of evil. The Eternal

Mother's forces cannot withstand it, or they would have done so already. This is Her final stand then; and the chances of defeat are greater than of success. Is that not an appalling thought, Master Kaan?'

Kaan blanched.

The Ging Si looked up into the prankish grin of the golden-faced Monkey, and wondered at its infinite capacity for mischief. He said quietly:

'Master Kaan, I beg you. Help me to prevent this hopeless bloodshed.'

'Help you, Ging Si? . . . An offer of poison with which to slake my thirst . . . How can you ever hope to understand, gwailo, what has come out of the Yellow Earth. Do you imagine that with your puny logic you have come up with a weapon with which to challenge psychic fact . . . The Maitreya has gone to commune with his God. The false world of the law of man, of which you are the cutting edge, must wait.'

This meditation was one of giant and tiring hindrances the like of which he'd not faced since he'd been a novice of that monastery, a journey that was burdened with questions of such vast distraction that at times he'd wondered if their encumberance was too much to bear. Should he not simply forgo all doubts, then, and retreat, and let things go on as they would? Of course he couldn't do that, because the very nature of meditation is a journey towards enlightenment, which not even a Buddha may shirk.

So he cooled his heart, and circulated his breath, and clung to the nourishment of his mantras. He fixed himself to a distant, inward point, and let light fall on it, and saw imprinted there the words, *Nothing is impossible*. And so the journey eased, and he progressed, and the vociferous questions became servants of the Master, and followed, quietly. His limbs filled up now with boundless energy, and his mind with pure joy. All around him the world lightened, and everything he touched became beautiful. The sun shone over a great lake, and rows of trees gave off the sweetest scent. There were gods in the valley, and distantly he could hear conversation, clear, but beyond his capacity to interpret.

He opened his eyes then and discovered that he was in a bright cloud, he looked downwards, searching for his body, but it was not visible . . . Then suddenly, as though caught in some soaring ecstatic jet-stream, he shot upwards, upwards, upwards, beyond the sight of all things natural into the limitless heavens. There appeared a light of unendurable whiteness and glory, incomparably brighter than he. In awe he stopped, unable to face it, yet knowing that he must not only approach it, but pierce it. For enshrined within this blinding emission, was God. He summoned all his energies and went in, and saw the invisible, and felt the unfeelable, and learned the unlearnable – every doubt vanished, and every question was answered with emblazoned clarity before it was even phrased.

He worshipped her.

The return from this incandescent orb to the World of Sorrow was as a spiralling gentle descent, and a slow return to mundane taste, touch and sound; a subtraction of radiance and its substitution with looming shadows, and the lustreless faces of two men, one of whom said:

'Forgive me, Maitreya, I could not prevent this. Here is the Ging Si; he insists you are to go with him.'

'There was brilliance,' said the Maitreya, 'such as the cloud that catches the sun. There was peace. I was nourished by the Source of all knowledge. I can go on, unafraid.'

'Maitreya; there will be no going on. Did you not hear what I said?'

'Yes, Brother, I recognize the Ging Si . . . Twenty years . . . Well, you've built a fearsome reputation in that time; though not altogether deserved. A big tree attracts the gale.'

'Tang Tsun,' said the Ging Si, 'you will have to come with

me I have a warrant for your arrest for offences under section thirty-four of the Societies' Ordinance . . .'

'A common triad criminal. Is that what you think I am? Ging Si, surely you don't believe a word of that!'

'Stop there!' Master Kaan stood, braced for action, with the flash of war in his eyes he afffirmed: 'We monks are ready to defend you, Maitreya.'

'There was a time when I would have asked for your protection, Master Kaan. But truthfully, there's no need for violence. It's right for me to go with him; it's part of Her design that the Ging Si is here. We're choiceless creatures, the Ging Si and I.'

'Will you come with me to Hong Kong?'

'Yes. Gladly, Ging Si.'

'Maitreya.' Master Kaan went to his knees and grasped the saffron cloth.

'It's all right . . . It's *all right*, Brother.'

'The Kalpa, Maitreya, who will see it through? Where will we go? What will we do? . . . Is it true that the forces of Evil are too great for the Eternal Mother to withstand?'

'Stand firm and have right thought. You, and all those in the Assembly are entrusted by Heaven to do that . . . As for the forces of Evil – they've come down from the north like a leaderless horde, uncontrollable, massively violent, lashing out in all directions at once, a hundred thousand headless, heartless monsters, too strong by far for any force that God or man could muster to oppose them . . .'

'Then there is no hope.'

'I did not say that, Master Kaan. There is hope.'

'Where is the hope?'

'Not just hope, but absolute certainty; a golden promise from the Eternal Mother, Herself. The ignoble legions finding no adversary, will turn aggressively inwards, and grind each other to the bone in a long and bloody self-slaughter that will have all of China as its arena . . . But as all things must end, the Armageddon will end. And over the blood and ashes of the decimated

367

armies, a white wind will blow, cleansing and repairing, and bringing an infant cry of new life . . . Write down what I have said, Master Kaan, on the Temple-scroll. For this is a true prophecy . . . Now it's time for us to go; come, Ging Si.'

The storm was over. They walked unhurriedly through the monastery gardens, the Maitreya and the Ging Si, hearing the splash of the waterfalls and the trickling calls of frogs in the deep green ponds, as though a bottle were being emptied. A sweet breeze puffed feather clouds through the sky above the mountain peaks and charmed the air in their clean-bathed valley.

They took the stone-paved pathway that wound past dripping wild loquat trees and camellias tipped with butterflies and ringing with cicadas, upwards towards the mountain called Ma On Shan. Here the Maitreya was told of his brother's tragic suicide. He walked with his head bowed for a while, shut off, it seemed, from everything but his sorrow. All that he said was: 'He is not dead.' When they had gained the summit, and were resting, he briefly returned to the subject of his brother: 'I loved him. I grieved for him more in life that I do in death. Be comforted. He will have another chance.'

'Yes,' said the Ging Si, wanting to say more, glad he need not.

'May we walk a little in this direction?' The Maitreya gestured towards a rocky spine. 'This is where Master Kaan brought me many times when he was my teacher . . . Are you afraid of heights, Ging Si?'

'No more than it's advisable to be.'

'Tell your men to stop here, then you and I will walk out a bit further . . . I was once afraid of heights. I couldn't even have attempted to walk where we're walking now.'

The path became a knife edge, falling away on both sides into a forested abyss. An eagle glided through the green-washed canyon beneath them in effortless flight.

'Look . . . Do you envy it, Ging Si?'

'It seems so free.'

'Yes it does. Let's go further on. The path ends at that spur. I'd like to go there, one last time . . . Shall I show you where Master

Kaan used to test me? He'd make me balance on the balls of my feet with my back to the drop. A bit further. Yes, here's the spot, I'll never forget it. This place I dreamed about; saw completely, and in every detail, long before I came to it. A mantra learned here gives you wings like that eagle . . . Listen to the purity. It gathers your mind. It cleanses.'

The two men stood quite still for a while. The breeze stirred the saffron robe, and the shadow of a cloud came by. The Maitreya smiled faintly, opening his arms wide like a cliff-bird, about to launch.

'A window into paradise . . . Look down, Ging Si. It's very deep.'

'A man falling from here would have time to think of many things before he struck bottom.' Forrester hurled a stone into the ravine and watched it curve inwards, and strike, soundlessly, long short of its aspired mark.

'I've tried that too,' said the Maitreya. 'Likewise, I could throw myself from this ledge now, and you could not do a thing to prevent it, Ging Si. You realize that, don't you?'

'Yes.'

'Your reasoning fascinates me. Why did you allow me to come here, in that case?'

'To allow whatever sacrifice you thought appropriate according to your understanding of things. Even to destroy yourself, if that was your need.'

'I believe you . . . Strange gwailo. You were putting *me* to the test.'

'It was not for me to decide . . . But I have learned.'

'And what have you learned?'

'Foremost, that you have the courage to go on . . . Maitreya, listen; the charges to be brought against you are well constructed. I developed the case myself. But all of it is just a stratagem. The reason; the true, but hidden reason for your arrest is that you have become an intolerable threat to the rulers of Beijing. To survive they must suppress all memories of good things of the past, and eliminate all influences that run contra to the ideals of the

Party. Old habits; old customs; old thoughts; old culture – the Four Great Dangers to survival of Communism must be ruthlessly rooted out of the minds of people. They did it in China, now Hong Kong is about to experience their hate for the past. And you, Maitreya, are a living reminder of that glorious and magnetic history that is their antithesis, and their dismay. That's why they will kill you.'

'The Communists are the Black Wind, Ging Si. That was taught to me today by the Eternal Mother. I saw her and She showed me the immutable truth of the Kalpa, for which I had been searching for so long. The Communists, *alone*, are the destructive force of this millennium, and *they* will see it to an end. It dazzles me this radiant truth, as brightly as a sunrise at sea. Was I blind then, that I could not see it before? They *are* the Black Wind.'

'They have such power for destruction?'

'Be glad of it, Ging Si. In their last days they will turn that vicious insatiable energy on themselves.'

'I have another belief – and this is my firm and absolute conviction, and my reason for coming to you here. It is that you are the seed of whiteness in the black; the eye of the placenta of *Tai ji*, which is the ruling principle of life. You are the Maitreya who will provide the rock of unbreakable faith upon which the Black Wind will ultimately falter, then die . . . Go into the minds of the people where you are indestructible, and bring the awful darkness to an end.'

'Heaven has promised a new world, Ging Si.'

'I believe it.'

Statue Square was a relic of bygone days and of colonial pomp. Once mighty Queen Victoria – three times larger than life – had been its absolute custodian. Her Majesty had been looted by the Japanese 38th Division, never to return. The genteel, gothic buildings that surrounded the square had all gone too, but for one worthy survivor of the days of colonades and cornices, which now served as home to the legislators of Hong

Kong. The single remaining monument in the square was the Cenotaph. As for the rest of Statue Square, parts of it were grass, most of it was paved, and a busy roadway cut it clean in half. There it lay in the plexus of the business district compressed by skyscrapers, mutely radiating echoes of the British Empire.

When the noonday sun broke up the canopy of wet gloomy clouds the knot of storm-wearied demonstrators took new heart. They unfurled their banners and emerged from the sturdy shelter at the base of the Mandarin Hotel; from thence to the square.

Mike Hempstead was on hand to observe the bedraggled procession; he counted twenty-two men, and seven women, twenty-nine all told, and made a mental note of that statistic. He was close enough to hear them being addressed by a chief inspector in the uniform of the Police Tactical Unit, who said evenly:

'This is an unlawful assembly. You must disperse at once.'

'Why is it unlawful?' A young girl in a white frock pointed that question at the inspector.

'It is illegal because the time allotted for this demonstration has long since expired.'

'So, protest must be measured in minutes. Tyranny may only be shouted at to the order of the hands of a clock.'

'That is the law.'

'It is not reasonable,' said the spokeswoman.

'Nevertheless, you must all obey it.'

'We're here to protest the show-trials and the wholesale executions of the Fascist Beijing regime.'

'You have already done so. Go home now.'

'Our protest will never end.'

The inspector glanced confidently from his watch to the woman, and predicted, 'It will end in five minutes, precisely.'

This entire conversation took place without heat or rancour. Mike Hempstead overheard it all, as did the inquisitive cluster of bystanders who had by now gathered. One of whom had this to say:

'Give them a chance. What's the harm? All they want is justice.'

Support for the protesters grew from there; a general murmur of approval for the stance of the students, and some reasonably good-natured digs at the police. The crowd grew thicker. The students drew themselves into a defensive knot around their main standard which read:

> *End the Terror*
> *Stop the Killing*

And that most reasonable demand became the refrain of their chant. Twenty-nine voices, even if delivered in absolute unison, is but a small sound, a wavering, and easily forgotten sound. But if it vibrates a sympathetic chord amongst those within earshot, it is likely to grow. So it was with those words:

> 'End the Terror
> Stop the Killing.'

The chant was simple to learn, and had near-irresistible contagion as it rippled outwards to the fringe of the small crowd. Absorbed and repeated, it called for more and more participants. It rolled around the square, lapping at the edges of the tall blockade of buildings, self-generating now, and with magnetic appeal, it escaped into the surrounding streets, engulfing all in its path. And this massive growth took place in minutes.

Now the time allotted for dispersal of the twenty-nine had certainly expired, and quite the opposite event had occurred. Before the very eyes of the police inspector, who had demanded that it go away, the softly spoken infant had grown into a vociferous monster. It flexed; it became aware of its potential.

There was a power of oneness cohering the people in Statue Square, a subliminal outpouring that bonded one man to the next, to the next, overcoming all barriers, smelting all schisms large or small into one completely integrated like-minded whole. It was a joy, a passion that took hold of heart and soul and swept away fear. Suddenly they had become triumphantly larger than life. Even Mike Hempstead's pale spirit was ruddied by it. At times he found himself quite stirred by this amazing unity.

He did not, however, forget for one moment that he was a policeman. Mike was entertained by the actions of the besieged PTU inspector, giving a rather interesting imitation of being cool, even blasé, and vastly commanding in the hub of a totally buggered-up situation. Not that any police action was needed, or desirable. For the crowd, despite its pumping fists and pithy slogans, was not in a troublesome mood, and would most probably quickly dwindle away after lunch.

Mike saw the chief inspector enter his vehicle and take hold of the radio-mike that would connect him to higher authority. The man spoke seriously for a while, then listened with equal diligence. Mike could not help wondering what message he had been given, for he knew that the main body of the Tactical Unit was deployed at the container terminal at the harbour, where the truckers were giving them hell. The inspector sat for a while with his head bowed, then, having re-composed his nonchalant face, he stepped out again, accepting as he did what looked like a sweet held out to him by a smiling youngster.

The group of twenty-nine moved on to the steps of the Cenotaph; an imposing setting; a good place to borrow dignity. Beneath that mighty marble wedge they set up their banners. A student wearing a white headband came forward holding a loud-hailer, and lifted his arms for quiet.

Mike would have liked to have heard what the fellow had to say, but lacked the time for it. He had a vital appointment with the securities manager at the adjacent Hong Kong and Shanghai Bank, and, thereafter, a potentially less comfortable interview with the Acting CSO, Organized and Serious Crime Group. The life, and death, of the unfortunate Connie Tam would be the subject of that discussion: poor Connie, who had been so bowed of spirit after her twin sister's tragic end, that she had followed on. Abric acid . . . Mike shuddered in vicarious anguish. 'A distressing time for me, sir, I don't have to tell you . . . I loved her very much.'

*

Bertie Humphries, perspiring so profusely that his shirt stuck transparently to his piggish pink body, took a photograph of that banner, and instructed his photographer (Chinese, unsweated and thin) to do likewise. Their cameras clicked and buzzed, and Bertie's tape recorders taped. Bertie, though he maintained a sharp and professional eye upon the goings-on at the Cenotaph, kept glancing about as though in expectation of newsworthy action from quite another quarter. He squeejeed at the sweat of his brow with the back of his thumb, and chewed on his lower lip, and worried about what was the greatest potential scoop of a scoop-filled career.

The man he was keeping such a sharp look-out for was Reven Forrester. For it was, amazingly, that most taciturn of all cops who had 'phoned him at his breakfast table with the promise of a story without parallel; a story of heroic dimensions, should he meet with him at this venue. But, where was the Ging Si? The crowd was banked up to the edges, some bright spirits had climbed on to the roofs of adjacent concrete shelters, and fresh banners were dancing up. The appointed time had come, and gone.

A hand touched Bertie's wet shirt: 'Mr Humphries? . . . Yes? . . . If you are Mr Humphries, you come with me.'

Bertie acknowledged his identity, then went with the man, a gawky-limbed Chinese with short-cropped grey hair and an umbrella, who did not look at all like a cop, but probably was. The man kept on glancing back as they wound through the crowd, to make sure that Mr Humphries was in tow. Of course he was. Bertie was energetically keeping pace. The old stone Legislative Council building seemed to be their target. They passed into its Palladian arcade, and from that long shady veranda into its museum-like interior. A broad teak staircase led them upwards, and into a vast second-floor office, with much more teak – a library from end to end, a corpulent desk, and french doors which stood open, admitting the undulating roar of massed humanity and the metallically expanded chatter of a bullhorn.

At first Bertie was drawn by the view, which was of the Cenotaph; of a human sea, tipped whitely with billowing banners. Then Reven Forrester came into the office.

'Mr Humphries.'

Bertie came forward, mopping with a handkerchief at his wetness. 'Ging Si. I never thought . . .' In the lap of a wing-backed leather chair, quite hidden until one had reached that point, sat a monk in saffron robes. One shoulder was bared, his slim arms rested lightly in his lap and one of his hands was lividly scarred. He had the peaceful face of a monk, but his eyes were not placid. His eyes brooded darkly, and there were regions, too, where sparks were struck from steel.

Forrester said, 'Maitreya, this is the writer I spoke to you about.'

The monk nodded, then smiled quite agreeably at Bertie: 'The man who will place the burning agony of China before the eyes of the world . . . Can you do that, Mr Humphries? The Ging Si says you've the talent to do it. If that's true, then fill your pen with grief and pain and bitterness . . . and hope. I'm the merchant of hope, yet all I possess of it is one tiny seed in a black-burned field. It's there amongst the acres of chaos. I'll find it for you. And I'll give to you . . . My plea to you is that you implant it in the minds of millions. Can you do that, Mr Humphries? The Ging Si says you have the talent, but talent is insufficient – have you the will, and the endurance?'

'I can do it,' said Bertie Humphries. 'Oh, definitely.'

'Then sit here beside me, and listen to the story of the betrayal and torture and death of a great nation.'

Bertie set up his tape recorder and braced his ring-pad on his thigh. He inclined towards Forrester a glance that was eloquent with thanks, then began to write.

'The Forces of Evil had dithered for a long time in the search for a captain; discarding one applicant after another for lack of sufficiently heinous intellect. Then, one day out of the mountains, at the head of a large army, marched the unmistakable genius of tyranny. His name was Mao Tse-tung . . .'

Now interesting things were happening all around Bertie, which were playing havoc with his concentration. There were three telephones on the desk to his rear, and at least one of them was constantly chirping for attention. And the man attending to them was Reven Forrester. His tone might vary from call to call – from hard-fisted command, to appeasing argument, with bewildering language hops from Cantonese to Mandarin, to English. Words, such as 'ex-patriate', and 'leader in exile', were tugging at Bertie's ear, and this was not the only distraction. A helicopter had come to hover, and its ruckus was beating down upon the square. Forrester shouted into a 'phone something to do with its immediate departure . . . and, lo! The noise lifted then whirred into the distance. Amazing authority was emanating from this office, and frustration, too. Bertie shifted the tape recorder so that its directional mike pointed at Forrester, then carried on scribbling. His mind was a mess of information, but despite all these diversions he had not missed a word that the Maitreya had said:

'. . . After the war was over, and all opposition beaten, Mao Tse-tung, with his Red Army, inherited Beijing; a sacred city of breath-taking splendour and absolute harmony; a city of exquisite gardens, of temples and palaces that took five centuries to build. It was the highest symbol of Chinese morality and culture . . . Mao set his maniac Red Guards loose upon it with sledge-hammer and dynamite, and ordered them to destroy everything old and beautiful. And they did. They smashed and burned and broke, year in, year out. They tore down the arches, pulverized the bricks of centuries. They used old carvings for firewood and shattered precious porcelain. But the worst destruction of all was invisible; they poured slow poison into the minds of the youth, corroding all good values, all virtuous memories. He gave them Communism instead. That, Mr Humphries, was the first breath of the Black Wind.'

First Breath, Bertie's pen fairly flew across the paper, *Black Wind*.

'And it blew through the length and breadth of China. Now Hong Kong must face this intractable force that will rape the past, and break down all things beautiful . . . But they must not reach the seed of hope; don't let them destroy the seed of hope . . .'

'They will not,' avowed Bertie Humphries.

'They're here,' said Reven Forrester. 'I tried. I couldn't stop them.'

There was a hush, a sough as though made of the indrawn breath of every person in the square. The sound of a lone child crying entwined the silence; a tremulous, solitary wail of misery from one timid lost breast, rising, waning, rising, waning.

'I just couldn't stop them.' Forrester's fingers pulled nervously at the skin of his neck. His face was bleak.

Bertie dashed to the window.

A column of olive-green trucks, open backed and filled with helmeted infantrymen, came nosing down crowd-choked Chater Road. At a whistle-blast the convoy halted. The tail-gates dropped with a clang that rang clear across the square, and the soldiers dismounted, jumping, two at a time, to the ground, with their AK rifles clutched tightly into their chests. Then they deployed in skirmishing formation. The crowd stared; as silently mesmerized as a colony of rats before the advance of this deadly olive snake.

'We are not afraid,' rang out the voice of the leader of the Twenty-nine. 'We stand firm before the naked aggression of the monsters of Beijing.'

They stood firm, as promised. But elsewhere Bertie perceived spasms of alarm; small shudders at first, that built by yell and shove into wild convulsions of panic that burgeoned and gripped rank after rank until the square was a rampage of people; shoving, lurching, screaming, wild-eyed people. And advancing with impassive step and tranquil bearing into this rip-tide of distress walked a man in a saffron robe.

And the chair where the Maitreya had sat was now vacant. Bertie gazed disbelievingly at the vacated spot: 'While we were turned from him . . .'

Forrester paced quickly towards the door that would lead him from the office, then just as suddenly stopped. He shrugged, and said, 'What's the good? I'm not his keeper, and never intended to be. I offered to arrange a safe exile; but that was never his intention.'

'He didn't finish; he didn't finish with his story.' Bertie watched the departing monk, in certainty that he would never speak to this man again, and felt more grieved than disappointed.

Forrester, without turning from the window, said: 'Had he spoken to you for a week, he wouldn't have been able to impart it all to you . . . I, on the other hand, have tapes of the Maitreya in my office. I have the Comprehensive Manual of the White Lotus Assembly . . . You will have no shortage of material, Bertie.'

'You'd give me all that?'

'I believe in him.'

'Is he truly the Maitreya?'

'There's no one who can reply to that but yourself.'

'Look, there he is. He's walking to the Cenotaph.'

And so were the men of the People's Liberation Army, with their rifles held at the port, as sweetly in step as though on parade. When they halted it was on the grass verge of the monument, with every helmet-tip, every gleaming boot and rifle-barrel perfectly aligned.

The group of Twenty-nine were defiantly unmoved upon the plinth, some kneeling, some standing, every one of them as still as if by some miracle they'd grown out of the very marble of that great memorial. The voice of their orator arose, ghastly with fear: 'We are not your enemies.'

The Maitreya walked onwards through the tattered remnants of the crowd. People turned to watch him pass, some stared and pointed.

'You should stop him,' said Bertie. 'Those soldiers are from a Hebei regiment. There's no love for the Cantonese in those northern hearts.'

'He fully understands the price of his actions; my role is up. I'm leaving Hong Kong, with Caroline, for good. I've no further part to play . . . You, on the other hand, Bertie, have a vast obligation and debt.'

'Where are those policemen of yours, Ging Si? I don't see one of them left on the square.'

'Reserve that question for the Commissioner; a man of the North.'

'It's a matter of face now, Ging Si. Someone is going to have to back down, and quickly.'

And if that was so, then it was not going to be the soldiers. There came a rattle of metal as the infantrymen worked their cocking handles. The Maitreya's steps faltered, but whether it was that deadly clatter that had stopped him was uncertain. He had by then arrived at a position midway between the Cenotaph and the line of soldiers, and there he squatted, cross-legged on the grass, facing the northerners as a tongue of yellow on the green – a small, unwavering flame.

And there they shot him.

Some fool had hurled a missile at the soldiers; a well-aimed bottle that smashed brightly on the rim of a green steel helmet, staggering the wearer out of true. Was that the reason why in that instant the rifles came up, thundering with flame and smoke, and death?

Bertie Humphries felt sick and weak, and his hands were trembling so he could hardly write. But write he did. The title to his story came easily:

Black Wind Blowing.

He poised his pencil for a moment, deeply, fearfully in thought. But the fear was transient. Pushing, thrusting through the dark, with the vigour of a germinating seed, came a young tap-root of certainty. It left no room for anything but courage. He began to write:

I saw them shoot the God of Hope . . .

Hold My Hand
I'm Dying
John Gordon Davis

'This is the best novel coming out of Africa that I have read for a number of years. *It is Africa today*. It has the inevitability of a Greek tragedy . . . both moving emotionally and full of adventure.'
Stuart Cloete

The great heart of old Africa is dying. Joseph Mahoney, the last colonial commissioner in the spectacular Kariba Gorge, is there to witness the death throes. Somehow, he must also ease the birth pangs of the new Africa that will take its place. His companions are Samson, his Matabele servant, and Suzie, the girl he loves.

But Mahoney and Suzie are drifting apart, and now Samson has been accused of murder. And all too quickly, it seems, the country is heading towards a bloodbath of revenge.

Hold My Hand I'm Dying – a compelling story of freedom, friendship and love in the face of hatred, violence and death.

'A great, compassionate and deeply moving book. I did not know how to put it down.'
Marguerite Steen

FONTANA PAPERBACKS

The Fireman
Stephen Leather

A high-powered thriller set in London and
Hong Kong, by the author of *Pay Off*

Young, talented, in love with life, why should Sally
have thrown herself fifteen floors to her death? But
suicide is the verdict of the uncompromising Hong
Kong authorities and Sally's brother, a London-based
crime reporter, is forced to begin his own
investigations.

As he delves into the details of Sally's unaccountably
opulent lifestyle, her mysterious work as a journalist,
he is forced to recognize a very different girl from the
fun-loving kid sister he remembers. And he uncovers
a trail that leads him through the decadent haunts of
Hong Kong ex-pat society, the ruthless wheeler-
dealing of international big business and the violent
Chinese mafia underworld – to an ultimate, shocking
act of revenge . . .

Pay Off, by the same author, is also available in
Fontana.

FONTANA PAPERBACKS

Sacrificial Ground
Thomas H. Cook

Even as a corpse, Angelica Devereaux is beautiful, and as enigmatic as the means by which she met her violent end. After the shattering suicide of his own teen-aged daughter, the Devereaux case is the last thing Atlanta cop Frank Clemons needs.

But like everybody whose life is touched by Angelica's, Frank cannot escape her irresistible allure – even from beyond the grave. It will drive him to probe ever deeper into the short, troubled history of a child-woman too dangerously desirable not to be killed. Before he knows it, Frank is trapped in an obsession, treading a serpentine path of corruption, loneliness and thwarted love, which will lead him out of the tortured past – or destroy him . . .

'This is the sort of novel that really delights all the senses: the suspense dark and intriguing, a compelling, twisted story.'
John Katzenbach, author of *The Traveller*

'Taut and engrossing, rich in atmosphere and character, a memorable and literate thriller.'
Jonathan Kellerman, author of *When the Bough Breaks*

FONTANA PAPERBACKS